WILD DE

Katie Fforde

MICHAEL JOSEPH
LONDON

MICHAEL JOSEPH LTD

Published by the Penguin Group
27 Wrights Lane, London w8 5tz
Viking Penguin Inc., 375 Hudson Street, New York, New York 10014, USA
Penguin Books Australia Ltd, Ringwood, Victoria, Australia
Penguin Books Canada Ltd, 10 Alcorn Avenue, Toronto, Ontario, Canada m4v 3b2
Penguin Books (NZ) Ltd, 182–190 Wairau Road, Auckland 10, New Zealand

Penguin Books Ltd, Registered Offices: Harmondsworth, Middlesex, England

First published 1996
1 3 5 7 9 10 8 6 4 2

Copyright © Katie Fforde 1996

Set in 10.5/13pt Plantin Light Monotype
Typeset by Datix International Limited, Bungay, Suffolk
Printed in England by Clays Ltd, St Ives plc

A CIP catalogue record for this book is available from the British Library

ISBN 0 7181 4134 2

The moral right of the author has been asserted

For my children, who of course bear no resemblance
whatsoever to any of the characters in this book

ACKNOWLEDGEMENTS

To Jane Fearnley-Whittingstall who unknowingly gave me the idea. To Mike Miller and his team at Clifton Nurseries, including Bob Scrutton and Nicki Harvey for being so generous with their time and expertise and for allowing me to roam freely around their site at the Chelsea Flower Show. To Alan and Minn Hogg, the children, parents, teachers and governors of Rodborough County Primary and Horsley Schools, as well as their opposite numbers in France. To Anne Rafferty and Laura Stewart who gave me valuable ideas. Also to dear Sarah Molloy and Richenda Todd for their constant support and supreme tolerance. And to everyone else who may have unwittingly triggered my unconscious and helped this book on its way.

CHAPTER ONE

'Mum,' said a voice, reproachful yet forgiving. 'Have you been drinking orange juice straight out of the carton again?'

Althea made a gesture of admission and apology tinged with indignation at being found out. 'It had gone all thick, anyway, you wouldn't have drunk it.'

Her seventeen-year-old son shook his shaven head in mock reproof.

'I didn't want to dirty a glass,' she went on. 'I only wanted a drop.' Asserting her motherhood, she continued: 'If you ever rinsed out a mug, or even loaded the washing-up machine, you'd appreciate my economy.'

'A dishwasher is what we call it nowadays.'

'I don't care what you call it, sweetie, just occasionally put something in it!'

William, tall, slightly spotty and to his mother's eyes quite beautiful, marred his looks with a grin full of metal. The train-tracks, top and bottom, added a bizarre touch to his broad smile. The combination of smile and braces was irresistible and she smiled back.

'Juno's coming round soon.' Althea was hoping that her son would take the hint and help her tidy up.

'Is she? That'll be fun for you.' William didn't approve of Juno, she was too materialistic and bound up in 'self'. But then, as a Buddhist, he applied this epithet to most people.

Althea sighed. 'Do give me a hand. You know how critical she is.'

'She's your sister – your *younger* sister. If you don't mind living in a mess, why should it bother her?'

'I don't like living in a mess. It's just something that happens to me. And it does bother her, you know it does. She tells me off.'

'That's your problem, Mum. You allow people to walk over you.'

'Yes, and you've got the biggest feet.'

'Nonsense. I only want the best for you.'

Althea scowled. There was a point when role-reversal ceased to be funny. 'The best for me right now would be a little help in the kitchen.'

William lobbed an apple core in the general direction of the rubbish-bin. It missed.

Althea noted where it fell. 'I thought Buddhists were supposed to be nice to their mothers . . .'

William made a face. 'Oh, all right. I'll blitz the kitchen, but I won't hang around and join in your trivial conversation. I've got work to do.'

'School work?' Althea hardly dared to hope. William spent a lot of time studying enormously expensive Buddhist texts, but didn't think A levels were important. Lacking them herself, his mother did.

William shook his head and picked up a cloth which he dabbed under the tap. 'No, mother dear. I've got to study a bit on detachment.' He made a swipe in the direction of the tea-stained work surface. 'I'm leading the discussion tonight.'

Althea sighed, got up from the table and kissed him. 'Think what good karma you're building up. I'll run round with the vac.'

She ran, bumping the furniture but avoiding actually moving anything, while her mind chewed anxiously at the knowledge that very soon she would learn whether or not she still had a job.

It was cruel, she decided, making people apply for their own jobs. Except in the eyes of the Whickham School – soon to become Whickham and Dylan's Combined Primary and more than doubling its size – it was not her job she was applying for, but that of secretary of a much grander operation. For although she had run Whickham School to everyone's satisfaction, the great and the good in charge of the new operation and of her fate might well consider that a younger, brighter, better qualified – albeit less experienced – person might suit their needs better. Mr Edwards, the head teacher she had worked with so happily for so many years, was taking early retirement.

Having examined the worst-case scenario many, many times, Althea concluded that telling her sister Juno she was out of a job would be the worst part. Juno was a strong woman, who had Althea's best interests at heart and felt these interests were best served by knowing and advising on every detail of Althea's life. She would have a lot to say about Althea's unemployment, which, Althea suspected, she would hear even if she did get the job.

William, who was sluicing the germs around in the cups so they covered every surface, watched critically as his mother swept a pile of papers off the kitchen table and put them on the dresser, where they would join other papers swept up there on other days, and disappear.

'You really shouldn't do that, Mum. Tomorrow you'll be frantic looking for Rupert's report and turn the house upside down. Why don't you be more organized?'

Althea, knowing he was right, made a face. 'I get bored with being organized. I am organized at school. At home, I am who I want to be.'

'No, you're not, or you wouldn't be flapping round like a blue-arsed fly because Juno's coming. You're a victim of your desire to conform.'

'I'm a victim of my bossy sister and my bossy children.'

'Then it's time you took control of your environment, like I do.'

Althea, who'd grown accustomed to such statements over the past year, snorted. 'I'm doing my best! You only manage to keep your room so minimalist because you keep your junk in the sitting room.'

'That's not junk, it's the school work you consider to be so important.'

'Well, it takes up a lot of space. I'd be grateful if you'd take it up to your room.'

'Yeah, Mum, like you always keep all your stuff in your room.' He dumped a cleanser-covered necklace which he'd found in a cup into her hands. 'That's me done. I'm just going to make some scrambled eggs.'

Althea added the necklace to a couple of others which hung from a hook on the dresser. 'No chance of you making them in the microwave, I don't suppose?'

3

'They're not the same in the microwave.'

'Then please wash the pan afterwards.'

'I always do!'

Althea reflected that her children wouldn't realize that putting cold water into a saucepan isn't the same as washing it until after they had left home and run out of saucepans.

She opened a packet of digestive biscuits and put them on a plate. Juno was an advocate of food combining and Althea could never remember what time of day she could eat what, but the biscuits were a gesture. Absent-mindedly she put a broken half into her mouth and, realizing what she'd done, started guiltily. Someone at school had given her a fridge magnet which said, 'Little Pickers wear Bigger Knickers.' Its trite, essential truth always flashed into her mind a moment too late.

At four o'clock – exactly the time Juno said she would call – the doorbell rang. Althea checked her face for crumbs and went to answer it. As much as she loved her sister, she was always a little nervous of her. Juno was one of those people who actually do put face powder on their cheeks while they make up their eyes so it's easier to remove any smudges. Althea didn't know anyone else who'd bother.

'Hello, darling,' she said, kissing Juno, who was, as usual, perfectly groomed and smelt marvellously of some new and unpronounceable perfume. 'Come in.'

Juno returned the hug. 'I've brought some magazines I've finished with, and a pair of shoes I bought in a sale which are far too big for me. You might like to try them.'

'Angel, how lovely.' Althea depended on her sister's passion for bargains for all her smarter clothes. 'Now come in and have something. What would you like? Tea? Coffee? Drink?'

Juno followed Althea down the passage to the kitchen. 'It's far too early to start drinking,' she said firmly, although Althea had actually meant something soft, 'but I'd love a cup of tea.'

William was draining the kettle into his personal cafetière as they entered the kitchen.

'Hi, Juno!' he greeted his aunt. 'How are you? Want some coffee? If you do, I'll make it. There's some technology' – he indicated the cafetière – 'Mum just can't get behind.'

'There's a lot of technology you can't get behind,' snapped

4

his mother. 'Like the broom and the duster, and Juno's having tea.'

'I'll make it for you, then,' said William, revealing his orthodontistry with great charm.

'Thank you, William,' said Juno, slightly taken aback. 'That would be kind.'

Althea knew that William's kindness was likely to degenerate into teasing at any moment. 'Shall we go through into the conservatory?'

'If there's actually space in there for people. When I was here the other day, it had the last remaining corner of the rain forest in it.'

Taking this as a compliment, Althea picked up the plate of biscuits and led the way to her favourite room in the house.

It was packed with plants and smelt of scented geraniums, damp soil and the lemon tree Althea had grown from a pip. As always the scent made her nostrils crinkle with pleasure.

Like many properties in the area, the house was on the side of a hill, and so the conservatory was elevated. From it, there was a panoramic view of where the Cotswold hills flattened out into the Severn Vale. On winter days with the leaves off the trees and just a hint of rain in the air, Althea could see the curling snake of the river and beyond to Wales.

Now, in early May, the south-west aspect of the conservatory made foreign holidays unnecessary, even if she could have afforded them. But even without the views, Althea could never have torn herself away from the garden in summer.

Bozo, her small spaniel, was sitting on the one decent wicker chair, guarding a vegetarian sausage. Not being vegetarian herself, Bozo didn't actually want to eat the sausage, but was anxious that none of the cats should get it. She had been carrying it around for days.

Bozo, seeing Juno, got down from her chair and leant her paws on Juno's legs, blinking affectionately. Juno patted the dog's head, which Bozo hated, and took her recently vacated seat. Althea took the chair opposite and offered the plate of biscuits. Bozo, forgetting the sausage immediately in the presence of something edible, waited, head on one side, for her share of this snacklet.

Juno declined the biscuits and Bozo turned her attention to her mistress, always an easy touch. Althea defiantly broke off a corner of digestive, waited for the little dog to sit, and then gave it to her.

'Honestly, you shouldn't encourage that dog to beg,' said Juno.

'She doesn't beg, she just asks nicely,' said Althea.

'It comes to the same thing. Now, tell me how the interview went?'

Althea shrugged. 'I don't know. I didn't like the new head teacher of the combined school much. His mobile phone was practically welded to his ear the whole time I was showing him round. And during the interview, he hardly looked me in the eye once. He kept talking about "dragging the new school into the new millennium", and asking what my "attainment targets" were.'

'Well, Mr Edwards was rather old-fashioned.'

'Mr Edwards was a dear who loved the kids and loved his school and let me run the office. He'll miss it all terribly when he retires.'

'When do you expect to hear?'

'Any day now.'

'You must be worried sick.'

Althea shrugged. 'I'm not sure I could work with that man anyway. As a school secretary you have to work very closely with the head. It's worse than being married, sometimes.'

Juno, whose own husband was well under control, tapped her foot impatiently. 'But you've got a good chance?'

'Well, I have been doing the job more or less for seven years, but the others were younger. And more glamorous.' Althea sighed and noticed an ant emerge from between the floorboards. Damn, how was she going to get rid of an ants' nest with a Buddhist in the house?

'You could be glamorous if you took a little time and trouble,' said Juno, but without conviction. Getting her big sister to smarten up her act was not yet a lost cause with her, but it was one of the tougher tasks she had set herself. And at the moment, the timing was against her.

They lapsed into silence, Althea hoping that Juno wouldn't notice the ants which were now forming an orderly queue

6

behind a biscuit crumb. If Juno spotted them, she'd demand kettles of boiling water and other instruments of death, William would get upset and there would be the nearest thing to a row as was possible when one of the contenders forbade himself to feel anger.

'Have you heard from Frederick lately?' asked Juno, still in ignorance of the trail of sentient beings at her feet.

Frederick was Althea's ex. He had decamped when Merry, who was now twelve and perfectly civilized, was a tiny, colicky baby, constantly crying or pooing. Now, he bullied Althea from afar, reminding her how unreasonable she had been by refusing to send the boys (Merry's education wasn't so important, seeing as she was a girl) to boarding school. If ever there was the tiniest hint that his offspring might not be getting As in everything, he told Althea it was all her fault for sending them to the local comp. Consequently, when she could have done with a bit of support in getting them to buckle down, she couldn't possibly ask for it.

'He rang William the other day, but you know I don't speak to him unless it's really necessary. He nags me about the children's school work.'

Childless herself, Juno, who agreed totally with Frederick on the matter of private education, pursed her lips. She knew Althea was deliberately vague about letting Frederick know how the children were doing at school and disapproved thoroughly. 'Well, you'll have to tell him if you're unemployed. You won't be able to keep up the mortgage payments.'

'It isn't a large mortgage. I wouldn't be unemployed until the end of August. And I would get redundancy money.'

'How much?'

'I don't know.'

'I bet it's pathetic.'

So did Althea. And Juno was right, if she lost her job, she would have to tell Frederick, who, with much muttering and I-told-you-so-ing, would probably make the payments. But he had always wanted the house for himself and his girlfriend. Would letting him pay the mortgage for a few months give him a larger stake in it than the one quarter he already possessed? Perhaps she should give up the struggle sooner rather than later.

7

'I think I'd rather move than let him pay.'

'But why should you?' Juno's wavering loyalty instantly corrected itself. 'It's your home – your *children's* home.'

'William'll only be here for another year and I've got to sell it anyway when Merry's no longer in full-time education. Unless I can afford to buy Frederick out. Which doesn't seem likely at the moment.'

'But it would break your heart to leave your garden!'

'Probably, but I could always make another one and, really, I can't afford to be sentimental.'

'I'm sure Frederick wouldn't mind paying. He can certainly afford it, and whatever you say, he's always seemed pretty reasonable to me.'

Althea actually felt Frederick had always seemed more than just 'pretty reasonable' to Juno. 'Pretty damn attractive' might be a more accurate summing up of her opinion. But Frederick had long since ceased being able to cause Althea pain, and while deploring her sister's taste, she didn't hold the secrets of Juno's heart against her.

However, she was not above making little digs at Juno's perceptions of the proper way to carry on. 'I could of course take in lodgers to help with the mortgage. A couple of Job Seekers on full benefit might cover it.'

Juno was horrified. 'You couldn't do that.'

'Why not? I've got a spare bedroom with a wash basin, and separate loo and shower.' Althea had only mentioned lodgers to annoy her sister, but now she thought of it, the idea had its advantages. 'Seriously, a nice quiet lady teacher would be no trouble.'

'A nice quiet lady teacher would never cope with sharing your kitchen.'

'Why not? I'm not in the least territorial.'

'Maybe not, but you are extremely messy. No, Frederick will have to support you.' Juno rearranged her beautiful legs, her unscuffed heels leaning at a graceful angle, and obviously considered her sister's unemployment a foregone conclusion.

'But he won't. You know he won't.'

Juno tsked and swept some non-existent crumbs off her skirt. 'Only because you're so awkward about the boys' education.

He'd have paid you alimony as well as their fees if only you'd sent them to decent schools.'

Althea suddenly felt very tired and anxious about her job prospects. 'Oh, let's not go into that again.'

'Yes, well, we did agree to disagree about that years ago. And I must say that, on the whole, the children are a credit to you.'

Althea gazed out of the window at her pond, grateful that Juno didn't know her children's academic results were less impressive than their interpersonal skills. 'Thank you.'

'But thinking about education,' Juno went on briskly. 'If you did lose your job you could go back to college and retrain. You could do a teaching degree. Then you'd still have the summer holidays off.'

Althea shuddered. 'I don't want to go back to college. There are so many women of my age doing it. They immediately start dressing like students and smoking dope. Besides, I don't think I could cope with all those essays.'

Juno, who had a degree in business studies, considered this. 'Mmm, and there is the little matter of your having no A levels.'

'I could probably talk my way in,' said Althea immediately, who only needed to be told she couldn't do something to want to do it instantly. 'Or even take a couple of A levels, but I couldn't hack the clothes. And the language. Sounding like a hippy is all right if you're eighteen, but not if you're knocking forty.'

'You are not knocking forty,' said Juno firmly, who was only two years younger. 'You're thirty-eight.'

'Nearly thirty-nine.'

Juno sighed. 'Well, I'll say this for you, your hair's a mess, you could do with losing a stone and your taste in clothes is pretty eccentric, but you don't look thirty-nine.'

Juno did not often compliment her sister. Althea found herself blushing slightly. 'Why, thank you . . .'

'You've got good skin and teeth which helps, as well as having naturally dark eyelashes and eyebrows . . .'

'Juno –'

'But you could look a whole lot better, if you took a bit of trouble – thought about what you ate, went to a proper hair colourist for once. And I dare say you've lost those tweezers I gave you last Christmas. But it's your figure which lets you down.'

Althea was spared a lot of dietary advice and a year's membership of a fitness centre by the entrance of her second son, Rupert. As tall as his older brother, he had a lot more hair and no braces on his teeth. 'Hello, darling. You've brought the tea in. How lovely. Good day?'

'Yeah, fine. Hello, Juno. Where do you want this?'

Juno smiled, even her critical heart unable to resist Rupert's shy smile, which lacked the teasing quality of his older brother's. 'I'll make a space on the table.' This she did by putting last Sunday's papers on to the floor.

'Are you joining us?' asked Althea. 'Get a mug.'

'Ah – no thanks, Mum. I've got work to do.'

Work keeping abreast of the soaps, calling it Media Studies, no doubt, thought Althea, hoping her ex-husband wasn't right about sending the children away to school. If the children all did badly in their exams, she would never hear the end of it.

'Which reminds me,' said Rupert, putting down the tray and pulling out a letter from his pocket. 'This was delivered by hand. It's for you, Mum.'

Recognizing Mr Edwards's writing, Althea's heart joined the ants on the conservatory floor. He would make sure she heard as soon as possible. And it had to be bad news. If she'd got the job she'd have been telephoned. She opened the envelope hoping her interested audience wouldn't see her hand trembling and her heart pounding through the thin fabric of her shirt.

> *Dear Mrs Farraday,*
> *We regret to inform you . . .*

She didn't bother to read any more. 'Oh bummer,' she said. 'I didn't get it.'

CHAPTER TWO

A bumble bee, trapped by the glass, buzzed noisily. Bozo started pursuing a flea in the middle of her back and fell off Althea's lap. The silence thus broken, Rupert and Juno began to talk at once.

'Bad luck, Mum . . .'

'Now, don't panic, Ally . . .'

'I can get a paper round . . .'

'You know, if there's anything I can do to help . . .'

'It's all right,' Althea said, sounding to herself very far away. 'Actually, I'm relieved.'

It wasn't how she'd expected to feel. She had expected devastation, anxiety, a ghastly void, with nothing but panic to fill it. Instead she felt slightly euphoric, as if a great pressure had been released. Exactly, she reflected, still from a distance, how she had felt when her husband had told her he wasn't coming back.

'Don't worry,' she said to her sister and son. 'Everything's going to be fine. I'll just make a go of my gardening. Get a few more clients. Raise more plants and sell them at car-boot sales instead of giving them away. No more school! It'll be heaven! People always want help with their gardens,' she added for the sake of her audience.

Juno took a deep breath. 'Sweetie, you're mad. Barking. You cannot keep yourself and three adolescent children on what you earn as a gardener. What do you do? Keep three old ladies' gardens in order for three pounds an hour?'

Althea's balloon of euphoria deflated a little. 'Of course, I'll put up my hourly rate, do more hours and perhaps get a part-time job at a garden centre,' she said, in order to pump it up again. 'Pricking out.'

Juno shook her head. 'You might earn enough for groceries in summer. You won't earn a bean in the winter.'

'It's only May . . .'

'Believe me, Christmas will be on us before you can say plastic holly.'

Althea, who never did say plastic holly if she could help it, was reluctant to accept the truth of what her sister was saying. 'I'll do dried flower arrangements, make wreaths for people's doors. That sort of thing. It'll be fine, really.'

Juno and Rupert regarded her anxiously, and were joined by William who, hearing sounds of agitation, came in to join them. 'Bad news, Mum?'

'Terrible. Your mother's lost her job,' said Juno.

William, his perception well honed, saw his aunt taking the situation far too seriously and his mother not seriously enough. 'You can always get another one, Mum. I'll fetch the paper.'

But Althea, elated by the knowledge that she would not have to spend her days in close proximity to a man she thoroughly disliked, being told how to do what she'd been doing for years, showed little interest in the 'Situations Vacant'. The 'Opportunities to earn money in your spare time, all you need is a telephone and your own car' occupied her a little longer, but when she got to the property section, she found herself brought up short. Here was a real calamity.

'Oh my God! The house has been sold.' Before, the prospect of being jobless seemed a golden opportunity for new ventures, a fresh start. Now the downward tug of reality pulled at her, making her limbs heavy with despondency.

'What house?' Juno jumped up to read over Althea's shoulder. 'Has Frederick put it on the market without telling you?'

'No, no, no!' said Althea. 'Not *this* house, silly. The house with the greenhouse where I raise all my plants. Look! This really is bad news.'

Juno took the paper from Althea's slackened grasp and returned to her chair. 'Oh, *that* house! Well, who would have thought it. I wonder who's bought that?'

'It's either another supermarket chain or a complete idiot,' said Althea, taking the paper back. 'It's not fit to live in.'

'The supermarkets were all turned down,' said Juno. 'It must be an idiot. Does it say?'

'No,' said Althea. 'It just has "Sold" flashed across it.'

Juno reappropriated the property section. 'There's a bit about it in the editorial. It's gone to a private buyer who intends to restore it to its former gracious elegance. It's probably a family of Arab sheikhs. They'd be the only ones who could afford it. It'll cost a fortune to do up.'

'And it has a fabulous walled garden and a tumbledown glasshouse, neither of which Arab sheikhs are likely to appreciate.'

'Actually,' said Rupert, 'the Arabs are very keen on their gardens –'

'But how did you get to grow plants there?' interrupted Juno. 'Did the previous owners give you permission?'

Althea put her hand on Rupert's arm to indicate that she appreciated his input but couldn't use it right now. 'I work for Mrs Phillips, who's right next door to it. I slip through a hole in the fence. I've been doing it for years.'

'You'll just have to find somewhere else for them.' Rightly assuming that her sister had not asked permission, Juno decided to postpone her lecture on the Criminal Justice Bill and Aggravated Trespass until a more auspicious occasion.

'But where? I haven't possibly got room for them here, and I'm unlikely to find another unused greenhouse anything like that size.'

'Then you'll have to find out who's bought the house and ask them if you can go on using theirs for a bit.' Juno was remarkably calm. 'The house will need loads doing to it. No one's going to move in for ages.'

Althea, who, if it was the right house, would willingly camp in one room while the rest of it was rebuilt around her, regarded her sister thoughtfully. It was unlikely that the buyers of Barnet House would have such a low comfort threshold – no one rich enough to buy such a house possibly could have. No, they were more likely to be like Juno, who wouldn't move into a new home if the paintwork needed touching up, let alone if the fitted kitchen or en-suite bathroom were not yet installed. Which could give her valuable extra time.

'How do I find out who's bought it?'

'Leave that to me. Networking is one of my strengths. I'll find out, then all you have to do is ask for *permission* to use the greenhouse.' Her sister's Cambridge blue eyes held more than a hint that that was what Althea should have done in the first place.

Brushing this aside, Althea asked, 'You don't think I could just carry on? Using the greenhouse without asking? They wouldn't find out for ages.'

'They may not find out, but they might send in the bull-dozers.'

'Oh God. What an awful thought. But supposing they say no? Or only speak Arabic?'

Juno ignored this lapse into flippancy. 'You'll be no worse off. And they're bound to give you time to find somewhere else.'

'But where? I've got a whole lot of French children coming this summer.'

Juno sighed. 'One at a time, I hope.'

'Oh yes,' said her sister. 'They're no problem. But it means I can't fill the spare bedroom with seed-trays and pots.'

'Well, I'll find out who's bought it as soon as I can, and then you can go and see them. Unless the builders want to knock down the greenhouse straight away, it probably won't be a problem.'

Althea scanned the paper for hints about who had bought the house, and whether or not they were likely to destroy a dilapi-dated glasshouse. Not finding any, she asked, 'And you really think they'll let me?'

'Of course, if you look respectable and honest. Don't worry about it. I'll lend you something to wear. I've got a suit which is quite baggy. You might just fit into it.'

Somehow this promise did not add to Althea's confidence about the situation.

Too tired to garden, and needing to relax when Juno had gone, Althea fetched the pile of magazines Juno had brought with her and took them into the conservatory. They were her favourites, full of beautiful gardens and luscious, unaffordable kitchens. Putting aside her pressing problems, she leafed through them, sighing wistfully at south-facing walled gardens and pleached hedges and tutting disdainfully at expensive, unimaginative planting schemes.

One of them had a competition. She could never resist a com-petition and quite often won things. Unfortunately, so far, none of the things had been remotely useful. Nothing loath, Althea found a pen and settled down to think up a really good tie-breaker to explain in twelve words why it was so important for her to have a holiday in the Algarve.

Later, when Merry came back from her friend's house, she found her mother engrossed.

'Hi, Mum. After another fitted kitchen you won't win?'

Guilty, Althea put down the pen. She should have been reassessing her marketable skills and updating her c.v., not day-dreaming about orange groves.

As yet unaware of the catastrophe which had befallen the household, Merry went on: 'All you ever win are boring things, like salad spinners and tickets to football matches. I don't know why you bother.'

'This one's for a fortnight in a villa in Portugal. You'd like that, wouldn't you?'

Merry nodded slowly. 'Only if I could take Ronnie.'

'Of course you could.' They both knew that no one would go to Portugal but they both enjoyed the day-dream. 'Hungry?'

Merry shook her head. 'I had a massive plate of pasta at Ronnie's. *Her* mother makes the sauce *herself*.'

'Well,' said Althea brightly. 'Perhaps if you asked her nicely she'd show you how to make it. But just now, there's something I've got to tell you.'

Merry took it extremely well. As long as she could still have the same best friend and go to the same school, she didn't much care where her mother worked. It was because, Althea realized, her daughter had no real concept of what being unemployed meant. Which was also why she herself was being so calm about the situation. She still had that airy feeling she had had when she left school, or, as she had reflected earlier, when she knew she no longer had to live with Frederick.

Juno rang back later that evening. 'Listen, I've found out who's bought that house.'

'How on earth did you do that so soon?'

Juno, who ran a highly active social life as well as a high-powered job, a combination made easier by her having no children, a tidy husband, and a cleaner, was blasé about her achievement. 'Well, Diana Sanders is the sister-in-law of the estate agent. She told me.'

'So who is it?'

'He's an architect who's just joined the Greenwich Partnership. Divorced, with a grown-up family and a meaningful relationship with his secretary, who came with him.'

'Do they make them fill in a questionnaire to get on the mailing list?'

'Of course not. But the important thing is, we know his name and where he works. All you have to do is arrange to visit him. It's simple really, darling. I'll bring round that suit. You needn't give it back, you'll be needing it for job interviews.'

Thanking her sister meekly, Althea determined to give the suit back the moment she had secured her glasshouse.

Althea pulled her silk blouse well down and pulled in her tummy. The suit was reasonably loose around the waist but was far too tight lower down and had a tendency to ride up. However, with the jacket to cover her hips, she was moderately content with her appearance. She had ignored her sister's advice that a single strand of pearls and pearl studs were what she wanted, and had put on a string of vivid glass beads and matching earrings. This shocked the navy suit out of its complacency, and made it clear to it that it was not after a job.

Tweaking her hair into place and on the lookout for signs of crow's feet, Althea decided the beads were a smidgen too long. In many ways she was careless about her appearance, but she was particular about the placing of brooches and the length of necklaces.

Lacking a safety-pin and not having time to find fuse-wire, she twisted them behind her neck to shorten them. But they were too tightly strung, and instead of the beads holding the loop, they snapped and bounced free.

'Oh, bugger,' muttered Althea, scooping up the beads as they fell about her. 'Now it'll have to be the pearls.'

She raced upstairs and plunged her hand into the bowl where she kept her jewellery, pricked her finger and found the pearls.

As it turned out, the pearls were a good choice: they gave her a much needed dignity.

As usual, she had arrived early and had to walk about until she felt it was the right time to get her knocking knees through the pretentious pillars and inside the shiny glass doors of the building. After instructions from the kind man at the desk, she had got on to the right floor and out of the lift.

Now, faced with a glamorous young woman in a short skirt and sleeveless top, showing not the slightest sign of pudgy knees or upper arm flab, she felt the pearls gave her the dignity of middle age. Which, in the face of such vibrant youth and overt fitness, was her only refuge. She could never compete on equal terms. This creature would patronize her at the drop of a hat.

'Do come in, Mrs Farraday, although you are a bit early,' said the woman, who was presumably Patrick Donahugh's 'significant other', the secretary Juno had told her about. 'Does Mr Donahugh know why you want to see him?'

Althea smiled, feeling old and stubborn. 'No.'

'You can tell me. I'm his personal assistant.' The woman revealed teeth that were unnaturally even and almost definitely capped but none the less dazzling for being artificial.

Althea ran her tongue over her own teeth, undoctored, and possibly lipstick-smeared. 'Then I'm sure he'll tell you. But I really can't go into it all twice.'

Miffed, but making a good job of not showing it, the woman ushered Althea to a waiting area. 'Your appointment's not for five minutes, you know,' she said, rubbing in what Althea already knew. 'Do sit down.'

Reluctantly, Althea let herself sink down into a sofa she might never climb out of and watched the woman disappear into the inner sanctum. She would not allow her boss to emerge a nanosecond before the appointed time.

Althea took a copy of *Country Life* and flicked to the gardening section. Her fingers went automatically towards a bowl of something she took to be tasty snacks for the hungry and anxious. Just in time she realized that they were wood shavings and tree seeds and not edible. How many people, she wondered, had carried them to their mouths, only to have to spit them ignominiously into their hankies?

At last the beautiful secretary reappeared. 'He'll see you now,' she said. She watched until Althea had hauled herself to her feet, then ushered her into the office.

Patrick Donahugh got up from behind a huge desk, so over-laid with plans and papers that Althea was reminded of the fair-ground game when you throw coins on to already heaped piles, hoping yours will be the coin to dislodge all the others. He was in his shirt-sleeves, which was understandable, considering the temperature in his office. His eyes exactly matched the blue of his shirt. Without doubt, the shirt had been bought for him by his girlfriend.

'Patrick Donahugh.' He held out a hand. 'What can I do for you?'

He had thick, rather untidy hair which could have been bleached fair by sun and wind, or have gone grey. His nose and mouth were large, set haphazardly in his face, which made the way he looked at Althea, straight in the eyes, more intense. He had a foreign-looking tan – not from the Caribbean, Althea decided, but somewhere salty, like Brittany.

Her wait had not lessened Althea's tension. She hated asking for favours, and having to ask one of someone she didn't know made her more nervous than ever. She took the hand, trying not to feel flustered by his gaze. 'Althea Farraday. Nothing too difficult, I hope.'

'Do sit down. Coffee? Topaz, would you mind?'

Althea, burdened with a mouthful of a name herself, felt a moment of sympathy for Topaz. This was dispelled by Topaz's flashing smile and swaying walk which somehow implied that she had been christened Tracy but had called herself Topaz. It also occurred to Althea, with something of a pang, that Topaz had a foreign-looking tan too.

She turned her attention to the matter in hand. Patrick Donahugh was still looking at her with close attention, which paradoxically made Althea feel he was really thinking about something quite else.

'I gather you've bought Barnet House?' she said firmly, to make sure she had his attention.

'Yes?' He didn't say, 'What has that to do with you?' but she could tell he was thinking it.

'Well . . .' What had seemed a fairly simple request now seemed

18

on a par with asking for a kidney donation. 'You know the green-house? At Barnet House?'

'Not well, but we have been introduced.'

Couldn't he just have said yes? Did he have to be facetious? 'Well, I don't know if you're aware ...' She'd worked out what she wanted to say days ago, why hadn't she brought her notes?

'Yes?'

'That I've been using it.'

Patrick Donahugh sat back in his chair as if this revelation had solved a mystery. 'I was aware that someone was. I didn't think all those plants got there on their own, like the dry rot and the death watch beetle.'

'Dry rot and death watch beetle? Bad luck.' Althea tried not to feel pleased. A house with those problems would have to stay empty for aeons.

'Yes. And seed trays in the glasshouse. There's no end to the problems of that property.'

Althea pulled at her skirt, wishing she'd worn one of her own, longer, drapey ones, which were easier to sit in. 'The seed trays aren't a problem, I put them there.'

'And presumably you can take them out?'

'Yes, but I don't want to. I mean, can I – Would you mind, if I left them there for a bit?'

Topaz sashayed in with the coffee. She had, Althea noticed, the sort of muscles in her upper arms that indicated regular work-outs with weights. She set the tray down on a small table which was empty save for another bowl of wood shavings and flower heads. They looked even more appetizing than the ones outside.

'What's that?' Topaz asked – rather sharply, Althea thought.

Althea turned to her. 'I was asking if it would be possible for me to go on using the greenhouse of Barnet House until I can find somewhere else for my plants.'

'I'm afraid that wouldn't be at all convenient,' said Topaz, without reference to her boss. 'We're having builders in.'

So they were actually living together. Did Juno's spies know this? And if not, should Althea tell them?

'Are you going to pull down the greenhouse? It would be an

awful shame. It certainly needs restoring, but basically, it's in good condition . . .'

'Mr Donahugh's not at all interested in gardening. So we're having an indoor swimming pool. The whole lot's going,' said Topaz, obviously a fifty-lengths-before-breakfast woman.

'But not immediately, surely? Don't you want to see to the dry rot and stuff first? You ought to, you know. It can spread terribly.'

Topaz handed Althea a cup of coffee. It had milk, no sugar and was nerve-janglingly strong. 'Of course. Patrick knows all about that.'

'As an architect, one would,' said Patrick, who took his coffee black and showed no signs of being affected by too much caffeine.

Althea wished she could start again. She felt dreadfully hot inside Juno's navy-blue suit, and wondered if she would look fat if she took off her jacket. 'What I'm trying to say is, or rather, what I'm asking is, can I keep my plants in your glasshouse for a bit longer? Just until I can find somewhere else for them?'

Topaz perched on the table and crossed her legs, causing Althea to speculate if the muscles in her calves weren't a bit too well defined. 'Well, I suppose . . .'

'Why did you put them there in the first place?' asked Patrick.

Althea compressed her lips into a smile. 'They just grew . . .' Seeing this answer wasn't satisfactory, she went on: 'I couldn't bear the wasted space. All that glass, ideal for raising plants, growing nothing but Traveller's Joy.'

'And why do you need to raise plants? Are you a gardener?' asked Topaz.

The way she said it made Althea feel as if she ought to be wearing corduroy trousers with strings round the knees and talk in an unintelligible country dialect. 'A garden designer, actually,' she said. That sounded much more the thing, very double-barrelled and posh.

Topaz obviously thought so too. 'Oh, really? Who have you worked for?'

Althea reeled off the names of her gardening clients. As she was given a totally free hand with all three of them, and had rearranged their gardens, she wasn't really lying. She'd just never thought of calling herself a designer before.

'So you needed the space for professional reasons?'

Althea looked at Patrick Donahugh and gulped. 'Yes.'

'So how long is it likely to be before you can find new premises?'

She shrugged. 'I don't know. Possibly for ever. But of course, that's not your problem,' she added, hoping fervently he would disagree with her.

'No, it's not,' said Patrick. 'But I don't see why you shouldn't leave your plants where they are for a couple of weeks, or even a month. But I do want them out by then.' He seemed to think this offer was generous.

'And we'll work out a suitable rent,' added Topaz.

Althea felt the sweat bead her hairline and took off her suit jacket. Fat or not, she would burst into flames if she didn't cool off. 'Of course.'

'I mean, if you're a professional garden designer, you probably charge a lot for your plants,' went on Topaz.

Althea only ever took money for plants if it was for charity. She took a deep breath. 'Could I arrange to pay you after a specified time? Say, three months?'

Patrick's blue eyes seemed suddenly rather cold. 'I did say three weeks to a month. And surely it would be more business-like to pay weekly?'

'Not in my business. As a designer I am paid for completion of a contract, as I'm sure you are.' How lucky she'd read that in one of Juno's magazines in the loo that morning.

'Do you have cash-flow problems, then?'

'Not at all,' said Althea indignantly. Her cash didn't flow so much as pour, all in one direction.

'Then you must be the only person running their own busi-ness who hasn't. However, if you prefer, we can arrange for you to pay when you take the plants out.'

'Thank you. Work out how much you want, and let me know.' But don't make it more than a couple of pounds a week, she added silently, through a forced smile.

'You know' – Patrick swung in his chair – 'it's a funny thing, but there was nothing in any of the papers that said the glass-house had a tenant.'

'Wasn't there?' said Althea, standing up rather hurriedly. 'How odd. But there again, there probably wasn't anything in them about the dry rot, or death watch beetle, either.'

'No, but they did crop up in the survey and I am accustomed to dealing with them.'

Althea hung the suit jacket over her shoulders wondering if she could become accustomed to dealing with him. In better circumstances, it might not be a hardship. 'Well, of course, I will get out of your way as quickly as I possibly can.'

'We do want to get on with the swimming pool,' said Topaz. 'I love to swim.'

'Naturally,' said Althea with dignity, putting on her jacket. Unfortunately, the action of raising her arms made the waistband of her skirt drop for a crucial second. She made her exit to an accompaniment of emerald green beads falling from her body and bouncing on to the marble floor.

CHAPTER THREE

A couple of weeks later, Althea was standing in the school office, first on one leg and then on the other, wishing her darling boss weren't so anxious.

'And so you're just looking after those five,' said Mr Edwards, handing her a sheet of paper. 'I wish I was coming with you.'

Althea, who had been briefed about the school trip to France every day for the last fortnight, felt she had already done the journey several times. She gave her boss a soothing smile. 'I'm sure everything will be fine.'

'It's so unfortunate that I can't come,' he said for the hundredth time. 'But I'm glad you're going to be there for Whickham Primary.'

'There are three other members of staff also there for Whickham Primary. Really, you've no need to worry.'

'I know, but none of them have been with me as long as you have, and their loyalties are shifting to the new head . . .'

'I'm *sure* they're not.' Her responses were on automatic, but even if she had her message of reassurance blazoned across the sky by an aeroplane, Mr Edwards wouldn't believe it.

'And you're happy to be paired up with Sylvia? I don't know very much about the lady you'll be staying with, except that she's a widow.'

'It'll be fine. We'll be fine.' Sylvia Jones was a nursery nurse at the school and a special friend of Althea's.

'So is there anything else you need to know?'

'I don't think so. I think I know the whole itinerary by heart. The coach leaves here at six a.m. sharp, tomorrow.' Wickedly, she added, 'If you could just give me a quick crash course in French, I'll be fine.'

Mr Edwards was horrified. 'Don't you speak any French at all?'

'Well, you know, O level, a thousand years ago.' She gave him a reassuring smile. 'I'm very good at mime, though.' She had confessed this when she was first invited to go, but Mr Edwards hadn't thought it mattered when he was expecting to be one of the party. Now, suddenly, it was an issue.

He appeared more anxious than ever. 'You'll be fine, really you will,' he said, obviously not convinced.

'I know,' Althea said firmly. 'Now I'm going home to pack.'

She also had exhaustive and complicated watering instructions to write for the boys. Merry was staying with a friend, but William and Rupert were in charge of Bozo, the cats and two guinea pigs who, though geriatric, resolutely refused to die. And, by far the most demanding, the plants.

Her packing was less important. Although there was to be a civic reception, there were only so many clothes one could wear during a weekend of coach travel punctuated by meals. Comfort seemed more important than elegance. Althea, trusting that her hostess wouldn't be unbearably chic, had decided to rely heavily on navy blue, brightened by scarves and jewellery.

Althea had been invited to go with the school to France as a special sorry-you're-being-made-redundant treat, and as an extra adult pair of hands. Each adult had been assigned groups of children which, with luck, matched their ability to handle them. Althea's group of girls were not angels, the angels being reserved for less resilient members of the party, but she was very fond of them all, and felt she could rely on them not to let her down.

The trip was the brainchild of the new head. Each year for five years, Geoffrey Conway (so he told everyone) had taken a small party of children to visit a school in France. This year, he had invited Mr Edwards to send a party too, as a 'team-building exercise' for the two schools. It was, he said, a chance for some of the staff to get to know each other in informal circumstances.

Mr Edwards had liked the idea, only – instead of handpicking children from nice homes who had been to France before – he threw the offer open to all those of the right age group on a first-come, first-served basis. This piece of democracy meant that instead of the bright, well-motivated children with whom Mr

Conway would be representing his country, Whickham Primary were putting up a mixed side, some of whom even the doting Mr Edwards described as 'lively'.

'Mrs Farraday! Mrs Farraday! Have you heard? Miss Jones can't come.'

One of Althea's brightest and 'liveliest' girls broke this news to her as she staggered through the school gate at ten to six in the morning, weighed down by bags and lack of sleep. She had woken every hour since three, in case her alarm didn't work. When it finally did go off, Althea was having her only deep sleep of the night.

'Oh, Lorraine, are you sure?'

'Yes! Her mum's poorly.'

Mr Edwards, who, although not of the party, was there to see everyone off safely, confirmed the depressing tidings. 'I'm afraid Lorraine is right. Sylvia rang me last night to say that she was too ill to come.'

'So we're an adult short?' Althea's tired heart sank. 'Do you want me to take her group?'

'No thanks, Althea, though it's kind of you to offer. I rang Geoffrey Conway to tell him and he said he'd find someone else. He's going to swap his groups around a bit, and their nursery nurse will take Sylvia's children because she's met some of them at the District Sports.'

'It's Julie Coulthard, isn't it? Pretty girl with long dark hair?'

'That's right! How clever of you to remember!'

'We did teas together at the Sports.'

'So you did. So perhaps you wouldn't mind just keeping a weather eye on her? I feel some of our lot might be a bit much for someone used to younger children.'

'Of course,' said Althea. Just then a cry of 'Here's the coach' rippling through the playground interrupted further specula-tion. Mr Conway's school, which was more accustomed to being dragged into the European Community than Whickham Primary, was already established on the coach. This was a disappointment to her charges but a relief to Althea. There was something about the back row of a coach which invited bad behaviour from even the most respectable senior citizens. Any group of children sitting there, unless actually handcuffed and gagged, would definitely become rowdy eventually.

Althea steered her children to somewhere in the middle of the coach and, having seen them safely established, went to put her bag in the luggage compartment under the floor.

She recognized Geoffrey Conway from the back and wondered if she was part of the 'team building'. He was talking to a late arrival who also had his back to her, and Althea hovered, not wishing to butt in.

'So who's this woman I'm supposed to be staying with?' asked the latecomer.

Althea thought she recognized the voice, but couldn't place it. He was taller than Mr Conway and was wearing the sort of casual clothes that were shockingly expensive but lasted for ever.

'Mrs Farraday, Alison – something like that. She's the school secretary at Whickham's. Bit of a –'

Althea cleared her throat as noisily as she could before she heard what Mr Conway thought of her. Eavesdroppers never hear good of themselves. 'Hello,' she said. 'I just want to put my bag in . . .'

Both men jumped and turned round as if she'd said 'Boo!' A moment later, she jumped herself. The man with Geoffrey Conway was Patrick Donahugh.

'But you're . . .' said Patrick.

'Mrs Farraday,' said Mr Conway. 'This is Patrick Donahugh. He's going to join our board of governors. He's very kindly agreed to step into the breach, so to speak.'

Althea managed a forced grin. 'Hello.' She owed this man quite a lot of money, and she had no idea how she was going to pay it. Perhaps she'd win the lottery in time.

'Hello, Mrs Farraday. How are you?'

'Do you two know each other?' Geoffrey Conway's eyebrows shot up.

'No,' said Althea quickly, 'but we have met.'

Geoffrey Conway's eyebrows reached his hairline and stayed there.

'Yes,' said Patrick. 'I thought you said you were a garden designer.'

'And I thought you said you were an architect.'

26

'I am an architect,' said Patrick crossly.

'Mr Donahugh – Patrick,' broke in Geoffrey Conway, rather put out that Althea didn't seem to have grasped this the first time, 'is going to be a governor at the combined school. He very kindly offered to stand in for Miss – er – Jones.'

'Golly,' said Althea whose general opinion of school governors was not high. 'Coming on this trip's going beyond the call of duty, isn't it?'

Patrick gave the impression that he was not necessarily there on purpose, as if circumstances had conspired against him and dropped him in it. 'Possibly. I don't know what being a governor entails, yet.'

Althea smiled sweetly. 'Please don't ask me to enlighten you.'

Geoffrey Conway did not look happy. He had not been impressed by Althea at her interview to be secretary at the combined school and had only agreed to her coming because she was known to be good with children. Patrick Donahugh was his new, prize governor, persuaded to the role with some difficulty, – probably, if he were honest, only because, apart from his colleagues at the architectural practice, Patrick knew very few people in the area except him. He had pounced on Patrick as fresh, influential blood, playing on a small prior acquaintance the moment he heard about Patrick's new appointment.

'Right, Mrs Farraday – or should that be Alison?' he went on hastily, before Althea could say anything awful. 'Let's get your luggage on board.'

Althea surrendered her bag. 'It's Althea, actually. Catch up with you both later,' she added quickly. 'I'll go and find a seat in the coach.'

The moment she found the place saved for her by Lorraine, she begged a passing child to sit next to her. It was unlikely that Patrick Donahugh – or worse, Geoffrey Conway – would willingly sit next to her, but if they didn't get in the coach soon, they would be forced to sit wherever there was a space.

As it turned out, Geoffrey Conway had a place saved for him in the front, and Patrick Donahugh ended up next to Julie Coulthard, the pretty long-haired nursery nurse from the other school. Somehow, Althea wasn't surprised.

'Want a sweet, miss?' asked Althea's seat-mate.

'No thanks, it's a bit early for me.'

Ellie, her companion, unwrapped a liquorice toffee, guaranteed to rip the fillings from anyone over twenty. 'Say if you want one later.'

Althea, having promised that she would, shut her eyes, in a vain attempt to catch up on some sleep before the singing started. When it did, a few moments later, and the children were all howling out pairs of names – *Kristen and Alex up the tree! K-i-s-s-i-n-g . . .'* – Althea was just very slightly tempted to suggest to Lorraine, who was the initiator, that the names 'Mr Donahugh and Miss Coulthard' were given a verse, but she resisted. That sort of thing could so easily backfire.

Having been told to please turn round and sit down at least a dozen times, Lorraine at last confessed that she fancied one of the boys in Mr Donahugh's group. How she had worked out who was in whose group, Althea couldn't begin to guess, but Lorraine was obviously like Juno when it came to networking.

'So can I go and sit nearer him?' asked Lorraine.

'No. All the seats are taken. Besides, he'd know you fancied him if you did that.'

Lorraine subsided for the time being and Althea bit back a smile. If she knew Lorraine, a powerful, liberated young woman, who had no truck with the old-fashioned notion that the boy should make the first move, Patrick's charge wouldn't be left in peace for long.

'Do you really want to start eating now, Ellie?' she asked her seat-mate who, having eaten half-a-dozen sweets, had now started on her lunch. 'It's still only seven in the morning!'

'My mum packed masses,' said Ellie. 'Want a cheese roll?'

Althea declined politely. All the children had their packed lunches out and were tucking in merrily. They continued to sing and eat for the entire journey to Dover.

'Right, girls.' Althea confronted her group, having successfully counted them all off the coach and into the lounge area of the ferry. 'If you're good, we can go into the duty free and spray ourselves with samples. But if you make a noise, Mr Conway will make us all sit here until we reach France.'

In Althea's opinion, Mr Conway lacked imagination when it

came to dealing with children. He wanted to keep them severely controlled at all times. Althea felt a few rewards and a few outlets for high spirits were more likely to achieve the desired effect. It was while she and her girls, all smelling intoxicatingly of French perfume, were on deck, that they met Patrick Donahugh. He was in despair. All his group, a hastily handpicked bunch of high-fliers, destined for great academic achievement, had escaped.

'Leave it to me, sir,' said Lorraine. 'I'll find them.'

'OK,' said Althea. 'You go with her, Angela. But you others stay here.'

Patrick, with less experience and therefore less confidence in Lorraine's ability to sniff out her quarry, was still concerned. 'I swear I only stopped to buy a paper and the whole lot of them vanished. They could be over the side by now.'

'They won't be,' said Althea. 'Lorraine will find them and bring them back.'

'But how do you know?'

'She's very strong-minded and, in case you hadn't noticed, very attractive.'

The rest of Althea's group lolled over the side of the ship, checking out the talent and spotting their schoolmates, shooting sidelong glances at Mr Donahugh. They liked Mrs Farraday, and although she was probably past it, she might like an equally ancient boyfriend. Mr Donahugh would do.

'Can I buy you a cup of coffee?' Patrick asked Althea when his troop had been found and, under the supervision of Lorraine and her mates, were all playing Street Fighter Two in the games room. 'I owe you something for finding my boys for me.'

'It was Lorraine you owe, she fancies your Darren. And we mustn't leave the children for long, but I certainly need something.'

Having told Lorraine they were going, they found a table and Althea waited for her coffee. Patrick was bringing it when Geoffrey Conway swooped on them. 'Hello, Patrick, Ali – Alison?'

'It's Althea, Geoffrey. A bit of a mouthful, I know,' she replied smiling sweetly.

Geoffrey sat down. 'I'm glad of an opportunity to talk to you both. As you know, *Althea*, Sylvia Jones was supposed to have been sharing your accommodation, and so far, I haven't been able to get in touch with the person you were staying with. *However*, the head teacher in France has assured me that there will be no problem accommodating *you* both.'

'You mean we won't find ourselves expected to share a bed, like in the coffee advert?' said Althea.

Geoffrey Conway didn't watch commercial television and had no idea what Althea was talking about, but was suitably horrified at the suggestion. 'No! Certainly not.' He laughed embarrassedly. 'We couldn't have that, could we?'

'Apparently not,' said Patrick, bland and ambiguous.

'When we actually arrive,' Geoffrey went on, after a startled glance at his star governor, 'the head teacher, the Mayor and all the village dignitaries will be out in force to meet us. So I'd like you, Patrick, to be with me when we get off the coach, to greet them. My French isn't all it might be, and I'm sure yours is far better.'

'Mine's not all it might be either,' said Patrick. 'But it's better than my German.'

'But I thought Ms – er – Topaz – when I rang up – she said your French was excellent!'

Althea suddenly began to feel sorry for Geoffrey. Topaz, wanting her boss and lover boosted, had obviously exaggerated his linguistic abilities.

Patrick raised his hands in an extremely Gallic gesture. 'Sorry!'

Just then, Lorraine appeared at Althea's side. 'Can you come, Mrs Farraday? Kirsty's fallen down and cut herself and it's bleeding really badly.'

Althea got up. 'Excuse me, gentlemen.'

'Don't hesitate to ask for help, er, Althea,' said Geoffrey. 'I have got a current First Aid certificate.'

'And I've got a sticking-plaster in my bag,' said Althea, 'which I think we'll find is more to the point.'

The children were still eating and singing when the coach finally drew up outside the village school, where, as Mr Conway had promised, a huge body of people awaited their arrival.

One of Patrick's group had been coach sick, and Patrick, quite unable to deal with it himself, had asked pathetically if Althea could help. Because she felt extremely sorry for the little boy in question, Althea had spent all the journey since arriving in France bathing his head with eau-de-cologne wipes and trying to keep her own lunch down while he lost his. Short on sleep before she started, Althea now felt fit to drop. The children seemed ready to party all night.

Geoffrey Conway and Patrick, confident that they were not smelling of sick, made their way with the other teachers to the front. Being less confident, Althea cadged a squirt of duty-free perfume from Julie Coulthard and they followed more slowly, letting the children stream off in front of them.

The school-hall was *en fête*. Vases of flowers were wedged into the small spaces on the tables not covered with food. Flags, both French and British, wound their way round the walls.

Julie had immediately disappeared into the bosom of her French hosts, but Althea, feeling like an evacuee, had not been claimed. She smiled vaguely at everyone, trying to look pleasant and friendly, feeling suddenly abandoned. Patrick was in a thicket of dignitaries, flanked by Geoffrey. If only Sylvia had been able to come, she'd have been enjoying herself.

'Please,' said a voice. 'Eat!' A kindly Frenchwoman pushed Althea towards the table where plates of quiches, pâtés, trenchers of bread, piles of exotic pastries and gâteaux fought for attention. The children, who had all found their host families and mingled with the French youngsters with delightful homogeneity, all grabbed handfuls of food and disappeared into the playing field to play football. One boy had a whole baguette, filled with ham and salad at least a foot long. It was, Althea noted without surprise, the boy who had heaved ever since Calais.

'Hello.' Patrick appeared at her elbow with a full glass of champagne which he thrust into her hand. 'I've just had a word with the French headmaster. It's a bit unfortunate, the woman we're staying with is a nurse on night duty and couldn't get time off to be here. Apparently we're having dinner with the headmaster and his wife, and Geoffrey. And then the headmaster will drive us to where we're staying. Someone's already taken our bags to the house.'

'Oh.' How like a man to dump his vomiting charge on her, to

disappear in a cloud of dignitaries and then saunter up and deliver this sort of information. Still, she had no right to expect anything better. 'It seems a bit rude arriving in the middle of the night without even saying hello,' she commented. 'And will she know that we've got to have separate rooms, and stuff?'

Patrick shrugged. Not for the first time Althea reflected that not speaking the lingo was no bar to acting it. 'I suppose so. Geoffrey promised he'd got it all sorted out and I told the headmaster that we weren't married and he said it was no problem. "*C'est pas grave*" were his exact words.'

'That could mean anything,' said Althea, gloomy with tiredness and champagne.

Patrick put a large hand on her shoulder. 'I'm sure it'll be fine. Look, there's the *directeur*, trying to catch our attention. It must be time for dinner.'

'I couldn't eat another thing,' said Althea, who had managed a cube of cheese only with difficulty.

Patrick made a face. 'Sorry, but you're going to have to. Francine, that's the headmaster's wife, made it clear she's been cooking for days.'

CHAPTER FOUR

After a hair-raising journey squashed in the back of the headmaster's car, they arrived at his house. After a brief moment to wash their hands, another bottle of champagne was opened.

Althea could have quietly dozed off on the sofa, but as Francine spoke no English at all, her O level French had to be hauled out and its pathetic inadequacy revealed. After a short and painful interval, valiantly trying to find some meaning in Althea's utterances, Francine sprang to her feet and summoned them to the table. 'Now, we eat!' she said proudly. And meant it. Althea thought she must have been cooking for weeks, not days. She certainly did not believe in her guests going hungry – even if they had been the army Francine had prepared food for.

Althea ate all she could and then some more. Somehow she got through four courses. She exclaimed in wonder at the terrine, a poem of pale green avocado, crab and strips of pepper. She marvelled over the tenderness of the salmon, cooked in foil and sea-salt. She tried three of the half-dozen cheeses on offer, choking down a musty goat's offering with something approaching a smile. She ate the luscious Charlotte Russe, wishing she had more appetite for it.

And there was not only the food to get through. Every course had its own wine to be tasted, savoured and then consumed in terrifying quantities.

'Now coffee!' said the *directeur*, just as Althea's eyelids finally closed. '*Et pour le digestif – cognac!*'

'It's good. I have a key!' The *directeur*, now known as Philippe, triumphantly dangled some house keys.

Althea, alone in the back of the car, had been fast asleep from almost the moment the first rabbit had narrowly escaped death.

'Some poor creature trying to commit suicide,' she had muttered to Patrick, who was in the front.

'But he failed,' he murmured back. 'It must only have been a cry for help.'

After that, Althea had firmly shut her eyes. There was no point in worrying about what you couldn't alter. Now, Patrick's imperative hand on her shoulder brought her back to the present. It took her a couple of moments to come to, by which time Patrick and Philippe were tiptoeing into the house.

'*Les enfants sont ici.*' As Althea joined them, Philippe opened the door to what was obviously a sitting room converted temporarily into a dormitory. There were little sleeping-bag cocoons on the sofa and on the floor. One longer cocoon indicated a teenager, presumably the babysitter.

'Bathroom.' He opened another door. 'Kitchen. *Et voici*, bedroom.'

Although still fuzzy with sleep, Althea noted the horribly singular nature of this announcement.

'And in here?' She pointed eagerly to the last remaining door.

'Nothing. Just a – cupboard?'

He had the right word. Behind the door was nothing more than the selection of polishes, brushes and brooms required for cleaning the ceramic floor tiles which were everywhere. Not reassuring under the circumstances.

'Ah, *bon*. You are tired, Alt'ea. Go quickly to bed!' Philippe opened the door of the bedroom, touched a switch, and the room was instantly bathed in pink light from a pair of bedside lamps and one above the dressing table. 'Quickly!' he commanded, as if she were a recalcitrant child and he an impatient father. He didn't notice her reluctance to enter, for the moment she was in the room he took her hand and kissed her cheek. '*Bonne nuit. Dormez bien.*'

Alone at last, Althea forced herself to contemplate the bed. And while it couldn't quite have been described as a double – more an oversized single – there were two sets of pillows on top of the bedspread and it was obviously meant for them both.

It was an extremely feminine room. The frilled curtains matched the bedspread and the scatter cushions. The kidney-shaped dressing table was crowded with cosmetics and perfumes and swathed in pink tulle like an opulent but vulgar ballerina.

There must be another bedroom somewhere, she thought. Philippe was probably showing it to Patrick this very minute. She'd just been confused by the layout of the house. There were probably a whole lot more rooms round a corner or something. Too little sleep and too much to drink had fuddled her brain. There was no earthly need to panic.

She clung on to these hopes while she extracted her sponge bag, even when she spotted Patrick's case next to hers. After all, Philippe – or whoever it had been – had probably just put both bags in one room for convenience. They couldn't know who wanted to sleep where. She decided to use the bathroom. A good splash of cold water would restore her sense of direction and reveal the second bedroom.

All it revealed on her return was a rueful Patrick standing by the window in her bedroom. The pink light and the frills didn't really suit him.

'Oh,' said Althea. 'So it really is like the coffee ad?'

He nodded. 'There isn't anywhere else to sleep, if that's what you mean. The children are sleeping in the *salon*, and this must be Madame's room.'

Althea looked about her. There were photos, ornaments – even a full-length mirror. It couldn't have been a spare room.

'The children's room must be somewhere,' she said.

'But if they're in the sitting room now, Madame must be planning to come home sometime during the night and use it. Finding a strange man already in occupation would be a nasty shock after a hard night's work.'

'Yes, I suppose it would.'

'I'll sleep on the floor. It'll be fine.' He spoke in the hearty tones which Captain Oates had probably used before he disappeared into the Antarctic night.

Althea glanced down. The floor, like that in the rest of the house, was tiled. A thin nylon rug by the bed was its only covering. 'Did you know this was going to happen?' she asked, procrastinating.

'Not until it was too late, I didn't. We can't ask to go anywhere else at this time of night. Besides, this is Madame's room. She's moved out of it just for us. It would be dreadfully churlish to make a fuss.'

He wasn't telling her anything she didn't know, but it was still depressing. Exhausted, she sank down on to the bed. It sagged alarmingly, dislodging the scatter cushions.

'Or there's a chair,' went on Patrick stoically, probably having noticed how cold and unyielding the floor was.

The chair, spindle-legged and upright, upholstered with a small, frilled cushion, was presently occupied by a pierrot doll. It was hardly more welcoming than the floor and would not be comfortable for anyone more substantial than Columbine.

'You'll freeze.'

'I'll be fine,' said Patrick, still in Captain Oates mode, but sounding less noble.

Althea made a decision. 'Listen, let's be grown up about this. I'm a married woman – or at least I was, and I'm sure I can trust you. If you promise never to tell a living soul, we can share the bed.'

'Can we?'

She was expecting some sort of protest. 'Of course. There's no need to be prudish about it. Just go and use the bathroom while I get changed. I'll be about ten minutes.'

While he was away, she got undressed rapidly. She did trust him not to jump on her in the middle of the night, but she wasn't entirely sure he wouldn't come back while she was still struggling with her tights.

She put a T-shirt on over her nightie – not, she admitted to herself, to conceal from him the rather generous amount of cleavage it revealed, but to cover the little pouches of flesh which lived between her bra-strap and her armpit. She cleansed her face, leaving just enough mascara so she wouldn't look too naked in the morning, then turned down the bed.

When Patrick came back, his chest was bare and his hair was wet. He had obviously had a shower.

'Right,' she said firmly, still adopting her crisp, no-nonsense stance. 'I'll go and brush my teeth.'

Once in the bathroom she wondered if she should shower too. If he had had the courtesy to do so, perhaps she should. She ran the hot tap, but no hot water came out so she abandoned the idea. They weren't lovers, and even if they were, she'd have to be very much in love to face more than a splash of cold water at this time of night.

Patrick, his chest now covered with crisp, Marks & Spencer cotton pyjama, was standing by the bed. 'Well, get in then!' she ordered briskly, as if to a small child.

'Althea . . . I really don't think this is a good idea.'

'We don't have a choice! I always get so irritated with that woman in the advert who seems to think the sky will fall in if she has to share a bed with a man.'

'Do you?'

'Well, don't you?'

'I always see it from the man's point of view myself.'

'Which is?'

'You are *so* naïve. Listen, you get into bed. I'll manage somehow.'

Althea shook her head. Her nightdress went down to her ankles, and with her T-shirt, she was covered up to her neck. There was no way she presented any form of temptation, even if he wasn't attached to Topaz. 'I wouldn't be able to sleep if you were on the floor. I'd feel too guilty.'

He sighed irritably. 'There must be a way round this.'

'There is. It's called sharing the bed.'

He shook his head. 'There must be something I can sleep on in here.' He opened the wardrobe and started rummaging through Madame's collection of frou-frou nighties and negligées. 'Ah! Thank God for a woman who hasn't heard of political correctness.' He pulled out a fur coat. 'This'll do.'

'It would if you were four feet tall, certainly.'

'It'll do now. Watch.' Patrick took one of the pillows. 'Can you spare a blanket?'

'Of course.'

He took one, folded it in half lengthways and laid it on the floor. He put the pillow up one end and laid the fur coat on top of him.

'So which bit will you keep uncovered? Your head and shoulders or your feet?' Althea asked.

'I'll be fine.'

It was Althea's turn to sigh. In the past she had always thought

37

chivalry a noble thing, something to be admired. Now she thought it was a damn nuisance. 'No you won't. Let me help.'

She rummaged through both their luggage and pulled out all their jumpers, sweatshirts and T-shirts. She made a pad with some of them which she put at the foot of Patrick's attempt at bedmaking. She took another blanket off the bed, which left her with one and the bedspread.

'Get in. I'll have to make it round you.'

Patrick's expression became pained, but he lay down obediently. His feet now rested on the pad of clothes and she laid two blankets on top of him, tucking them under his feet. The fur coat went on top of these. Another pad of clothes kept his head and shoulders off the stone floor.

'How's that?'

'Fine.'

He didn't sound fine, but there was nothing else she could do for him, given that he was being so silly. She got into bed and realized she was cold. Too much to eat and drink always had that effect on her. She got out again and found a bundle of clothes she hadn't used on Patrick's bed. She wrapped her feet in a T-shirt and laid the others carefully over herself.

Althea was aching with tiredness, yet she knew that she had no chance of getting to sleep. She was far too tense. What she needed was the World Service to bore her into somnolence, or failing that, hot milk and whisky. She stifled a sigh. Patrick shifted. She was obviously keeping him awake.

'Sorry. I am finding it rather hard to relax. It's been a long time since I've shared a bedroom with anything bigger than a miniature spaniel.' And how she longed for Bozo now. A furry hot-water bottle was just what she needed. 'Are you sure you're all right down there?'

'I'm fine.'

'I'm sleeping there tomorrow.'

'Go to sleep.'

'Sorry. Goodnight.'

In the middle of the night Althea awoke, sweating. She sat up and took off her T-shirt, but even though she was cooler now, she did not doze off.

She could hear Patrick on the floor beside her. He wasn't

snoring exactly, but his breathing had that emphatic smugness which declared that he was asleep and she was not. She listened for a while, finding the rhythm soothing.

What had Frederick sounded like when asleep? When they were first married she probably slept too deeply and never heard him. And then when the children came along, alarmingly soon, he had spent most nights in the spare room when Althea, terrified of cot deaths, refused to put William in his own room the moment he came home from hospital. She had insisted on having him by her bedside. Frederick found this an invasion of his personal space and things had gone downhill from there.

Twice, after Frederick left, Althea allowed herself to be persuaded into having an affair. Both men had been good friends to start with and both insisted that sleeping together would enhance the relationship. It didn't. Both men separately decided that things could not go back to how they had been before and went, one to Canada and the other to the Outer Hebrides. Althea missed their talents with lawnmowers and ballcocks, but not the sex, and afterwards resolved to keep her friends and her chastity.

When the children were little, they quite often spent the night with Althea in the big double bed. But that stage was long over, and it was only Bozo, her little Cavalier, who was allowed in her bed on windy nights, or if Althea was feeling particularly depressed. But Bozo was always over-heating or scratching, which made her a restless bed-mate. Thus compared, Patrick was very little trouble.

When Althea woke again, Patrick was standing by her urgently repeating her name.

'Althea? Wake up! Madame has breakfast ready and we have to be at the school in an hour.'

'Oh God! What time is it?' A glance at her watch told her it was half past eight. 'How can I have slept so late? Have I time for a shower?'

'If you're quick. And by the way, we've been married for twelve years and have three children.'

'Oh?' she chuckled. 'And what are their names?'

He grinned. 'I left that entirely up to you.'

'Typical. How old are they and what sexes?'

'You've got children, haven't you? I thought we could use them.'

'Not if we've only been married twelve years, we can't. My eldest is seventeen.'

'Oh.' He looked put out. 'You don't look old enough.'

'I was a child-bride.' She fiddled with the sheet, hoping he wouldn't notice her blushing.

'Obviously. And do you like tea or coffee?'

She chuckled. 'How did you explain not knowing that?'

'I said that usually you drank tea, but you might like coffee. As we're in France.'

She nodded. 'That probably covers it.'

'Now hurry up. The children all had breakfast ages ago and she wants to show us the garden before we go.'

Althea pulled herself upright. 'She speaks good English, then?'

Patrick appeared momentarily confused. 'Er, not really. But I'm quite good at making myself understood. Now hurry! I'll sort out all this bedding.'

When Althea appeared, Madame got up from the table and embraced her warmly, breaking into rapid speech and indicating that Althea should sit down.

Althea apologized for the paucity of her French and sat at the table which was laden with coffee pots, baskets of croissants and a huge brioche which sat on a tea-towel. By the time she had fought off everything except a croissant and a bowl of coffee, she felt exhausted.

Madame spoke rapidly and animatedly to Patrick who shrugged and referred to Althea. Madame appeared confused, but then turned to Althea and continued at the same rate. Althea explained that her husband did not speak much French and took refuge in another croissant. While she was eating, not even Madame, who had a personality as generous as her ample figure, could expect her to speak.

'That was exhausting,' said Patrick as, late, they hurried to the school where the bus was waiting to take them on a scenic tour of the country.

'I knew it would be,' Althea panted, forced into a jog by the pace.

'So did I, really.' Patrick, though not so hung up on punctuality, was longer-legged and therefore merely walking briskly.

'So why did you come?' For her the weekend was 'getting away'. Part work, part pleasure, it was France, and it was free, apart from spending money. And if Sylvia had been able to go too, as planned, it would have been fun. With Patrick as a companion, 'fun' no longer covered it.

'Personal reasons.' He put a wealth of meaning into these two words, including the fact that he did not want to go into details.

'Oh.' Althea was dying of curiosity but she suppressed it. 'Do look at the way those tiles are hung. It looks as if the roof has slipped off, like melting icing.'

'Oh yes.' His mind was on other things. 'Now, Althea, we're going to have to be really careful if anyone asks about our accommodation.'

'*If* anyone asks? Are you mad? That'll be the main topic of conversation! What did you eat and what was your room like?' She paused to catch her breath. 'I reckon we've got about a hundred yards to think up a room for you. I'll keep the one we had as more people will ask me.'

'OK. What'll we have? An attic?'

'Not in a bungalow, no. A small room off the garage. Single bed, single light bulb but very comfortable. OK?'

'I suppose so. But only one pillow, and the bed was rather on the short side.'

Althea raised a suspicious eyebrow. 'You're quite good at this pretending business, aren't you?'

'Sometimes I surprise myself.'

He certainly surprised Althea. The lies tripped glibly off his tongue as he described to Geoffrey Conway how Althea had volunteered to have the smaller bedroom with the short bed, but how he had insisted on her having the double all to herself.

She realized, as Patrick was carried away by Geoffrey on a tide of obsequiousness, that she missed him. She wanted him by *her* side, not with Geoffrey, or worse, in the youthful clutches of Julie Coulthard, who pounced the moment Geoffrey released him.

41

For Althea, other women's men had always been completely off-limits, a high moral stance made easier to maintain by the fact that she didn't remotely fancy any of her friends' husbands. But Patrick was attractive, Topaz was far away, and being thrown together in deceit had given them a common bond. Unfortunately, she couldn't take advantage of it – take his arm in a proprietorial way, or demand to sit by him in the coach, or tug at him to point things out, however much she wanted to. She would have to content herself by admiring his broad shoulders and athletic stride from afar.

Unlike Lorraine. Lorraine, in short shorts, black tights and big boots, had no scruples. Eleven going on nineteen, she oozed sexual confidence and was intent on adding Darren to her tally of conquests. Darren went to the 'other school', which gave him a glamour not shared by her classmates. He defeated all comers at arm-wrestling during the coach journey and was therefore worthy of her attention.

With a mixture of horror and envy, Althea watched as Lorraine got her prey in her sights and followed him the moment he left the coach. The rest of her group were as keen to see how Lorraine fared as Althea and it was easier to follow than to try and get her back. Aware she was taking the easy rather than the right option, Althea and the others pursued their strong-minded leader.

Patrick's boys were also willing to trail along behind Lorraine and Darren. There was only half an hour to explore the 'typical French market' they had been driven to see, so it was essential that everyone got a chance to buy their souvenirs but not an opportunity to wander off.

Althea was just helping a girl choose between one pair of cheap earrings and another, a task which seemed to take longer than painting the ceiling of the Sistine Chapel, when suddenly she heard an oath from Patrick, and saw him cut through the crowds with surprising speed.

'What happened? Did anyone see?'

'It was Darren, miss,' said a boy. 'He and that girl went off.'

'Oh no!' Althea almost stamped her foot in frustration. Why hadn't she kept a better eye on them? It was all her fault. Now Lorraine and Darren would miss the coach, she'd have to wait for them, and somehow get them back to the village. Geoffrey Conway had been very strict with regard to stragglers. Anyone who was late wouldn't be able to see the windmill or the canal lock which was the deepest in Europe, treats likely to tempt the palette of the most seasoned traveller – or so he thought.

It was kind of Patrick to chase after them, but there was no doubt who was responsible for their absconding. She would have to be the one to wait for them.

Wearily, she ushered her enlarged, mixed flock along the aisles of the market. When they reached the coach, there was still no sign of Patrick and the truants. Althea had to confess what had happened to Geoffrey Conway, and was then forced to listen to his strictures on people who couldn't keep their children in order.

'Really, Mrs Farraday' – he hadn't been happy using her Christian name and was glad for an excuse to revert to titles – 'Mr Edwards assured me you were very responsible and good with children. I am disappointed in you.'

Althea, who wouldn't have spoken to her own children like this, let alone an adult, seethed silently, adding this humiliation to her score with Patrick, who was by now, unbeknownst to him, responsible for the entire fiasco.

As Geoffrey was confiscating the last piece of chewing gum and muttering about leaving, Althea went in search of the truants herself. She knew Geoffrey Conway wouldn't leave without Patrick, whoever else he abandoned.

She saw them coming out of a bar. Patrick, a bulky package under his arm, was chatting amiably to the barman, who was raising his hands and clapping Patrick on the back. Althea couldn't hear which language was being spoken, but she was willing to lay money that the barman wasn't speaking fluent English.

She met the party near the coach, hands on her waist, eyes narrowed, considering how to chill them into obedience.

The children, seeing that Miss's rage wasn't confined to them, skipped neatly on to the bus, leaving Patrick to take the flak.

'I found them in a bar, little devils,' he muttered. 'They'd ordered Pernod. I should have made them drink it. It would have served them right.'

He then explained charmingly to Geoffrey what had happened while Althea stalked into the bus.

'He talks French really well, Mrs Farraday,' said Lorraine as Althea sat down behind her, instinctively knowing this would redirect Althea's rightful wrath. 'Jabbered away like anything.'

Althea had had a very *mauvais quart d'heure* waiting for them. She had been genuinely anxious and she had been tongue-lashed by Geoffrey Conway. To have her dawning suspicion that Patrick spoke not only French, but good French, confirmed, did nothing whatever for her fraying temper.

'You liar!' she accused him as he sat down next to her, her lowered tones doing little to soften her anger. 'You told me you couldn't speak French.'

His blue eyes glowed with amusement under his raised eyebrows. 'You told me you were a garden designer.'

'I *am*. Or at least, sort of. But you really *lied*.'

Like Lorraine and Darren he didn't seem to comprehend the enormity of his crime. 'I didn't actually say I couldn't speak French, did I?'

'*I* don't know. But you didn't speak it, which comes to the same thing.'

'I did confiscate their fags,' he offered, by way of apology.

Althea ignored this. 'Fancy letting me make a fool of myself with my O level French I haven't used for years.' Her whisper spat and hissed like a furious firecracker. 'Besides, if you speak French, surely you could have made it so we didn't have to share a bed?'

His breath was hot in her ear and made the hair on the back of her neck stand on end. 'We didn't share one, remember?'

'That's hardly the point!'

'Look, I realized pretty early on that it would have been very difficult to change our accommodation, and I thought, as adults, we could cope. Which we did.'

She conceded this point with reluctance. 'OK, I understand that part. But why didn't you let on you could speak French?'

'Because I'd have had to interpret for Geoffrey the entire time.'

That was true. Geoffrey was clinging to him quite enough without using him as a translator. She huffed. 'It still seems very odd and quite unnecessary.'

Suddenly she became aware of how much attention their whispered conversation was drawing. The girls in front had turned right round in their seats, their avid curiosity revealed by their open mouths. Althea cleared her throat. 'Oh look, there's a river,' she said loudly, pointing out of the window.

'It's a canal, actually,' said Patrick.

'Why should I believe you?' she demanded, but she was no longer angry, just confused. She felt like a servant wench who'd been taken advantage of by the young master. Except, she realized with a pang of regret, she hadn't.

'At least I've bought a sleeping bag,' he whispered.

CHAPTER FIVE

❂

'We're here!'

The cry woke Althea from a fitful, much-needed doze. Worn out and thoroughly bored with travelling, she could have done with another ten minutes' sleep. Unlike the rest of the party, who'd fallen in and out of sleep from the moment they'd set off on the return journey, Althea's eyes had only closed when they were nearly home. A glance at her watch told her it was only four in the afternoon. It felt like midnight.

She looked out of the window to see William leaning against his ancient Ford Escort. Bozo was dancing on the end of her lead, prepared to bark at everyone who got off the bus.

Next to the Escort was a pale blue, low-slung sports car with its top down, not new but classic and hideously expensive to insure. Waiting by this was Topaz in perfectly pressed linen shorts and a silk vest. Rather to her horror, Althea realized that William and Topaz had been talking.

She had been annoyed when she and Patrick had got separated after the last stop and were no longer sitting together, but now she was relieved she wouldn't have to make introductions. She couldn't rely on William to stick to bland social niceties and Topaz was bound to sense her guilt for what hadn't happened, or hadn't even been likely to happen.

Althea spent a few minutes rummaging in the luggage rack, handing down rucksacks and trying to sort out plastic carriers, all identical on the outside, but all belonging to different people. While making sure there was no litter left, she did a little vital sorting in her brain. Why had she felt a pang of guilt when she saw Topaz? Nothing had happened. There had been no hand holding, no furtive kiss. And there had been nothing wrong with them ducking out to cool off for a few moments during the country dancing. As neither of them smoked, they hadn't even

46

gone behind the bike sheds – if they had those in France – and shared a Gauloise. But as they had returned to the school hall, she had been aware of speculative eyes upon them. And inevitably, because they were sharing accommodation – thank God no one found out about the bedroom – they were regarded as a couple.

A less rigorous conscience than Althea's would have been clear. But she couldn't forget how they had described where they were staying to the adults in the party. It had become more elaborate with every glass of wine. They seemed to know just what the other was going to say, and as far as she knew, no one had suspected a thing.

There had been the galling jealousy she had felt when Julie Coulthard had swept Patrick off to the bar on the ferry, leaving Althea with all three sets of children. She had complained mildly about the children to Julie, but couldn't say a word about what really bothered her.

By the time the children were all off the coach, Topaz was entwined with Patrick in a way which made Althea think of snakes. If it had been a quarrel (and Althea was certain it was) which had sent Patrick off in a bus to northern France with a whole load of schoolkids for the weekend, it was all made up now.

Bozo, seeing her mistress, leapt up and down, desperate to get close to her. Althea picked the little dog up, and through practice, avoided having her nose bitten. She then greeted William with more affection than he usually tolerated and, tiredness forgotten, was suddenly very glad to be home.

'Hello, darling! How are you all? Did everything go all right? Did you remember the guinea-pigs?'

'Let's get your bag, Mum. Everything's still alive, even the plants.'

Althea allowed herself a brief glance at Patrick, but he was busy, so she didn't say goodbye. She just got into William's car and back to real life, mentally designating her weekend non-affair with Patrick as a pleasant fantasy, safely unfulfilled. She had all she wanted in life: her home, her children, her dog and her garden, so why yearn for something which would spoil everything?

*

The house gleamed and smelt strongly of polish and bleach. The kitchen table, which for once in its life was clear, had a vase of flowers on it. Overcome with love and maternal pride, Althea embraced Rupert and Merry, nearly banging their heads together in her enthusiasm.

'So how was it, Mum?' asked Rupert when he could breathe again.

'It's nice to have you home. Did you have a wonderful time?' Merry kept one arm round her mother. 'We've tidied the house!'

Indeed they had. Apart from the collection of tote-bags and carriers that Althea had brought with her, it no longer had that 'just burgled' look, and a pile of letters, neatly stacked, was waiting on the kitchen table.

'Open them, Mum,' urged Merry.

'Can't I have a cup of tea first?' Time enough for the final demands and 'free silk headsquares if you order in fourteen days' after a hot drink and, possibly, a biscuit.

'I'll get you one,' said Rupert.

'There's all sorts of goodies in my bag. Wine, chocolate, cheese. Have a rummage.'

'Sounds like a recipe for migraine,' said Rupert, filling the kettle.

'Oh *do* open your letters.'

'Why? It'll only be bills and stuff.'

'No! You've won something! I'm sure!'

Althea sat down again, resigning herself to winning £50,000 but only if her name were drawn out of a hat with 50,000 other names in it. She took the envelope which was causing Merry such excitement and opened it.

A moment later she said, 'You're right! I have!'

'I know! We could tell by holding the envelope up to the light. But what have you won? The holiday in Portugal?' Merry demanded.

'A fitted kitchen?' asked Rupert.

'A car?' asked William, hopefully.

'No,' said Althea slowly. 'Nothing like that.'

'Then what?' her children shouted in unison.

'I've won a chance to actually be a garden designer, as opposed to just telling people I am.'

'What?' said William, fingering a parcel of very ripe camembert.

'You know what a garden designer is, surely?'

'I think so, Mother. I meant, who have you told that you're one?'

'It doesn't matter. But this is wonderful! I've actually got an opportunity to see if I can design a garden from scratch.'

The children tried to share in her enthusiasm for a moment.

'What did you buy us, then?' said Merry.

But Althea was re-reading her letter under her breath.

> *If your garden is picked, you'll have an opportunity to create it at the famous Chelsea Flower Show, and have it judged by RHS judges, alongside the professional gardens. You will be given £1,000 . . .*

'That sounds a lot.'

'It's not much for a garden,' said Althea. 'It's only because it's so tiny . . . Oh, and they'll be sending me a cheque for two hundred pounds. Hang on, there's a catch.' She read aloud:

> *'Remember creating a garden in just three weeks is extremely challenging . . .* Why don't they say "hard"? *Innovation is essential to make a winning garden, but please make sure your plans will work in a practical way. We suggest you use your £200 to experiment before designing and drawing your garden. Should your garden be chosen, you will receive £1,000 as an outright prize, which you may choose to use to purchase special plants for your garden at Chelsea.'*

'Oh good,' said Merry, 'You won't need to bother with any of that. We can spend the money on something else.'

Althea exhaled and bit her lip in the way that parents do when they've bad news for their children. 'The trouble is, though I've designed several gardens, it's always been on the spot. I've never worked anything out on paper first. The only way I can do this at all is to create the garden first, and draw it afterwards. I might need your help there, Merry.'

'But surely that won't cost two hundred pounds?' asked Rupert.

'And the rest, which we haven't got.'

'Oh.' Merry was disappointed but not devastated. 'How boring. I thought you might have won something really interesting.'

'Well, it is interesting to me,' said Althea. 'And it might lead to a whole new career. Which I could do with right now.'

'What did you have to do?' asked William.

Althea looked at the letter. 'Can't really remember. I think I only had to put names to photographs of famous gardens and say Why I Like Gardening in twenty words or less.'

'Perhaps if you've got tie-breakers cracked,' said Merry, 'you might win something better.'

'Yeah,' said Rupert. 'If you put your mind to it we could get some good stuff.'

Althea laughed. 'Pass me that bag and I'll see what I've got for you all.'

'Ally? Are you back?' Juno didn't sound her usual cool self. 'I've *got* to come round.'

Before answering, and almost unaware she was doing it, Althea considered how much work the house would need doing to it. Then she remembered that the children had blitzed it while she was away. Apart from her bags, which had exploded into heaps of dirty washing and the other detritus of travel, things weren't too bad. 'That would be lovely,' she said, as if Juno had actually asked if she could come. 'When will you be here?'

'Twenty minutes,' said her sister, and rang off.

Althea moved her bag from the kitchen table, abandoned the idea of an evening asleep in front of the television with a glass of wine, and brushed her hair. The fact that she had spent most of the weekend on a bus would cut no ice with Juno. There was never an excuse for looking untidy.

Juno looked as soignée as ever, if a little tight-lipped. For one horrible moment Althea wondered if she could have found out that her elder sister had spent two nights in a bedroom with a strange man, but dismissed the idea as paranoia. They had been such chaste nights, no earth-moving vibrations could possibly have reached even Juno's information net.

Althea drew her firmly past the half-unpacked bags to the

conservatory. 'Do sit down. Can I get you anything? Glass of wine?'

Juno sank down into the chair and looked about her. 'This room looks less cluttered than usual. Fewer plants. I suppose it's because you've been away.'

'I put most of them outside to make it easier for the children to water them. Was that a yes or a no?'

'A yes. I think.'

It was unlike Juno to be so indecisive. 'Mmm?'

'The thing is, I'm not sure if I ought to.'

'Ought to what?'

'Have a drink. The thing is, I'm pregnant.'

Althea didn't move or speak, trying both to take this in and work out if Juno thought it good news or bad. The wrong reaction would be fatal. 'Well, I think a glass of wine is a good idea,' she said after a moment. 'I'll bring the bottle.'

She took a bottle of white wine and one of fizzy water from the fridge and brought them with some glasses back to the conservatory, where Juno was cuddling Bozo. Basking in attention from this unaccustomed source, Bozo was lying with her legs in the air, blissfully happy.

'How about a spritzer?' asked Althea. 'That couldn't do you any harm.'

'Don't you think so?'

Althea, who had been pregnant before it had been considered necessary to give up everything that made life worth living, had gone off alcohol of her own volition. But had she felt like a spritzer, she would have had one. 'No,' she said, after a few moments' desperate consideration.

Juno took her drink with unaccustomed meekness. 'Thank you.'

Althea's wine was undiluted and she took a huge gulp of it before sitting down opposite Juno, prepared to be supportive. 'So, are you pleased?'

'I don't know. I don't even know how it happened.'

Althea's mouth twitched. She felt very tempted to run the facts of life by Juno one more time, but refrained. This was no occasion for flippancy.

'Did you want it to happen?' Althea spoke very gently, prepared for a vehement denial.

'*I* don't know.' Juno, usually so certain about everything, seemed to have lost touch with herself. 'I just thought we couldn't. And we haven't done anything about contraception for years. And now, just when my career is really going well, and we've had the house decorated and booked a holiday in Africa, *this* happens.'

'Are you going to – I mean – you're not going to – you know, do anything about it?' Althea spoke as blandly as she could. Abortion wasn't an option for her, but if that was the route Juno was planning, she didn't want to appear judgemental.

'I don't *know*. I don't think so.'

'How does Kenneth feel about it?'

'He doesn't know. I felt I had to tell you first.'

Althea was touched. 'But do you think he'll be pleased? I mean, you might not be able to go to Africa, but nothing else need change just yet.'

'*I don't know!* You keep asking me questions when I haven't a clue about anything. I mean, do you think I'll be able to have a baby?'

'Why on earth shouldn't you? It's not all that difficult, you know. Once you're pregnant, the body mostly gets on with it by itself.'

Juno was silent for a shocked moment. The idea that her body should do anything without her caring, informed intervention was obviously appalling. 'Oh, no. That wouldn't do for me. You have to manage your pregnancy. I mean, if I'd *meant* to get pregnant, I'd have been on a pre-pregnancy diet for *at least* two years.'

Althea, heartily relieved that the old, decisive Juno was emerging from her shell-shocked doppelganger, suppressed a smile. 'But you eat very healthily anyway, I shouldn't think you need to worry.'

Juno sighed impatiently. 'But don't you see? Eating healthily isn't enough. I haven't been eating the right way *for pregnancy*!'

'Well, you must have been doing something right,' said Althea. 'Or why did you get pregnant now, after all these years?'

Juno shrugged. 'I don't know . . .'

William would say it was nature's way of curing a control

freak. Juno, who had every aspect of her life running on oiled wheels, compartmentalized down to the last note to her milkman, had had her life-plan sabotaged by a chance meeting between two cells invisible to the human eye. 'You didn't have your tubes blown, or anything?'

Juno shuddered. 'No. I never wanted children, so why go through all that pain and humiliation in order to have them?'

'I've heard it is terribly painful, but hardly humiliating.'

'That's really not the point now, is it? I'm pregnant, with or without having dye forced through me.'

Althea nodded. Anything she said now would be wrong.

'So I'm going to get a reading list, start studying and get enrolled in some decent natural childbirth classes. I want the birth to be totally natural, possibly in water. With no mechanical or chemical intervention.'

Althea had to bite her lip again. Apart from the water, she had wanted all this too. But with William, things had not gone quite as described in the NCT handbook, and she had ended up begging for all the mechanical and chemical intervention the hospital was willing and able to give her. 'Of course,' she said.

'We could have a birthing pool in the study,' Juno mused on. 'Then I could have a home delivery as well.'

'Have you any idea when the baby's due? How did you find out you were pregnant?'

'I bought a test. I was ten days late.'

'Well, I think you ought to make an appointment to see your doctor. He'll give you a due date.'

'*She* will, you mean. You don't think I'd let a man fiddle about with me, do you?'

You must have let Kenneth fiddle with you, or you wouldn't be in this state now, said Althea to herself. 'Well, whoever. Then you can make plans. But really, it isn't nearly as complicated as you seem to think. You can carry on pretty much as normal, unless you get horribly sick, like I did.'

Juno was not going to get horribly sick. She just wouldn't allow it. Her body had got away from her on one occasion, but wouldn't be allowed to do so again. 'I'm sure if you'd done the right things, eaten the right diet, you would have been perfectly all right.'

Althea nodded meekly. She'd done everything known to science, pseudo-science and old wives, and still she'd vomited for nine months. 'I'm sure Kenneth will be pleased. You should go home and tell him.'

'*You* may be sure, but I'm not. He may not like me when I'm all fat and misshapen. Frederick hated it when you were expecting.'

'Frederick is different. I was pregnant so often, so close together. And it wasn't the pregnancy he didn't like, so much as the screaming babies.'

'You know, I'm sure if you'd tried William with a cranial osteopath, he wouldn't have cried so much.'

'It was Merry who had colic.'

'Well, whichever, you should have tried it.'

'I expect I would have if I'd known about it. But things like that weren't so available in those days.'

'No, well.' Juno stopped bossing and suddenly sighed deeply. 'But at least you were the proper age for having babies. I'm going to be an elderly primigravida.'

Trust Juno to know the technical terms even before her first antenatal visit. 'You're going to be a wonderful mother. There's a lot of evidence which suggests that the children of older mothers are more intelligent.'

'If they're not handicapped.'

'Juno, please stop worrying. You're only thirty-six, which is not old. You're extremely fit and healthy and you've got a husband who loves you. Really, you're a very lucky girl.'

Juno sighed again. 'I know all that, really. But I'm *frightened*, Ally.' Her voice broke and she started to cry, shock and hormones overcoming her usual reticence.

Althea put her arms round her younger sister. 'It'll be all right, really it will. I'll be here to help you.'

'But you were such a *disgusting* mother!' Juno sobbed.

This was going too far. 'What do you mean? God! I know I was a bit sloppy, but . . .'

Juno sniffed. 'I distinctly remember on one occasion you actually wiped William's nose on your skirt!' Juno dabbed at her own nose with a freshly ironed linen hanky.

Even Althea was shocked. 'Did I really? How awful. I'd completely forgotten.'

'Well,' Juno conceded, 'those wrap-around Indian skirts were in that summer, and it may have been his face you wiped.'

'Oh, was that all? You had me worried for a moment.'

'Even so,' Juno went on. 'You were very slutty about everything. I don't ever remember seeing a bottle sterilizer.'

'That was because my babies were breast-fed, and then went on to cups.'

Juno shrivelled further into her chair. 'Oh, God! I know it's supposed to be best and you were completely shameless about where you did it, but I don't think I can bring myself to breast-feed.'

'Well, don't then. And I wasn't shameless, I was very discreet.'

'No you weren't. You did it everywhere! Even in the supermarket. I saw you.'

The mists of Althea's erratic memory cleared for a moment as the incident came to mind. 'But nobody saw, or knew about it. *You* only found out because you came to tell me off for contemplating the Pot Noodles and I had to tell you I was only reading the ingredients on a pot as an excuse to stand still while Merry had a quick suck.'

'I know, but . . .'

'A crying baby is offensive to everyone. A feeding baby need be offensive to no one, provided the mother is discreet.'

'You sound like an extract from *Breast is Best*,' said Juno, a glimmer of humour breaking through her distress.

'I know. That's probably where I got it from, but I do believe it.' She was just glad that owing to clever tricks involving magazines, scarves and baggy jumpers, she'd never had to ask a burly publican who suggested she feed her babies in the Ladies how he would feel having to eat his lunch in a lavatory. Whereas if Juno got over her revulsion, she would relish such battles and would campaign for separate railway carriages and whole sections of aircraft to be provided for nursing mothers.

'The idea just makes me curl up,' said Juno. 'It's so sort of – sexual.'

'Babies do very well on formula. You don't have to breast-feed if you feel like that about it.'

'I suppose not. But you know how strongly I feel about proper diet, it seems silly to feed my baby on God-knows-what chemical rubbish when my milk would be so perfect.'

Althea suppressed a sigh. There was no winning with some people. 'Well, you don't have to think about it now, you may feel differently when the time comes.'

Juno got up. 'I know. I'm being neurotic. I'm just so thrown by the whole idea.'

Althea gave her another hug. 'I know, but there's really so much time to get used to the idea of everything, you'll be feeling fine about it long before the baby's born.'

'If you say so.' Juno returned the hug.

'When are you going to tell Mummy?' They moved towards the front door arm-in-arm.

Juno grimaced. 'Not before I have to. She'll want me to have it at Queen Charlotte's, with a dozen male specialists in attendance. She's so *bossy*.'

Althea spotted a clump of cat hair on the floor which had been missed by Merry's attack with the vacuum. It was both sad and funny that Juno and her mother were so often at loggerheads when they really had so much in common.

'Well, I must get on. I do feel a bit better about everything now.' Juno became aware of Althea's luggage. 'And you must be dying to unpack and get yourself organized. I can see how chaotic everything is.'

'Oh Juny, I bet you'd arrive home in the middle of the night from a twenty-four-hour flight and still put the washing-machine on straightaway.'

'Of course,' said Juno. 'I have it all in a bag ready sorted. And that way you can take advantage of the Economy 7!'

CHAPTER SIX

Althea felt her unpacking could wait. A lot had happened since her return home and she needed time to think things over, read her letters and contemplate being an aunt.

A glass of wine later Althea realized she was pleased about Juno's pregnancy. She loved babies, and couldn't expect grandchildren for years yet. And though not a 'primigravida' she was more elderly than Juno, and as a single woman, couldn't have any more children herself.

But Juno had never been terribly good at sharing her toys, and Althea might not be allowed to play with the baby very much to begin with. But as reality eroded Juno's high-flown ideals about childrearing, she might be very glad of a pair of loving arms where she could safely dump her screaming infant.

Althea smiled as she speculated on the plans for the birth. No military campaign ever devised would be more detailed or better organized. Juno would slice through red tape like the proverbial knife through butter. For once Juno had decided upon a course, mountain ranges would melt in deference to her determination. This baby's birth would be attended by every 'natural' expert available. In fact, Althea doubted if there'd actually be room for anything so allopathic as a midwife, unless she was prepared to take off her clothes and deliver the baby naked in a birthing pool.

No, there'd definitely be an aromatherapist, an autogenic trainer and a homoeopath, possibly a shiatsu practitioner, Alexander Technique teacher and a cranial osteopath. But how many doctors without huge tolerance to complementary medicine would be permitted was doubtful. Kenneth, the baby's father, would be there, but only if he'd completed the right training course and passed the exams. Juno would probably make him read the baby politically correct fairy stories in the womb, from week twelve.

'No, it'll be weeks before I'm allowed to touch it,' Althea said to a bumble bee, who was kindly pollinating her *jasminum officianale*. '"It's not that I don't trust you, Ally dear," she'll say. "But you must admit your fingernails are always filthy."' Althea did admit it. She could never keep her fingers out of the pots which filled her house, and even a trip into the garden for some herbs always included a little tug at a weed or two.

She chuckled as she imagined being asked to splash through disinfectant barriers and wear a surgical mask and gloves before picking the little mite up. Then she yawned and stretched before refilling her glass and picking up her letters, remembering with a frisson of satisfaction that she had actually won a competition. Juno's news had put her success out of her head.

But the next letter rapidly blotted up her pleasure. It was from Dicky, her builder-cum-handyman-cum-good-friend, and it was not good news.

Dicky had first arrived in her life when her roof had leaked badly. He had fixed it up amazingly cheaply, and had kept the house together more or less ever since. He always charged as little as possible, and if he thought Althea could do the job herself, would show her how to do it. She called on him rarely now, only when her painfully acquired DIY skills seemed inadequate.

Just before she'd gone to France, she'd knocked off some plaster in William's room and found something which looked suspiciously like dry rot. Dicky, who came almost immediately, confirmed that it was. He had now sent Althea a written estimate for dealing with it, and although she knew no one else would do it so cheaply, it was still a lot of money.

The bumble bee was now trying to escape through the glass and Althea got up to steer it to a less solid exit, cursing at the gods which snatched back with one hand what they had given with the other. Once the bee was free, Althea drained the bottle into her glass and read the letter again. So much for the prize money being spent on plants, a bit of pool-liner and some stone. Now it would have to go on a lot of plaster dust, some extremely toxic chemicals and new wood, all of which would eventually need decorating.

Still, she told herself firmly, at least she *had* the prize money –

or would have when the cheque came. Without it she would have been in a real spot. She wasn't due for her redundancy money for ages. Besides, that was likely to be a tiny amount and would have to be eked out, penny by penny, not spent in two-hundred-pound lumps. No, without this windfall, she might have had to ask Frederick for help. She shuddered.

But her disappointment remained. She'd been looking forward to getting out her 'Plant-Finder' and enjoying a little authorized indulgence. Now, she'd have to create a garden for the competition without buying anything. She riffled through her mail to read the letter telling her she'd won again. But although it was cheering, her initial euphoria didn't come back. She was far too tired. She'd feel better tomorrow, after a hot shower and a good night's sleep.

Upstairs, the bathroom was full of steam, wet towels and damp clothes. The smell of aftershave told her the previous occupant had been male, and a rummage in the airing cupboard added the information that they had also finished off the meagre hot-water supply. Althea sighed, switched on the boost, and resigned herself to a wait before she could wash herself.

Rather than find herself dozing off in her chair, Althea decided to go and look at her plants in her borrowed greenhouse. It was only seven o'clock and the sight of things growing always cheered her up. Because of the wine, she would have to walk, but it was a pleasant evening, and although she was tired, she had spent most of the day cooped up in a coach. It would do her and Bozo good to stretch their legs for twenty minutes or so.

Bozo was thrilled to be invited, though she insisted on ducking away from Althea several times as she tried to put on the lead.

'How you'd have driven Frederick mad,' said Althea. 'What a relief we don't have him any more.'

Althea often counted her blessings, and Frederick's absence was always blessing number one. She called up the stairs to her children and set off.

Bozo was familiar with the journey and had pushed her way through the hole in the fence before Althea had even reached the crumbling mansion which Patrick Donahugh had been inconsiderate enough to buy.

In the seventeenth century it had been planned as a mill, but before it had been completed, the mill-stream had been diverted leaving the building redundant. Fifty years later, some enterprising builder had eventually turned it into a gentleman's residence which subsequent generations had found too big to live in and too historic and beautiful to pull down.

Althea was in no hurry to catch her dog up, being less enthusiastic about her secret greenhouse now she knew she might not have it for long. She was quite used to losing things: keys, bills, her handbag; all had independent means of transport and delighted in evading her. But just recently she had started losing things that mattered, like her job, her glasshouse, and now her prize money. Her children would start leaving home soon and then she'd be lonely as well as poor. How would she cope with only Bozo, three cats and two guinea pigs for company?

She lifted open the gate to the derelict garden. I could always child-mind for Juno's baby, she thought, but then shuddered. Having Juno as a sister was challenging; having her as an employer would be impossible. No, stick with being a garden designer – if you can make a new garden with no money. Plants might be as demanding as any sister, but at least they didn't verbalize their criticism. If they had any complaints they merely wilted, shed their leaves or died in silence. And they never told you that you needed to lose weight.

Bozo was scratching at the door when Althea caught up. Althea was just about to chide the dog for her foolishness in knocking at the door of a deserted building, when the door opened and Bozo went in. A moment later she yelped and shot out again, fleeing to Althea with her tail between her legs. Patrick's large form filled the narrow doorway to the glasshouse.

'What are you doing here?' said Althea when she had calmed Bozo's shattered nerves. Then wished she'd thought before she'd spoken. It was his greenhouse. She was the trespasser, not him.

'I just came for a breath of air and to have a look at what you get up to in here. Topaz is cooking dinner.'

Althea could imagine. It would be fish cooked in some fat-free way, garnished with fresh herbs and served with steamed vegetables and a few new potatoes if he was lucky. They'd drink a little cold chardonnay and follow it with fresh fruit, poached, possibly, or baked in the oven with vanilla pods. Even if it did come from some anorexic Hollywood starlet's 'High Fitness, Low Fatness' eating plan, and contained nothing more sustaining than a trace element or two, Althea suddenly felt hungry and full of cheap wine.

'Well, let me show you,' said Althea, trying not to sound resentful. It was a shock to see him again so soon, although now, only a few hours later, their weekend away seemed a long time ago.

She pushed past Patrick and led him to the end of the greenhouse where the glass, though cracked and broken in places, was clean. It covered an area about ten feet long. She unhooked some lengths of green shading material, revealing that some of the frames were glazed with polythene held in place with masking tape. But the benches underneath were sturdy enough and were covered with plants, pots and seed-trays. A stand for compost, sharp sand, perlite and coir, a peat-substitute, was nearby, and a huge, chipped clay flower pot held a selection of handtools.

'There you are. Here is my plant-producing business.'

He obviously found it difficult to come up with a suitable reply. It *was* fairly pathetic, and added little to her claim that she was a garden designer, but it was all she had.

'I've just won a competition, actually,' she said, fighting the desire to fling her body over everything, like a child over a picture when it doesn't want anyone to see.

'Jolly good. What for?'

Remembering that she would have no money to fulfil the brief, she backed down. 'Oh, it's to design a garden, a small one.'

He shot her a bemused look, but took the hint not to press the point. 'What's this stuff?' He pointed to a tray of tiny green leaves.

'Mind-your-own-business,' she said, unable to resist the temptation.

His untidy eyebrows jerked upwards.

'I mean, it's a plant called "Mind your own business", or *Soleirolia soleirolii* if you want to be formal.'

The eyebrows settled. 'Oh.'

'I make balls and things with it. It's like topiary, only it doesn't need clipping, or take twenty years to grow. It's nearly instant.'

'Very clever. Was it your own idea?'

She shook her head. 'I got it from a television programme.'

'I see. And these?' He pointed to a row of pots with polythene bags on them.

Althea took one and shook away the condensation. 'These are going to be morning glories.' She peered through the bag. 'Yes, they've germinated.' She took off the bag. 'See? The cotyledons are huge, aren't they?'

'I'm afraid I don't know anything about plants. My idea of a perfect garden is a paved courtyard with perhaps a fountain.'

Althea sighed. 'Very few men do understand plants. Even those who are supposed to don't. I've got a brother-in-law who's a horticulturist and I've watched him mow wild orchids.'

'That bad?'

'They were only pyramidals, not specially rare or anything. But *really*. It was in a beautiful part of Scotland, next to a dear little wooden house with wonderful views. But he thought it looked untidy. I expect some man will invent a domestic napalm for people like him to use.'

'*Amok with a Mower: the story of a horticultural hitman,*' said Patrick. 'Available to rent now.'

Althea couldn't help smiling. 'My ex-husband – it was his brother – once asked him to tidy up my garden for me. It took the place five years to recover. I haven't let a man do anything in it since.'

'What about your sons? Don't you let them help?'

'It isn't so much a matter of letting them, but getting them. They'll only mow the lawn if bribed.'

'So I'm the first man in your greenhouse then?'

Althea nodded. 'The male aphids usually avoid it, too.'

'I consider myself honoured.'

'Don't bother. I wouldn't have let you across the threshold in a month of Sundays if you hadn't owned the place.'

He laughed. 'Difficult for you.'

62

'Very.'

There was a silence which went on long enough for Althea to feel forced to break it. 'So what do you plan to do with this? Enclosed by the walls, it's very sheltered. It would make a lovely swimming pool.'

'Don't you consider that on a par with mowing orchids?'

'Well, yes, I do. But it's not my house, and different people have different hobbies. I just don't happen to like swimming very much.'

'What do you think about an orangery, or something? Or a proper conservatory?'

'With a pond? And all sorts of huge palms and things? And proper wooden furniture, not the kind that ladders your tights, and jugs of Pimms . . .' And Topaz looking gorgeous in something diaphanous, making love with Patrick in the scented, humid night, the air heady with citrus trees . . . Althea forced herself back to earth. 'This might be a good time to discuss rent,' she said, to give herself a metaphorical cold shower.

'You haven't told me if you approve of the orangery idea. I would value the opinion of a garden designer.'

'There's no need to be sarcastic.'

'I wasn't. Would an orangery be nice?'

'An orangery would be fabulous, and you know it. You can build Topaz a swimming pool somewhere else. I don't imagine you're planning to resuscitate the vegetable garden. There'd be room for a covered pool and all the extras.'

'Another woman who thinks I'm made of money.'

Althea laughed. 'I certainly hope you are. Think what it'll cost just to repair the roof.'

'I have. I do. It keeps me awake at night.'

'But if you're not a millionaire, why did you buy this place? You of all people should know what it'll cost to restore.'

There was a hint of tightness about him, as if he'd had this discussion many times but had never completely convinced anyone. 'I bought it when I took the job with the Greenwich Partnership and discovered it was on the market. I hated the thought of it falling further and further into disrepair, and I needed a challenge. And besides, after planning permission for everything had been refused, it was very cheap.'

'But still, even if they gave it away, it'll still cost –'

'Then I'd better charge you an exorbitant rent to re-coup some of my losses.'

There was enough acid in his tone to make her anxious. 'You'd better make it something I can afford, or I'll have to just ship out.'

Patrick shifted so he could straighten up, collecting a large cobweb on his hair as he did so. He looked down at her and smiled, but as the fading sunlight was behind him, the subtleties of his expression were lost to her.

'I don't think your five bob a week'll make a lot of difference. Why don't we just forget the question of rent?'

'But I couldn't, I mean, it wouldn't be right . . .'

'If anyone says anything you can say it's because you've slept with your landlord. It's nearly true, after all.'

Suddenly lighthearted, Althea laughed. 'But what on earth will you say to Topaz? Or are you planning to tell her what happened?'

'Certainly not. Unlike you and me, she'd have no compunction about making a huge fuss in the middle of the night in a foreign country if everything was not exactly to her taste.'

'Really? So what will you say when she asks about the rent?'

'I'll think of something suitably vague. But if she asks you . . .'

'She won't. Our paths aren't likely to cross again.'

'And what about *our* paths?'

Althea felt as if she had been paddling in shallow, sunny waters when the ground had suddenly shelved away beneath her feet; if she didn't step back quickly, she would find herself out of her depth.

'Oh . . .' She was deliberately vague. 'I doubt they will. You're not planning to go on any more school trips are you?'

He laughed. 'Well, no. But I am planning to move in here fairly soon.'

'What!'

'Don't shout. It's quite usual to move into property you've bought, you know.'

'Not when the property is as dilapidated as this is, it isn't! What about the roof, for one thing?'

'There's a section of roof which has been replaced quite recently. There's a good four rooms plus a large scullery which are perfectly habitable, if a little dusty. I shall move into them.'

'But *why*?'

'Because when the builders start, I want to be on the spot. Otherwise I'll have to do a day's work, then come here and find it's all gone wrong behind my back. If I'm on the spot, I can sort out the builders before I leave for the office. It's a perfectly practical idea. I don't know why everyone's getting so worked up about it.'

Althea had little difficulty in interpreting whom he meant by 'everyone'. 'Does this mean you'll want me out sooner?'

He shook his head. 'I don't see why it should.'

'But what about Topaz? She might not like me poking about in the greenhouse.'

'She might not, but she's unlikely to know about it. She's staying where she is for the moment.'

The question she had been pondering for the past forty-eight hours was finally answered. 'So that was what it was,' she said, without thinking.

'What what was?'

'What you quarrelled about. I mean, you *must* have quarrelled. Otherwise you would never have gone to France at such short notice. You're not so friendly with Geoffrey Conway that you'd give up a weekend like that without an ulterior motive.'

'Oh?' He suddenly sounded cold and dignified.

Althea set about mollifying him. 'I don't suppose anyone else suspected a thing. But being so close to you, so to speak, I couldn't help speculating . . .'

Althea's children said that she was nosy. Althea claimed that she was merely interested in people. Patrick looked as if his vote would be with Althea's offspring. He released a sigh which seemed to have been pent up for some time.

Althea went on rather quickly, '. . . and rather than risk another quarrel, hadn't you better go back and have your supper?'

A distinctly adolescent mulishness took possession of Patrick's chin.

'I mean, if Topaz has gone to a lot of trouble cooking you a meal, you must be there to eat it.'

'You sound just like my mother.'

'Do I? I am sorry. I do it to everyone. I'm trying to give it up.'

'Well, do. It's very irritating, especially when I'm several years older than you.'

'You don't know that.' Althea hoped it was true, but it was hard to tell these days.

'Yes I do. I'm forty-two.'

'Oh, ancient.'

'And you must be older than you look, if you've got teenage children.'

'Must I?' She didn't mean to be coy about her age, but really, a woman was allowed some secrets, surely?

Apparently not. 'So how old are you?'

The thought that she might refuse to tell him flickered momentarily through her mind. He had a very determined expression and she did need to keep in with him. 'Thirty-eight.'

'Topaz is twenty-eight.'

Lucky Topaz. Young, beautiful and attached to Patrick. 'Well, at the risk of sounding like your mother again, unless you want the age gap to look even larger, I suggest you take that cobweb off your hair.'

'Where?' He brushed his hand over his head, missing the cobweb.

Althea stood on tiptoe and teased the cobweb away. Patrick's hand flew up and caught her wrist and then, as if he'd originally had something else in mind, slowly brought it down.

'You'd better go and eat,' said Althea.

'Yes.' He released her hand. 'I'd better.'

CHAPTER SEVEN

Merry was doing her homework at the kitchen table. Althea was procrastinating. 'I can't think of anything to do for this garden competition,' she said to her daughter.

Merry licked her crayon and turned a block of children who were driven to school bright purple. There were more of them, Althea noted, breathing over her daughter's shoulder, than children who walked or took the bus.

'When have you got to have the plans in?'

'The first of September.'

'You've got three months, nearly.'

'That's nothing in gardening terms. I've got to start soon. If only I could draw, I wouldn't have to actually create the garden. But I just can't.'

'Then you'll have to go out there and get digging,' said Merry. 'Something will come to you.'

'But I've spent years getting my garden right. I really don't want to dig a twelve-foot crater in it.'

'There must be a corner you can spare. What about that bit by the compost heap?'

'It's on a steep slope, and is covered in weeds. In July it's a touching display of pink convolvulus. I'll never get all the roots out.'

'You're always telling us to relish challenges.' Merry wanted to get on with her homework in peace. 'Nothing worth having in life comes easily.'

Althea nodded reluctantly, recognizing the words as having come from her own lips and the wisdom in them. 'But it's raining.'

'I thought you liked gardening in the rain. You always say the roses smell better.' Merry sounded sceptical.

'Well, they do. And my Buff Beauty's looking superb. You're

right, darling. Grasp the nettle, or in this case, the fork and spade. I'll go out now.'

'But it's nearly lunchtime!' Belatedly Merry remembered that once in the garden, her mother wouldn't be seen for hours. 'I'm starving!'

'Then you'd better get yourself something to eat, poppet. There's lots of pasta but try not to leave grated cheese all over the worktop.'

Merry sighed. This role-reversal thing had its down side.

It was not hard for a garden to look beautiful in mid-June, when all the roses were out and everything was flowering so generously. Althea's garden, having been lovingly worked on since Frederick left, since when she had needed a relationship which repaid effort, was superb.

And for Althea the rain added a pleasing melancholy to the swathes of blush pink, apricot and cream which clambered through trees, up fences and over walls. Each blossom had such a short moment of glory, yet gave of its beauty so willingly, from bud to drooping cluster of petals, whether there was anyone to see them or not.

She wandered from plant to plant, inspecting her lilies for slug damage, peering at the leaves of a self-seeded geranium, trying to decide if it was from a proper garden variety or from the pink, quasi-weed she had dug up from the field. She plucked the dead head from a late peony, wondering yet again if she really should have a whole bed of them, or if their season was just too short. Knowing she would never reach a decision, she moved down to her pond, delighting to see it full for once and her bog garden satisfyingly damp. She reckoned the height of her newly planted gunnera, wondering if it would ever reach the promised eight feet or if the ground was just too dry for it. Only after she had visited each plant and considered its well-being did she turn her mind to the competition.

It was perhaps a shame that the only bit of garden which Althea didn't mind digging up was such a difficult site: steeply sloping, full of weeds and short on topsoil.

But, she reasoned as she put a stone on the end of her tape measure, no garden plot is perfect. If she could create a garden which overcame common problems, rather than one which relied on being south-facing on Lincolnshire loam, with a stone wall on which to grow fruit, and several antique statues which just happened to be lying about, she'd at least have something useful.

She wondered, as she poked a bit of stick into the ground as a peg, if she could photocopy plans of her garden and sell them at car-boot sales, with the sweet-williams, foxgloves and hollyhocks she now gave away. But she decided not. The thought of people offering ten pence for something which had been such hard work to create and was going to be such agony to draw was too disheartening. No, she'd just have to think of this garden as part of her own, and make it something she was really happy to give space to.

Her twelve-foot-square plot marked out, not without consider-able difficulty and a lot of slipping and swearing, Althea stood and looked at it, the rain splashing gently on the hood of her waterproof. Now what she had to think of was a theme which would make her garden attractive to judges. In the space and within the budget, they wouldn't be expecting the Hanging Gardens of Babylon, but they would want an idea which brought together a variety of plants, with year-round interest, and various different features in the form of walls and fences, and which looked attractive.

It would have to have water in some form or other – no garden had a hope at Chelsea without. Which – given the sloping char-acter of her plot – presented a few problems.

If only she had the money, she could at least consider spending it all on a pump and a fountain, and painting it with yoghurt to encourage algae. This, having swallowed up her budget, would be the centrepiece of a few choice varieties mixed with common, beautiful things. Ivy-leaved toadflax, pale pink oxalis and common ivy would together recreate some tranquil corner of a forgotten stately home.

But not only had the promised cheque not yet arrived, but it was already accounted for. To pay Dicky for fixing the dry rot, she had added horribly to her overdraft. She badly needed to bring it down to something acceptable for her bank manager's sanity and her own need for sleep.

Thinking of Dicky gave Althea an idea. A few years ago, he

had replaced a badly cracked wash basin for her. She hadn't let him take it away in case it came in useful. Well, now it was going to! Gleeful and muddy she tramped down the path to the garage, too small actually to keep a car in, but jolly handy for the bikes and garden tools. There, creating tenement housing for a host of insects, all of which William would claim she should leave undisturbed, was her wash basin.

'All it needs,' she explained to the creatures made homeless by her creative outburst, 'is a bit of pool-liner draped over it, and I have a raised pond. In fact' – inspiration spiralling to dizzy heights – 'if I had another couple of them, I could have a waterfall.'

By the time Althea had heaved the basin into the wheelbarrow, got it to the chosen spot, and found enough stones to wedge it upright, she had thought of a theme. She would create a garden on an absolute shoe-string. The sort that young couples could still afford after the mortgage and paying for the wedding.

She went into the house, suddenly desperately in need of a wash and a sandwich. One of the children might think of a snappy title for her – something like 'Out of the Skip and on to the Lawn' or 'The Ten-pound Garden', or however little she thought she could get away with paying.

She was standing in her kitchen in her muddy boots, her hands as yet unwashed, when the phone rang. She picked it up. 'Hello?'

'Hello, Althea.'

It was Frederick. Althea often felt she ought to ring Frederick about various things, and even more often found good reasons for not doing so. The best was that she never knew what time it was in Hong Kong, and didn't want to find herself waking Frederick's girlfriend in the middle of the night. He, of course, had got the timing spot on.

'Oh. Hello.' Althea scanned her conscience frantically but re-membered that, as she hadn't had the children's reports yet, she couldn't have sent them to him. Nor had she asked him for money for the dry rot, still hoping for the cheque to arrive. There was, of course, the little question of her redundancy, but as term still had a few weeks to run, that could wait. 'Frederick. How are you?'

'Fine. Children all right?'

'Yes,' she said doubtfully, wondering if she should slip in something about them being better if they had a bit more pocket money.

'I'm ringing to say I'm coming over.'

Panic rushed in like a rip-tide and then receded as she realized it was highly unlikely he would leave London once he'd got there. 'Oh? On business? Or for shopping?' Claudia, the high-powered businesswoman with whom he shared his tasteful home, was probably suffering from Beauchamp Place withdrawal symptoms.

'Strictly business. Claudia's not coming with me.'

'Oh. Do you want to see the children?'

'Naturally,' he said huffily, as if he were entitled to a Father-of-the-Year award. 'I also thought I ought to come and see you.'

Althea felt cold all over and had to sit down. As there was no chair within reach, this meant the floor. 'Really? Why do you think that?'

'We haven't seen each other for twelve years, Althea. I thought it was time to get a little more civilized. I'd like to come and stay.'

'Frederick, I'm frightfully busy just now . . .'

'Oh, I know all about that garden competition thing. Merry told me.'

Althea was beginning to sweat. What else had Merry told him? She had suggested to the children that their father needn't know just yet that she was losing her job, but knew they found conversation with him hard enough, without having most topics banned.

'Althea! Are you still there?'

'Of course. I was just thinking. When are you coming? It's really not very convenient . . .'

'If you don't know when I'm coming, you can't know it's not convenient,' he said with horribly undeniable logic.

'Well, I've got a series of French children coming in the holidays . . .'

'I know about them. I was planning to come before the holidays.'

Which wouldn't give her much time to clear up. If Juno was picky and critical about Althea's housekeeping, at least her intentions were good. Frederick was just picky. And he would be delighted if Althea was driven to throwing a pot of jam at him when her ability to take criticism finally expired.

'I really am looking forward to seeing you again, you know.'

'Are you? Why?'

'Really, Althea, you seem to have forgotten we were married.'

'Well, you seem to have forgotten that we're divorced.'

'Not at all. I'm just trying to be civilized about it. I'm flying in on Monday, that's tomorrow, and I'd like to spend the weekend with you. I'll stay at the Dog and Fox. You don't have to put me up.'

This was marginally better. But he must know what havoc his visit would cause. 'I'll check the calendar.' Althea got up and looked. Next weekend was terrifyingly blank.

'The children said there was nothing written down.'

Damn them! 'Well, I suppose next weekend's all right. But you can't come until Saturday. I've a meeting after school on Friday night.' It was not so much a lie as damage limitation. She needed at least Friday to get herself and the house in a fit state for his visit.

'Saturday it is. I'll be with you at about seven p.m. Oh, and I'll be taking you out to dinner.'

Althea's stunned silence crossed ten thousand miles and eight time zones.

'Goodbye, Althea. I'm looking forward to seeing you.'

'Er – goodbye, Frederick.'

Dinner? Goodness. He'd stopped taking her out for birthdays and anniversaries about two years into the marriage. Claudia must have completely reprogrammed him.

Althea found she was shaking and no longer hungry. Trust Frederick to want to come and stay, so, instead of spending the rest of Sunday gardening, she'd have to clean the house. Well she wouldn't. He could have a quick wizz round with the hoover, a flick of a duster, a spray of that polish with silicone in it he always disapproved of so much, and no more. If he wanted to come and see her after all these years, he could see her as she was – almost. It was bad enough him mucking up one weekend, without encroaching on to this one too.

She rinsed the worst of the soil off her hands, wondering who she was kidding. Of course she'd blitz the house, just as she did for anyone who gave any notice of their arrival. But so she couldn't start now, she decided to go and see how her morning glories were doing in the greenhouse.

She stopped washing and dried her hands on her jeans, not wanting to dirty a towel. Why on earth did Frederick want to see her after all these years? And why dinner? What could he possibly want from her? There were a couple of items of furniture that had belonged to his mother. If he wanted those, he had only to arrange their transport to Hong Kong and they were his. And he must know that.

It must be something more, bigger, like the house. Well, he wouldn't get that, not one moment before she was legally bound to sell it and pay him his share. And if there was any possible way of keeping her hands on it, like winning the lottery, she would. She called the dog, put on her lead, and shouted up the stairs where she was going. Despite nonchalantly carrying on with her Sunday, she was already starting to feel worked up. And by the time she had panted up the hill and let herself into what was now a full-scale building site, she was almost in a state.

But whatever else Frederick told her was wrong with her, the words 'Let yourself go' would not pass his lips. When he arrived he would see a confident, attractive woman, not the tired and dithering wreck he had left behind – even if that was how she felt sometimes.

She had read years ago that knowing one was going to meet up with an old flame after many years was the thing most likely to make you go on a diet. An ex-husband now living with Super-woman came a close second. Of course, there was no time to lose the amounts Juno declared were necessary, but a couple of pounds would make her feel better. Instantly, her hunger returned. Why was it whenever she told herself she was on a diet, she immediately craved crisps and chocolate and all those other things she managed without perfectly most of the time? Blast Frederick! It was just as well there was nothing to eat at the greenhouse, or she would have fallen on it.

Checking her plants was harder now Patrick was in residence in one corner of the house. She had to pick her times. For she had made a decision to avoid him. Not because she didn't like him, and enjoy the way their conversations led almost to flirting, but because he was spoken for, and therefore off limits. Unfortunately for her plants, this fact alone was not enough to make him unattractive to her. It should have done – it always had in the past. But not this time. So she restricted her visits to when he was likely to be out. If she saw his car, she turned round and went home. On a rainy Sunday Patrick would be holed up with Topaz in their flat, not pigging it in the mud. Topaz would see to that.

Perversely, she was disappointed not to see his car, and know there was no chance that he would come and say hello to her.

However, her plants were all doing well, which, if not quite compensation for not seeing Patrick, did please her. She pricked out some of the larger seedlings, did the watering, and pulled back the shading. She would grow some of her plants for her garden from seed, as poor young couples would have to, and try not to rely too much on her established garden. You could always buy plants from open gardens and car-boot sales, but she'd have to work out the cost. And for town gardeners, this would be harder. For her garden to work, it mustn't rely too much on kindly neighbours. Besides, kindly neighbours usually gave you a whole carrier bag of plants, not just a tiny plastic potful. It would take lots of plastic potfuls to make a good show.

The pond-liner would be a fairly major expense, she thought, until she spotted the builder's polythene flapping over a pile of bricks. She trod carefully over to the spot. It was flapping really quite badly. In fact, a good gust and the whole thing would blow off – away even.

Looking the other way, so she would not actually see herself doing such a dreadful thing, Althea moved the planks which held the polythene in place. It fluttered a little and slid to the ground. There you are, she said, picking it up. It just blew off. What a good thing the builders had used black, not the bright blue they usually went for.

She rolled it up, stuffed it under her gardening coat, called Bozo and furtively went home, certain that someone would see her and report the theft. She was not temperamentally suited to this sort of behaviour. If ever she felt a burning urge to steal a bit of plant material from outside someone's house, or by the canal, she always got Merry actually to do the deed. And she still felt bad.

By the time she got back she felt so hideously guilty that she rang Patrick's office number – it was the only one she had, the flat would be bound to be ex-directory – and left a message on his answering machine: 'I've stolen a bit of polythene, I hope you don't mind.'

It didn't make her feel entirely happy about her action. Topaz would get the message first, and would have a lot to say on the matter of squatters who stole from those kind enough to give them a place to squat. But at least it gave Patrick an opportunity to say that actually, he did mind, and would she give it back. To purge herself some more, she went into the garden and dug a base for the wash basin. It was incredibly hard work. She fervently hoped the fictitious young couple, who were becoming more and more real in her mind, didn't have back problems or were expecting a baby.

In spite of all her muttering that if you added together all the time you spent cleaning and cooking and making yourself look respectable you'd have a whole day extra per week, she still found herself washing the bedspreads she flung over the sofas and digging out an ancient tin of hard polish in honour of Frederick's imminent arrival. Bozo greatly appreciated having clean covers to lie on but barked at the vacuum.

'Anyone would think that I never cleaned at all,' muttered Althea crossly, 'when I jolly well do. It just never lasts more than five minutes.'

Althea and Merry tackled the house together the Saturday of the visit, Althea agreeing that Merry should be paid lavishly for her work. After all, if the boys didn't help too, it was only fair.

Merry tended to be of the put-all-these-papers-out-of-sight-in-this-cupboard-and-just-ram-the-door-shut school of tidiers, which gave a good impression but caused havoc afterwards. Althea, who liked to leave piles of papers where she couldn't forget about them, sometimes for years, hurried behind her on a forced march of sorting and discarding. She pinned the most pressing bills on the notice board, hoping that Frederick might take a fit and offer to pay them.

Between them, they made a pretty good team. By the time Merry had been paid and had gone into town to spend her winnings on cheap jewellery and make-up she wasn't allowed to wear, the house looked as good as it could.

The next job was to fill it with vast flower arrangements. Not because Frederick would appreciate or even notice them, but because they hid those disaster areas which dwelt in every house over a certain age which was not constantly repaired and refurbished. Frederick felt because he still had a quarter stake in the house, it was Althea's duty to keep it in a good state of repair for him. She wanted to avoid the lectures on setting money aside so when something needed doing, you could nip the problem in the bud, and not let things get really bad.

Althea had just put a large glass sweet jar full of rambling roses which would drop by morning in a corner which had an ominous crack in the plaster, when she had an idea. How about asking Frederick for the dry-rot money? After all, dry rot was something that just happened, no blame could really be attached to her. If he wanted something from her badly enough to take her out to dinner, he might feel like dishing out the odd two hundred.

For reasons of pride, Althea had put as much thought and effort into her own appearance as that of her house. She had had her hair professionally highlighted – necessary to hide the grey hairs which had hit her so cruelly early. Usually she just used some proprietary brand which sometimes worked quite well, and sometimes turned her hair a strange shade of pink. But for Frederick, she had endured the masochistic experience of having a rubber helmet put on her head and strands of hair pulled out with a crochet hook. It took hours and was so exquisitely painful that having one's hair washed afterwards was as exquisitely pleasurable. And it was such a relief to have the whole thing over, you didn't much care what colour it all came out.

But the hairdresser had done a good job. She looked sun-kissed and golden instead of greying, and the trim they insisted on giving her gave her hair a bit of extra bounce.

She had plucked her eyebrows for the first time for months. She had rejected all Juno's offers of navy-blue suits and round-necked jackets which made her look fat, and had borrowed Sylvia's black dress, which, Sylvia had promised her, never failed. And for a nursery nurse, Althea always considered, Sylvia got around.

The dress was a smidgen too low-cut for respectability, but since Frederick had always maintained that all that breast-feeding would ruin Althea's breasts – a part of her he had felt possessive about – she wanted him to know, in the subtlest way, of course, that it hadn't.

She applied her make-up very carefully, sharpening her pencils and drawing little squiggles in the palm of her hand to warm them. She borrowed Juno's eyelash-curler, and when her new mascara stuck them together, separated her lashes with a pin. She'd even gone so far as to paint her nails with scarlet polish, although this was mostly because it was easier than getting the mud out from under them.

Juno, who, to Althea's irritation, had insisted on 'popping over to see Frederick', was conditionally approving.

'You see. You can do it when you make an effort. Just make good grooming a *habit* and you could look like that all the time. Well, not quite like that, I hope. But if you took some proper aerobic exercise, got off that extra stone or two . . .'

If Althea hadn't spent so much time and effort getting ready, she'd have wiped it all off and put on her baggy trousers. Instead she just sprayed on more scent.

CHAPTER EIGHT

Frederick, who had always been handsome, had improved vastly with age. Tanned, fit and immaculately dressed, the years had taken away the matinée-idol gloss which, with the benefit of hindsight, Althea realized had made him just slightly too much like the plaster groom on top of a wedding cake. Now, she considered, he was almost without flaw, if you could overlook the myriad defects which made up his personality.

Althea was not sure she could, although she did see that she must make the effort. But any dormant passion Juno might have nurtured would rush into full flower when she saw him.

'Do you want to see the children?' said Althea, shaking with nerves almost the moment she had opened the door.

'I've come to see *you*.' He smiled and looked warmly into her eyes. 'I've arranged to see the children tomorrow.'

Althea was taken aback. Frederick had been a figure of odium for so long, and now he was here, living and breathing in her hallway, smiling at her as he had done when he rescued her from that dreadful party all those years ago. Suddenly Althea found him difficult to hate. It must be living with a Buddhist.

She smiled, feeling like a schoolgirl on her first grown-up date. 'Come in. Juno's here.'

'Babysitting? How kind.'

'No, actually. The children haven't had a babysitter since William turned sixteen. She's here to see you.'

Juno emerged from the sitting room holding out her arms. 'Hello, Frederick. Let me look at you. You look *marvellous*. How about a glass of sherry while Althea gets herself ready? I remember you liked a nice chilled Tio Pepe.'

'Juno!' Frederick embraced her warmly. 'You look magnificent! Not a day older. . .' He didn't let her go.

Juno hugged him back and allowed him to lift her off her feet a little and twirl her round. They laughed into each other's eyes, both being uncharacteristically skittish for two such basically serious people.

Althea looked on, rapidly developing indigestion as a turmoil of emotion bubbled inside her. She'd always thought that Juno and Frederick were rather cold fish, but they'd all of a sudden become terribly touchy-feely. She was grateful when Bozo wandered sleepily into the hall to see what was going on.

'And this is Bozo,' she said loudly.

Frederick and Juno put each other down and Frederick regarded the little dog. 'Er – hello.'

Bozo decided not to reply and retreated back to the comfort of the sofa. Althea was relieved. Bozo only barked at people when it was embarrassing for Althea. She'd let any old meter-reader into the house without a murmur.

'Well, now,' said Juno, pink with pleasure. 'I'd better go. I told Kenneth I'd only be a minute. He does worry about me so.'

'Does he?' said Frederick.

Juno made a self-deprecating gesture with her hands which showed off how well kept they were. 'Althea will tell you.'

'I'll call the children,' said Althea, trying not to sound sour.

'Don't disturb them. I told you, I'm taking them out tomorrow. This evening I want to see *you*. Properly,' he added, as if anticipating her snapping, 'Well, you've seen me now.'

'But you'll come and see us tomorrow, after you've seen them? Or bring the children over for tea?' said Juno. 'Kenneth would be so disappointed to miss you.'

'There's no danger of that. I'm going to be over for a few weeks.'

Althea's depression deepened. Juno collected her bag and gave Frederick's suit sleeve a quick stroke. 'Oh *good*,' she said. 'I'm thinking of giving Althea a little party, for her birthday, you know. This means you'll be able to come.'

For the most assertive female since Germaine Greer, thought Althea, Juno could be maddeningly sycophantic. As for her little parties . . .

'Are you ready?' Frederick interrupted Althea's mental growling. 'Shall we go?'

In spite of having exercised it so vigorously, Althea's patience

was still rusty, and she felt grumpy as she searched for her handbag, which, as usual, had gone into hiding at the vital moment.
However, once she was in Frederick's sleek, hired car, driving
through the country lanes to one of the country's most exclusive
restaurants, she relaxed a little.

When she had first met him, Frederick had been an up-and-
coming young businessman. Now he had definitely arrived, and
was bending over backwards to be charming. Having all this
effort directed at her, and not her younger sister, she found it
easier to handle.

'Where are we going?' she asked.

'Jeremy's. It always was the only decent place to eat round
here, and I don't suppose that's changed.'

Althea would have liked to have told him about several
new restaurants which had sprung up recently, serving subtle
and innovative dishes in the manner of Raymond Blanc, but
she didn't know of any. 'We could have eaten at the Dog
and Fox.'

'We could, but I think Jeremy's is better.'

It was certainly more expensive, but Althea didn't mention
that. It would sound too wifely. 'Did you book?' she said instead.
'It's always frightfully full.'

'Of course. My secretary rang them when I first knew I was
coming over.'

'For me?' She could count on the fingers of one hand the
amount of times he'd taken her out to dinner after they were
married.

'Of course, for you. As I said, it's been a long time since we've
seen each other. I wanted the occasion to be memorable.'

Well, it was so far. Althea sat in silence for the remainder of
the journey, looking at what would have been beautiful scenery
if it hadn't been flashing past at such a rate. Frederick had
always driven a little too fast for her taste so that at least was
familiar.

He parked the car and took her elbow as they walked across to
the house which had once been a vicarage and was now a restaurant. As it was rather far out into the country, it had a few bedrooms to cater for people who didn't want to drive. Something
about the way his fingers caressed the inside of her arm made

80

her wonder if he'd got his secretary to book a room as well as a table. A little more of this sort of behaviour years ago and they might have stayed married.

'You look – different,' he said when finally they were sitting opposite each other over a plate of hot canapés and a bottle of champagne.

'The word you're looking for is "older".' The acid in Althea's solar plexus had abated, but it remained on her tongue.

'It's more than that. You're more confident, more assured. Would you be offended if I told you that you've changed from a pretty girl into a beautiful woman?'

'How could I be? At my age, those words are music to my ears.'

'Don't be sarcastic, Ally. I mean it. I left you a quivering wreck and now you have style, elegance –'

'My best friend's dress,' she murmured.

'What was that?'

'Nothing. Do go on.'

'I wondered if there was a man on the scene.'

'No, there isn't.' She smiled blandly, silently commiserating with him that there was no one willing to take her on, forcing her to sell the house so Frederick could have his share.

But Frederick seemed genuinely pleased. 'Oh good.'

'Why "good"?' She was immediately suspicious.

'Because it means you're free, that's all.' He added a touch of boyish shyness to his ex-wife-charming act. 'I'd like to drink a toast, to you, Ally.'

Still wary, Althea picked up her glass and they clinked, but she'd hardly got her glass back to the table before she was aware of Frederick's eyes homing in on someone behind her. No, he hadn't changed that much.

'Who are those people?' he asked. 'They seem to be looking our way. They must know you.'

Althea turned and saw Patrick and Topaz. Topaz was half naked in an off-the-shoulder dress which made her look like Diana the Huntress, all well-toned muscle and safely tanned skin. Patrick looked rumpled and grumpy in a cream linen suit and dark blue silk shirt. He didn't smile and gave the impression of being here under sufferance.

Althea gave them a brief flex of her mouth muscles and was surprised when Topaz got up and prowled over. In the time it took her to arrive, Althea wondered if it was like calling to like.

'Hello, Althea, how lovely to see you here.' Topaz looked expectantly at Frederick.

'And you. Let me introduce you.' Her patience was working hard. 'This is Frederick Farraday, Topaz — I'm afraid I don't know your last name?'

'Oh, Parker. Ms Parker. But your name is Farraday? Does that mean . . . ?'

'Althea and I were once married,' said Frederick, helpfully.

Topaz gave Althea a quick glance as if checking to see if this could possibly be true. How had frumpy old Althea ever attracted this gorgeous beast?

'Well, I won't disturb you,' she cooed. 'You must have a lot to talk about.'

'No, not really,' said frumpy old Althea, pointedly unpossessively. 'Why don't you and Patrick come and join us?'

'We couldn't possibly.' Topaz's throaty chuckle sounded well rehearsed. 'You're obviously set for a romantic reunion.'

Althea felt trapped. Frederick must have seen her panic and made a decision. 'How about having coffee and liqueurs together?' His eyes narrowed into charming slits. 'Afterwards?'

'What a good compromise,' said Topaz. 'We'll meet up later.' She waggled her fingers. 'Bye now.'

Frederick met Althea's questioning look. 'I want to meet your friends, Ally,' he explained reasonably. 'You don't mind, do you?'

'I suppose not, but Patrick and Topaz don't qualify as friends. I mean, I hardly know them.' Althea had consigned her weekend in France to a previous incarnation. 'Now we'll have to make small talk.'

'I'm sure that won't be a problem. Topaz seemed charming.'

Althea sighed, recalling that her ex-husband's ability to remember names and to 'seem charming' were part of the reason he was so successful. He and Topaz would probably have a lot in common.

'Shall we think about what we want to eat?' She picked up her menu and gloomily surveyed it.

It was short and esoteric with a strong emphasis on goats' cheese and entrails. Althea was not fond of either and her gaze skated over coy descriptions and recherché culinary terms, hunting for something identifiable. She found a pasta dish as a starter extremely similar to what the children were eating at home, only with a more exotic name and probably costing enough to keep them in food for a week, and then something which might well be a lamb chop.

Frederick would have liked her to hand the menu to him and say, 'You choose.' He was that sort of man. But even if she could have trusted him to order something she liked, she wouldn't have indulged him. She felt, rightly or wrongly, that at nearly forty, she was old enough to choose her own food.

'Well, I've chosen. What about you?'

Frederick raised a quizzical eyebrow – a look he had perfected over the years. 'That's very decisive. You used to dither so over menus.'

'Did I? But then, it's been a *very* long time since you last took me out to dinner.'

'Not as long as all that, surely.'

'About fifteen years.'

'Come off it. We haven't been divorced that long.'

'No, but after I had Rupert, we stopped going out to restaurants. The occasional pub lunch was about all I got in the way of breaks from the kitchen.'

Frederick was hurt and disbelieving. '*Surely* not?'

Althea nodded. 'Oh yes. I was very fussy about who I'd let babysit, and you . . .' She paused. It was childish to bring up old grievances. 'Well, it was difficult then.'

'We did get married very young.' Frederick tried to sound wistful and sorry but didn't quite make it.

'*I* was very young. You were twenty-seven.'

'Whatever, you're very different now. As I said earlier, you're beautiful.'

And that was supposed to make a difference? Althea was saved from telling Frederick not to give her that crap by the appearance of the waitress. But in spite of her indignation, a tiny part of her needed to know if he really thought she was beautiful, or if it was all just because he wanted something.

83

The waitress was young and leggy and wore a badge saying 'Fenella, Table Assistant'.

'I'll have the pasta and then the lamb,' said Althea briskly.

Frederick smiled charmingly and ordered pan-fried venison liver with sage and tomato salad, followed by a ziggurat of lambs' tongues with white beans. Fenella wrote furiously on her pad and whisked away.

While desperately curious to see what on earth a ziggurat was, for once Althea was not sorry that Frederick was so opposed to the sort of companionable swapping of mouthfuls or sharing of puddings which Althea enjoyed. Still, with all that offal, he wouldn't be going short of iron. He studied the wine list while Althea concentrated on the champagne.

The waitress came up with a jug of iced water and collected his wine order and his instructions as to serving temperature. Frederick's gaze followed her departure thoughtfully. 'With legs like those,' he concluded, 'she should be a model.'

'I expect she's got a 2:1 in Social Sciences and is just doing this until she can get a proper job,' said Althea snappishly. She saw Frederick was beginning to utter something very non-p.c. about education being wasted on women, but he rapidly turned it into a cough.

'So what are *you* going to do until you get a proper job?' Frederick turned his most penetrative gaze full beam at Althea. Her heart lurched, stopped and started beating again, very fast.

'What do you mean?'

'The children told me you've been made redundant.'

'Did they?' She had specifically asked them not to and they were totally loyal.

'Well, let's say it slipped out.'

'Oh.' Had he tortured them? It seemed entirely possible.

'So, how are you going to manage? They're at a very expensive age.'

'Tell me something I don't know. Are you offering to help?'

'That depends. Maybe. I do think we should be a little more imaginative in our dealings with each other now. There were faults on both sides.'

'Were there?'

84

'Of course. If I hadn't felt so dragged down by the children, the mortgage . . .'

'Me?'

'Well, you were totally wrapped up in the babies. All your clothes were stained with baby puke and you never had time to get your hair done, or do anything to make yourself attractive.'

'So meeting Claudia on a business trip had nothing to do with it?'

'Not really, no.'

Althea swallowed down this essential truth with a gulp of champagne and belched discreetly into her napkin. She was spared the effort of finding a suitable comment by Fenella returning with the wine.

Frederick tasted it, passed it fit and turned his attention back to Althea.

'Well, it's all water under the bridge. Isn't it?'

He was obliquely asking if she bore him any resentment, and really, she didn't. He'd done them both a favour when he'd left, but those early years had been very difficult. He'd stopped paying maintenance for her the moment the children were old enough to go to school and she could go out to work, and for them, the moment the question of secondary education had caused such a rift. If it hadn't been for the fact that the mortgage was small and that her parents helped with things like shoes for the children, she would never have managed.

'I expect so,' she said, the hardships softened by time and alcohol. 'Let's just enjoy our meal, shall we?'

Althea's pasta was perfect, almost good enough to make her forget whom she was eating with. But not quite. His plate looked like a pool of blood. It was like sitting opposite a ritual sacrifice.

'I'm thinking of coming back to England,' said Frederick, happily shovelling.

'Oh? Why?'

'The moment Hong Kong goes over to the Chinese, I'm out of there. There are other places in the East I could try, but I have a yearning for England.'

'And what about Claudia?'

'I don't know about Claudia. We'll have to see. We're having a time apart.' He looked hurt, momentarily very like his second son.

Her sympathies heightened by this likeness, and too much champagne, Althea put her hand on Frederick's. 'Oh, I am sorry.'

It was a mistake. Frederick's free hand covered hers in an instant. 'Don't be. I thought it might be an opportunity. . .'

'What sort of opportunity?' The champagne abandoned her, leaving her unsympathetic and suspicious.

'For us to . . . consider our relationship.'

Althea put both her hands firmly back in her lap. 'I don't think that's a good idea at all.'

'You haven't thought it through. You're out of a job and the children need a father. Who better than me, their real father?'

Almost anyone, thought Althea. 'You abandoned them before they were conscious, so I don't think they'd accept your authority now. Besides, I'm not "out of a job", I'm having a career change.'

'What? Gardening? I'm sorry, my dear, I don't mean to sound patronizing, but it's hardly a career . . .'

'I'm planning to be a garden designer. I've already won an opportunity to create a garden at Chelsea,' said Althea sweetly and not quite truthfully. 'And here's the main course.'

Frederick, who'd restricted himself to one glass of champagne and one of wine, had not forgotten what they were talking about when they were both finally served. 'What do you mean, at Chelsea?'

'They have a flower show every year. You must have heard of it.'

'You mean the Chelsea Flower Show?'

'Naturally. My design will be seen by thousands of people, and if I get any sort of award, I can put it on my prospectus.'

'Good God!'

'Don't blaspheme, Frederick, and eat your ziggurat.'

Frederick didn't fill her glass again. Althea ate her chop and went to the ladies. On the way back, she passed Topaz and Patrick. Patrick was getting through a pillow-sized portion of bread and butter pudding, and Topaz was toying with a mint which would make wafer-thin seem chunky.

Althea decided against having a pudding, although they were her favourite part of a meal. If the helpings were all the size of Patrick's they'd be here all night. Topaz and Patrick would get bored with waiting and go home, and Althea would have to contend with Frederick on her own.

She told Frederick this when she arrived back from the ladies. He nodded his approval through a mouthful of white beans. 'Good idea. You're carrying a bit of extra weight and puddings are empty calories.'

'A moment ago,' said Althea, wondering if she would get through the evening without throwing something at him, 'you said I was beautiful.'

'You are. But just a little bit plump.'

At that moment Topaz appeared, in time, Althea was certain, to hear Frederick's last remark.

'Hello, you two. We thought it would be nice to have coffee and liqueurs in the lounge. Would you like to join us when you're ready?'

'I've got a better idea.' Frederick put down his knife and fork. 'Let's go back home and have it. I brought a really good bottle of brandy with me, and if we have the equivalent here, it'll cost an arm and a leg.'

'What do you mean "home"?' demanded Althea.

'Well, you know. Where we used to live. Where you and the children still do live. You don't mind, surely?'

Patrick hove into view behind Topaz, apparently still bored and unwilling. 'Darling?' Topaz addressed him. 'Frederick's just suggested we go back to Althea's for coffee and brandy. I think that's a lovely idea, don't you?'

'What does Althea feel about it?'

'I'm not sure I've got any decent coffee.'

'I only drink herb tea, anyway,' said Topaz. 'Do you have that?'

'Yes,' she hissed.

'Then that's all right,' said Frederick. 'Bill, please!'

Althea waited in the foyer while Topaz was in the bathroom, refusing to share a mirror with a vision of loveliness who had just heard her referred to as fat.

★

87

'You had no right to invite people to my house uninvited,' she said, the moment the car moved off, followed by Patrick and Topaz who looked respectively grim and feline.

'Oh, come off it. It seemed the obvious thing to do. We don't want to pay restaurant prices for things we can get cheaper at home. And they seem like a nice pair.'

'Topaz's pair is not as nice as mine,' she muttered, looking out of the window.

'What's that?'

'Nothing. I just hope the children have gone to bed.'

'Why? They're nice kids. I'm proud of them.'

For the sake of peace, Althea kept her opinion on his right to feel pride when he'd had so little to do with them to herself.

The children had not gone to bed. They were watching a video, probably something quite unsuitable. The sitting room which, when Althea had left the house, had been hoovered and immaculate, was now a graveyard for take-away pizza boxes, bowls of cereal and cola bottles. Popcorn and tortilla chips littered the carpet like autumn leaves. Bozo had ripped up a paper napkin and was now eating a slice of pepperoni and pineapple on the sofa, smearing tomato sauce generously over the covers.

Everyone except the dog, who growled, stood up as the adults entered the room.

'Sorry,' said Merry. 'We were going to clear it up. You're back early.'

'So we are,' said Althea, pushing her party bodily into the conservatory, which thankfully was still as she'd left it. 'It's nicer in here, anyway.' She switched on the table lamps, casting huge exotic shadows on to the roof blinds. 'Do sit down, I'll go and make the coffee.' She left the room quickly, not giving them a chance to disobey.

In the sitting room, the children were more mortified than she was. Merry was snapping at her brothers, who were gathering pizza boxes and putting them in the fireplace.

'Not in there,' said Althea, as she had many times before. 'It's all right in winter, when we have fires, but this is summer. Please use the wastepaper basket.'

'It's all right, Mum, we'll do it,' said William, feeling that they'd let their mother down and that it was mostly her fault.

'OK,' said Althea mildly, agreeing with him. 'But go and say hello when you have. Daddy wants to introduce you.' Their groan was audible from the kitchen.

Althea extracted her enamel coffee pot from the corner under the worktop. It hadn't been used for ages and was terribly dusty. Bitterly, she remembered the silver one which Frederick had taken with him. She hadn't minded at the time, or at any time since, only now. But even if she had had it, she told herself firmly, it would take more than a rinse under a hot tap to get it clean. She heard footsteps behind her. It would be William with the cereal bowls and glasses, wanting an explanation for their early return.

'Bloody Daddy!' She pulled out a tray. 'Inviting people back here, to *my house*, without so much as a by-your-leave. I hate making bloody coffee. You do it for me, there's a love.'

'All right,' said Patrick. 'If you tell me where everything is.'

CHAPTER NINE

Althea turned round, appalled. 'Oh God, I'm so sorry. I thought you were William!'

Patrick smiled. 'That's fine. I'm sure I can make coffee just as well as he can.'

Althea wanted to hug him and not only because he looked irresistibly rumpled. His smile was so calm and undemanding. He appeared to have lost his irritation of earlier and had come to help.

'Do you think so? I would be so grateful. I must do something about the sitting room and be there to stop William saying something outrageous.'

'He can't say anything that terrible, surely?'

'Frederick's idea of outrageous is different from mine, and he might feel obliged to assert his authority.'

'Feeling the young stag is challenging the old stag?'

'Something like that. Only in this case it's more like the young Buddhist challenging the old capitalist. Just as gory, though.' Althea leant on the kitchen counter, reluctant to leave Patrick's undemanding company.

'It appears that William and Topaz have met,' said Patrick.

'Oh? Oh, yes.' The weekend in France came flooding back and she blushed, the first blush causing further embarrassment and more blushing. 'They picked us up from the coach, didn't they?'

Althea's embarrassment seemed to cause Patrick some amusement, and she saw him bite his lip. 'She seemed enchanted.'

'Did she?' Cross with herself for blushing and at Patrick for smiling, she suddenly became very brisk. 'Well, she won't for long. He's a sweet boy, but entirely unpredictable. There are the beans, there's the grinder and the jug. The cafetière's too small. Damn! I suppose I've got to get out the good coffee cups.'

'Don't bother on my account . . .'

'It's not that. I haven't got anything else half decent but Frederick doesn't know I've got them.'

She hadn't meant to keep them, they'd just been put away in a box for safe keeping, and when all the grisly carving up of their lives had been going on, quietly stayed there, unremembered by either protagonist. She set them on a tray, prepared to fight for them, knowing she might lose. They'd been a wedding present from Frederick's aunt.

The sitting room looked a lot better after the children's blitz. The pizza boxes and cereal bowls had gone, and only a fine layer of popcorn, chips and torn tissue covered the carpet. But the conservatory was the site of a potential social disaster.

The children, summoned by their father, were lined up inside the door, but refusing to move too far from their escape route. Bozo had taken a dislike to Topaz and was barking at her, ducking her head away at Topaz's attempts at reconciliation. Frederick, who wanted to show off his children, was thwarted both by their refusal to co-operate and the dog's high-pitched yaps, and was getting increasingly angry.

Althea summed up the situation at a glance. Merry was terrified in case her father kicked her dog. The boys, held in check only by the knowledge that Althea would be mortified if they were rude, were ready to run.

'You lot should all be in bed by now,' she said crisply. 'Specially you, Merry.' Althea hadn't worked at a primary school for years without picking up a few tips. 'Off you go, all of you, and don't forget your teeth. Take Bozo with you.'

Merry picked up the dog and ran. Her brothers were set to follow her, tolerating their mother's peremptory manner only because it got them out of a spot.

'Before you go,' said Frederick to William, 'catch!' He tossed his car keys at his eldest son who caught them as a reflex action. 'There's a bottle of brandy in my car. Fetch it, will you?'

William gave his father a look which should have withered him, had his father enough awareness of others to notice. 'If you want to put a thief in your mouth to steal your brains . . .' he said, and went.

There was a box of chocolate fingers in the cupboard, she remembered. She must find an opportunity to take them up to William's room, where her children would be finishing the pizza and watching the rest of the video. They would not, however, cover his floor with litter: he was much stricter than Althea.

'William's a Buddhist,' Althea explained. 'He doesn't approve of alcohol.' He didn't approve of being treated like a bell-hop, either, but that was another issue. 'We can move back into the sitting room, now,' she added, in the same brisk tone she had used to her children. 'Or are we all right here?'

'We're all right here,' said Topaz who, no longer in fear for her ankles, had made herself comfortable on the sofa. 'This is a lovely conservatory.' She slipped off her sandals and tucked her prettily painted toes under her.

Slightly mollified, Althea put down her tray. 'I'm glad you like it.'

Frederick saw his opportunity and sat down next to Topaz, putting his arm along the back of the sofa, ready, should the opportunity arise, to drop his hand on to Topaz's bare shoulder. Would Topaz notice it hovering there? Althea wondered. And did she mind? Judging by her expression, probably not. And Frederick was a very attractive man on the surface, who knew how to make a woman feel flattered.

'I'll go and get the coffee.' Depressed, Althea returned to the kitchen where Patrick was hunting for teaspoons in all the places she most liked to keep private. She felt annoyed with Frederick all over again for inviting people to her house, treating her children like servants and flirting with Patrick's girlfriend.

'So which is it to be?' asked Patrick. 'Sitting room or conservatory?'

'Conservatory, thank goodness. I really didn't want to have to get the hoover out at this time of night.'

'Surely we could have coped with a few crumbs?'

'Usually I can, but not when the house is full of strange people – oh God! Did that sound terribly rude?'

Patrick nodded. 'Don't worry, I'm getting used to it. Now, the coffee's made. All we need is milk and sugar and another tray. Oh, and Topaz's tea. Have you got herb tea?'

'Yes, William drinks it all the time.' Althea retrieved a tray, gave it a wipe with a damp cloth and put it on the kitchen table. Patrick put the coffee jug on it and looked expectantly at her. 'The sugar will have to be plain old white gran,' she went on. 'I haven't got any coffee sugar, or lumps, and I expect my brown sugar would have to be hacked at with an ice pick just to get it out of the jar.'

'That's OK. I don't have it anyway.'

'But Frederick –'

'Does,' he finished for her. 'I thought you two were divorced. Why do you worry about him so much?'

Althea poured some milk into a jug, deciding not to heat it. 'He's invaded my territory. He covets my house. He treats my children as if they were his, which of course they are, but not like that. And having him here has brought back all those memories of what he was like to live with.'

Why, she wondered, was she telling Patrick all this, when she hardly knew him? She opened a cupboard and spoke with her back to him.

'Topaz can have twig tea, which is almost caffeine-free, Fruits of the Forest, Summer Loving, or Raspberry Zinger.'

'Camomile is her favourite.'

'There might be some somewhere. Oh yes, here it is. It's a bit old, I'm afraid.'

'As long as it tastes of cat-pee, it'll be fine.'

'It's very soothing, they tell me,' said Althea, who liked her tea strong and full of caffeine.

'They tell me that too. I don't believe them.'

There was a moment of electricity when their eyes met and Althea felt herself blush with pleasure and then with shame. She quickly put the milk and sugar on the tray. He belonged to another woman. He was off limits.

'You could take the coffee through,' she said. 'I'll make Topaz's tea.'

'OK.' He didn't move.

Althea found a mug without a chip in it, poured on the boiling water, and prodded the bag with the spoon. 'Does she like honey or anything in it?'

'No.'

'Well, come on.' Althea sighed. She didn't want to move. She

93

wanted to stay in the safety of her kitchen with Patrick. 'Hell! I forgot the brandy. I'd better find some glasses.' She put the tea on the tray, picked it up and put it firmly into his hands. 'You take it. I'll be along in a minute.'

The back of his linen suit was terribly crumpled. She always avoided linen for that very reason, although Juno had told her that linen being crumpled was different, it showed it was linen. But until she saw Patrick wearing them, Althea had never thought of creases as a fashion accessory.

Topaz was pouring coffee into the little strawberry-decorated demitasses Althea so loved. To her paranoid eye, Frederick seemed to be about to ask some awkward questions. The saner side of her realized he would hardly start demanding his share of them in front of guests, particularly when he was so taken with at least one of the visitors.

'Can't you find any better glasses than these?' demanded Frederick, when he saw the small tumblers Althea had produced.

'No.' Rightly assuming that he would have more use for brandy balloons than she would, she had let him have the whole set when he left, but kept quiet about it now. He might have forgotten about the cups, but mention of the glasses was sure to remind him.

'These are fine,' said Patrick, watching Frederick pour generous measures. 'Darling, are you willing to drive home?'

Topaz smiled. 'I should hope so, sweetheart. You must already be over the limit. I only had a spritzer and I never drink spirits.'

Althea winced. Juno didn't drink them either, and they were both a lot thinner than she was. Perhaps she should give them up.

'Jolly good,' said Patrick, unabashed.

Frederick laughed. 'I'm hoping Althea can put me up. If I drink any more, I shall be well over.'

'You've only got to get to the Dog and Fox. And they're expecting you.'

Frederick put on a superior expression. 'That's hardly the point. And I can easily give them a ring.'

Althea, who never drank anything if she was going to drive, wished she hadn't drunk so much champagne. One glass less and she might have made an exception and driven to Sylvia's for the night. As it was, she would have to endure Frederick for another twelve hours or so.

'We've got the Elan, otherwise we could give you a lift,' said Topaz.

'Oh don't worry. I'm sure I can stay here for the night, can't I?' Frederick asked, a lot less nicely than he should have done.

'As long as you don't want to sleep in my bed,' she said sweetly. Everyone laughed, as if she had made a joke.

Tension pulled her into a ball as she huddled into the broken wicker chair and watched the others enjoying themselves. Bloody Frederick! It was all his fault. Inviting first Topaz and Patrick, and then himself into her house. The fact that it had once been Frederick's, and that he would like it back, made everything worse. His presence made her looming redundancy and new career plans seem something to be dreaded, not the bright new opportunity she had come to regard them as.

Topaz was enough to make anyone depressed, especially anyone older and fatter who envied her Patrick. If she were a Topaz, instead of an ageing divorcee with three teenage children, she might make a play for him. Topaz could always find another man, after all. But she wasn't. She was dear old Althea, nearly forty years of age and nearer forty round the hips, with inconvenient morals. She sipped her brandy and tried to keep her expression pleasant.

At last Patrick got up, announcing it was time to go. Topaz slipped from under Frederick's arm and put her own around Patrick's waist, a statement of possession which Althea could have done without.

'Oh no, really?' said Althea, meaning 'about time too'. 'Won't you have some more coffee?'

'No, thank you,' said Patrick. 'You might ask me to make it.'

Althea felt it was unfair of Patrick to look at her in that teasing way in public, when she couldn't reply. She put him in her bad books along with the rest of the party.

'No, we really must go,' said Topaz. 'I've a hot date with a swimming pool at my club at six a.m. tomorrow. Which reminds me, Althea. Have you had any luck finding anywhere else for your plants?'

'Er – no. Not yet. I'm still working, you see. I haven't had a chance to look properly.'

'Well, don't leave it too long. When the builders are ready, we'll have to go ahead. It would be a shame if your plants got spoilt.'

'What are you talking about?' asked Frederick.

'Nothing much. I'll tell you later.' Blast Topaz, she thought. I should have given her dandelion tea and made her pee all night.

Eventually, Althea got the spare-room bed made up. As she'd left the old sheets on since her last guest, it meant a frantic search in the airing cupboard for new bed-linen. And, of course, as it had been her mother who had last stayed, all the nice matching pillowcases, sheets and duvet cover were dirty. If Frederick hadn't known that she hadn't made up the bed for him, she'd have just put him in it and hoped he wouldn't notice the smell of Chanel No. 5 and face powder.

In her own bed at last, with Bozo for company, it took Althea a long time to sleep. She was too jizzed up to relax, in spite of too much to drink and a long, busy day preparing for Frederick.

Of course, it was all Frederick's fault, trying to kiss her good-night. A peck on the cheek would have been all right, but he had tried to make it something more. Even that would have been endurable if Althea hadn't found herself responding. It was humiliating. The combination of his aftershave and the strength in his arms triggered off some primitive response which mentally she totally rejected.

She managed to push him away before he realized what was happening and took advantage, but it had shaken her terribly. Might they have ended up in bed together as Frederick had probably intended that they should? The thought was utterly repulsive, so why hadn't his kiss been?

Sylvia, her friend and the owner of the black dress, would have said she'd been too long without a man. It was sexual frustration, simple as that, and nothing to get worked up about. But Althea wasn't accustomed to having sexual feelings without liking the object of them. Sexual attraction started in the head. If you know someone's a complete low-down toad, how could you want to hold or touch them? Or let them touch you?

Sylvia, whose absence was not preventing her taking a major part in this conversation, would say this was not a problem. Some women, and here Sylvia would sigh, find low-down toads, who you know are going to two-time and dump you, very attractive.

Althea rearranged her pillows, punching and shaking them with all the irritation she felt with herself. She was not Sylvia, young and single and distinctly frivolous. She was Althea, school secretary, mother of three teenagers. She did not fall in love with cads, as her mother would describe them. In fact, she told herself very firmly, she did not fall in love at all.

So she could stop thinking about the man she was certainly not in love with. Althea switched on the radio and listened to the World Service. She heard the news three times, each time seeming more dreadful than the last, and finally fell asleep during a very interesting programme about the history of roses. Bugger Frederick.

'I'm glad to see you've got a new dressing gown at last.'

Frederick's voice made her nearly drop the kettle. Now why had he got up so early? She just wanted a few moments on her own in the kitchen, tidying up.

'Hello, Frederick,' she said coolly, not responding to the dig about the dressing gown. 'You're awake early. Would you like some tea?'

'Yes. But please make it in a pot. Tea-bags are so sloppy, don't you think?'

Althea didn't answer. She made Frederick, who was fully dressed and shaved, a pot of tea, and herself a cup made with a tea-bag. Sharing his pot would imply agreement.

'Why don't you take yours through to the conservatory? I just want to tidy up a bit.'

'The children did make a bit of a mess, didn't they? I would have thought they'd have grown out of that by now.'

'Well, they haven't. And nor have I.' She opened the dishwasher and started to unload it. Frederick watched her. She didn't want him offering to help, rummaging about in her cupboards, but she did wish he wouldn't just watch her like that. 'Are you going back to the Dog and Fox for breakfast?' she said hopefully. 'There's not much here that you would like.'

'I think now I'm here, I'd like breakfast, if that's all right.'

Althea could hardly say it wasn't. 'But you'll have paid for breakfast at the Dog and Fox and they'll give you eggs and bacon. The best I can do is toast and cornflakes, unless you like sugar-free muesli, which William eats.'

'Toast and coffee is all I have these days. I have to keep an eye on the old waistline.'

'Yes, it is just a tad older than mine,' she said wickedly.

'And more than just a tad firmer,' he replied.

Althea pulled back her shoulders and tightened her belt. 'If you don't mind, I'll go and have a shower before I make breakfast. Can you amuse yourself until I come down?'

'I think I'll go and get the Sunday papers. It's nice to have a chance to read them in peace.'

Just how long does he think it takes me to have a shower? wondered Althea, hoping against hope that Frederick didn't mean to spend the whole day in the house. He'd take the children out somewhere, wouldn't he? She turned the temperature up to hot and switched on the shower. But where could he take them? Seventeen, fifteen and twelve, the petting zoo at the local Rare Breeds park was hardly going to fit the bill.

Frederick didn't leave until tea-time.

'I'll be at the Dog and Fox for a few days,' he said as he kissed her goodbye. 'And after that, I'll be in London for a while. So this isn't really goodbye at all.'

Althea closed the door deliberately quietly and went back to cope with the mountains of newspaper which littered the house.

'Daddy was really nice today,' said Merry, reading *The Funday Times*. 'Not nearly so stuffy.'

'Was he?' Frederick had taken the children out for a pub lunch and would have taken Althea as well had she not refused to go, saying she had too much to catch up with.

'Yeah,' said Rupert. 'He offered to buy us beer and everything.'

'And did you drink beer?'

'No,' said William. 'But it was nice of him to offer.'

Althea went into the kitchen and slammed all the cupboard doors shut. She couldn't even have a good moan about the blasted man. He was their father, and if he'd made an effort to be nice to them, she couldn't sound off at his unreasonableness in front of them. Althea was about to drop a mug from a great height, just to hear it smash, when something stopped her. It was William.

'Don't do it, Mum. Anger always rebounds on the person being angry. And that's your favourite mug.'

Althea smiled ruefully and put it down. 'I know. I just feel a bit hemmed in today. It's the Sunday papers, they always do that to me. All that paper, all those trees, what a waste if I don't read them all.'

'Don't worry about it. Go and find the gardening section and read that. After all, the papers are produced whether you read them or not. And Dad's thrashed through the business, the motoring and the current affairs. That just leaves you with the arty farty bits and the gardening. I'll bring you a cup of tea.'

Althea sighed deeply, letting her pent-up emotions out with the sigh. 'You're a good boy, William. I don't care what they say about you . . .'

William grinned. 'I know.'

CHAPTER TEN

❀

'But how can you organize a party when you're being so sick?' Althea drew a stylized rose on her gas bill, the receiver tucked under her chin. The thought of the birthday party threatened by Juno actually taking place was unnerving. Juno had rather formal ideas when it came to entertaining.

'If I sip peppermint tea all day, I'm only sick until midday and then I pick up,' said Juno. 'I'll get someone in to do the catering, of course. I can't face cooking.'

'But, Juny, that'll be frightfully expensive. I couldn't possibly let you.'

'Well, normally, I would have waited until your fortieth. But I can't see myself being able to do anything which requires organization when I've actually got the child.'

'You can get a nanny, Juno!' Usually, this was the last thing that Althea would suggest, but circumstances altered cases.

'I will, but I'm still doing a party this year. Fortieth birthday parties are rather a cliché anyway. Kenneth suggested a surprise party, but I thought that was rather childish, don't you?'

'I suppose so.' Actually, Althea had always rather fancied a surprise party, all the fun and none of the work, but Juno would be upset if she'd told her. However bossy and managerial she was, Juno was basically kind and wanted people to be happy. Althea decided to change the subject, in the vain hope that Juno would forget all about parties, fortieth or otherwise. 'Have you thought any more about how you're going to have the baby?'

'Of course I've thought, but I haven't made any decisions. It's not due until January, you know.'

Althea did know, but Juno was a girl who liked to plan ahead, and might easily have got her case packed by now. 'So has Mum picked herself up off the floor yet?'

Juno chuckled. 'She was staggered, but terribly pleased. I was rather touched. She's got grandchildren already, why should she be so excited about another?'

'Because it's yours, Juny. And there hasn't been a baby in the family for ages.'

'No, well. And she isn't being at all bossy about it. She's happy for me to have the baby in exactly the way I think best.'

'Oh good. I am glad.' Her tactful intervention had been worth the agony then – if only it would last. 'So which method do you think you'll go for?'

'I've told you, I haven't decided, and that's not why I rang you, Althea.'

Althea bit back an automatic 'Sorry'.

'Frederick told me he's going to still be in England, so I asked him. And you must give me a list of everyone else you'd like to come. It could double as a leaving party from school if you want.' There was a pause long enough for Juno to draw breath. 'And I thought Topaz and Patrick would like to come.'

'Topaz and Patrick? I didn't know you knew them.'

'Topaz and I go to the same gym. She's a nice girl, very sensible . . .' Althea added thorns to the rose while Juno thought up how to phrase what she wanted to say next. 'You wouldn't consider joining us at the fitness centre, would you? I mean, it would be nice to get fit for your party, wouldn't it?'

'Why? Are you organizing a home Gladiators' competition, or something? If so, I'll have to buy a new leotard.'

'Don't be silly. It would just be nice to lose a few pounds, have a flatter stomach, things like that.'

'Out of the question, I'm afraid. I'm really frightfully busy at the moment. I've got this garden to design, and school is frantic, preparing to move to the new site, and joining up with Geoffrey Conway's lot. And I might be getting a lodger, a newly appointed teacher. They'll be having two Year 1 groups now.'

'There's always some excuse with you, Ally.'

'Yes, and it's always the same excuse. I haven't got time. I haven't, really.'

'Topaz and I have both got full-time jobs that don't finish at three-thirty in the afternoon.'

'But you haven't got three children and a dog, who gets a walk every day, very often twice. I don't need to pay a fortune to get exercise,' said Althea crossly. Then, feeling suddenly remorseful for snapping at her sister, she went on, 'Are you sure you've got time to organize a party? Your energy levels must be lower now you're pregnant.'

'Of course,' said Juno coolly. 'Organize is the word. If you just thought things out logically, made a plan and stuck to it . . .'

'Juny, I've got to go. Something's burning in the oven.'

Sylvia went with Althea to Cheltenham to help her buy a new dress for the occasion. Althea had the money sent to her by her mother as a birthday present. Althea's mother had also offered to lend Althea money while she found a new job. Althea provisionally accepted the offer of the loan, if she really needed it, but refrained from telling her mother that she wasn't exactly looking for a new job, more a new career. And not one her mother would think of as 'proper'. Althea could be firm with her mother when Juno's well-being was at stake, but for herself, she just avoided confrontation.

'Well, I think you should have a red dress. Red is a good colour,' said Sylvia, parking her car. 'Strong, statement-making.'

'Juno would say at my age I should stick to black or navy blue,' said Althea.

'Nonsense. It's your party, you should draw attention to yourself.'

'It's awfully sweet of Juno to arrange one for me, but I can't help feeling I'd rather just spend the day letting the children make a fuss of me. Or we could have gone out for a meal somewhere.'

'I think the party's a better idea,' said Sylvia. 'Here we are. This is my fave dress shop. And if you don't find anything here, there are plenty more shops to choose from.'

Althea went home with a stunning, sexy dress in bright scarlet. Juno would say it made her look too voluptuous but she didn't care. If she was about to descend rapidly over the hill, at least she could approach the brow with flags flying.

Sylvia came home with her and they slumped on to the sofa in the conservatory, kicked off their shoes and opened a bottle of white wine.

Sylvia, in her late twenties, was stunningly attractive, had the dirtiest laugh Althea had ever heard and was what Merry would describe as 'forward going'. It was an equestrian term which exactly suited Sylvia's glossy black hair and strong eyebrows.

Althea was grateful her sons were both out. Sylvia had taken to looking at them a touch lustfully lately. If they appeared, as they well might, hot from playing basketball, shirtless and in shorts, Sylvia might forget whose sons they were and take them aside to 'show them the way'. In theory, Althea was perfectly happy with the thought of her sons having a sex life, she just didn't want them having it with her best friend.

'So,' said Sylvia, taking a gulp of wine. 'How's your love life?'

'How's yours?' replied Althea, prodding at the compost round a plant with her fingers. 'It's bound to make a more interesting topic of conversation.'

'I see. No progress with Patrick, then?'

'What do you mean "progress"? We've never even started. He's firmly attached to Topaz, who's younger, prettier and in possession. I may find him attractive, in a purely intellectual way, but I wouldn't do a thing about it, even if I had a chance.'

'According to the staff-room gossip you got on very well in France. *Very* well.'

'You shouldn't listen to gossip, Sylvia. It only leads to disappointment.'

Her friend sighed. 'I thought it might lead to a blow-by-blow account of what went on, but . . .'

'Nothing did. Sorry to be so dull and predictable, but what do you expect with the older generation?'

Normally truthful to a fault, Althea had no compunction about lying to Sylvia. If she had so much as a sniff of shared accommodation, let alone beds, she would worry at Althea like a terrier until she'd got enough information, speculation and imagination for a full-length block-buster.

'Perhaps something nice will happen at your birthday party,' said Sylvia.

'I doubt it. There won't be any men there I don't know.'

'Won't there? How dull. Still, I expect the food will be good. Or will it all be low-fat and healthy?'

'Well, it's being catered, so I expect it'll be delicious. By the way, I thought I'd ask that girl who may be my lodger. Can't remember her name, but you know who I mean?'

'Oh, the new Year 1 teacher for Dylan's?'

'You mean Whickham and Dylan's Combined Primary, don't you?'

'But for how long do you think they'll have that mouthful for a name? You mark my words, it'll be Dylan's before they've used up the first order of letterheads. Do you know, they're having a new hall built and God knows what else? The government can find money for things like that, and then cut back on books.'

Althea sighed. 'I'm glad to be out of it.'

'I know.' Sylvia emptied her glass and went on. 'But it's very kind of you to ask her, whoever she's working for. I could put her up after the party, if you like.'

'Could you?'

'Yup. Geoffrey told me she was coming to the area quite soon. To give her plenty of time to case the joint, I suppose.'

'Oh, it's Geoffrey now, is it? I called him that in France, but since then we've reverted to Mr and Mrs. He and I just didn't hit it off.'

'All it takes is the right kind of smile, Althea. You're too moral, that's your problem.'

'Did Geoffrey give you any indication when she was coming?'

'I can find out. Asking her to the party is a sweet idea.'

'Well, as I'm not having a separate leaving party, this would be a good opportunity for her to meet the staff informally. And if I don't like her, I don't have to offer her my spare room. I only told Mr Conway I might be able to put her up, I didn't make any promises.'

'Won't you mind having a stranger living in your house?'

'She's probably a sweet young thing, who I shall take to my bosom like anything. And I'd rather share my house than let my children starve.'

'It won't come to that, will it? Why don't you get a job at Tesco's or something?'

'I would if we were really starving, but I've got to get the drawings for my garden in by September, and for me, that means creating the garden first. I'm too hands-on for a garden designer, really.'

'You'll get over that. If you have to keep turning your precious garden into whatever your clients want you'll soon learn to put it on graph paper.'

Althea refilled Sylvia's glass. 'It's learning to draw that's bothering me. Merry's much better at it than I am.'

'Get her to draw it, then.'

'That would be cheating.'

Sylvia sipped her wine and put her feet up on the occasional table, which was still thick with Sunday papers from Frederick's visits. 'So what do you plan to do about paying the mortgage, the bills and the Council Tax and stuff?'

'My redundancy money will tide us over for a while, and when I've got the plans in, I can look for another job. There's bound to be jobs about in the run-up to Christmas.'

'Do you fancy being a barmaid, then?'

'Well, *I* wouldn't mind, but they probably want them young and attractive, and able to give people the right change.'

'You must stop putting yourself down! You may not be in the first flush . . .'

'Actually, that usually comes nearer fifty, and I haven't hit forty yet.'

Sylvia threw the Innovations catalogue at her. 'You know what I mean. You're an attractive woman.'

'And look,' replied Althea, who had opened the catalogue and was scanning through it. 'This is what I should wear under my new dress. It's a sheer body stocking, helps you avoid V.P.L.'

'What the hell's that? They keep inventing these new diseases . . .'

'Visible Panty Line, idiot.'

They spent the rest of the afternoon speculating on the catering arrangements and what shoes Althea should wear with her dress and whether black tights looked silly in summer. Althea was pleased Sylvia enjoyed talking about clothes so much otherwise she might have found herself mentioning that Patrick was going to be invited to her party. That was all it would take for Sylvia to get completely carried away.

It transpired later that the sweet young thing would not be able to come to the party. She was abroad, refereeing a rugby match.

★

Althea did spend most of her birthday being spoilt by her children, eating the chocolate cake they had made her. But then, at six o'clock, she selected some of the bath unguents given to her by Merry and set out to make herself glamorous. When she emerged, some time later, her children pronounced her beautiful. It was a shame that the man she had made so much effort for would be harder to please.

They arrived at the party, as requested, at half past seven. Juno's husband Kenneth opened the door. Without giving him time to say hello, Juno diverted the children into the kitchen for a few last-minute instructions. Althea hoped their determination not to let their mother down would survive this initial onslaught.

'You look wonderful, Ally,' said Kenneth, kissing her cheek. 'Just as a birthday girl should.'

'You look fairly wonderful yourself. Potential fatherhood must agree with you.' Althea was very fond of her brother-in-law, who, although thoroughly bullied by Juno, loved her dearly.

Kenneth grinned. 'A bit of the turn-up for the books, eh? It's just such a long time to wait.'

'That's nature's way of making sure by the time the little mite does appear, you're all really keen.'

Kenneth patted her shoulder. 'Come and have a stiffener before the crowd arrives.'

Juno's house looked marvellous. It was on an exclusive estate where genuinely old houses mixed with tasteful reproductions and 'architect-designed' modern homes. Juno's was one of the latter. All the windows were geared to make the most of the stunning views to the front and the climbing woodland to the rear. Inside, acres of natural wood flooring set off the strong colours of the curtains. The furniture was all handmade by local craftsmen and fulfilled all the Pre-Raphaelite requirements of beauty and usefulness. There were a few huge paintings on the wall of the genre Althea described as 'beautiful but difficult' and for the party, massive flower arrangements were placed at strategic intervals. Not to hide areas of damp or peeling wallpaper, as they would have done in Althea's house, but to conceal fragile ornaments, or pieces of furniture which resented glasses being put on them. Althea greatly admired Juno's taste and her ability to avoid clutter. Things would change a bit when she had the baby, of course, but not in a way noticeable to the casual observer.

'Juny! You look stunning! Are you really pregnant?' Juno was wearing a coral-coloured crêpe de Chine shift, calf-length, scoop necked, slit to the thigh, under which there was certainly no V.P.L. and no obvious sign of a bra, either.

Juno laughed. 'Well, something's making me awfully ill in the mornings.'

And something's making you dress up in a very sexy way, and probably not darling Kenneth, thought Althea anxiously. Of course, Juno was far too organized and sensible to make a fool of herself over Frederick, but she usually looked as if she were wearing more than just a couple of yards of silk.

'Frederick's coming early,' said Juno, adding to her sister's anxiety. 'So we can have a drink together before the scrum.'

Althea accepted the glass Kenneth put into her hand. Surely her sister didn't mean to sound rude when she referred to her friends as the scrum. But Althea knew some of the teachers at school weren't really Juno's type. And Sylvia she definitely considered a bad influence.

Althea had long since stopped looking for Patrick and Topaz. At first, every time the doorbell rang and new people arrived, she looked up expectantly; but now, an hour and a half into the party, she had told herself they weren't coming and set about enjoying herself.

A lot of the people were friends of Juno and Kenneth, known only slightly to Althea. Althea moved among them, laughing and chatting, appearing to have a good time. But inside she felt unsettled. If it had been her house, and her friends, she would have been busy, seeing everyone was happy and had someone to talk to. But here, she was out of her environment, half hostess, half guest, and she felt uneasy, even a little lonely.

She was on her way to get herself another drink when suddenly Patrick appeared in the corner of her eye.

'Hello, Althea. Happy birthday,' he said and kissed her cheek.

Althea jumped as if scalded. It was so unexpected. His hot breath, the quick graze of his newly shaved chin, his cologne, all combined to resurrect her carefully damped-down hormones so rapidly her legs felt shaky.

'Don't look so startled,' he said, laughing. 'It's perfectly de rigueur to kiss the birthday girl.'

'Is it?' Althea was struggling to breathe normally. He was wearing his rumpled linen suit and dark silk shirt, substituting sexiness for sartorial elegance. Unlike Frederick, who was one of the few men wearing a dinner jacket.

'Of course. You're not telling me there's a man here who hasn't kissed you?'

'Well, no.' There had been a good many friendly pecks on the cheek. 'But you sort of came up behind me. I wasn't expecting it.'

He chuckled. He had wonderfully laughing blue eyes. 'Next time I'll give you a bit of warning.'

Althea swallowed hard. 'Is Topaz with you?'

'Over there.'

She was with Frederick and Juno. Frederick was laughing and had an arm round both women's shoulders, handsome, debonair and well tailored. Topaz was looking sleeker and fitter than ever in a dress even sexier than Juno's. They made a glamorous, sophisticated trio. Althea began to wonder if scarlet had been a mistake.

'Were you on your way to the bar?' said Patrick. 'Can I get you something?'

'A glass of red wine, please.'

'With or without mineral water?'

'Without,' she said firmly.

'So that's one still water, one fizzy with a splash of white and two glasses of red.'

'Can you manage all that, or shall I come with you?'

'Come with me.'

He went first and she indulged herself for a few moments admiring his broad shoulders, his neck, the way his hair grew at the back, and then she lowered her eyes and tried to think about something else. She was far too old to worship from afar and although they might have shared a bedroom for a couple of nights, he was still way out of reach.

She was following him back to Topaz and Juno, carrying the two glasses of red wine, when someone came up to her.

'Quick! You must come! There's a policeman at the door for you.'

Someone took the wine from her shaking hands. Rapidly she went through the reasons why a policeman might call. Her children? No, they were all here somewhere, being obliging, thoroughly bored. That was all right then, it could only be that her house had been broken into. She arrived at the door relatively calm.

'Are you Mrs Althea Farraday?'

'Yes.' The policeman looked extremely young and had an earring, but that was a sign of getting older, thinking that policemen were young.

'Well, I'm afraid I'm here to inform you . . .'

Something was wrong – it was a fine summer night, and lots of guests had spread themselves on to the paved area in front of Juno's house. And lots of them had cameras. Why were they all ranged round the door looking at their friend talking to a policeman, cameras poised?

'. . . that as it's your birthday . . .'

Her first reaction was relief. It was a strippergram. Horrible, embarrassing and about as un-p.c. as someone dressed as a P.C. could be, but not threatening.

There was an explosion of flash guns, and Althea caught a glimpse of Sylvia looking triumphant and wicked. Her nearly retired boss, Mr Edwards, was smiling awkwardly, trying both to join in the fun and disassociate himself.

Althea had a very short time to make a decision. She could be snooty and dignified and ask the man to leave, or she could go along with it. She really had very little choice. Her friends had probably spent a fortune on getting this young thing there and if she reacted badly, they would all think they had made a terrible mistake in going along with Sylvia. They had of course, but it wasn't their fault. Althea had made a few mistakes herself by going along with Sylvia.

And so she played out the comedy. She watched him take off his clothes, which was slightly less exciting than seeing her own boys undress. She took off his boxer shorts, at arms' length and with the tips of her fingers, and revealed his prosthesis which was crude enough to send a hiss of shock through her audience. And she endured his jokes and his kiss and wondered what he did for a day job. And when it was all over, she invited him and his minder, who was the roly-poly-gram on the nights she was working, to have a glass of wine. Then she went back to face the disapproval.

CHAPTER ELEVEN

❁

Juno was furious, smiling tightly while she hissed her rage at Althea, knowing that it really had nothing to do with her, but not being able to express herself to anyone else.

'It was so undignified! You should have just told him you preferred not to participate.'

'But, Juny, he would have been so expensive, and none of my teacher friends have got any money.' Althea had felt perfectly all right about it before. Now she felt besmirched and degraded.

'I thought it was disgusting.' From nowhere, Topaz appeared, eager to back up Juno and wallow in Althea's increasing misery. 'How any woman of today could participate in anything so sexist, I don't know. Of course,' she went on, fluttering her eye-lashes in a disapproving way, 'it was awkward for you, if your friends arranged it.' She managed to make it clear that anyone who had those sort of friends deserved everything they got.

'Really, Althea,' said Frederick. 'You could have behaved with a bit more dignity at your age. But you actually went along with it! God! When I think that my children saw you behaving like that . . .'

'Hi, Mum,' said Rupert. 'You didn't mind, did you? Sylvia asked us about it, and we thought you'd be OK.'

Althea put an arm round her son and hugged him. 'It was fine, darling.' She swallowed hard.

'I think what your mother needs is a drink,' said Patrick after a moment, putting a glass of wine into her hand. 'And then do come and tell me how you're getting on with your garden.'

As she gratefully allowed herself to be taken away from the knot of disapproval represented by Topaz, Juno and Frederick, Althea wondered if anyone would follow. With luck, Topaz and Juno would be so eager to deplore her behaviour with her ex-husband that they wouldn't.

Patrick found an uninhabited corner of Juno's sunroom and sat her down. Althea felt very weak and feeble, horribly close to tears. He waited until she had drunk half her wine before speaking.

'I thought that was great fun,' he said. 'A wonderful piece of theatre. You handled the situation extremely well. After all, if you'd been snooty about it, all your friends would have felt they'd done the wrong thing and been miserable.'

Althea was resting her elbows on her knees being miserable for them, unknowingly giving Patrick a good view of her Gossard Wonderbra and what it contained. 'I felt all right about it at the time. I was so grateful he wasn't a real policeman, telling me some frightful news. But now I feel sort of raped.'

Patrick, who had been sitting opposite her, moved so he could put his arm round her. 'There's no need to feel like that, honestly. No one thinks any the worse of you. You behaved perfectly in the circumstances. You were humorous and lighthearted, you participated but kept yourself at a distance.'

'Topaz and Juno think the worse of me.'

'They're just jealous.'

'Don't be silly. How could they be? No woman in her right mind would want something like that to happen.'

'Maybe not. But they neither of them could wear that dress.' He indicated her scarlet silk-jersey.

'Nonsense! When you've got figures like they have, you can wear any dress you like.'

'Not without looking very dull in it, they couldn't.'

Althea had just about worked out what he meant when Sylvia appeared, obviously to find out if her friend was traumatized forever.

'I'm not interrupting anything, am I?'

'Of course not, Syl. Come and meet Patrick Donahugh.'

'Patrick Donahugh? My stand-in for the French trip? Now tell me, Patrick, just between ourselves, *does* Althea snore?'

'I think you having a lodger is a ridiculous idea.' Frederick paced round the kitchen once more, and then sat down, to give his point emphasis.

It was a week after Althea's party and Frederick still hadn't forgiven her for coping with the strippergram with some show of equanimity.

To get him off the subject, Althea had told him how she had heard from the refereeing probationer teacher. This young person would very much appreciate the offer of a room to rent until she could find a flat.

She also wanted to come right away, although her new job didn't start until September. Not one to turn down the chance of regular money in her hand, Althea had agreed. She had thought Frederick would have approved of this sensible approach.

'No, it's not,' she said, her patience getting more practice than it had energy for. 'It's entirely practical. This is a big house. It's silly to have empty rooms when I need the money. And it's not as if she's fresh out of Brixton or Holloway or wherever. She's a recently qualified teacher, come to this part of the world for her first job. It'll be nice for her to have somewhere homely to live.'

'Homely! It's a bloody mess.'

Frederick, nominally setting up a new partnership in London, but spending a lot of weekends at the Dog and Fox, had, by his propinquity, lost his status as someone to be cleaned up for. Particularly as, in spite of the goings-on at the party, where Frederick seemed much impressed by Topaz, Althea couldn't shake off the feeling that he was toying with the notion of them getting back together.

He had been very free with his kisses and hugs lately. And she, having quite recovered from her momentary hormone rush when he'd kissed her after he took her out to dinner, wanted to do everything she could to put him off.

'Only to you, Frederick. To me and the children it's home, and it's how we like it.' She was glad none of the children were around to hear this and splutter incredulously that if this were true, why she was always nagging at them to tidy up?

'She'll be horrified.' He shifted enough newspapers, shopping lists, catalogues and opportunities to buy books at vastly reduced prices to find room for his elbows. A lot of them slid off on to the floor. 'See what I mean?'

Althea rescued the pile and tossed a lot of it in the bin. 'It'll be good for her to expand her ideas. And she'll be company for me when the children are out. Oh dear,' she added. 'I suppose I'd better pay this.'

This was a mistake. Frederick spotted an opening and flew in. 'If it's company and help with the bills you want, I've got a much better idea.'

Oh, please don't let it be what I think it might be. 'What's that?'

'That you and I should make another go of it. You've said yourself that the children need a steadying influence right now. Who better to give it than their own father?'

'Oh, Frederick, you might be right about the children, but what about us? We drove each other mad all those years ago, why should anything be different now?'

'You've grown up since then, Ally.'

Althea glared at him. She might have grown up, but he was pretty much the same: more handsome, but with just as roving an eye. He and Topaz had seemed to be getting on like a house on fire at her party. If Patrick hadn't had Sylvia to entertain him, he might have been quite put out. Juno certainly had been. And he always had been unliveable with in every other way, critical, demanding and with a very boring taste in television programmes. And he had the nerve to imply their marriage had broken up because of her immaturity!

Althea spotted a kitchen knife which was lying in a pool of apple peel under the Lakelands Plastics catalogue. She didn't want to kill him with it, just stick it into his hand or something. A little wound which would put him off the idea of remarriage. However, to prove how grown up she was, she kept quite calm.

'You've said that before, Frederick, but it makes us less likely to get on, not more.'

'Oh?'

'Yes. I'm more of my own person now. I couldn't adapt to sharing my life with another adult.' Or sharing her husband with another woman – but she didn't mention that. He might think she was jealous.

'But that's exactly what you'll have to do if you go ahead with this lodger idea.'

'That's different. I can tell her the rules, give her parameters.

Like I do the children.' Or at least, how she would do with the children if she weren't so sloppy.

'And what about the children? Couldn't you put their needs first?'

'I could, I do, I always have. But I don't think having us living together, bickering and fighting all the time, is what they need right now. I've spent years working out my relationship with them,' she added more gently. 'It's subtle. You think they do what they like and walk over me. But they don't, not totally. And honestly, bringing up teenagers is hard enough if they like you. If you put their backs up you've no chance.'

Frederick picked up William's *Guardian* and started to read it. 'Perhaps you're right.'

'Why do you want us to start again? Why not try again with Claudia?'

'I could. She'd welcome me back with open arms. But this is – was – my home. And you were my wife, and you're still the mother of my children. Those things are precious to me.'

For a moment, Althea was touched. Then she saw exactly what was precious to him – the house. 'Would you buy me out if you could, Frederick?'

'Would you let me?'

'No. I won't leave this house a moment before I have to. It's my children's home.'

'Supposing you have a new relationship?'

For a moment a yearning for Patrick stabbed her. She breathed through it, like a woman in the early stages of labour, and it passed.

'It's highly unlikely, and I wouldn't dream of it with the children the ages they are. The boys would hate another man in their house. Even Merry would only tolerate it if he could afford to buy her a pony or something.'

Frederick put down the paper. 'Except, of course, it wouldn't be in their house. If you remember, if you remarry, or live with someone, you have to pay me my share.' He tried but failed to keep the satisfaction from his eyes. 'Which would probably mean you having to sell.'

'Of course I remember, Frederick. How could I forget? But the whole thing's hypothetical. I've no intention of having another relationship.'

Frederick seemed relieved. She would have been flattered if she hadn't realized it was just because he didn't want Althea to find a man rich enough to buy him out.

'Well, don't forget. I did ask. I would have given up Claudia for you.'

Althea sighed the sigh born of twelve years' single parenthood. 'It's a pity you didn't think like that twelve years ago.'

When Frederick had said his goodbyes to the children, promising them tickets to Hong Kong as soon as he was settled back there, and finally taken himself off, Althea set about cleaning the house. Frederick was right, it was a mess, and however enriching it would be for a young teacher to live in it, she might find it a bit of a culture shock, even after student accommodation.

She slapped a leftover tin of rose-white emulsion all over the spare room, including a fair chunk of the carpet, found a bedside light that worked, a rug to cover the paint splashes, and moved all the odd clothes in the chest of drawers up to the attic. She cleaned the basin, made up the bed and considered the room ready. She would put a bunch of flowers on the dressing table on the morning of her lodger's arrival, which was to be next weekend.

Given the tender ages of her sons, Althea might have preferred a rather different type of girl than the one who arrived on her doorstep the Sunday before the last week of term.

Jenny was blonde and bouncy and brimming with confidence, with an Australian accent which added to her larger-than-life personality. She wore a very white T-shirt with an environmental slogan and black lycra cycling shorts.

Althea had always privately thought that cycling shorts should be illegal for anyone over ten years old, and although there was nothing wrong with Jenny's figure – a fact obvious to all the world – seeing them on her lodger didn't make her change her mind. However, the girl was obviously as good-natured as she was enthusiastic, appealing and over-energetic, like a golden retriever. Bozo thought she was wonderful.

It came as no surprise to Althea to hear that Jenny had specialized in P.E. at training college. When she wasn't refereeing, her hobbies were women's rugby and water polo. She was planning to get mixed football into the new school within a year.

'And how did Geoffrey Conway react to that when you told him?' Althea asked when Jenny had flung her tote-bag on to the bed, and thus settled into her room.

'Oh, I didn't tell him! You need to creep these things up on people. If you get all in your face about it, you never get anywhere. They get anti and you'll never change them. No, once he realizes he can offer all sorts of after-school clubs now he's got me, he'll be eating out of my hand.'

'Golly. And are you sure this is your first teaching post?'

'Yeah, but it'll be a doddle. I come from a big family. I can handle myself. I was born in Australia, you know? And we're born self-reliant.'

'Golly,' said Althea again, feeling whingeing and Pommish.

'So, what do you do for fun?'

'Er – I garden . . . '

'Do you? Cool. We didn't have much of a garden at home, but I loved making mud pies.'

'Well, that's as good a place to start as any.'

'I love cooking as well. Veggie, of course. I hope I won't get in your way or anything. I plan to get my own place as soon as I can find the right person to flat with.'

Althea nodded. The word 'flat' as a verb was new to her.

'Hey, do you know anywhere round here that has a proper fitness circuit? It's really important for me to keep things up. Once the muscles go flabby' – she looked at Althea rather intently – 'it's really hard to get them firm again.'

'I know just the person to ask.'

'Oh, cool.'

At this moment, William and Rupert appeared, hot and sweaty from tennis, determined to denude the fridge of milk in five minutes flat. They paused in their assault when they saw Jenny sitting with their mother.

'These are my sons, Jenny,' said Althea. 'William and Rupert. Boys, this is Jenny. She's going to be staying while she looks for a flat.'

'Great,' said William, and grinned.

'Hi,' said Rupert, not quite meeting her eyes. Jenny was a

rather daunting prospect for a fifteen-year-old who didn't get out much.

Jenny looked them over with the critical eye of an outback sheep-farmer, picking out his stud cattle.

Seeing this, Althea hastily referred to her watch. 'Goodness. I nearly forgot. I've got to go and pick Merry up.'

'Do you want me to go, Mum?' asked William.

Jenny wouldn't really eat them. And she was at least nearer their age group than Sylvia. 'No, you stay and get acquainted with Jenny. I'll go.'

By the time Althea and Merry got back, the three of them were sitting round the table drinking twig tea and getting on like the proverbial house on fire. Merry soon joined the party and Althea felt that Jenny was going to be a good addition to the household, even if she did seduce her sons. But after a while, the boys drifted away, Merry went up to clear up her room, and Jenny still needed entertaining. She expressed an interest in seeing the greenhouse she'd heard the children talk about.

Althea had badly wanted a little time on her own. Although she knew it was unlikely she would see Patrick, the time spent among her plants, near where he lived, would cheer her. And if she did see him, well, that would be nice too.

Not, she assured herself, because of his laughing eyes, and loose-limbed, sexy body, but because of his kindness. He had been kind at her party when all about her had been disapproving. They had made a bad situation worse, he had striven to make her feel better. So it was only for comfort that she even dreamt of seeking him out.

But as she didn't quite believe her own high-mindedness, she allowed Jenny to invite herself along for the ride. Jenny would act as a metaphorical hair shirt, to remind her of her pure intentions.

And as Patrick's car was the first thing she noticed as they approached the property, she should have felt grateful that she was protected from impropriety by her bouncy Antipodean friend. William had been right when he had whispered to his mother that their lodger reminded him of Tigger. She was fun and outgoing and spoke before she thought.

Patrick saw them arrive and was there to greet them. Quite

why he was there on a Sunday, she couldn't ask, but he seemed preoccupied.

'Get a load of that!' murmured Jenny under her breath. 'Who is this gorgeous guy? Old, but perfectly formed.'

'I'll introduce you,' said Althea bleakly. 'It's Patrick Dona-hugh. He owns the greenhouse.'

The common name of one of the plants which grew at the base of the walls of Barnet House was 'Creeping Jenny'. It seemed an appropriate nick-name for her lodger. Not that she crept in a snake-like way, she was much more open in her approach. She found Patrick attractive and made no secret of it. He was not particularly welcoming and Althea quickly slipped away to the greenhouse. But Jenny would not be brushed off so easily.

When she finally dragged her new friend away, she lectured her sternly on the morality of homing in on another woman's man.

'You're crazy!' replied Jenny, unabashed. 'It's every girl for herself out there! If this Topaz person is silly enough to let a guy like Patrick out of her sight, she deserves to lose him.'

'He's a little old for you, isn't he?'

'Nah, I like the more mature type. They're richer.'

'And he's not really handsome. His nose is crooked and his mouth sort of lopsided when he smiles.'

'Those things don't matter. It's personality that counts. And his personality is dee-lish.'

Althea wanted to burst into tears, stamp her foot and declare, 'He's mine!' But she couldn't, for several reasons, the most important being that, in fact, he belonged to Topaz. She could make no claim on him. Nor could she alter her morals and home in on him herself, they were part of her, ingrained, and no amount of wishing would alter them.

I should have asked Jenny for more rent, she thought as they went home. I don't mind sharing my kitchen and bathroom, or even my clothes, for a bargain price, but sharing my dreams should be very, very expensive.

The staff at the school had all secretly arranged a farewell assembly for Mr Edwards, their departing head teacher.

Afterwards, there was to be a party, arranged by Althea, which was also a surprise. Teachers past and present, distinguished ex-pupils, governors and anyone else Althea could think of, had all been invited.

Althea didn't go to the assembly. The children had said goodbye to her the previous day. She didn't want to encroach on Mr Edwards's celebration and had a lot to organize.

She could hear the children singing in the hall while she set out piles of plates and folded paper napkins. This was the last time she would hear the jangly piano, the enthusiastic, off-key singing, the local accent exaggerated by the weight of numbers. She allowed herself a private tear. She would miss the children terribly.

But what, apart from the children, would she miss? The other staff, certainly, though she'd still see them. But with Mr Edwards gone and the school on another site, the working day would be very different. And with Mr Conway as head, they wouldn't be having much fun. No, on the whole, she was glad to be leaving. Jenny, who had gone to the assembly and was coming to the party, might be able to handle Mr Conway and his radical ideas, but she was young and full of enthusiasm. Althea was older, and though equally enthusiastic about what interested her, had gone off the National Curriculum.

She heard the thunderous cry of children cheering, a brief silence while Mr Edwards told them to keep safe during the summer holidays and not to put their parents to the trouble of taking them to casualty, and awaited the first trickle of teachers.

Sylvia was among the first. She alone of all the conspirators involved in the strippergram fiasco had not come up to Althea privately and told her that they hadn't thought it a good idea, but didn't like to seem a party pooper. Althea told each one that while it wasn't what she would have chosen, she had known they meant well and that it livened up what could have been a boring party. She added her fervent hope that they hadn't ordered the roly-poly-gram for Mr Edwards.

Reassured that they hadn't, Althea happily doled out the warm white wine, the orange juice and the elderflower cordial.

A jug in her hand, she was heading towards the chairman of the governors, a large, round woman, cheerful and efficient, when she spotted Patrick coming into the room with a group of teachers and governors from the other school, headed by Geoffrey Conway. She turned on her heel and marched swiftly back the way she had come.

Her first thought was for the catering. She'd only asked Geoffrey Conway because everyone said she had to, and he had said nothing about inviting new governors. The party was overcrowded as it was. The man was the bloody limit.

Her second feeling was embarrassment. It was something to do with Patrick seeing her in her working environment, among people who had seen them together in France. She felt caught on the hop, hot and unattractive in her rather faded cotton dress, which was clean and comfortable but a million miles away from glamour.

'I'm just going to get some water for the cordial,' she told the school caretaker, as an excuse to get away.

Not that he'd necessarily speak to her, she told her reflection as she splashed her face with cold water. He might not even see her in the crush. But he'd see Sylvia and Jenny, they would make sure of that. And was she prepared to let him be set upon by those two harpies, unprotected by her own motherly person?

She came back with the jug of water and made up the cordial. Then, taking the bull by the horns, took it to the corner of the room where Geoffrey Conway, Patrick, and the chairman of the governors, were all talking.

'Yes, thank you, I'd love some more,' said Mrs Jenkinstown, who combined her governorship with all sorts of other committees. 'And I'd like a word later, a little favour I want to ask.'

'Oh?' A quick glance at Geoffrey Conway told her he didn't want to ask it and would probably veto it if he could.

'Yes. It's about you staying on as Clerk to the Governors. It seems the new school secretary doesn't do shorthand. And we'll need someone to take minutes.'

Geoffrey Conway had the grace to look discomforted.

'I see,' said Althea, suitably staggered. 'Well, I'll have to think about it.'

'There is a small honorarium attached to the post,' went on the chairman. 'You've always dealt with it so efficiently in the past.'

'Well, thank you. I'm flattered, of course . . .'

'Rather a bore when you're planning a new career, but we are desperate.' Mrs Jenkinstown smiled. She had the pretty sort of face shared by many big women and ran half the community with a bracing kindness which told any hangers-back that if she could do so much for others, they could do a little. It always worked.

'Well, in that case . . .' Althea mumbled. 'I suppose . . .'

Mrs Jenkinstown twinkled. 'I knew I could rely on you, Althea.' Althea smiled back before moving on with her jug.

Patrick, she noticed when she dared steal a glance at him, was looking particularly tired and drawn about the mouth. She found her way through to him and offered to get him a drink.

'No, thank you. But like Mrs Jenkinstown, I'd like a word. Unlike her, I really do need it in private.'

Althea's heart began to pound. Had Topaz had the bulldozers in without telling anyone? Were her plants all buried under six feet of rubble?

'Is it to do with the house?'

'No, nothing like that. But I can't talk about it here.'

'Where then?'

'Perhaps you could give me a lift home. Among other things, my car's been stolen.'

'What! But that's terrible! Have you told the police?'

'Not yet. I think I know who's taken it.'

'But who would do a thing like that?'

'Topaz, to get her to the airport. She's gone, you see. To Hong Kong.'

CHAPTER TWELVE

Althea went hot and then cold. 'Oh, my God. How awful!'

'I thought I ought to tell you as soon as possible. Before you heard it from someone else.'

'But why would I?'

Patrick looked quickly over his shoulder. He bit his lip and spoke so quietly she could hardly hear him. 'I did say she'd gone to Hong Kong . . .'

It was if someone had put an ice-cube down her neck. 'You mean she's gone with Frederick?'

Patrick nodded. There was strain in his eyes which made him look older. Althea felt a sharp stab of anger which was rapidly followed by guilt. So Frederick wasn't content to philander with the hundreds of unattached women who would be delighted to run off with him, he had to choose Topaz. And while she didn't care about Topaz herself, Patrick obviously did. The guilt was because for some obscure reason she felt responsible for Frederick and his actions. And if it hadn't been for her, the runaway couple would never have met each other. She must do what she could to put the situation right.

'I'll get away from here as soon as possible.'

It took her fifteen minutes to make apologies, excuses and fond farewells. She managed to imply she was too overcome by emotion to stay and clear up – not a ploy that would work too often. She also asked Sylvia to take Jenny home and tell the children she had to go out and would ring when she knew what was happening. Sylvia agreed on the strict understanding that she would get a blow-by-blow account when Althea got back.

'We can't leave together,' Althea said to Patrick. 'I'll go first. Just give me a minute.'

'But I came with Geoffrey Conway,' said Patrick. 'I'll have to tell him I'm going, or he'll wonder how I got home.'

'Hell . . .'

'But it's all right, I'll just tell him you said you had to catch the bank and I asked for a lift.'

'OK,' Althea agreed reluctantly, doubting he would get away with anything so simple. Geoffrey Conway was the one person she hadn't said goodbye to. 'But I'll still go first. I don't want all my friends seeing us leave together and making five.'

Patrick frowned briefly. 'As you like.'

Althea didn't have to wait long before he joined her by her car. 'I didn't quite take in that this was your leaving do and I've dragged you away.'

'That's fine. It's not my leaving do, it's for Mr Edwards, and I'd only get dreadfully sentimental if I stayed any longer, not to mention saddled with the washing-up. And the people I'm fond of, I'll go on seeing.' Althea unlocked her door and reached across to Patrick's. 'I don't want to find myself exchanging addresses with a lot of people I never much cared for.'

'And besides, you're going to be Clerk to the Governors,' he reminded her, getting in.

'Oh hell, so I am.' Althea watched as he moved the seat back and finally folded himself into her car. 'Sorry, it's a bit of a squash for tall people.'

'That's fine. I'm grateful for a lift.'

Althea started the car and nosed her way out of the play-ground into the road. 'It was very noble of you to go to that do. I always used to invite governors to things and hardly any of them ever came.'

'I wasn't going to. In fact I'd forgotten all about it, what with one thing and another. But Geoffrey rang to give me the three-line whip and I suddenly realized you would be there. It was an ideal opportunity to see you.'

Althea gulped back the knowledge that this was not the compliment it sounded. 'Of course.'

'Where are you going?' Patrick asked after about five minutes, when they were driving along the common.

Althea slowed down suddenly. 'Oh I'm sorry. It's so thoughtless of me. Was there anything you wanted to pick up before we go?'

'No . . .'

And I've organized things at home, so we might as well press on.' She speeded up and overtook a pair of bicycles.

'Press on where?'

'To Heathrow, of course. To see if we can catch them.'

'Althea – Look, pull in, will you? I think we need to talk.'

'We can talk as we drive.'

'No we can't. We could be going in the wrong direction.'

'Could we?'

'Yes, pull in here. Please.'

Althea pulled into one of the laybys scooped out of the common to make a car park. 'I'm sorry. I'm going off at a tangent again.'

Patrick undid his seatbelt. 'Do you mind if we walk as we talk?'

'No, of course not. You must be dreadfully cramped.'

They set off across the common, avoiding the main path which was beginning to be dotted with people walking their dogs after picking up their children from school.

'Has this come as an awful shock to you, Althea?'

'Well, yes. I mean, I saw them getting on well at my party, but I never thought . . . Did you?'

He shook his head. 'No. Though I did know . . . ' He tailed off and started again. 'I wouldn't have had this happen for the world.'

'God no, nor would I. I feel so responsible.'

'You mustn't blame yourself.'

'But I do. Topaz and Frederick would never have met if it wasn't for me.'

'They're both adults. You can't feel responsible if they have the morals of tom cats.'

'But I always do. Guilt and oestrogen go together, you know.'

He grunted as a gesture towards this small joke. 'Really? Perhaps Topaz was light on oestrogen.'

Althea could almost feel his pain. 'Oh, Patrick, this must be so distressing for you. Would you prefer just to borrow my car and go to Heathrow by yourself?'

Patrick didn't answer for a moment, and then his arm came down and landed on her shoulder. The heat of his hand was noticeable through the thin cotton of her dress. 'What?'

'You said your car's been stolen. Though I must say, I thought Topaz had her own car.'

'I sold it. It drank petrol, cost a fortune to insure and had to be the most expensive fashion accessory around.'

'Oh.' An infinitesimal part of her sympathized with Topaz, having her car sold from under her.

'If she wanted a car,' Patrick went on, as if sensing Althea's thought, 'she could well afford to run one on her own money.'

'Oh.' Topaz as a kept woman deserved no sympathy at all.

Patrick squeezed her shoulder in an absent-minded manner, as if he didn't really know he was doing it. 'I don't know quite how to put this, but you've got to realize there's really no point in going after them. Their flight will have gone.'

'But your car . . .' Althea walked slowly lest she dislodge his arm. The feel of it, heavy across her shoulders, was incredibly pleasant. She just wished it wasn't there for the wrong reasons.

'I'll get that tomorrow, but I'm worried about you.'

'Me, why?'

'Is there anyone you can go to about this? Your sister, perhaps?'

It was Althea's turn to grunt. 'My sister will be furious and blame me entirely.'

'But how could she do that?'

'She's always fancied Frederick herself, you see.' She moistened her lips anxiously. 'He is a dreadful womanizer. I'm so sorry he picked Topaz.'

He stopped and brought her to a halt by taking hold of her free shoulder with his other hand. 'Is it worse because it's Topaz?'

The tired, hurt look had gone. His expression now was one of sympathy and understanding. She gazed up into his eyes, unable to stop herself, her compassion for him all muddled up with her baser feelings.

'Well, it must be a lot worse for you,' she said, wanting to add, but don't worry, I'll kiss you better.

'Well, not really. If she's gone, she's gone. I'm just sorry she chose Frederick. It must be so painful for you.'

Althea suddenly had the feeling she was part of the wrong conversation. 'Why would that be particularly?'

'Because he was your husband. You were trying to make a go of it.'

'Were we?'

He nodded. 'So Juno led me to believe.'

'How dare she!' She put what she really wanted to say, *bons mots* like 'interfering cow' and 'bossy old bag' on hold for later and contented herself with a growl.

'I'm sorry. You probably didn't want people to know.'

'Because it's not true! Juno of all people should know that. How dare she go around giving people that impression when I wouldn't have Frederick back silver-plated!' She shrugged off Patrick's arm and started walking much faster.

'Wouldn't you?' he asked, lengthening his stride. 'Then why are you making all this fuss?'

She stopped suddenly, confronting him. 'I'm not making a fuss, I'm comforting *you*, so *you* can make a fuss about Topaz!'

'Topaz! I don't want to make a fuss about that spandex-coated fitness-freak with permanent spendomania! As far as I'm concerned, Frederick's done me a good turn taking her off my hands. I just hope he can afford her. If she hadn't taken my car I'd be out celebrating!'

'Then why are we walking into this wood?' Althea demanded, feeling confused, angry and rather silly.

He shrugged. 'God knows. I thought I was comforting you about Frederick.'

'So you're not cut up about Topaz at all?'

'Not really. I feel bad about her, of course. But she insisted on following me here. I knew she wouldn't want to live in an unfinished house. And she must have realized after our initial fling that we were unsuited as a couple.'

'If you knew that, why didn't you finish it? You couldn't know she'd up and off with someone else.' They were still walking towards the wood but neither of them seemed to want to turn back.

'Oh yes I could. She upped and offed with me. And when Topaz has you in her sights you don't get much of a chance to say no.'

'I'm sure you tried really hard,' she said, as blandly as she could.

He shrugged. 'At least this way nobody got hurt.'

Althea's anger faded and she wondered if he was telling the truth. He must be hurting, even if he didn't want to admit it. He couldn't really be accepting his woman running off with an older man with such impunity.

'At least,' he went on. 'I hope they didn't. I'm just sorry it was Frederick.'

'Well, you don't have to be on my account. It doesn't make any difference to me who he goes off with. If you don't mind about Topaz, I certainly don't mind about Frederick.' They walked on in silence for a while. 'Perhaps we should go back. I mean, if we're both perfectly fine about this, and neither of us are in need of comfort, we can just go home.' This was his opportunity to talk about Topaz and get a bit of his unacknowledged hurt off his chest.

He didn't take it. 'If you give me a lift.'

Men always found it hard to talk about their feelings, Althea mused as they turned round. Perhaps her boys would be different. She had certainly always encouraged them to express themselves, to cry if they were hurt. She had just asked herself how, if ever, she would know if this had worked, when she was distracted by Patrick taking hold of her hand.

He turned her round and together they set off back towards the car.

He must need comfort really, thought Althea, or he wouldn't have put his hand in mine like that. He says he doesn't care because his pride is hurt, but of course he cares. Waves of compassion pushed aside the thrill of walking next to the tall, attractive man she'd fantasized about for so long. And then, when she stumbled and he caught her, brushing the inside of his arm against hers, feelings of desire swept aside her sympathy. By the time they'd reached the level area and were approaching the car park, she was totally confused.

'So what would you like me to do?' she asked, putting the ball firmly in his court, quite unable to do anything about it herself.

Patrick sighed. 'Oh Althea, you do ask some awkward questions.'

'Do I?'

'Sorry, I wasn't thinking for a moment. What I'd really like is to get some things from the flat to take to the house. I shall give up the flat as soon as I can, now. But I don't want to take up all your afternoon.'

'Not at all. I thought you wanted a lift to Heathrow, after all.'

'And you'd have taken me?'

'Of course. If you'd wanted to go after Topaz,' she added, thinking she'd sounded a bit too obliging.

'You're a very kind person.'

'Yes I am.' She burrowed in her bag for her car keys. 'Now where is your flat exactly?'

He directed her, and they set off, Althea trying hard not to feel put down. In spite of all her son's Buddhist teachings about cherishing others and compassion, she didn't want to be called kind, not by him. She wanted to be called beautiful and sexy. Bloody Frederick had done that, the very last person she'd wanted to hear it from. And Patrick, whom she yearned for, thought she was kind. She shot him a look that was anything but, but he was looking out of the window and didn't notice.

She turned on to the tarmacked drive and pulled on her hand-brake rather hard.

Patrick shifted round in his seat to look at her. 'I'm dreadfully sorry, I'm putting you out awfully. I've dragged you away from your leaving party under false pretences. Let me make it up to you with a long glass of something nice.'

'I never drink and drive.'

'Topaz had a whole range of non-alcoholic herbal things. Some of them are almost palatable.' He put his hand lightly on her shoulder, melting her anger. 'Please.'

'Well, I could murder a cup of tea.'

'Then come on.'

The flat was tidy, tasteful and dull – a stopping-off place. Inoffensive grey carpet, pastel paint and an exposed stone wall. There were few signs of anyone's personality.

'Would you mind if I used the bathroom?' said Althea, suddenly feeling very hot and sticky. She also needed a few moments alone, without Patrick's disturbing presence, to collect her thoughts.

'Through there.'

The bathroom was beautifully appointed, tiled, with a bidet

and twin wash basins, separate shower and a corner bath. The mirror-fronted cupboards were all open, presumably left that way after Topaz had packed what she wanted. But there were an amazing collection of cosmetics remaining. Was all that aloe vera the reason for Topaz's stunning appearance? Or was it youth and a carefree life? Whichever, it made her a very tough act to follow.

'Just as well,' said Althea to her reflection, 'that you are not aiming to do that.' She spoke firmly, as if to convince herself.

'Why not?' demanded the Althea who was a good friend of Sylvia, and could be a little wild.

'Because,' replied the mother of teenagers, 'he wouldn't be interested. And if he was, you don't go in for casual relationships. And it could only be casual, because the children wouldn't stand for anything else. So just put away all those nasty physical urges which threaten your way of life and concentrate on being nice. It may be boring, but it's safe, and it's what your children need you to be right now. Besides, now you're unemployed you have to keep your mind on earning a living, not on unobtainable men.'

She came out of the bathroom feeling positively nun-like, only to have all her resolutions swept away by the sight of Patrick leaning back in a chair in front of the little balcony. He had taken off his jacket and had his hands behind his head. His throat arched into his chest like a beautiful piece of sculpture. She had been right when she had told Jenny that he was not good-looking. But he had a beautiful body and a very interesting face and a mixture of laziness and vitality which was intensely attractive. Althea sighed.

'Tea?' she asked.

'I'm just waiting for the kettle. I took the electric one to the house.'

'No wonder Topaz left home.' Althea sat down opposite him in a shaft of sunshine wondering if it was too soon for levity.

He laughed. She watched his Adam's apple move and then looked away. 'She never had breakfast at home. She used to go straight to the pool, do her forty lengths and then have herb tea when she got to the office.'

'Goodness.' A thought suddenly occurred to her. 'I'd

forgotten! Frederick not only ran off with your woman, but with your secretary! How will you manage?'

'Fine. There's a sweet girl on reception, who's very efficient and who'll welcome a chance of promotion.'

'Oh. Oh good.' So she wouldn't be moving her workplace from a school to an architect's office then. Perhaps it was just as well. 'I expect the kettle's boiled by now.'

He got up slowly, like a tiger, and padded into the tiny kitchen. 'What sort of tea do you want?'

'The kind with caffeine and tannin in.'

'Bag all right?'

'Fine.'

He came back a moment later with two mugs, and a box of biscuits in his teeth. 'Have you tried these?' he said, when he'd put down the mugs and could talk. 'They're made locally.'

Althea accepted a biscuit. Comfort me with calories, she thought. I am sick with love. Her private misquotation brought her up short. Surely even she couldn't imagine herself in love with Patrick? In lust, sure, but love?

'That's a good cup of tea,' she said, deliberately mundane.

'Is it? Good.' He sipped his and then laid back and closed his eyes.

Althea took advantage of the opportunity to study him, pushing the word 'love' out of her consciousness. Lust was fine, a normal reaction of a healthy woman to an attractive man. But for a woman of thirty-nine, with three children at difficult ages, who didn't have a job but did have a mortgage, love was not an option. She drank her tea.

'I hate to hurry you, but I really ought to be getting back.'

Patrick had obviously been asleep. 'God! Of course. How thoughtless of me. I must have dozed off.'

'You were probably tired.'

He nodded. 'I started work on the house last night after I got home.'

'So you didn't come here?'

He shook his head. 'We had a row the night before.' He took a deep draught of his cold tea. 'Sometimes I find it hard to work out what I saw in Topaz.'

'Do you? Perhaps I could help,' she said primly. 'She's a very attractive girl with the body of a TV Gladiator.'

The faintest tinge of embarrassment lifted one corner of his mouth. 'Yes, well, one can go off sleeping with an athlete, you know.'

'Really? I'm not qualified to comment.'

'Mmm. Those iron thighs and washboard stomach were quite unforgiving sometimes.'

'You mean she had more stamina than you?'

He stood up and pulled Althea to her feet. 'No I bloody well don't! I just meant that sometimes a man wants something a bit more – yielding.'

He had hold of her upper arms and pushed his hands under the sleeves of her dress. Althea's senses leapt. She had no difficulty in interpreting his message. He wanted her.

But in spite of her own desire, she stepped back. If they made love now, or even kissed, it would be for all the wrong reasons. It would be because her husband had taken his woman and he wanted her to assuage his wounded pride.

'I'm sorry,' he said after a moment. 'I'm being very insensitive. I'll go and get my things together.'

Althea blinked away the tears which had suddenly formed. She was too damn fussy, that was her problem. If he wanted her, and for that moment he did, why couldn't she have just gone along with it, and not troubled herself with his motives, or the ghastly repercussions? Because I'm Althea, not Sylvia or Jenny or any other sensible person. Blast it.

'What will you do about supper?' Althea-mother-to-all-the-world heard herself asking as they approached the old house which was now almost completely obscured by scaffolding.

'I shall get a takeaway of some kind, I expect.'

'You could come and have supper with us,' she went on, surprising even herself with her masochism. Jenny would be there, and Sylvia. 'Although you may prefer to be on your own,' she added hurriedly, giving them both a let out.

'Oh no. I'd like a chance to see more of your children. I met them at your party, of course, but we didn't get to talk much.'

Her children. Another good reason for not taking him home.

132

'It'll only be spag bol or something else I can make with a pound of mince and some overripe tomatoes.'

'I've got a bottle of wine I could bring,' he said, not at all put off. 'Or would that mean you wouldn't want to drive me home?'

Well, I'm certainly not going to suggest you spend the night with Jenny in the spare room. 'No, I'm sure William will run you home. He's a Buddhist, he doesn't drink. Or you could walk. It's not far.'

Patrick seemed genuinely pleased. Althea wished that for once in her life she could stop offering to feed people just because they might be hungry. She didn't like cooking much and she could certainly do without the social strains the evening would put on her.

'Oh good. What will you do? Come and pick me up? Or, as you've just pointed out, I could walk.'

'It depends how long you want to be. But I need half an hour or so with my plants. If you were ready then, you could come back with me.'

Everyone except Althea thought the evening was a roaring success. Jenny and Sylvia went gaga over Patrick, entertaining him in the conservatory while she cooked. He offered to help Althea, but Jenny and Sylvia both insisted that she would be better off on her own. Even her children thought he was quite nice. Unlike Jenny and Sylvia, he knew enough about Buddhism, films and horses to have interesting conversations with each of them.

And when eventually, barefoot and red in the face, she got the meal on the table and summoned her guests, they all came and jostled round the table in a matey way, having a thoroughly good time. Had her heart not been occupied otherwise, it would have swelled with pride at the happy faces round her kitchen table.

Rupert came back into the kitchen while Althea was clearing up. William was driving Patrick home and everyone else had either gone, or gone to bed.

'He's not your boyfriend, is he, Mum?'

'No, he's not. Why should he be?'

'No reason, except Sylvia was making remarks. I just wondered.'

'Well you don't need to worry about it.'

'Good. Then that gives Jenny a clear field then.'

'What do you mean?'

'She fancies him. If you don't, then that's all right.'

Althea was touched. 'Would you have minded, if he had been my boyfriend?'

Rupert backed off. 'Well – a bit. I mean, he's a good bloke. But I wouldn't want him living here or anything. I wouldn't want anyone here. Dad's bad enough and he goes back to Honkers eventually.'

Althea thought Rupert was old enough to know about Dad going back to Honkers. 'He's run off with Topaz, Patrick's girl-friend. That's why I asked him round.'

'Dad did? Ran off with Topaz?' Instead of being shocked, he seemed to think this behaviour was impressive.

'He shouldn't have, you know. He ought to have gone back to Claudia.'

'They've been separated a long time. He didn't want you to know. But Dad and Topaz! I mean, he's *years* older than Patrick.'

'Yes, but he's probably also a lot richer. And with women like Topaz, that counts for more than a few wrinkles.' This could have been a most unwarranted slur on her character, but Althea was fed up with being nice, and needed to relieve her feelings in a little old-fashioned bitchiness. It helped.

'You don't mind about Dad, do you?' Rupert was unusually sympathetic for a boy of his age.

'Certainly not! They deserve each other.'

'Or Jenny and Patrick?' He looked eager, willing her to say no.

'No.'

'Cool!'

His feet pounding up the stairs would have woken anyone who'd been asleep. Althea followed him slowly. If she'd been in any doubt, and she hadn't, not really, Rupert had confirmed that now was not the time for her to have a relationship. Her feelings of lust and hankerings for love would have to go on hold for a little while longer.

CHAPTER THIRTEEN

With Monday came the start of the summer holidays and by eleven o'clock, Althea had one of the downsides of a six-week break from school brought forcibly to her attention. It was the constant presence of dirty crockery. It littered the table, the work surfaces, the dresser and the sink. And no matter how often she washed up, more seemed to generate itself by some process known only to science fiction writers and teenagers.

Now there were not only the remains of three people's diverse breakfasts, which included honey, Marmite, two margarine cartons, both half used, and an empty yoghurt pot tipped over by the spoon left in it, but Jenny's muesli bowl. Was having a probationer teacher in the house going to be like having another child?

Althea loved children, she told herself as she remembered that, shortly, she would be having a foreign one to add to her brood. But the children she was having were out all day, and it was only at the weekends that she would have to do heavy-duty entertaining and non-stop catering.

Her own children liked having foreign students because – as Rupert explained when she broke it to him that this summer it meant him having to give up his bedroom and share with William – that meant she would cook the occasional meal. A rare and beneficial consequence. As was the extra pocket money she paid them for the inconvenience and lack of privacy. The remuneration for having foreign students was not very much, but Althea reckoned that as the children always needed more money in the summer holidays they might as well do something to earn it and passed some of what she was paid on to them.

Although she was very relaxed about the fact that often in the summer she was either childless or had nine for tea, she did wonder if perhaps Frederick had been right about having a lodger as well, especially when she needed the summer holidays to finish her garden. If Jenny was going to be as untidy as her own lot, it would be a real nuisance.

No, Frederick couldn't possibly be right, not about anything. She would speak to Jenny, be polite but firm, and Jenny would respond positively. Althea sighed and stared out of the window, watching for flying pigs.

'Hi, Mum, how are you?' Merry came in. 'I've just tidied up my bedroom. Do I get paid?'

'No.' But then Althea had an idea. 'You wouldn't do the kitchen, though? Juno's coming this afternoon.'

Merry thought about it. When in the mood, she enjoyed cleaning – as Althea did. The trouble was, Althea was only in the mood about every eighteen months.

'How much?' demanded Merry.

'Pound.'

Merry shook her head. 'Tenner.'

'No way.'

'Way. Eight pounds?'

'Two pounds fifty.'

Merry sighed. 'Three pounds. I want to go to the cinema with Ronnie tomorrow.'

'OK. But I want it perfect, all the saucepans washed, dried and put away, and a clean cloth on.'

'You're not paying that child to clean up for you, are you, Mum?' William was disapproving. 'Merry, you're always getting money out of Mum. You should cherish her and do it for nothing.'

'Yeah, right,' said Merry, the only member of the household totally proof against Buddhism. 'Like you ever clean up.'

'I do, don't I, Mum? And when I do, I don't ask for money.'

'No, you want money to do your homework,' said his sister.

Blast, thought Althea. Merry's heard about the sponsored essay scheme. She was the only one who got her homework done without being asked about it. And she did it on Friday afternoon, explaining that that way she had the whole weekend free. Althea wondered how it was that Merry had grasped this after her first week at secondary school, when she had been failing to get the message across to the boys for years.

'I've got more important things to do than school work . . .'

136

'And I've got more important things to do than wrangle with you lot.'

Althea fled to the garden, where the problems were practical and didn't require tact to solve them. Her competition garden was nearly finished. Although a small plot, it was divided into separate areas by sections of trellis discarded by one of her regular clients, creating a zig-zag path to the end, where the wash basin pond made a focal point and sitting area.

Each trellis backed a bed with a different sort of plant. One bed was lined with builders' plastic creating an area for moisture-loving plants: primulas, astilbes and irises. Hostas were an obvious choice, but they were so prey to slugs that she had used hart's-tongue ferns instead. These grew wild in her garden and could, she was fairly sure, be obtained for nothing from other sources. While they didn't actually appear to flower, their foliage gave a very similar effect to hostas – and at least they got to keep it.

There was a tiny rockery planted with ivy-leaved toadflax, saxifrage and creeping thyme. The toadflax she transplanted from the wall and the saxifrage and thyme she bought from a WI stall. Even town-dwellers would have some access to cheap suppliers, she reasoned, as she noted down exactly how much she had spent.

Another area was for the sort of annuals you just sprinkle over the soil and wait to grow. Scarlet flax, cornflowers, sweet rocket and love-in-a-mist. This could double as a children's garden, if you added marigolds and clarkia, Californian poppies. She put this in the notes, but as she hated marigolds, although they were so willing and easy to grow, left them out of her version.

Her white garden – her gesture to taste and refinement – was mostly annual, though she had transplanted all her own self-seeded foxgloves which had obligingly pale flowers. Sweet alyssum, malvas, white love-in-a-mist and lavatera. This could be bought in a single, colour-coded packet of seed. Tall flowers, everlasting sweetpeas, larkspur, delphiniums and the hollyhocks she was named after, as well as a couple of clematis, concealed the trellis, so you couldn't see through to the next section and could believe the garden was huge.

A climbing rose, 'New Dawn', grown from a cutting, but

added to the budget for the purposes of the competition, made the garden look complete, its delicate pink flowers and apple fragrance adding maturity and continuity between the small beds. She was nurturing a few cuttings, but saving them in case she needed them for Chelsea. Among them was a seedling of *Rosa Glauca*, whose blue leaves, shocking pink flowers and later orange hips made it one of her favourites.

Looking at the garden today, she had reason to feel proud, but she would have to make it very clear she was not encouraging people to take rare plants from the wild when she used frog-bit for water lilies, and took water mint, forget-me-nots and king-cups from the canal. She was only telling people that common plants, which grew in huge quantities, could work well in a garden setting.

Part of the competition was to submit a dissertation on the use of plant and other material. Hers would have to be spectacular if she was to convince judges that a garden could be created cheaply with a little ingenuity and an eye for a bargain, but without actually stealing anything.

Anyone could have a lovely garden if they could afford to buy plants in threes and fives from top nurseries. Getting the plants to flourish and grow could be learnt by experience. But getting a plot, which most likely started out with a meagre inch of topsoil over several feet of clay, to look like a garden in less than three years and several hundreds of pounds was a real challenge. Other gardens could be Japanese, Impressionist or even Buddhist, but hers would be Cheap.

She went in later, starving to death and needing to wash her hands. Too late she remembered Merry, who would not be pleased if she covered her gleaming sink with mud and put crumbs on the work surface as she prepared bread and cheese. Dutifully she washed her hands in the downstairs loo, sure that Juno would never have problems of role reversal. Juno would do the telling and her child would wash its hands when it was told. Somewhere, Althea had made a terrible mistake.

With great tact and rapid clearing, Althea managed to have lunch without sullying the purity of Merry's kitchen. When asked, she duly handed over the money but wondered how much longer she'd be able to manage the luxury of 'help in the house'. When the money ran out, she'd have to stop inviting Juno for tea.

Then she had a go at the downstairs loo, as the most noticeable thing about Juno's pregnancy was her frequency of micturition, remembering Merry's expression when Althea explained this meant Juno needed to wee a lot. It asked quite plainly why on earth didn't Juno say that then? As this was a question Althea couldn't possibly answer, she was glad her daughter's query was both silent and rhetorical. She polished the wash basin with the handtowel and made a mental note to replace it with a clean one.

Juno arrived, her looks enhanced by the softening effect of her pregnancy, which was more evident in the quality of her skin than her bulge. Her stomach, swathed in a silk vest Althea would struggle to fit into unpregnant, was hardly bigger than a small melon.

But there was an awkwardness in her manner, which wasn't cured by being established in the best chair, Bozo quietly on her diminished lap, a cup of raspberry-leaf tea at her side.

Althea found herself having to start the conversation. Usually this was Juno's prerogative.

'So how's Kenneth? I haven't seen him since the party.'

'Oh, he's fine. He just loves being a prospective father. He's being very tender and caring.'

'He always was, wasn't he?'

'Oh yes, but – well, perhaps I just appreciate it more.'

'Because you're pregnant?'

'Yes, and because . . .'

Althea didn't speak, she just tried to look uncritical and accepting of anything Juno might need to say.

Juno sipped her tea and realigned the flower pot nearest to her, so its trailing occupant didn't tickle her arm. 'I've been a bit of a fool about Frederick.'

'Oh?'

'I had such a frightful crush on him when you and he were first going out, I always thought I chose Kenneth on the rebound. When he came back, and I was pregnant and everything, I just had another little crush. Very silly really, all to do with my hormones.'

'Probably. And you're a million times better off with Kenneth.'

'Oh I know,' said Juno crisply. 'He may not be as handsome as Frederick, but at least he'll stand by me, however much the baby cries.'

'That's the important thing.'

'And now Frederick's gone and done this!'

Althea held back her instinctive demand to know how Juno had found out so quickly. Juno might not know much at all. 'What? He told me when he was going back. It was a relief to get rid of him.'

'But did he tell you who he went back with?'

'Um – er, no.'

'Diana Sanders told me. It's so embarrassing, and so awful for you.'

'Is it?'

'It's that little cat Topaz! Poor Patrick, he must be so upset. And it's not very nice for you, either.'

Althea sighed. 'Juny, it's sweet of you to be concerned, but quite frankly I don't give a damn who Frederick runs off with.'

'No, but Topaz! Claudia was bad enough. But Topaz is *years and years* younger than Frederick. Than Patrick, even.' She paused, aware of something out of place. 'You're not even surprised. You didn't *know*, did you?'

Althea blushed, feeling distinctly guilty. And not because of her knowledge, but the circumstances under which she found out. 'Well, yes, I did, actually. Patrick told me. He thought I might be upset too.'

It was Juno's turn to blush. 'That's because I told him you and Frederick were getting back together.'

'He said. But why did you think that? Frederick and I are even more unsuited now than we were years ago.'

Juno fluttered her hands in a gesture of confusion. 'I suppose it was wishful thinking on my part. And because I – fancied him – I couldn't believe you wouldn't. And I definitely know he wanted to get back with you.'

Althea waited for the 'can't imagine why', but it didn't come.

'He told me,' Juno went on, 'he wanted to spend more time with the children, and he thought you'd . . .'

'Grown up a lot. He told me that too.'

Juno produced a freshly ironed hanky and blew her nose on it in a way that seemed to avoid getting it dirty. 'Sorry, Ally. I've been a twit. But getting back with Frederick would have been the answer to all your problems.'

'Would it?'

'Well, of course! He'd pay the mortgage and keep you and you wouldn't be permanently broke.'

'Juny, I'd rather be broke than trapped in a loveless marriage.'

'Would you? I'd hate being poor myself. And Frederick is so gorgeous . . . but I suppose I'm being twittish again.'

Althea felt a wave of love towards her sister. She was so much more endearing twittish than when she was being her usual efficient self. 'Pregnancy does funny things to people.' She put her arm round her. 'Come and see my competition garden. It's nearly finished.'

Juno wandered up the paths Althea had made, sat on the seat by the pond and wandered back down again. 'I must say, Althea, it's extremely impressive. I thought you were just being provocative when you said you were going to be a garden designer. But you obviously weren't.'

'Certainly not! I really meant it about seeing being made redundant as a chance to try something more challenging.'

'But won't you need some sort of formal qualifications?'

'Probably, but this would be a good start. It should get me on any course I might need to do. And perhaps even qualify me for a grant.'

'Oh? I thought grants were scarce these days.'

'Hen's teeth.' Althea snapped the seedhead of an Icelandic poppy and scattered it willy-nilly into what had once started out as a white border. 'But I'm sure I could manage without a course if only I could draw.'

'But Merry can draw.'

'I know. She must get it from Frederick, because I can't.'

Juno gave the problem her full attention while Althea pulled dandelions out of the path for the guinea pigs. While she was bending, a Siamese cat came and jumped on her shoulder, his claws painful through the thin cotton of her sun top. She winced and groaned but let the animal stay perched on her shoulder.

'You spoil your cats worse than you spoil your children,' said Juno. 'And if there's anything Kenneth and I can do, like lend you the money for a course of some kind . . .'

Althea put her arm round her sister and gave her a hug. 'Thanks, Juny, you're very kind. But I'm determined to do this on my own. Not just for money, which is why I've always worked in the past, but to give myself a future when the children are all gone.'

'It's odd that your children will be nearly grown up before mine is even at school.'

'They're really looking forward to the baby, Juno. All of them, not just Merry.'

Juno sighed. 'So am I, I think. When I let myself.'

Juno was not often in the mood to take pep talks from Althea, so Althea grasped her opportunity. 'It will change your life, there's no getting round it. But in such a beneficial way, you'll wonder how you ever managed without the baby to love and to love you.'

'Well, I hope you're right.'

As they walked up the steps to the house, Merry appeared sucking a tube of polythene out of which protruded a frozen stick of sugar and artificial colouring which called itself cola. 'Patrick rang. He said thank you very much for the other night, he really enjoyed it and perhaps you might like to ring him sometime.'

Althea concentrated hard on appearing unmoved by this news. 'Oh, OK.'

Merry skipped back into the house, still sucking her lolly. Juno treated her sister to her most inquisitorial gaze. Althea hadn't felt more put on the spot since Frederick left home.

'He just came round for a meal. Sylvia and Jenny and the children were there,' she said, sounding guilty even though she was speaking the truth.

'Oh I see. So there's nothing going on between you?'

'Certainly not.'

'Pity.'

It was Althea's turn to look surprised.

★

Althea didn't ring Patrick. She thought about it, wanting to do it, but good sense prevailed. Besides, she was busy. She had to get her garden finished, get her competition entry in, and entertain French children. In between times, she had to get her clients' gardens up to scratch, something she hadn't done properly since Easter. She couldn't spare the time to chase after dreams.

The first French child arrived at one o'clock in the morning, by coach, accompanied by fifty others and a couple of harassed teachers. William came with Althea to collect theirs, a ten-year-old waif called Véronique who took some time to identify. Together they guided their sleepy charge to the car, having been told to have it dressed and fed and at the Leisure Centre by nine the following morning.

'The poor little thing ought to have a lie-in,' she murmured to William. 'And she's so *young*! She's bound to miss her mother.'

'Don't worry,' said William, carrying the luggage. 'Judging by the weight of this case, she's brought her mother with her.'

But although she managed to avoid Patrick's physical presence entirely, watering her greenhouse only when she knew for certain he was out, he was harder to banish from her thoughts. His quirky, laughing mouth would filter into her mind at the oddest moments: when she was covering the builders' plastic with soil; when she cooked spaghetti; when she saw the coffee advert with the couple who were so coy about sleeping together. Just do it, she urged silently. You've got no children, no other responsibilities, just go ahead and have a good time.

She was clearing up the kitchen, determined to have another attempt at drawing her masterpiece in the couple of hours she had before she had to produce something Véronique, who was on a day trip to London, would eat, when Jenny came in.

'Hey, Ally. Do you mind if I cook now? I'm playing tennis later and I want the food to have a chance to settle down.'

'If you promise to clear up after you.' Althea abandoned her plan with little regret but some remorse. Véronique would have to have pizza again.

'Don't I always?'

'No.' Jenny cooked up cauldrons of pulses, woks full of stir fry

143

and jam jars full of half-sprouted beans with the same lack of awareness of their detritus as her children showed.

'Aw, sorry. I'll try and be better, really I will. I've just been busy.'

Feeling churlish for having spoken to Jenny as if she were indeed one of her children, Althea sat down at the kitchen table and asked, 'Planning your lessons for next year? New job and all, you must be getting prepared.'

Jenny laughed. 'Nah! I've been getting my backhand into trim. It's taken me ages to persuade Patrick to play tennis with me. Now I've finally done it, and with luck I'll be able to give him a run for his money.'

'Patrick? Patrick Donahugh?'

'None other.' Jenny opened a can of tomatoes and emptied them into a pan where she proceeded to break them up by squeezing them with her hand.

'Oh. I didn't know you knew him.'

'Course I know him. He was here that evening, remember? And a nod is as good as a wink to a blind horse.'

Althea had never quite understood this expression, but she didn't seek enlightenment from Jenny. 'I suppose so.'

'Of course men are always far stronger than women when it comes to sports. But I don't mind being beaten by a strong man.' Jenny laughed. Althea struggled to join in.

Jenny had made some attempt at clearing up after herself. She left her half-eaten meal in the saucepan, which at least prevented anyone else from using and therefore dirtying it. She rinsed her crockery under the tap and left it on the draining board, piled up so anything else added would send the whole lot into the porcelain sink. And she had wiped a wet cloth over the table.

After she had gone, cycling shorts gleaming like gloss paint over her well-muscled behind, Althea had dried the table, put away the dishes and got out the A3 pad of squared paper again. Then she had found a selection of Merry's pencils, a rubber, a ruler and a packet of biscuits. It was time to get down to some serious work.

She made serious inroads into the biscuits. There were crumbs among the swathes of rubbings-out, the pencil shavings and balls of paper. But there was little else recognizable on the fresh sheet on which Althea was now resting her elbows, as a prop for her hands and head. She was sitting like this when Jenny returned.

'I'm just going up for a shower,' she said breezily.

'There may not be any hot water,' said Althea, not looking up, not caring if Jenny's shower was cold.

'Why didn't you ring me?' said Patrick from the doorway.

Althea jumped like a cartoon character. 'Um, I've been busy.'

'Too busy to pick up a phone?'

'Yes.' Her throat muscles were tight, making her voice high and tense.

He stood there, larger than life in tennis whites, his hands on his hips, his expression distinctly unfriendly.

'Did you have a good game of tennis?' Althea asked after clearing her throat.

'Not particularly.'

Her instincts of hospitality wanted to offer him a drink of some kind, but she couldn't leave her garden plan exposed. 'I expect Jenny will be down in a moment to offer you something to drink.'

'I'm sure she will.'

'You can come in, you know. You don't have to stand there in the doorway.'

'Are you sure? I thought I might not be welcome, when you didn't ring me back.'

Althea licked her lips. 'Oh no. I've just been really busy, that's all.'

He took two long strides and ended up behind her, looking over her shoulder. 'What are you doing?'

'Er – I'm drawing a garden plan,' she said, keeping her hands flat on the paper and spreading her fingers so more of it was covered.

He pulled away her hands finger by finger, and then her arms, holding them apart so he could see her paper.

'I thought you said you were a garden designer when you weren't being a school secretary.'

'Uh huh.'

'But you can't draw.'

145

'Not very well, no.'

'Not at all.'

She cleared her throat. 'No.'

'When have you got to have your plans in?'

'By the first of September.'

'Then you've got a month to learn. Time enough.'

'Is it?'

'Of course. If you let me teach you.'

CHAPTER FOURTEEN

❁

Althea moved her tongue in her dry mouth, trying to get her voice to function. 'Er – it's kind of you to offer, but I don't think I'd better.'

'Why not?'

'Well, it would be cheating.'

'I'm not offering to do the drawings for you. I am offering to teach you the rudiments of drawing so you don't make a complete hash of it. Jenny tells me you've worked very hard on your garden. It would be a shame if you submitted a series of boy scouts frying sausages round a camp fire at the bottom of the Grand Canyon.'

'What!'

'That's what it looks like, all those wonky circles.'

William, who needed to eat approximately every seventeen and a half minutes, chose this moment to enter the kitchen for a snack.

'He's right, you know. It's either boy scouts or gnomes peeing into a pond.'

Rupert and Merry, vainly hoping for more than a snack, given the time, had followed their brother. They laughed.

'It's all very well for you lot to mock, you don't have to do something you're totally incapable of doing just to show off what you can do!'

'Don't we?' said Rupert. 'I thought that's what GCSEs were.'

'Yes,' William went on. 'You told me, when I was a little boy of six, that it was no good being a genius if no one could read my geniusness.'

'I'm sure I never . . .'

'Yes, you did!' William poked her affectionately in the chest. 'You jolly well made me improve my handwriting.'

'And here you are refusing to have drawing lessons,' said Merry, who didn't need them.

'Why don't you show me your entry,' suggested Patrick, possibly feeling a little overcrowded. 'Then I can get some idea of what your drawing should look like.'

'But you're not interested in gardening.'

'No, not in the slightest, but I am interested in getting an accurate picture of your garden.'

Althea got up from the table. 'OK, but have a glass of something cold first. You're sweating.'

Jenny joined them in the garden. She had showered and changed her black cycling shorts for a shocking pink pair. She bounced around, panting for Patrick's attention. At least she doesn't chew things and shed hairs, thought Althea, looking on the bright side and wishing she could send Jenny to her basket.

'This is the front,' Althea told Patrick, resisting the temptation to tell Jenny to get down. 'You have to imagine a small terraced house, halfway down a hillside.'

'And why is it halfway down a hillside?'

'Because this is the only bit of garden I could bear to dig up, and as you see, it's steeply sloping.'

'So you've terraced it. I see.'

'I'll have to put some trees in, for height, but I don't know what I'll be able to afford. I've got a *Rosa glauca* seedling, which I'll put on the plan, but will keep in case I actually win.'

'And what's this?'

'That's my damp bed. It's lined with plastic and heavily mulched to keep in the moisture.'

'My plastic?'

'No,' said Althea firmly. 'Only the pond is lined with your plastic. I'm sorry about that. I should have bought you some more.'

'It's all right. The builders did. They can well afford it, the amount of money they're getting from me.'

'Is it being dreadfully expensive?'

'Of course. It doesn't seem to matter how carefully you do your sums, add lumps on, make allowances, it always seems to cost far more than your most pessimistic estimate. I may have to do just half, and finish it when I've got some more money.'

'Well, it will be lovely, whenever it's done. And the garden could be fabulous.'

'I dare say it could. If I find the right garden designer.'

Althea suddenly spotted a bit of convolvulus which had escaped both her fork and her weedkiller. She knelt down to deal with it.

'I'm considering dividing the house in two,' Patrick went on, apparently unaware of Althea's evasive tactics. 'You could have two separate entrances, a bit of shared garden and a bit of private garden. It could work very well. Topaz wouldn't hear of it. Now she's gone, I can do as I like.'

'Of course.' Althea couldn't stay squatting at his feet forever without feeling faint.

'And it's not just that she was expensive to run. I can stop eating so damn healthily.'

Althea took a sneaky look. There was, as yet, no sign of a bulge over the waistband of his tennis shorts. And as she hadn't seen his legs before, she couldn't judge if they had changed. To her eye, they seemed perfect.

'Would you like to share my stir fry?' Jenny asked, glad of an opportunity to break into the conversation. 'I've got sprouted mung beans, miso and some of those baby corn on the cobs? If you've been living on junk lately, you ought to get some goodness into you.'

'No thank you,' said Patrick. 'It's sweet of you to offer, but I've promised to take Althea out to the pub for a meal. We'd invite you to join us, only we're going somewhere where they don't do vegetarian food.'

'I could always have a baked potato and eat my stir fry tomorrow.'

'No, you couldn't. Don't you know that vegetables lose seventy per cent of their nutritional value each day after they're picked?'

Jenny was horrified. 'Do they?'

'How do you know that?' asked Althea, incredulous and suspicious.

'Topaz told me. And actually, Althea, if we hang around here too long, we'll miss our table.'

'You can't book tables for pub meals,' said Jenny indignantly.

'I know,' said Patrick. 'But if you don't get there early, all the best things are off the menu.' He turned to Althea. 'I'll just run home and shower and be back to pick you up in half an hour.' He squeezed Althea's hand and bounded up to the house and a moment later, she and Jenny heard his car start up and drive away.

'He never said anything about taking you out for a meal,' said Jenny, still indignant.

'Didn't he?' said Althea, not mentioning that it was the first she'd heard of it, too. 'Oh well. I'd better go and get changed.'

Jenny had her revenge by forcing Althea to have a barely tepid shower, having used up most of the hot water. And had Jenny realized the panic Patrick's casual, high-handed non-invitation caused Althea as she stood, shivering, in front of her wardrobe, she'd have felt totally mollified.

Althea scanned her clothes, tightly packed into her small wardrobe. Only about a third of them was wearable ever, and very few were wearable now. She had to think quickly, or there wouldn't be time to put on any make-up. Althea had got used to Patrick seeing her in her gardening clothes, but she didn't want him to sit at a table opposite her while she wasn't wearing mascara.

She should have refused to go, she thought, hastily ironing a black cotton T-shirt. After all, he hadn't invited her properly. It was very high-handed of him just to tell Jenny they were going.

But what was his alternative? she asked herself, sliding the iron equally quickly over a skirt. They would never have shaken off Jenny, who would have gone on offering him meals in her, Althea's, kitchen, which Patrick would in the end have accepted, and Althea would, no doubt, have found herself washing up after. No, this was far better. She skated downstairs to the cloakroom to put on her make-up, the only place in the house where the light was right.

'Trowel working all right, Mum?' asked William, seeing her there.

'Yes, thank you, darling,' said Althea, ignoring this old joke with ease, defiantly dabbing powder on her nose with her finger, having lost her powder puff.

'Ya Mum's going out with Patrick,' said Jenny in a tale-telling way, as if William was in a position to forbid her to go.

'Only to the pub, for a meal,' said Althea with her mouth open, putting on lipstick.

'But what about us?' squeaked Merry.

Althea bit her lip, guilt suddenly swamping all her girlish excitement. 'Bloody hell! I've forgotten Véronique. She needs picking up at nine-thirty.'

'I'll do it, Mum, and look after you, Merry,' said William, digging his sister in the ribs. 'You let Mum go out and enjoy herself at the pub, leaving her poor starving children at home and her little European visitor waiting forever at the Leisure Centre. We'll find a stale crust of bread and some water . . .'

'I'll pay you petrol money, and you don't have to starve,' said Althea, relieved at William's good-natured offer. 'The freezer is groaning with food.'

'But it's all vegetarian,' complained Merry.

'I'm sure there's a bit of carcass in there somewhere,' said William. 'I'll do chips. We'll make popcorn.'

'Chips!' shrieked Jenny. 'How unhealthy can you get! Can I have some?'

'Popcorn?' Althea sighed. 'OK, but *please*, not all over the carpet. And oven chips only, and do eat something sensible as well.'

'Yes, Mother.'

'Do I look all right?' Althea presented herself after the fastest make-up job ever.

'You look wonderful,' said Rupert, who ambled into the hallway having finished watching *Three Colours White* on video. He gave his mother a hug. 'Have a lovely time. I'll take the dog out.'

Althea waited for Patrick in the front garden, pulling out weeds and examining seedheads for ripeness, trying not to get her hands dirty. If she'd stayed inside, guilt might have made her decide she had to collect Véronique, cook everyone a meal, walk her dog, water her plants, and do the thousand other domestic chores which were daily obligations. If Patrick had been longer than the half-hour he'd said, she might still have succumbed to her conscience.

'You're ready quickly,' said Patrick, getting out of the car.

'I know. If I gave myself time to think, I wouldn't have come. There's a French child due to be collected, the children haven't had supper, Jenny's all put out, and the dog usually gets a walk around this time.'

'Well, would you like me to amuse myself while you cook and walk the dog? I might even get Jenny off your back.'

'Oh no,' said Althea hastily. 'Do let's go.' She got into the passenger seat and he shut the door behind her. 'Even though you didn't invite me.'

She said this while he was moving round to his side of the car, but he seemed to hear her anyway. 'If I'd invited you, you wouldn't have come. You'd have made some excuse.'

Althea adjusted her skirt, noting forlornly that one of the buttons was missing and therefore, unless she kept her eye on it constantly, her knees would escape. They were nice knees, but dimpled, and she didn't want them unfavourably compared with Jenny's or Topaz's.

'You would, you know you would,' he went on. 'Otherwise you'd have returned my call.'

Althea looked out of the window.

'I had to kidnap you.'

Althea sighed. 'I suppose you're right. Now, where's this pub where they don't serve vegetarian food and all the best things are off the menu if you don't go early?'

'I don't know. I was rather hoping you'd tell me.'

The corner of Althea's mouth twitched, a sign her children would have recognized as meaning she wasn't cross any more and would laugh, given half a chance. 'We'd better go to the Dun Cow. I don't know what the food's like, but the views from the garden are fabulous.'

The food at the Dun Cow was plain but served in generous portions. Patrick, who declared himself to be starving, regarded the blackboard with relish and ordered a starter and then pie, chips and peas. It was hard to convince him that Althea only wanted pâté and salad.

Having ordered, they took their drinks outside and found a seat under a tree, from where they could see across one valley

152

and into the next. A church spire rose from the trees, horses grazed in a nearby field, and swifts swooped and whistled across their line of sight, chasing unseen flies. It was such a picturesque, rustic scene and so beautiful, Althea felt quite melancholy. She almost wished they'd sat inside with the fruit machines.

'So, did you enjoy playing tennis with Jenny?' she said brightly, making an effort to be jolly.

Patrick nodded, sipping his lime juice. 'She's got a very good backhand, and her forehand's not bad either.'

'I don't play tennis, so I don't suppose I have any hand at all.'

Patrick took possession of the one she had left lying carelessly on the table. 'Yes, you have.' He inspected it. 'Small, capable, and a little grubby.'

'That can't draw,' she said awkwardly.

'That hasn't yet been taught to draw.' He replaced her hand. 'I understand your reluctance. You feel me teaching you to draw would put us in very close proximity. Well, it would, but if I promised not to jump on you, would you let me?'

'Patrick, I never. . . '

'The reason you didn't ring me was because I nearly jumped on you back at my flat, wasn't it?'

'It's not like that . . .'

'I did think we had something going for us. I still think it. But I may be going too fast for you. And if you're anxious that I might get carried away at any moment, you won't be able to draw a straight line, let alone draw an aerial view of a patch of dahlias.'

Althea was forced to laugh. 'I haven't got dahlias in my garden. They're too fiddly for beginners.'

'Oh good, because they're probably hell to draw as well.' He looked at her very intently, holding her attention with his vivid gaze. 'I make you a promise, Althea, that while I'm teaching you to draw, I shan't touch you in a way that could possibly make you uneasy or nervous. And if we eat together or go out for a drink, it'll be as friends. OK?' he added softly.

Althea licked her lips, shifted her glass, pulled her skirt over her knees but eventually found herself forced to give him an answer. 'Well, if you really wouldn't mind . . .'

'Good God, woman! Would I have spent the last five minutes trying to convince you I've got no ulterior motive, trying to persuade you to let me teach you to draw, if I minded? Of course I don't mind!'

'Oh well, that's all right then.'

After that, Patrick set out to entertain her, though he was careful not to let entertainment turn into flirting. He talked about books, television, the latest films, nothing you couldn't discuss in front of your maiden aunt, apart from the fact that his choice of these things would be considered slightly avant garde. While she greatly enjoyed his company, and his sense of humour, his efforts to keep his conversation strictly neutral did slightly take the edge off her pleasure.

'There's no pleasing some people,' she muttered, letting herself into the house after being chastely delivered to the door, her offer of coffee refused. She picked up Bozo who was scrabbling painfully at her bare legs. 'I avoid him because I'm afraid he'll make a pass, and then when he promises not to, I miss the not knowing when a chat will slip into something more.'

She went into the kitchen to make herself a hot drink. Far from being the mess she had imagined, it was perfectly tidy. Everything was washed and put away. Only the tiniest trace of popcorn sullied the floor. Merry had moved all her papers on to the dresser, out of harm's way.

Her heart swelled with love for her children. They were such good kids, helpful, kind, likeable. They might never achieve the sort of academic success which everyone else's children seemed to have, but she couldn't have been more proud of them as human beings if they'd all got scholarships to Oxbridge when they were ten. And because they were such good companions, as well as being her children, she would never do anything to upset them, like bring a step-father figure into their lives. There would be time enough for her to think about having relationships when they'd left home.

Would Patrick still be unattached? No, it was highly unlikely. He was a man who liked a woman in his bed and wouldn't hang around for a couple of years waiting for one. No, she could either go for Patrick now, and mess up her children at this tricky stage in their lives, or wait until they left home and hope to find another Patrick. And it wasn't really a choice at all – she would do what was best for her children.

She sighed deeply, and took the tea-bag out of the mug. Of course, it might have been Jenny who had tidied the kitchen so well. In which case, she would have to forgive her for playing tennis with Patrick and using the hot water. And she'd better learn to live with the idea that Jenny was after Patrick, and that he, being only human, would probably allow himself to be caught. She knew that he was attracted to young, athletic women, viz Topaz. And Jenny was a lot jollier.

She took both the tea and Bozo up to bed with her. She seemed to need the comfort of the little dog's presence more and more often these days.

Patrick was true to his word, he taught her to draw with a doggedness which would have eventually got through to the most untalented pupil. Althea considered herself only one rung up from this standard and had to work extremely hard.

She spent a lot of time incarcerated in what Patrick pretentiously called his study, one of the few rooms in his new house which had plaster on the walls and floorboards underfoot. It had good natural and excellent artificial light. One day, Althea was sure, it would be a study. But until it had more than just a drawing board and an old-fashioned typist's chair in it, it wasn't.

'You'll be wanting me to have a Swiss Cheese plant next,' he grumbled at her, when she brought in a wastepaper basket from home so that all her failures didn't land up on the floor.

'Swiss Cheese plants have no function,' she said crisply. 'And may I remind you it is August the twentieth.'

'Then stop gossiping and get back to work. Have you got a pencil with a decent point on it this time?'

The day she got the plans in the post, she invited Patrick for dinner. She would have taken him out, only she couldn't afford it. As it was, she found herself having to work for two extra hours in the blazing sun laying paving slabs for one of her clients' nieces to afford a decent bit of steak and some wine. Not to mention all the little treats for her children she used to salve her conscience.

Merry decided to help Althea prepare. Then Merry decided

that it would be really nice if Althea and Patrick dined in the conservatory.

'The dining-room table's covered with junk and the carpet smells funny,' Merry argued. 'You can't eat in the kitchen because we'll all be there. It'll be so nice in the conservatory. I'll get out all the best glasses and things.'

'But, darling, he might get the wrong idea if it's all too romantic!'

'And Ronnie and I will serve you, so you don't have to do a thing.'

'Except cook,' put in Rupert.

'Yes, and you do have to keep your eye on steak. It's so easy to overcook,' said Althea. 'It would be much better if you lot ate first, and then we had ours afterwards.'

'In among the ketchup bottles and soy sauce?' said William. 'Very nice for a celebration dinner, *not*. Besides, when will Jenny get a chance to cook and eat?'

'God! I'm beginning to wish I'd just bought Patrick a bottle of champagne. It would have been cheaper and a lot less bother.'

'But you've asked him now,' said Rupert. 'You can't uninvite him.'

'I could say I've changed my mind. Or it's no longer convenient.'

'But you've bought half a dead cow. Not to eat it now would be compounding your crime,' said William.

He had a point. She had bought two large steaks she couldn't afford. William was a vegetarian, Rupert didn't like steak, and Merry, who did, was always full after two mouthfuls. She would have to eat steak for days, and she wouldn't enjoy it, not under those circumstances.

She toyed with the notion of taking the steak to his house to cook, but only briefly. When she'd last been in there, his kitchen consisted of a camping stove and a formica table which wobbled.

'OK. If you and Ronnie want to set it all up in the conservatory . . .'

'Goodie! I'll ring Ronnie and tell her. Can she stay the night?'

'I suppose so.'
'And how much do we get paid?'
Althea picked up her daughter and hugged her, very tightly.
'All right, all right. I was only joking.'

CHAPTER FIFTEEN

Althea decided to stop worrying about Patrick thinking she was trying to give him a romantic meal. Even he must realize that however many candles the room was lit with, and how many vases of flowers stood about, there was no chance of romance in a house full of teenagers.

She had also decided that she would tell him that their relationship had no future – if she needed to. Seeing the conditions under which she lived, never alone, always surrounded by people who not only demanded her attention, but who were entitled to quite a lot of it, might do the job for her.

But it was with a somewhat apologetic air that she opened the door and ushered him in. Keith Jarrett issued loudly from the kitchen tape player. Something that William would scathingly describe as 'pop' music was floating down the stairs, and Jenny was playing 'The Moonlight Sonata' on the piano in the dining room, well, if somewhat repetitively.

Althea accepted his kiss of greeting with what equanimity she could muster and ushered him in. It was a shame that in order to get to the conservatory, Patrick had to run the gauntlet of the kitchen, at present the territory of Merry and her friend Ronnie.

The two girls had decided to dress up for the occasion. They were both wearing tiny pinafore dresses over cropped T-shirts over which they had pinned linen table napkins as aprons. They had gelled their hair into total rigidity and put on as much make-up, consisting of clear mascara and brown lipstick, as they thought they could get away with. Althea had sprayed them both lavishly with the scent Frederick had given her for her birthday, to save the house from smelling of something vile. They both collapsed into giggles the moment they saw Patrick.

The boys, never far away from the food-source, accepted his appearance with a casual hello, and introduced their friend, a curly-headed giant with an engaging smile and familiar manner. He shook Patrick's hand warmly. Bozo, who had decided that she liked Patrick, scrabbled at his leg for attention. At least Jean-Claud, who had replaced Véronique, was staying with his best friend, who was billeted nearby. Althea got Patrick settled in a chair.

'Right. Now tell me, what would you like to drink?'

'What is there?'

'Wine or gin. Not a wonderful selection, I'm afraid.'

'What, no tonic at all?'

'Of course there's tonic! And ice and lemon, I just meant . . .'

'A gin and tonic would be lovely.'

It would indeed, she thought, filling a glass with ice-cubes, I just hope I have more than a minute to sit down to have one.

The meal was as ready as it could be in the circumstances, and as simple. Not that any meal which involves so many cooks is ever completely straightforward. But Althea had made a Master List of everyone's allotted tasks. Most of hers were ticked off. She only had 'Cook steak', 'Clean downstairs loo', and 'Iron blouse' left in her column. She had worn a blouse that didn't need ironing, and squirted something toxic but quick round the loo.

Apart from the steaks, which were lying in a film of olive-oil, out of the way of the animals, the meal was more or less cooked. She had made kipper pâté as a starter. It was easy, it was cheap, and, unlike the steak, didn't involve any last-minute attention. Merry and Ronnie had spent all afternoon and a whole loaf of bread making melba toast and butter curls.

Merry was also responsible for bringing out the deep-fat fryer which Althea had won in a competition, but never used. This would no doubt be excellent for the sauté potatoes, but it had taken a whole bottle of oil to fill. As Rupert said, next time she would have to try and win a more sophisticated model. Althea, as exploitative as the next mother, used this criticism as an excuse to get Rupert to take responsibility for the potatoes. They were lying parboiled and sliced in an untidy grey heap in the larder, the top of the freezer being the only space available for the deep-fat fryer.

The salad, filled for the vegetarian's benefit with avocados and blue cheese, was made and the vinaigrette, made by Rupert, ready to pour on. The puddings – two individual portions of chocolate mousse, and a pudding basin full of it for the children – only needed cream and grated chocolate. It was not a gourmet menu, and if Althea had had the place to herself, she would have cooked something more sophisticated, but she knew as long as it was nice, Patrick wouldn't care.

Althea went back into the conservatory with two drinks and a bowl of pistachios. Even as she cracked open the first one, she knew her kitchen floor was being covered in shells as the children fell on the rest of the packet.

'Well, here's to the competition,' said Patrick, raising his glass.

Althea picked up hers. 'And here's to my drawing teacher.'

'To our combined success.'

They clinked.

'This is a stunning view,' said Patrick. 'In fact, it's a really fabulous house.'

Althea took another sip of her drink and nodded. 'Yes. I love it. It would be the nicest house in the area if I didn't live in it.'

'Why do you say that?'

'Because I can't afford to keep it in the condition it deserves. And even if I could, it would still be dreadfully cluttered. I'm so untidy.'

'It always seems fine to me.'

'I've probably always just tidied up.'

Patrick shrugged. 'Maybe. I never really notice things like that.'

Althea settled more comfortably in her chair. 'How is your house getting along? That will be fabulous, when it's finished.'

'When it's finished.' He picked up a handful of nuts and started opening them rather forcefully. 'I'm running out of money.'

'Perhaps you could let part of it.'

'Only when part of it is fit for habitation. But then I could, yes. It's too big for one.'

'Would you sell it?'

He shook his head, shrugged, made a small, querying gesture with his hands. 'I don't know. I'd certainly never want to. But who knows? I may be forced to.'

'That's just how I feel about this. I have to sell when Merry's no longer in full-time education, to give Frederick his bit. But I'm hoping that somehow I'll have enough money by then to buy him out.'

'Have you got much saved?'

Althea laughed. 'Five pounds and twenty-five pence.'

Patrick leant forward, as if to take her hand, but stopped when Merry, followed by Ronnie, came in. They had found some bits of old net in the dressing-up box and tied them round their heads.

'Would sir and madam like to eat now?'

'Er, yes,' said Patrick. 'I think so. How does madam feel about that?'

'You wouldn't like another drink first?' asked Althea.

'Oh no. You mix a pretty hefty g and t.'

Althea finished hers rather quickly.

Merry removed their drinks and the nuts from the small table and spread a cloth over it. Ronnie produced knives and forks and set the table. Althea and Patrick sat back and watched the cabaret. By the time they had finished, adding flowers, candles and a bottle of wine, there was hardly room for the plates. But somehow, the girls squeezed everything on, and with many flourishes and sirs and modoms, left the diners in peace.

'I tried to get them all to go out,' explained Althea. 'But they wouldn't. They insisted they wouldn't get in the way.'

'Why should they go out? It's their house, they live here.'

'True, but were the situations reversed, I'd go out – or at least retire to my bedroom.'

'Well, I like having them around.' He looked up, a curl of butter balanced on his knife. 'We'll be alone when I ask you to dinner at my house.'

Althea licked her lips, suddenly panicked. She had intended, almost from the moment she asked Patrick to dinner, to tell him that this meal was a sort of goodbye, that she couldn't cope with a relationship right now. Quite what she planned to say if he said he didn't want a relationship anyway, and couldn't they just be friends, she hadn't worked out. Which didn't help her nerves, seeing that was precisely what he would say.

On the other hand, with the house full of children and noise, he might realize how impossible the whole thing was, and stop asking her out anyway. So instead of telling him that she couldn't go to dinner at his house, she just smiled. Entertaining one's lover with a house full of teenagers would be a nightmare. But if on the other hand the man was not your lover, and you wanted gently to point out how impossible it was that he ever could be, until after the teenagers had all left home, it was not a bad way of letting him know, without actually having to say anything.

The evening rumbled on, from near-disaster to near-disaster: Rupert forgot about the sauté potatoes and one batch were decidedly too brown. Ronnie cut her finger on a cooking knife and while Althea was holding it under the cold tap, some of the blood splashed on to the salad and the steaks overcooked. Althea offered Patrick a second helping of chocolate mousse, only to find that the children had eaten every scrap, even wiping the bowl with their fingers. She had to go back into the conservatory with a cheese board hastily made up of sweaty vegetarian cheddar, a heel of stilton and some cream crackers, most of which were broken.

Patrick coped with everything totally calmly, accepting with enthusiasm anything that came his way. He was the perfect guest – totally unfazed by the chaos of the evening. The whole family sat in the conservatory for coffee – instant – made by Henry, William's friend. Patrick appeared to enjoy himself thoroughly.

'Right.' Patrick got up in the manner of a man about to make an announcement. 'Althea is going to show me her garden.'

'But you've seen it loads of times,' complained Merry.

'I want to see it again.' He was very firm. He pulled Althea to her feet, into the garden and along to the rustic bench. It was made by a local craftsman and she had put it there so when she was tired from her gardening, she could sit and admire her pond.

'It's probably covered in mould,' she warned him as he made to sit down. 'I never got round to putting wood preserver on it.'

He took off his coat and spread it on the seat. 'Sit down,' he commanded. Meekly, she obeyed.

'Alone at last,' he said, putting his arm along her shoulders.

Althea ducked from under his arm and turned to face him.

'Patrick, I don't know how to tell you this, but I don't think we can go on seeing each other.'

He stiffened. 'What do you mean, "seeing each other"?'

'You know perfectly well. Tonight was supposed to be a thank you for your teaching me to draw, but really . . .'

'Really what?'

He was sounding dreadfully distant. This was getting worse and worse. 'I hoped it might – well – give you a hint.'

'What sort of hint?'

'That I'm not a free agent. I can't go out with you – with anyone – seriously.'

'What about frivolously?' His eyes, which could be so warm, became like the stormy wastes of the North Sea.

Althea chewed her lip and crumpled her skirt with her hands. He was obviously determined to make her spell it out. 'Listen, Patrick, you've said, you know you have, that you think we've got something going for us.'

'So?' His eyes snapped, as if he'd deny ever having said any such thing.

'Well, we haven't.'

'Why not?'

'My family.'

'But your family like me. Even your damn dog likes me!'

'I know, but them liking you, when they see you occasionally, on a casual basis, is different from them seeing you – often.'

'They've told you this, have they? They've said that they don't mind me sometimes, but they wouldn't like me hanging round the house all day?'

'No . . . That's not what I meant . . .' lied Althea desperately.

'Then what the hell do you mean?'

Althea shut her eyes, but Rupert's anxious face still hovered behind the lids. *I wouldn't want anyone here* . . . 'I mean, I can't have casual relationships. I'm emotionally incapable of it. And while the children are still at home, I can't have serious ones.'

'I see. And which do you think I was after? A quick lay? Or till death us do part?'

'I don't know.' Althea wanted to cry, but knew she must postpone it. 'Probably neither. But whatever you did want, you can't have it.'

163

'I don't remember asking you for any sort of relationship, but thank you for sparing me a knock back. At least I know where I stand in case a violent blow to the head causes me to ask you out for a meal, or anything else likely to disturb your children's delicate psyches.'

'There's no need to be sarcastic! It's not like that, you know it's not.'

'Althea, I don't think you know what the hell it's like. You don't know what you want, but if you did, you wouldn't let yourself have it, in case your children didn't like it. You're so bloody contrary.' He got up and put his hands on the arms of the bench so she had to remain seated. 'Goodbye, Althea, thank you for a very pleasant evening. Because it was pleasant, up until now. But as you've made it quite clear you don't want to have anything more to do with me, I won't invite you back. Good night!'

Althea watched him storm through the garden and out of the gate. When she heard it slam behind him, she burst into tears.

When the children found out, as inevitably they did, that Althea had 'dumped' Patrick, as they put it, they were furious.

'But he was OK. Played tennis. Good taste in music,' protested William.

'Yes. I liked him,' said Merry. 'He wore nice clothes. He was coo-erl.'

Rupert, at least, was less critical, merely enquiring, 'Did you have a row?'

'Not really,' said Althea, swiping the work surfaces more viciously than usual. 'I just decided it would be better if we didn't see each other.'

Jenny, on the other hand, was very understanding. 'Don't be hard on yer mum, kids. A girl's gotta do what a girl's gotta do.' And she left the house rapidly, giving Althea the strong impression that what that particular girl hatta do was Patrick.

For the first time for years, Althea was not joining her children in the new term. Usually she started work a bit before they did, but they all experienced the First Day of Term syndrome together.

The worst part was the night before, sorting out bits of uniform. Usually, some part of it was lost, and first cross-country runs would have to be done in one proper sock and one ordinary. Some part would be new, a sweatshirt, a pair of shoes, or just more socks, which had to be marked, with a pen. The yards of different nametapes which filled Althea's sewing basket were not to be used, for they, it seemed, were akin to having your gloves sewn on bits of elastic, and just too embarrassing.

Then there were the clothes that had been grown out of, un-noticed, which required promises of replacements as soon as possible. And now Merry was at secondary school, there were skirts which were always the wrong length, the fashion in school skirts having changed during the holidays. Last year they had to be nearly ankle length, this year, two inches below the backside. Althea, who refused to cut off the extra fabric in case the fashion changed again, was forced to make giant hems, and teach her daughter to roll her skirt over from the top.

But the worst were the things discovered mouldering in bags, where they had lain since the summer half-term holiday. Some-how, these had to be washed and dried ready for school, with all the stains, which time and micro-organisms had ground into the fabric, removed.

At the end of every term, she frisked the children, searched their rooms, and shook out every carrier bag in the house, looking for their clothes to prevent this happening. And at the beginning of every new term, there was always something.

'You know what I hate most about school uniform?' she asked Jenny, the only member of the household she was still speaking to. 'The fact that they make me wash over the weekend.'

'It's supposed to be good for kids all to wear the same things. It stops the rich kids dressing better than the poor ones.'

'Rubbish!' said Althea. 'If you think kids can't tell who gets their school skirts from Peacocks and who get them from Cav House, you're kidding yourself.'

'I was only quoting –'

'Yes, I know. I'm sorry to sound off at you, particularly when you must be anxious about tomorrow.'

'Yeah well, there are a few butterflies in the old tum. But I'm well prepared and my room's looking fab. I've got lots of ace posters up, and all the children's names are stuck on the desks. It looks darling.'

'I must come and see it. I've got to go over to the new school next week. Bloody governors' meeting. I don't know why I let Mrs Jenkinstown con me into being the Clerk to the Governors.'

'Because you're soft?'

'In the head,' agreed Althea. At that moment Merry came in.

'Can I make something to eat now, or are you still in a moody?'

'I'm still in a moody,' snapped Althea, and stomped into the conservatory to read the paper.

Jenny joined her a little later and handed her a glass of wine. It was Althea's wine, but it was a kind thought.

'You have been quite hard on the kids lately. Are you cut up about Patrick?'

'No, of course not! I'm just worried about having no job and no money!'

Patrick had sent his apologies to the Chairman and was absent from the governors' meeting. Althea couldn't help wondering if it was because she would be there, or if it was, as he said, due to a prior engagement. While everyone signed the attendance book, she decided it was arrogant of her to assume she had anything to do with it.

Although it was in a different setting, with different governors, the meeting was – as were almost all the other meetings Althea had attended – mostly about money, and how there wasn't enough. But Geoffrey Conway had one piece of good news: their school had finally been allocated the money for the new buildings.

'We've got the funding. Now all we have to do,' he said, 'is decide which plans we'll go for.'

'Yes, but there's not time to look at each plan individually during a meeting,' said Mrs Jenkinstown. 'Can all the governors who are interested make time to look at the plans here, at the school, during the next couple of weeks? Then I'll call a special meeting and we can discuss them.'

This being generally agreed, Althea made the appropriate notes and got up to make the tea.

'Althea, dear.' Mrs Jenkinstown caught up with Althea just before she got the key into the lock of her car. 'Before you go. *Big* favour to ask you. But I do hope you'll say yes.'

Althea accepted this announcement with a wariness she didn't try to hide.

'It's a terrible imposition, I know, but . . .' Few impositions would be too terrible for Mrs Jenkinstown. 'You know the French school are coming for a return visit?'

'Yes,' said Althea slowly, wondering how on earth this could affect her.

'Well, it's Patrick Donahugh . . .'

'What about him?'

'He promised he'd have the Mayor and his wife to stay.'

'So?'

'Well, my dear, he can't, can he? His house is uninhabitable except for him and the mice and he hasn't even got his girlfriend.'

'Well, someone else will have to have them.'

'They can't! Everyone else I've asked is either having someone already, or hasn't got enough room. I'm desperate. It's Patrick or nothing.'

'Talk to Patrick about it then.'

'Althea dear, don't sound so haughty. If he can't have them, there's only one person who can . . .'

'Mrs Jenkinstown, I can't! My children have only just got their own rooms back after a whole summer of sharing because of the French children. I can't ask them to shift about again now. It's term time, and although they don't often do it, they do have work to do.'

'But my dear, Patrick's partnership has submitted plans for the new school buildings – far the nicest, and nearly the cheapest – and Geoffrey Conway won't be able to resist choosing his plans if he has been so obliging.'

'But *he* won't have been obliging, *I* would! How would that help Patrick?'

'Geoffrey would think that Patrick had persuaded you to have them. He's feeling frightfully guilty himself because he's got the builders in and he can't have anyone to stay.'

'And what does Geoffrey suppose I stand to gain? Patrick's

undying gratitude, I suppose. Well, it's not enough. And surely Patrick can't vote for his own firm's plans?'

'Of course not, he won't even be at the meeting. But Geoffrey Conway has a vote, and some of the other governors won't even look at the plans, and will just go with the cheapest unless Geoffrey leads the way.'

'What's wrong with that? The school can use any money over for books, or something useful.'

'Now, don't be like that, dear. The cheapest plans are ghastly, quite the worst sort of concrete and glass. I can't bear the thought of them despoiling the landscape.'

'I don't care about the landscape.'

'Yes you do, you know you do.'

'So I've got to have two grand French people to stay in my chaotic household, just to get Patrick out of a spot and to make sure the school which made me redundant has beautiful buildings? I don't think so.'

Mrs Jenkinstown appeared defeated. 'I agree that put like that it does sound totally unreasonable. And I could put my aged mother out of her cottage and into a hotel for the weekend, hire a couple to act as host and hostess for the French people in her house, but she won't like it . . .'

Althea let out a sigh which could have doubled as an expletive. 'Oh, all right I'll have them! But you're a bully and a blackmailer!'

Mrs Jenkinstown squeezed Althea's shoulder affectionately. 'I know I am, dear, but you should meet my mother!'

CHAPTER SIXTEEN

✿

Althea was furious. Unfortunately, she had to go shopping and was prevented from ringing Patrick up and telling him just how furious immediately. But rather than risk her white-hot rage diminishing to mere pique, she fed her anger as she planned how to feed her family, striding up and down the aisles of the supermarket, flinging things in her trolley, her mental invective getting more inventive with every tin of beans and packet of peas. The telephone would spontaneously combust before she'd finished with him, and if he wasn't in when she rang, she would use up all the tape on his answering machine telling him where to get off.

She reversed out of her parking space, narrowly missing the C Zone post, and drove home in a cloud of blue exhaust smoke. But the telephone was spared. Patrick, instead of being at his office, where Althea could have a good go at him, was sitting at her kitchen table, dunking biscuits in his tea with her children. She confronted him, hands on hips, eyes crackling with rage.

'Oh God, Mum's going ballistic,' muttered Rupert. 'Who's done what? Where? How?'

Patrick got up, holding out his hands in a gesture of peace and disassociation.

'I know, I know, Mrs Jenkinstown told me. I've come to apologize and tell you to take no notice of her. I'll sort out the mayor some other way. You don't have to have them.'

Althea, who had a short anger-span, most of which had been expended in the supermarket, found herself beginning to relax. But she was determined not to let Patrick see that. 'Out!' she said to her children dramatically, so they would know it was nothing personal. 'I'm going to tear this man apart, and I don't want witnesses!'

The children, laughing heartily, left her and Patrick facing it out across the kitchen table.

'I swear I had nothing whatever to do with it,' he began. 'When she told me what she'd done, I was as angry as you are. It's a terrible imposition. Don't even think of doing it. I'll think of something else.'

As 'terrible imposition' was on her list of things to say, she felt thwarted. He was taking the wind out of her sails and using it against her. Her brain worked frantically as she filled and switched on the kettle, thinking up another damning phrase. All she came up with was, 'But what can you think of?'

Patrick shrugged. 'I don't know – a hotel or something.'

This feeble suggestion gave her an opportunity to be angry again. 'You can't put them up in a hotel! Not after the hospitality they showed us. It would defeat the whole object of the exchange. Those people took us into their homes and entertained us like princes. You can't leave them to the mercies of the Dog and Fox . . .'

'Well, I could clear out my bedroom . . .'

'And what about a bathroom?'

'There's a perfectly good bath – even a bidet.'

'But they're not plumbed in! And the only working loo is the one outside.'

'The French aren't so hung up on plumbing as the English are . . .'

'They still need water to wash in. And what would you cook on?'

'There's a perfectly good stove . . .'

'With only two burners that work!'

'Why are you making all these difficulties?'

'I'm not making difficulties. You're the one living in a building site!'

'A historic building site,' he murmured, offended.

'I'm just looking at the problem realistically,' Althea went on. 'Mrs Jenkinstown was quite right when she said your house was only fit for you and the mice.'

'She said that? How dare she? One of the loveliest houses in Gloucestershire and she says that about it?'

'Loveliness alone is not enough. You need a roof, windows, walls . . .'

'Yes, well, that's a matter of opinion.'

Althea poured water on to the tea-bags, glad of an excuse to turn her back and hide her twitching lips. 'It may be, but honestly, Patrick, you must admit you can't put the mayor and his missus up in your house.'

'Well, I'll have to think of an alternative then. Why can't someone else have them?'

'Everyone else is having someone else, or can't, because they haven't got room. She wouldn't have asked me if she hadn't been absolutely desperate. Mrs Jenkinstown explained it all to me.'

'Mrs Jenkinstown is an interfering old bat!'

'No she's not! She's extremely kind and public spirited! And do you know the reason she asked me to have them? So Geoffrey Conway would vote for your firm's plans for the new school!'

'Why should you having them make any difference to how Geoffrey votes? We're not exactly married.'

'No, but she seems to think that Geoffrey would assume you'd persuaded me, which apparently would make him vote for your firm's plans out of gratitude.'

'Oh, I see. And why is Madame Jenkinstown so keen on my plans being adopted?'

'Because she likes them! Honestly, you're so unreasonable! Here's a very genuine, caring person, who does a very great deal for the community, putting herself out so your firm can earn thousands of pounds, and all you can do is snipe at her.'

'But don't you see? It's not her putting herself out at all, it's you! Why doesn't she have them?'

'Because she's having the head teacher and his wife. Geoffrey's got the builders in and can't.' She chuckled. 'It's funny when you think about it. He's probably having a patio done, or something. And you – well – what *aren't* you having done?'

'Hmmph.' Patrick was not prepared to see the funny side. He rearranged the dozen mugs that littered the table into orderly rows, as if working out a plan of battle. He seemed a lot angrier than Althea had been. She carried her tea over to the table and sat down.

'Listen, I'm not saying it'll be particularly convenient. I'll have to ask the children and Jenny to swap their rooms round again, so the spare room's free. And we've only just got back to normal after the French children, but it's not impossible. And it certainly isn't worth getting all worked up about.'

'Isn't it? You seemed fairly worked up when you came in.'

'Yes, well. I was for a while, but really, it's a lot easier for me to have them than for you to think of something else.'

'I'm not convinced. I just haven't had a chance to come up with a plan.'

'Well, don't stress yourself. I do owe you a favour, after all.'

'Do you?' He seemed genuinely perplexed.

'You taught me to draw, remember?'

'What's that got to do with the price of kippers?'

Althea wished she hadn't reminded him. She felt his anger switch from Mrs Jenkinstown to her. 'Well, you know, a quid pro quo, or whatever it is . . .'

'I taught you to draw because I wanted to.'

'And I'm offering to have these French people because I want to.'

'Oh, don't give me that! You were steaming with rage at the very suggestion!'

Althea cleared her throat. 'Well, I know, but I've had a chance to calm down now, and see that there's no alternative. And there isn't,' she interrupted his protest. 'There really isn't.'

'I suppose not.'

'So will you let me have them?' she asked gently. 'Honestly, I don't mind.'

He took a deep breath and let it out slowly, with feeling. 'Very well, under certain conditions.'

'What?'

'Number one, you don't spend a single penny on anything they, or your family, eat while they're here. I'll pay for everything.'

His eyes had become very glittery, his mouth firm and determined. Althea decided it was time to capitulate. 'Fair enough. But I have conditions, too.' He wasn't going to have it all his own way.

'What?'

'That you speak French. No pretending that you can't.'

Having won a major point, Patrick subsided into his normal

state of relaxed amusement. 'But I didn't when we were at the reception.'

'I don't care.' Althea's eyes were sparkling now. 'I'm not doing all that cooking and cleaning –'

'I'll pay someone to do the cleaning for you.'

'Don't be silly – but I'm not doing it and carrying the whole burden of conversation as well.'

Patrick chuckled. 'But think how your French improved.'

'If you make me do all the talking,' she told him through clenched teeth, 'your French won't just improve, it'll come out of a strange part of your anatomy!'

Instead of being shocked, Patrick laughed even harder. 'All right, all right, I'll admit to speaking French, though not, I beg you, in front of Geoffrey.'

'And there's to be no pretending to be married, or anything like that. They must be quite clear that you go back to your own house at night.'

'But won't they think it an awfully odd arrangement?'

'I don't care.'

'But why should you be doing all this entertaining for me, when we're not even engaged?'

'Because I'm an extremely kind and compassionate person,' she growled.

'If you really think they'll believe that . . .'

'Of course they will. They'll realize that for a single man, entertaining is very difficult.'

'No, no, not that part. It's the going home at night bit which'll stretch their imagination.'

'Nonsense,' said Althea. 'The French are much more broad-minded about these things.'

'That's what I mean.' Patrick raised his hands in self-defence. 'OK, OK, whatever you think best.' He paused, his eyebrows raised and a tiny, challenging smile lifting the corner of his mouth. 'If you think we'll get away with it.'

She scowled at him. 'Honestly, anyone would think we were doing something immoral.'

Patrick regarded her thoughtfully, as if he might say something, but instead, he gathered up the mugs and took them over to the sink.

Gratified by this helpful gesture, Althea said, 'If you like, I'll give them my room and sleep with Merry. It would save Jenny being put out of her room again.'

Patrick stopped washing mugs and spun round. 'Don't even think about it! And I'll pay Jenny's rent. If she's moving out to accommodate my guests, it's only fair. And I'm sure she could do with the money.'

'Oh. All right.' Althea had in fact given Jenny a rebate when she'd had to use Merry's room, but for just a weekend, she wouldn't have thought it necessary. 'She doesn't pay very much rent, you know.'

'I know. But she's saving every penny she can to raise a deposit for a flat.'

'Mmm.' Althea nodded. She knew that, of course. But Jenny and Patrick must be closer than she realized if Patrick knew it too.

'And your children. They should be compensated, too.'

'Patrick, this'll cost you an absolute fortune.'

'I can afford it.'

'Can you? With all your building expenses?'

'If I've said I can, I can, OK? And I mean it about paying someone to clean for you. There's no reason for you to do it all.'

'Can I come in and get a drink?' asked Merry, peeping round the door. 'Or are you two throwing things?'

'No, no, we're being perfectly peaceable,' said Althea.

'Unless you go on refusing to let me pay for a cleaner,' said Patrick.

Althea settled down to explain how you couldn't just get a cleaner into a house like hers, how she'd have to tidy up first, and how she wouldn't want a stranger silently tutting at the dust on her picture frames. She was halfway through when Merry interrupted.

'I'll clean, if you pay me. I'm good at it, and I know how sordid everything is.'

'True,' Althea agreed.

'But are you really good at it?' Patrick asked Merry. 'I only want the best for Althea.'

Althea laughed. 'Believe me, Merry is the best for me. I really don't want someone I don't know coming in.'

'OK. You let me know the hourly rate and how long it takes you,' he said to Merry.

'So that's settled,' said Althea. 'Now what do you want me to give them to eat?'

By the time Patrick finally left, having been fed, with the rest of the family, by Jenny, on one of her high-fibre, low-cost vegetarian feasts, everyone except Althea stood to gain financially from the planned visitation. He would have paid her too, had she not flatly refused. As far as she was concerned, it would make them quits. He had taught her to draw, she could entertain a French couple for two nights.

In fact, they worked out, it was only for one dinner, two breakfasts and two lunches, as Saturday night was to be spent in the neighbouring village hall, to the accompaniment of music, country dancing and a bring and share supper. Before anyone else could use her idea, Althea quickly told Mrs Jenkinstown that her contribution to this would be a trifle – not cheap, but so quick.

For the other meals, they agreed that only the best of English produce should appear on the table. Between them they devised a menu that would impress, but would stay within the bounds of Althea's cooking abilities. Once, years ago, she had been a good cook, and had produced meals Frederick had been proud of. But lately, she'd got bored with cooking and gone on to gardening instead. However, once she got the cookery books out, some of her old enthusiasm returned.

Patrick gave her a hundred pounds in notes crisp and hot from the machine. Clutching it, Althea went forth, shopping for England's honour.

She bought a huge piece of beef, organic and guaranteed to be well hung. She bought English cheese, mature Cheddar with the rind on, smoked Double Gloucester and Stilton from the market. Also fruit and vegetables, hand picked by her, painstakingly packed by the veg. man. She bought specially thick and expensive double cream from the health food shop. She only stopped when the boot of her car was full and over half the money was gone. There was still the supermarket shopping to do.

Patrick was in charge of the wine, but they had decided not to push patriotism too far. Beef, cheese and vegetables could be relied on, but they neither of them knew enough about English wine to risk it.

By the time the four of them, Henri and Paulette, Patrick and Althea, turned up at the barn dance, they had eaten roast beef and Yorkshire pudding, roast potatoes and a selection of vegetables, a dish with chicken breasts, mushrooms and cider, an Autumn version of Summer Pudding, and gooseberry fool.

Every meal had gone well, the fact that Althea had used frozen Yorkshire puddings had not been discovered, but she was dead on her feet, and would rather starve than ever cook anything again. But, as she kept reminding herself, there was only a traditional English breakfast to do tomorrow morning. They were taking them out to a traditional English pub for lunch so Henri could try some locally brewed beer and the coach was leaving at two.

They were a delightful couple. Neither of them could speak a word of English, but even when Patrick wasn't there, they managed to convey their appreciation and enjoyment of everything. With the end of her cookathon in sight, Althea was looking forward to an evening where the food was not her sole responsibility, although she had brought her trifle, sprinkled with toasted almonds and borage flowers and covered with cling film.

Althea had seen the evening as a break from the huge pressure of entertaining. What she hadn't anticipated was the stir her arrival with Patrick would cause.

Everyone was very pleased to see her. She had been popular as a school secretary and no one had wanted her to leave. But when she appeared with Patrick, albeit chaperoned by a substantial French couple, the gossip rose like midges on a summer's evening.

'You cow!' said Sylvia. 'You told me, categorically, that there was nothing going on between you.'

'There isn't anything going on. Keep your voice down!'

'Oh, don't be silly! No one can hear us with this row going on. Are you sleeping together?'

'The row', in the form of a young band of musicians sounding out ye olde English folke tunes, suddenly ceased as the second fiddle, nine years old if she was a day, snapped a string.

Althea, convinced the whole barnful of people had heard Sylvia's question, turned the colour of the blackberry fool she was standing by.

'Ah, Althea.' Mrs Jenkinstown bore down on her and Sylvia. 'It is *so* kind of you to help us out of this little spot. And no, dear' – she turned to Sylvia who had suddenly taken on the appearance of a schoolgirl – 'there is nothing going on.'

But in spite of this witness for the defence, the murmurings still went on, so Althea took refuge in the kitchen, washing the constant stream of dirty glasses. Patrick eventually dragged her out and made her join in a country dance which involved a lot of clapping and kissing. But she avoided eye contact wherever possible.

Fortunately their guests thought that Althea's stint in the kitchen was just another aspect of her self-sacrificing character, and commented on her public-spiritedness all the journey home.

Patrick, however, digging out the remains of Frederick's brandy, refused to allow her any brownie points.

'I can't think why you made such a fuss!' he muttered, so their guests, in the next room, wouldn't hear. 'It's only Sylvia getting her ideas in a twist. And so what if people think there is something going on between us? There very well might be!'

Althea was polishing the glasses. 'We've gone into all this before. I have a family to consider!'

'So have I. I have two nearly grown-up daughters. They don't restrict my actions at all.'

Althea, torn between a desperate desire to hear all about his family, and a need to keep him in his place, hissed, 'And where do they live?'

'OK, so they're studying abroad, in Canada, but even if they weren't. . .'

'My family live with me. You've seen for yourself how crowded the house is. I have no time for relationships! Now, do let's get the brandy on the tray. I'll find the After Eights.'

'If that's your last word, I won't trouble you any further.'

Patrick picked up the tray and carried it out of the kitchen. Althea suddenly thought she was going to cry. 'Pull yourself together,' she ordered. 'You're very tired, and it's making you over-emotional. When you've recovered from this you'll be glad to be rid of him.'

She *was* tired, and her smile, as she brought in glasses and the mints, was very forced. But she knew she would miss Patrick. If only she'd met him when the children were little, and still adaptable. Or, alternatively, met him in five years' time, when the children would have mostly left home.

She let herself sink into silence while the others spoke in French, sparing herself the concentration needed to follow. What will I look like in five years' time? Will I still be able to attract any man, let alone a man like Patrick? Lots of people did, of course. But they were the sort of women who hadn't 'let themselves go'. Gloomily, she helped herself to another mint.

The following morning she felt more cheerful and was merrily grilling bacon when Patrick arrived, looking every inch the host with the most in his navy canvas trousers and dark tan cotton shirt. They still had breakfast and the pub lunch to get through. She couldn't afford to be too distant and stand-offish. She smiled at him warily. 'Coffee? Or tea?'

'Coffee, please. Are they up yet?'

'No. I thought I'd leave them until breakfast was nearly done. They must be exhausted. They haven't had a moment to themselves since they arrived.'

'It was the same for us, remember.'

She laughed, wiping her greasy fingers on her apron. 'Well, almost. It's just as well Madame de Villeneuve couldn't come. We would have been in a frightful pickle. We might be still, if she and Paulette are best friends.'

'They're not. I asked, and she said only to nod to.'

'Well, that's a relief. We're very lucky. Most people are having the people they stayed with over. It was a shame Madame couldn't come. But it would have been awkward.'

'There would only have been one of her.'

'But I couldn't have coped with pretending to be married all over again. It would have had to have been the quickest divorce in history.'

'It was all right for you,' said Patrick. 'At least you got some sleep.'

'So did you! I heard you! You practically snored.'

'I was pretending.'

'Oh, pretending. You're very good at that, aren't you? Do you get a lot of practice?' Althea tried to sound light-hearted, but found in fact her heart had started to thump rather heavily.

'Some,' said Patrick at the grill, turning over the bacon with his fingers. 'But I only do it when necessary. And never about anything important.'

Althea started slicing mushrooms. 'Then why did you pretend to sleep then?'

He shrugged and hesitated before answering. 'To save you from having to make conversation when you weren't asleep.'

'Can you pass me the butter? It's in the fridge. And why didn't you sleep? Too cramped?'

He handed her the packet. 'Something like that.'

Althea was not quite happy with this explanation. There seemed to be a sub-text that she was missing. But time was getting on, and she had the feeling that he wouldn't be more specific even if she did enquire more closely.

'That was wonderful,' said Althea, when at last the coach had disappeared and she could stop waving. 'But I'm glad it's over. I'm exhausted.' She was also full of cider and that, combined with the heat of early autumn, was making her incredibly sleepy.

'I'll run you home,' said Patrick. 'And then you can have a nap.'

'There's so much I ought to be doing.'

'You'll do it better if you're rested.'

In spite of her resolutions, she invited him in for a cup of tea. 'I always get dreadfully thirsty if I drink at lunchtime.'

He followed her into the house and, at her insistence, sat in the conservatory to wait for the tea. When she came in with it, he appeared to be fast asleep, and although she wondered if he was pretending, she didn't call his bluff. She closed her own eyes. The house was quiet for once, all the children and Jenny having dispersed to friends or colleagues, to work or play, depending.

It was a beautiful day, hovering between summer and autumn,

as if undecided which was the more lovely. Althea lay with the sun on her eyelids, appreciating the silence, broken only by the dog shifting on her lap, Patrick's gentle breathing, and the snoring of her cat.

This is peace, she told herself. This is happiness. Grasp it. Don't think of the future or the past, just take the moment. She slept.

Then Patrick stirred and woke, waking her. Nothing very much had changed, but the moment had gone, Althea's anxiety and sadness were waiting to return the moment she gave them space.

'This is nice,' said Patrick. 'What happened to the tea?'

'It went cold,' said Althea. 'I'll make some more.'

'Don't bother. Let's just sit here.'

Althea sat, but not relaxed, as she had when he'd been asleep.

'Topaz and I never did much of this.'

'Well, no. I suppose it's an occupation for older people.'

'Older yourself! But it's not. Just sitting, being together, is important in a relationship.'

'I'm sure you and Topaz found lots to occupy you. Lots of tennis, squash, stuff like that.'

'Shopping was what Topaz liked best, spending my money. I hope Frederick's got plenty.'

'Oh yes.'

'But she could have spent every penny I had and I still couldn't have given her what she wanted.'

'What was that?'

'Commitment.'

'Mum?' called a voice and the front door slammed. 'I've brought some of the lads to play basketball. OK?'

'Fine, darling,' she called back, then asked Patrick, 'Would you like that tea now?'

He regarded her very intensely, his eyes made bluer by the sky in which small, autumnal clouds had begun to race. 'If that's all that's on offer.'

Althea got up. 'I'm afraid it is.' She didn't add that she would want commitment too. She didn't want to hear him tell her that she couldn't have it either, although she knew that's how it was.

'So even after all we've gone through together, what you said the other day still stands?'

She nodded. If she spoke, he might hear the tears in the back of her throat.

CHAPTER SEVENTEEN

That was the last day of summer. After that, autumn came rushing in, stripping the leaves from the trees, sending away the swallows without giving them a chance to say goodbye. And with autumn came a melancholy which settled on Althea like a cotton blanket – it weighed her down without providing any warmth.

She missed Patrick desperately. He was not missing her, having accepted perfectly calmly her ending the relationship. She heard constant reports of how calmly, through Jenny, who seemed to be contributing to his well-being in her own, inimitable way. Althea couldn't ask if they were sleeping together, but she was sure that they were. Otherwise, how could she explain the extra bounce in Jenny? It surely couldn't be explained by a first term's teaching – enough to wear down the strongest and most experienced. Yet Jenny, the ink on her certificates not yet dry, was full of beans and plans for the school panto, which she seemed to be organizing single-handed. Sylvia, not intending to depress her depressed friend still further, had come to the same conclusion when she called in one Friday afternoon.

'She's got a man. There's no other explanation.'

'Well, she's young and fit. Teaching obviously suits her,' said Althea, trying to convince herself.

'Nah – it's got to be more than that. Has she said anything?'

Althea shrugged. 'Not really.'

Actually, Jenny was naturally confiding and would have told Althea everything if she'd expressed an interest. But Althea had held her off in self-defence. Jenny might not confine herself to telling her landlady how interesting Patrick was, or how kind. She might launch into detailed descriptions of how he was in bed and this was not the sort of information Althea wished to learn second hand.

'And you and Patrick?' Sylvia asked. 'You're not seeing each other?'

Relieved that Jenny had not yet confided to the staff room, Althea shook her head. 'No.'

'So you wouldn't mind if I turned my antennae in that direction?'

A vulgar suggestion that other parts of Sylvia might work better remained unexpressed. She didn't want to give Sylvia ideas. 'Not at all.'

Easily convinced, Sylvia changed the subject. 'So how are you coping money-wise?'

Althea tried on a bright, optimistic smile, but decided it didn't suit her, and took it off again. 'If I don't spend anything on Christmas, I'll be all right until January. After that, it's a well-paid job or sell the house.'

'You can't do that!'

'People keep saying that, but actually I can. It will hurt like the devil, and the sorting out will be a nightmare. But quite honestly, it's always been too big and expensive for me to run, really. And a few months without a job has forced me to be more realistic.'

'Well, get a job!'

'I have tried, believe me. But there's nothing locally. And if you've got to pay to get there, wear smart clothes and buy convenience food because you're too tired to cook, you have to be earning much more. And while of course I'll go on looking, my heart's not in working for an insurance company.'

'There are lots of perks.'

'I know, but can you really see me fitting in to one of those places? I like to run my own show, not conform to some sort of manual.' Althea inhaled deeply, but decided she spent too much of the time sighing lately, and let her breath out silently. 'I am going to be doing odd jobs for an old lady who's just come out of hospital.'

'For sixpence an hour? If you charged properly for your little odds and ends of gardening jobs, and doing shopping for old ladies –'

'They wouldn't be able to afford me so I'd be out of work completely. Those little jobs do suit me. I fit them in round everything else, half an hour here, an hour there . . .'

Sylvia sighed. 'And all for tuppence ha'penny.'

Althea nodded. 'So you see, selling up, paying off Frederick and the mortgage, living in a house which is easier to heat and maintain makes a lot of sense.'

'Yes, but it doesn't sound a lot of *fun*.'

'No, well, I think I'm too old for fun.'

'Oh, Ally!'

'I'm making all my Christmas presents this year.' Althea stuck with the smile this time. 'I've got loads of hyacinths in bowls which should be in flower for Christmas.'

'I find hyacinths smell a bit strong.'

'What about a nice egg cosy then?' Sylvia didn't laugh. 'Oh, OK. I'll make you fudge.'

'But what about the children? You can't give them egg cosies or hyacinths.'

'No, but with luck my mother will give me money, and I'll spend it on them.'

'But that's dreadful!'

'It's real life! It's how women like me have always managed! Someone gives you gardening vouchers, or book tokens or something, for your birthday, so you save them up and do your Christmas shopping with them.'

'But don't you feel dreadfully short-changed and resentful?'

'Sometimes, yes. Mostly you just feel relieved you haven't had to spend money you haven't got. But honestly, what I wanted most when the children were little was what no one could give me.'

'What was that?'

'Enough sleep. Poor old Juno. Think what's in store for her.'

Sylvia had never got on with Juno, and was not in the mood to sympathize with her now. 'New babies do make people irritable. Did you hear about John Campbell?'

'In Mary's class?'

'Well, he's in Harry's class now, but yes, him.'

'No. What?'

'His mum's just had a new baby and he was off school for a week, with no note or anything. It turned out he had a black eye.'

'He could have come to school with a black eye, surely?'

'Yes except his mother wouldn't let him. Apparently' – here

Sylvia lowered her voice confidentially, although they were alone in the house – 'it was her new husband who did it. Too many broken nights. It got to him and he lashed out at John.'

'How awful!'

'Yup. There's something about step-parents. I saw a programme about lions once. The male lions always kill the cubs that the lioness had by a previous relationship.'

'Sylvia, I don't think animals have relationships in quite that way . . .'

'Well, it's nearly the same thing, isn't it? It's something to do with the selfish gene. It seeks to destroy other genes.'

'I didn't realize you were such a fan of wildlife programmes.'

'I'm not. But when I go home to see my mother, we have to watch them because it's all my step-father likes. There – another example!'

'Making you watch David Attenborough is hardly child abuse. I quite fancy him, actually.'

'That's not what I meant! What I meant is, step-parents, especially men, hardly ever get on with their step-children.'

'Oh, I'm sure that's not true!' She racked her brains for an example which disproved this theory but failed to come up with one.

'Well, in my experience it is,' Sylvia persisted. 'He's very nice to everyone else. It's just me he can't stand.' She laughed. 'Still, Fulham is handy for the shops, so I refuse to take the hint, and keep right on visiting.'

Althea chuckled. 'Come on, let's have some tea.'

Sylvia looked at her watch. 'It's past six o'clock. We could open a bottle.'

'I haven't got a bottle. It's tea or nothing.'

'Golly, Ally! I hadn't realized things had got that bad!'

'Things are bad when I start making my own wine. While I can manage without it, things are OK.'

'Mum! Post!' Merry called up the stairs, her voice full of enthusiasm.

'What is it?' called Althea through a mouthful of toothpaste.

'It's from those competition people. You know, the gardening ones.'

Althea spat, rinsed and wiped, trying to keep calm. It was bound to be a letter regretting that unfortunately . . . but until she knew for certain, she could still hope. She galloped down the stairs.

'Good news?' asked Merry a moment later.

Althea nodded, rereading, trying to take it all in. 'I've been selected for the final three, the ones who are actually getting to build their gardens at Chelsea.'

'Yippee!' said Merry. 'Will they give you money?'

'I hope so.' She referred to the letter again. 'Yes, they're sending me a cheque for a thousand pounds to create the garden.'

'Golly! That's a fortune!'

'No it's not, not really.' Then, seeing Merry's crestfallen face, she added, 'But it should cheer up Christmas.'

Althea knew it was madness to use the money for anything other than her garden. But she also knew she couldn't tell her children they couldn't have much for Christmas when she had a thousand pounds in her bank account. She decided to compromise – some would go on her children's presents, and the rest would be assigned for its proper purpose.

'What a good thing my whole theme is cheapness,' she said aloud.

'Mmm. You shouldn't have to buy a single plant,' said Merry, hopefully.

'It's not the plants, it's the labour. I'll have to have help building the garden.'

'Don't the competition people do that?'

'Only up to a point. It says here we each have a labourer to help us for a day, but then any more labour we need, we have to pay for out of the budget. I'm bound to need more. My garden's on a slope.'

'Couldn't you flatten it out?'

Althea shook her head. 'Unfortunately not. If your garden deviates too much from the original drawings, you'll be disqualified.'

'That's tight. Still, Patrick will be pleased, won't he?'

Althea didn't answer.

'You are going to tell him, aren't you?'

'Well, I haven't actually won, you know. I've only got through to the next round.'

'You will have to tell him. I mean, he spent hours teaching you to draw. And you were hopeless.'

'I wasn't hopeless!'

'Well, it was hard work for him.'

Althea sent him a postcard, brief and to the point. He didn't reply.

If it had been possible, Althea would have stopped using Patrick's greenhouse. But with summer over, lots of plants had to come in for protection over the winter, and her own conservatory was completely full. She also had to produce a huge amount of plants for her Chelsea garden, far more than would eventually end up in it, so only the most perfect specimens need be used.

In fact, without saying anything about it to Patrick, she was forced to spread herself and her plants into the most dilapidated part of the glasshouse. With a borrowed staple gun, bubble wrap and builders' plastic, she made the area as weatherproof as possible. It was far from satisfactory. One good gale and her plants could be cut to pieces by broken glass, or smashed under falling panes. But she had to have the extra space.

She watched the weather forecast daily, and if high winds were predicted, she would rush over and cram all her plants under the staging, so if anything happened, they wouldn't be damaged. It was just as well, she told Sylvia, trying to sound cheerful, she hadn't got a job. With one, she wouldn't have time for all the running around.

One day, a particularly strong wind was forecast. Although it was not due to hit until the following day, she decided it was better to make them safe while the weather was relatively calm, rather than wait until the gale started. She called her dog and set off.

Rather to her surprise, she saw Patrick's car in front of the house. She hesitated for a moment, wondering why he was there during the day, and if he would speak to her if she went to her greenhouse. Just as she had decided to carry on with her errand, she heard the front door open and Jenny's voice float merrily out.

'It's really nice of you to help me like this,' she said. 'You must let me know how I can return the favour.'

Patrick's laughing reply was made inaudible by a sudden gust of wind, but still Althea turned and ran, abandoning her plants, tugging Bozo's lead with unusual fierceness. It was one thing to think that your lodger and the man of your dreams were having an affair. Seeing them together and confirming it was quite another.

Later, while she was peeling potatoes, Jenny came in, full of happiness and good health. 'Great news!' she said. 'I've found somewhere to live! Patrick's been helping me move in.'

Althea's heart stopped and then started again, beating rapidly. 'That's wonderful. Where?'

'Quite near. Handy for school and everything. But I can't stop now. Patrick's taking me to the pub for a meal.' Jenny was good-natured and had not an ounce of bitchiness in her, but even so, she looked at Althea for a few seconds too long, to gauge her reaction to this news.

Althea kept her expression neutral. 'Oh good. Well, tell me about it some other time.'

'Sure. It's great, isn't it? You'll like having me out of your hair.'

Althea forced a smile. 'Maybe. But I'll have to get someone else. And better the devil you know . . .'

Jenny grinned. 'I'm not a bad girl really, now am I?'

Althea shook her head. 'You're a great girl and we'll really miss you.'

'Oh, you won't need to miss me! I'm not going far, I'll be popping in all the time, you'll see. Hell! I must fly.'

Tears blurred her vision, but Althea carried on with her task. She didn't need to see to peel potatoes. She was mad to assume Jenny was going to live with Patrick – she'd only seen them coming out of his house together, after all. It was the most cir-cumstantial of evidence. But the vision of Jenny's youthful figure and the sound of Patrick's laughing voice burned into her brain. Of course he'd want her, she was young, keen and athletic.

She went to bed early, turning off the lights behind the chil-dren as they fled up the stairs, anxious lest they be asked to switch on the dishwasher or bolt the front door. And being tired, she fell asleep quickly. But just after midnight, she woke, stiff with anxiety. A moment later, she heard why she had woken, and why she had woken so frightened. The gale, forecast for the following day, had begun.

A gust so strong the whole house shook got Althea out of bed and pulling on whatever clothes came to hand. Her plants were all out on the staging, exposed to every element. Some of them were irreplaceable. It was already raining hard.

Without giving herself time to think how lunatic her actions were, she wrote a note to the children, in case they woke and found her gone, and allowed the dog to go upstairs and creep into her warm bed. Then, after much searching, she found a torch and set off.

The car didn't start. 'Oh come on! Don't do this to me!'

She pulled out the choke and tried again, willing it to turn over. She found herself sweating as she kept the key turned, her foot pumping up and down on the accelerator. Eventually, when she realized she'd flooded the engine, she gave up. She would have to walk.

She was too anxious and jittery to take the time to go back into the house to get a proper coat, and besides, the dog might wake up, and then wake the chilen. The rain on her face was chastening, running into her eyes and making them sting. But she refused to listen to the voice of sanity in her head which told her no plants were worth walking through a gale for, risking being hit by flying roof tiles.

It was only when the house was out of sight that she started to be frightened of the dark. It was such a familiar journey, and she would never usually dream of being anxious about making it on foot, whatever the time of day or night. Whether it was the storm or her generally wound-up state, she found herself terrified of being jumped on, raped or mugged.

But she wouldn't let herself turn back. She held her torch like a club, determined to fight for her virtue with it if necessary. Her plants were her future, she must look after them. If anything happened to them it would be her fault. If she'd seen to them before, instead of running away, she wouldn't have to be doing this now. She'd abandoned her plants for the feeblest of reasons, and this was her penance.

And if all her plants were ruined, it would be indirectly because of Patrick and Jenny. Which in some confused way would mean they had somehow taken her chance of a new career as well as her happiness.

Althea's already leaking deck-shoes splashed through a particularly deep puddle, submerging them completely and soaking the hems of her trousers. She walked faster, her anxiety increasing as she got wetter and wetter. Bloody Patrick, bloody Jenny! And with Jenny leaving, she'd have either to do without her money, or find another lodger. It was all so unfair!

At that moment, a streak of lightning rent the air, swiftly followed by a thunder clap. One day, maybe even tomorrow, she would laugh at the pathetic picture she presented, soaking wet, hair clinging to her head in rat's tails, clutching on to her torch, scared out of her mind. Steven Spielberg couldn't have done it more convincingly. But now she couldn't laugh, she could only walk as fast as she could. She jogged for the last bit, only slowing down as she ducked through the fence.

It was difficult, picking her way through the deep trenches, holes and piles of spoil which were everywhere, slipping and sliding on the heaps of clay. But at least she was in her greenhouse. And while here she was in more genuine danger than she had been up to now, she felt comparatively safe.

Her torch revealed that so far, nothing had been damaged. She shone her torch up round the roof, to see if any more panes of glass had broken, but as yet, none had. But it was only a matter of time before the wind got underneath the panes and started flinging them about like tiddlywinks. She'd have to clear the bench completely instead of only moving the most delicate plants. And first she had to make more space. At present, there was only enough space underneath the bench for a few trays. It would have been a daunting task on a fine spring morning, now it seemed too huge even to attempt.

Something bounced on to the glass at the other end of the greenhouse and crashed off again, not breaking it. It forced Althea into action. The glass not breaking was pure fluke, she couldn't hope that the next loose tile would bounce off. Topaz had wanted the greenhouse pulled down. This gale might very well do the job for her.

Althea started to pull things out from under the staging, finding space for them further along. Luckily the staging was all in reasonable order, but under it were boxes and boxes of clay flower pots, broken crocks and ancient bottles of weedkiller, all left there for years.

When she thought she had enough space, she started to shift tray after tray of seedlings, the myriad pots. It took a long time, but at least the effort kept away the tears, which had been hovering all day. And the lightning, which was obligingly frequent, meant she could manage without the torch most of the time. The sound was deafening.

When, in a moment of quiet, she heard a voice behind her, she screamed. She knew, even before she'd drawn breath to do so, that it was Patrick, but her instinctive reaction was faster than her brain and the scream came out and her heart pounded.

'What the fucking hell are you doing here?' He was wearing jeans and a jumper, but nothing else. His hair was all over the place. His expression was a mixture of confusion, anger and amazement.

'What's it look like I'm doing here?' His swearing gave her backbone and she faced up to him. 'I'm getting my plants under the staging so they don't get damaged by broken glass.'

'For crying out loud, woman! You must be stark, staring mad!' His confusion and amazement had gone, leaving his anger undiluted and a hundred per cent proof. 'Never mind your fucking plants! You might have been killed! There are tiles falling off all over the place, it would only take one to come through the glass and you could be cut to pieces!'

A clap of thunder drowned the last of his words. Althea waited for it to rumble away before retaliating.

'Well, don't just stand there swearing, give me a hand! And put some shoes on! There's broken glass down here already.'

Patrick looked for a moment as if he might snatch her up and fling her through the greenhouse into the storm. Althea felt like she'd just picked an argument with The Terminator – having right on her side was just not enough. She lowered her eyes.

'I'm sorry, it's the mother in me,' she apologized, without looking at him. She turned away and went back to shifting boxes of flower pots.

Her heart ached for a moment, when she realized he'd gone, but she had no time for feelings just now, there were still so many trays to move. She was dragging a huge stone crock filled with hand tools, bags of fertiliser and coir, when she felt the weight of it taken from her, and two wellington-booted feet appeared under her gaze.

They worked together, and when everything was moved, Patrick banged pieces of batten over the bubble wrap Althea had put up, making the whole place less vulnerable. 'That should keep the worst out,' he said.

'It doesn't matter so much now, anyway,' said Althea. 'Now the plants are safe.' She suddenly felt achingly tired. She shivered convulsively. While she was working, the effort had kept her warm in spite of her soaking clothes, now they clung to her, ice-cold. Her teeth started to chatter.

'You're freezing. Come into the house,' he said.

Althea opened her mouth to refuse, but he had put his hand on her shoulder and, without exactly pushing, was manoeuvring her ahead of him, out of the door, across the building site.

'You need a hot bath. Yes, it is plumbed in,' he added, forestalling her next question. 'Go upstairs. There's loads of hot water. You'll have to use my towel, but it's fairly clean.'

CHAPTER EIGHTEEN

The bath was white cast iron on ball and claw feet. The wash basin matched it. In one corner there was a shower cubicle, obviously unplumbed. There was tongue-and-groove boarding along one wall, which was obviously intended to extend to all of them. It made a change from tiles, she thought. Would the tongue and groove be painted or just varnished? she wondered.

One day, it would be a bathroom to die for. At the moment, the floor was dirty plywood and the curtains were obviously a stop-gap – the merest concession to modesty made necessary by the harsh single bulb which lit the room. But as promised, the water was hot and plentiful and the bath was fairly clean. She watched the water steaming into it as she pulled off her clammy clothes.

It was boiling, but, reluctant to add any cold, she got into it inch by inch, not sure if the water was really too hot, or if it was just the contrast to her own shivering flesh. Eventually, she lay down full length and sighed the sigh of a true voluptuary.

After a while she washed her hair and soaped herself, but it was an effort to do anything but lie there. Knowing she would fall asleep if she stayed much longer, she dragged herself up, her body as scarlet as any boiled lobster. Dizzy from the heat, she padded across the bare floor, leaving wet footprints on the plywood and enveloped herself in Patrick's towel.

It was hanging on a heated rail under a bathroom cabinet. It smelt of maleness and his aftershave, and for a few moments she buried her head in it, breathing in his scent, until she felt less faint. Then masochism mixed with curiosity made her open the cabinet.

There was nothing feminine in it at all, no shampoo other than the supermarket brand he favoured, no female deodorant or perfume. Whether she'd really been expecting to see a bottle of Jenny's Tea Tree Shampoo, her organic deodorant or fennel toothpaste, she didn't know, but not seeing any trace of her lodger in Patrick's bathroom was a huge relief.

She felt better, but not better enough to wipe the condensation from the mirror. Wet hair and a bright red face only worked on the very young, and her streak of masochism wasn't strong enough to make her confront her reflection.

She dried herself slowly. After being so het up and strained for such a long time, it was as if the elastic had snapped. Her limbs were heavy, she felt sleepy and totally relaxed. She looked at her clothes lying in a puddle on the floor and knew she couldn't put them on again. They were cold, wet and dirty and had not been overly attractive when clean and dry. She had been wearing baggy, comfortable, patterned trousers, with a loose cotton top, in bottle green. Individually, William told her, they were nice clothes. It was the combination that created the Pregnant Clown look he objected to. What she yearned for was a soft, old, full-length cotton nightie she could just go to bed in. The thought of fighting her way back through the storm was too horrid to contemplate. She gathered up her unsavoury bundle and went in search of an airing cupboard. Patrick would have something he could lend her.

There being no airing cupboard as yet, she found herself looking at Patrick's open bedroom door. Her need for clothes was genuine, but it was her burning, dangerous curiosity about what she would find there that led her across the hallway to the open door. She felt like Bluebeard's wife as she stepped inside.

She hadn't heard him come upstairs, so his presence by the unmade bed startled her.

'Oh, I'm sorry,' she said. 'I was just looking for something to put on.'

The room was lit by a single bedside lamp. A book was open face down next to it. A glass of water had been knocked over and a puddle lay on the bare floorboards. He had obviously got up in a great hurry.

'Of course, there should be something.'

He crossed to a huge Victorian chest of drawers, one of the

few pieces of furniture in a room so large it could have taken several such pieces without being over-crowded. Althea's room was small, even with only her in it. The view from this room would be wonderful. Now, the night sky pressed against the glass; the lightning, further away now, gave the room brief, blue floodlighting. It was not a room to be alone in.

She watched as he sorted through clothes, aware that he was still angry with her. She thought, when he'd invited her in, that he'd forgiven her for disturbing him. But she could tell from his back that he had not.

'How did you know I was in the greenhouse?' she asked.

He stopped rummaging and turned. 'Not sure. The thunder woke me, I suppose. Then I saw your torch moving about.'

'And you thought I was burglars?'

'No. I thought it was you.'

'So why did you come rushing down?'

Lightning, much further off now, flicked across his face, throwing up sharp shadows from his large nose and jutting chin. 'So you wouldn't get yourself killed.' He spoke matter of factly, but his mouth was tense and his expression cold.

Althea tried to add a little levity to the occasion. 'You might have got killed yourself.'

He made a small gesture. 'You did say you needed something to put on.'

'If you don't mind lending me something. My clothes are wet.'

'Some clothes would certainly be a good idea.'

He turned back to the chest, sitting on his heels. She came to see what he was finding for her. She didn't want him producing a pair of size ten jeans discarded by Topaz, knowing she wouldn't get them past her knees.

'Would you mind not doing that?' he said curtly.

'What?'

'Coming up behind me.'

Hurt, she backed off. 'Sorry.'

'I'm not a goddam saint,' he growled. 'You're a woman I've wanted for some time now, you're naked, and you're in my bedroom. Please don't stand too close.'

Althea's cooling body heated up again with embarrassment at

his words and shame at her own actions. She was not a girl, she was a grown-up woman and some part of her was aware of what she was doing, even if it wasn't the thinking part, the part with morals.

'Sorry,' she said again, holding the towel more tightly.

'I would hate to have you accusing me of rape,' he went on bitterly, pulling jumpers and pairs of jeans about without apparently looking at them.

'I would never do that,' she assured him, anxious to calm his growing anger.

He rose up from his haunches like a giant. 'Wouldn't you? Not even if I did this?' Although she had moved almost to the other side of the room, it took him only two strides to reach her. Then he wrapped both arms round her and held her very tightly, crushing her ribs, looking into her eyes as if trying to bore through to her mind, willing her to reject him, to demand to be released.

Althea licked her lips. Breathing was difficult, and not only because it was restricted. 'Probably not.'

He looked into her face for a second longer, then his gaze transferred to her mouth. She swallowed and licked her lips, then she closed her eyes.

The crushing, suffocating feel of his mouth on hers was a relief in spite of the turmoil it created. She hadn't been certain he wouldn't push her away, and if he had, she didn't think she could have borne the rejection.

Her arms went round him, hugging him as hard as he was hugging her. She gave him back kiss for angry kiss, her teeth clashing against his, scrunching his hair in her fingers, relishing its wiry strength. They clung as shipwrecked mariners cling to rocks, as if their lives depended on getting as close as possible. And when he lifted her off her feet and carried her across the room, still kissing her, still crushing her to him, and she landed on the bed which was warm from his body, she felt she had come home.

'Are you sure?' he breathed. He'd pulled off his sweater and his hands were at the button of his jeans. 'You've always seemed so –'

'Yes, yes, I'm sure,' said Althea quickly, before the million defence mechanisms which kept her safe had a chance to operate.

'I'll find something to put on.' He turned away and started rummaging on the side table for his wallet.

Althea closed her eyes. Hurry, hurry, she breathed, before my good sense comes back. But even as she tried to hold it off, it filtered through her initial passion, cold water on a sun-warmed back.

'It's all right,' he said. 'I've got a condom.'

Althea swallowed. She couldn't tell him that she'd changed her mind, not now. That would be the worst form of coquettishness. If only he hadn't stopped to find a condom, she thought. It would have been fine – more than fine, it probably would have been wonderful – if complete insanity. But it was no good. She'd gone this far, she'd have to go through with it. She tried a smile but it didn't work and she turned it into a cough.

'Do take off the towel,' he said, watching her, still wearing his jeans. 'I'm not sure it's your colour.'

'No.' She couldn't. Yet a few moments ago she wanted him so badly she would have risked Aids. Now she couldn't bear the thought of him seeing her naked. 'You go first,' she added.

Patrick smiled, all his anger gone, a man who knew he could have the woman he wanted, and was prepared to wait for his pleasure. 'All right.' He stripped off his jeans slowly and Althea saw he wasn't wearing underpants. He must have got dressed in even more of a hurry than she did.

Althea swallowed, fighting back the prickle of fear which the sight of a naked man gave her after so many lonely years. He was in splendid shape: all that tennis and squash, all those foreign holidays with Topaz had made him lean and tanned, long-legged and athletic.

Her own pale, plump flesh seemed unworthy to lie next to his well-honed body. She felt too old, too marked by childbirth to expose herself. He got into bed next to her and she shuffled away to one side, still keeping her towel tightly around her.

'This bed isn't big enough for three of us,' he said, tugging at it.

She held it tight. 'Yes it is. We've shared smaller beds than this – nearly.'

'Maybe, but for what I've got planned, we need space.'

'This is a big bed.' It was no time to get cold feet and she couldn't possibly back out, but the passion which had led her into his room and more or less into his arms had vanished, leaving her as terrified as any virgin bride. There seemed no alternative but to lie back and think of England.

'Darling, what is it?' He turned to her, propping his head on his hand. 'What's the matter? Why have you gone shy on me?'

'At least you said shy and not coy.'

'Why don't you want me to see your body?'

She buried her head in the pillow so she couldn't see him watching her. 'I'm nearly forty, I've had three children' – she swallowed – 'and Juno thinks I should lose two stone.'

He laughed. Hearing him, horrified, she opened her eyes to look at him reproachfully.

'I'm sorry,' he said. 'It's just so ridiculous. You've got a luscious figure and you're years younger than me. What are you worrying about?'

'You haven't had babies.' She shut her eyes again and muttered 'cellulite' inaudibly into the duvet.

'Have you changed your mind?'

He didn't sound angry, but he was definitely tense. Althea didn't blame him. 'No, of course not,' she squeaked, her voice high with anxiety.

'You don't need to lie,' he said softly, the tension still apparent. 'I'm not an adolescent about to tell you that I'll be terribly damaged if you don't let me make love to you.'

'No.'

'So you have changed your mind?'

Althea hated herself. She felt so strung up every part of her seemed about to snap. 'A bit.'

Her voice was so soft and croaky, she didn't think he'd heard. Just as well. It would be better if he just went ahead and made love to her. It didn't matter if she didn't enjoy it, she really couldn't deny him now. In her heart she wanted him, had wanted him, for a long time. It wouldn't be rape, even if she hated every minute of it.

His hearing must have been excellent. He exhaled very slowly, and turned out the light. 'I'll tell you what.' He spoke softly into the darkness. 'We won't make love, we'll just cuddle.'

Relief and disappointment made her relax her grip on the towel and he tugged it out of her hands. She would have pulled it back again except that before she could, their bodies had touched. The feeling of skin on skin was so delicious, warm and soothing that Althea's tension lessened immediately.

'Turn over with your back to me,' he ordered. 'Then you won't feel threatened. I'll just cuddle you from behind, like this.'

He tugged her pillow so her head was supported. It was so comforting lying in the arms of a man, Althea felt she could have lain there all night. For a few moments he kept perfectly still, his knees drawn up under hers, his arms supporting her body, his chest warm against her back.

Then his hands shifted so they enclosed her breasts, one in each hand. This felt better still. She liked the feeling of his warm hands cherishing her body. In fact it was all fine, perfectly chaste, perfectly safe. Until he started to move his thumbs.

It was only when their movement had an instant, dramatic effect that she realized that his thumbs were directly over her nipples. As rapidly as it had faded, her sexual desire started galloping back. But she didn't say anything. Changing one's mind might be a female prerogative, but not even the saint he declared he wasn't would tolerate a libido like a revolving door.

The movement of his thumbs continued, until, unbidden, a little groan escaped her. His hands took up the refrain, so not only her nipples were being stroked, but her breasts as well.

He didn't speak, or move, or indicate in any way that he wasn't perfectly happy to go on stroking her breasts all night. It was Althea who spun round in his arms and flung herself against him, all her doubts and fears washed away by passion.

'At last,' he breathed. 'I've wanted this for so long.'

'So have I,' she replied.

He was a patient, painstaking lover, and soon she'd forgotten all about not wanting him to see her naked. She made no complaint when he turned the light on, but revelled in the feelings he excited in her, her heart and mind at one with her passionate body.

Later, seconds before the moment when foreplay became the

torture of deprivation, when he asked her, his voice husky and breathless, if she wanted to change her mind again, she bit his shoulder, pushed him over on his back and climbed on top of him.

She no longer felt fat and frumpy, she felt beautiful, sexy, triumphant. It was only in the very furthest recesses of her mind that she realized sex had not been like this before. The feeling was new and empowering and strange. Never before had she felt able to use her body in a way to produce such extreme emotions both in herself and the man she loved.

Together they rolled around and around, until eventually they fell out of bed and landed on the bare floor, pulling the duvet with them. It was there that they finally came together, then fell apart to lie, panting, sweating, exhausted.

They lay in silence for a while until Patrick suggested they get back into bed. 'Otherwise we'll be terribly stiff in the morning.'

'I can't be here in the morning!' she said, feeling as if a bucket of water had been tipped over her. 'I must go home, now.'

Patrick protested, but not much. He could see she was set on returning home, and understood her reasons. Her children couldn't wake up and find their mother missing. Nor could she creep home in the dark of the dawn.

'I'll drive you,' he said. 'I'll find you something to put on and take you home.'

'Thanks.' She didn't try and dissuade him. If she'd protested and he had agreed that there was no point in them both going out into the night, she'd have wanted to kill herself. Remorse would come with the daylight, and with it a douche of reality which would be unbearable. She couldn't face the journey home alone, on foot, and in the rain.

She made him drop her a little way away, so no one would hear his car. Now the storm had passed, the night seemed preternaturally silent. She let herself into the house, her body still warm from the quick bath she'd taken before getting into his jeans and jumper, her limbs still softened and relaxed by their lovemaking. But her heart was already having regrets.

She had been mad, she had behaved like a woman with no family, no responsibilities, instead of one with plenty of responsibilities but no job. It was like being drunk, she decided, not quite drunk enough to forget everything, but drunk enough to know you would have a hell of a hangover in the morning. It was when you started drinking pints of water, litres of orange juice, in an effort to stave off the inevitable, and sometimes it worked. But no amount of vitamin C or fluid would prevent the devastating reaction she knew she would have. She got to sleep with the aid of two aspirin, a hot-water bottle and the World Service, and woke up late.

She banged on William's door. 'It's half past seven, time to get up!' She opened his door and his duvet shifted.

'Mum! I don't have to go in until half ten!'

Althea retreated, wondering if she would ever get used to William going to school just for lessons now he was in the sixth form. She went up the stairs to the attic, where Rupert slept.

'Darling?' She put her head round the door. 'Time to get up.' While her son groaned and rolled over, she gathered up socks which were scattered about the floor. 'Now I know why you boys are always running out of socks,' she said. 'They're all up here. You haven't gone back to sleep, have you?'

Merry was much easier to wake. She liked to get up early, to give herself plenty of time to pack her bag and do her hair. The children were supposed to make their own sandwiches. They were, they all agreed, quite old enough. But Althea could never relax until she'd seen them put lunch boxes into their bags, although she knew perfectly well they wouldn't die if they forgot and had to go hungry.

This morning, groggy from aspirin and lack of sleep, not to mention a guilty conscience worthy of a mass murderer, she was especially worried. She gave them a time check every five minutes until Merry told her she was worse than the radio.

'OK, but do keep an eye on the clock, or you'll miss your lift.'

'When I was Merry's age, I walked to school,' said William, who didn't have to hurry. Althea ignored him.

'Have you done your teeth?' she said to Rupert, who was eating a bowl of muesli oat by oat.

'After my breakfast, Mum!'

'OK, but have you done your lunch?'

Rupert put on a pleading expression which never failed him. 'Could you?'

Althea found rolls in the freezer, fished Merry's games skirt out of the washing machine, gave it a cursory iron to dry it and came back into the kitchen, assuring her daughter that wearing it wet wouldn't give her pneumonia. Someone had put on a tape, and Althea, as usual, found herself yelling, 'Will you please tell me what do you want in your rolls?' across the kitchen, while her children had a deep, meaningful Buddhist discussion about death.

But at last the kitchen was empty and silent. She had her hand on the telephone to ring Patrick, to tell him that last night was a one-off, a never-to-be-repeated experience that they had better both forget, when it rang. It felt like an electric shock under her shaking fingers, and when she heard Patrick's voice she nearly dropped it.

'Ally? Is that you?'

Hearing him use her pet name made her weak with longing. 'Yes, is that you, Patrick?' She sounded very crisp and business-like. Good. She pulled a chair from under the kitchen table and sat on it, the first time she had sat all day.

'I meant to tell you last night, but there never seemed a moment . . .'

'What?'

'I've got to go away. It's been booked for ages – I would have mentioned it . . .'

'When are you going?'

'I'm leaving for the airport at ten. I have to go to Madrid.'

'Oh.'

'Are you all right? I wouldn't dream of leaving like this if I could help it.'

'It's all right, I'm fine.'

'We'll talk when I get back. It should be before Christmas.'

'Fine.'

'You don't sound fine.'

'I am. I'm just a bit harassed after getting the children off to school. It was better when I was going out to work too, I didn't have time to fuss over them.'

'I see.'

It was the perfect moment for Althea to end the conversation, but in spite of all her regrets, she couldn't bring herself to. 'Why Madrid?'

'The firm's got a branch there. We're designing an office complex.'

'Oh good.' She swallowed. 'Well, must get on.'

'Yes, I must.' He paused. 'Ally, you'll be all right, won't you?'

'Of course. I always have been, you know.'

She hadn't meant to sound hard and detached, but she could tell by his curt 'So you have', that she had done.

'Goodbye, Althea.'

'Goodbye, Patrick.'

It was only when the house was empty, and she had made sure that she'd put out the dustbins, fed the guinea-pigs and put on the washing, that she allowed herself to cry

CHAPTER NINETEEN

'I really want to have them here,' said Juno, adjusting the little mat under her cup of raspberry-leaf tea. 'I can't travel all the way up to Scotland in my condition.'

'You can't have a family Christmas in your condition! I'll have them at my house. With Jenny gone, there's plenty of room. You and Kenneth can come and spend the day. It'll be fun.'

This was not what she meant, but Althea felt strongly that doing Christmas for their parents, herself and her children, Kenneth, and a very large bulge, would be too much even for Juno.

Her sister, always reluctant to accept advice, thought otherwise. 'Nonsense. You know how critical Mummy is about your house and how you've never got enough matching plates. And besides, you can't possibly afford it.'

'I would accept charity, you know. You could buy the turkey.'

Juno was adamant. 'No, I want this last Christmas at home. You can help.'

'Juny!' It was more of a plea than a protest. 'It's not a last Christmas! Have it next year and it'll be the baby's first Christmas. It'll be magic, little hands pulling off wrapping paper, more interested in the boxes than the presents . . .'

Althea may have been touched by this picture, but Juno obviously wasn't. 'I've already asked them. The parents will arrive on Christmas Eve. We'll have the neighbours in for drinks at six, as usual. I'm much more organized than you. It'll be less hassle all round to have it here.'

'Well, you must let me help. And I'll bring a pudding.'

'Actually, I've already ordered one from the National Trust.'

'Oh. A cake?'

'Chatsworth. They do a *really* good one. And I've ordered two dozen mince pies from a woman in the village. She uses organic, wholemeal flour, soya margarine and vegetarian mincemeat.

Much healthier than all that suet. Not that I shall eat any of this of course, but Daddy appreciates it.'

Knowing full well that her father hated anything which smacked of health food and would much prefer her own light-as-air mince pies, Althea resolved to give him some as a present.

'Well, I shall make a trifle,' she said firmly, half hurt, half relieved. 'I get terribly sick of all that dried fruit.'

'That would be lovely,' said Juno, belatedly aware of being less than gracious. 'And, of course, I'd love a hand with the veg.'

'Of course,' Althea agreed, aware that if she wasn't careful, by Boxing Day she would be nursing a bad case of sprout-peeler's thumb.

'Mummy will help too, I'm sure.'

'It'll be fine. My children will help with the spuds.'

'Oh good.' Juno hesitated. 'You wouldn't like me to invite anyone else, would you? Patrick, perhaps?'

Althea almost felt herself go white. 'Oh no, I don't think so. He's bound to be busy, and we're not – seeing each other, or anything. In fact, he's away and may not even be back.'

'If you're not seeing him, how do you know he's away?'

'Well, he told me. Just in passing.'

'But he might like to be invited. You know how it is for divorced people without new families.'

'Yes I do. But there'll be so many people already.'

'I know. That's why one more wouldn't make any difference. My table's big enough and my dinner service does twelve.'

Althea wondered briefly whether, if she had begged Juno to invite Patrick on bended knees, Juno would have refused if she couldn't have provided him with a matching plate. 'I really wish you wouldn't. He would be terribly embarrassed and assume you were trying to push us together.'

'It seems such a shame that you haven't got a boyfriend. I mean, you're quite attractive and everything.'

'Well, I don't think it's a shame. I mean, I've decided that I really can't have relationships with the children the ages they are.'

'Why not? They know the facts of life, don't they?'

'Knowing them is one thing. Imagining their mother doing them is quite another.' Althea compressed her lips together between her teeth. 'I'm their only role model. With Frederick running off with Topaz like that, I have to do the right thing. And the boys would hate me to bring another man into their lives. It's Oedipal, they couldn't help it.'

Juno, usually quick to react, to judge, to advise, was silent for some time. 'Is that what being a parent is all about? Sacrificing everything for them?'

Althea thought for a moment before answering. 'I don't feel I've sacrificed very much worth having, but yes, I suppose it is.' Althea saw Juno take this in like a dose of nasty but efficacious vitamins. 'Would you like me to make you a wreath for your front door this year?' she added by way of a spoonful of honey.

Juno turned her mind to this new problem and for a moment looked as if she was about to say, no thank you, she'd ordered one from Moyses Stevens, but thought better of it. 'That would be lovely. And in fact, I've got one or two friends who'd like one. Could earn you a little extra money.'

'That would be useful.' Not as useful as a lot of extra money would have been, but every little helped.

'In fact' – Juno leant as close to Althea as she could, given her advanced state of pregnancy – 'Diana Sanders was saying just the other day that the part she really hates about Christmas was decorating the house.'

'Really? That's the part I like best. It's the shopping that gets me down.'

'So I was just thinking, why don't you offer to do it for her? For a fee, of course.'

'You mean she'd let a complete stranger go in and put up her Christmas decs?'

'Why not? She had an interior designer to choose her bath-room fittings.' Juno shot Althea an anxious glance. 'As long as it's all neutral greenstuff and tartan ribbon, nothing tacky.'

'But I wouldn't know how much to charge, or anything.'

'Leave all that side of it to me. I'll ask Di and see if she's got any friends who are just as busy.' Juno made a leap of faith. 'You can start with me. You know I have absolutely no imagination.'

Althea did know. Juno was fine with colour charts and swatches, but when it came to knowing what to do with half a holly bush and several metres of ivy, she was lost. 'I'll tell you what, I'll do your house, for nothing, but early. Then you can have Diana round and ask her if she'd like me to do her house. I would make sure that every design was totally individual.'

'What a good idea. But are you sure I can't pay you? I know how strapped you are just now . . .'

'I'm sure. I may be poor, but I have my pride.' Althea patted Juno's hand to reassure her that her feelings weren't really hurt beyond repair. 'I must go. I promised I'd call in on Sylvia. I haven't seen her for ages and there's a governors' meeting next week I've got to take the minutes for. I need to know if there's anything I need to know.'

It still felt odd to be taking minutes at a governors' meeting when she was no longer a member of staff. She handed round the attendance book, wondering how many governors would turn up for this special meeting. They jolly well ought to, she mused, seeing another couple of cars draw up. New buildings were important.

It was, of course, a huge relief that Patrick wouldn't be there. He was still away, and wouldn't have come anyway, seeing that he was directly involved and unable to vote. But she couldn't keep away the nagging yearning sensation which haunted her these days. Although his presence would have been acutely embarrasing, knowing he wouldn't appear was depressing.

'I think we should press on,' said Mrs Jenkinstown, who had been elected Chairman of the governors of the new school, as no one else seemed willing to do it. 'Anyone not here who hasn't sent apologies?'

The table was respectably full. Mrs Jenkinstown was pleased. But could all these eager governors be trusted to make the right decision? Althea realized that she would be very cross and upset if they didn't.

'Have we all had a good look at the plans? Is there anything that needs clarifying? No? Good. Then shall we briefly remind ourselves . . .'

Althea's hand moved over the paper automatically. Why couldn't Mrs J go straight into a vote, and put her out of her misery? But she was an old hand at committee work. You got more done by going through the drill than by cutting corners. Indeed, Althea had got up and made the tea before the voting stage came. But when it did, she was pleased to note in her most careful shorthand, that the result was resoundingly in favour of the plans submitted by the Greenwich Partnership.

'Would you mind awfully telling Patrick?' Mrs Jenkinstown asked under the hubbub of circulating chocolate digestives. 'I mean, I know you and he are special friends. And you should be the one to break the good news because it was partly down to you, you know.'

'Was it?'

'Oh yes. The governors were all very impressed by you entertaining that French couple so well. They saw it as Patrick doing his bit for the school. And when he's such a new governor, and unlike most of them, not actually a parent, it looked well.'

'I should think Patrick would prefer his designs to be chosen on merit,' she said primly.

'Oh, this lot wouldn't know good design if it got up and bit them! And I know Patrick would prefer you to tell him.'

'That's as may be,' said Althea, allowing her asperity to show. 'But as he's out of the country, he'll have to hear it via the firm.'

'Oh, shame. He's such a nice man, you know.'

'I know,' said Althea. 'But he's nothing to do with me!'

Juno, who had taken maternity leave and was therefore bored, spent her spare time bullying her friends into having their houses decorated for Christmas by Althea. Althea enjoyed doing it. It didn't take long, they all gave her a completely free hand, and it allowed her to snoop inside other people's houses and very often ravish their gardens for greenstuff. It also gave her an opportunity to tell them that if ever they wanted their gardens remodelled, she would be able to help.

With a supplement from the precious thousand pound prize money, it was thus that Althea scraped together enough money to provide her children with Christmas stockings and presents. All her other presents were homemade. Juno and her mother were getting massive arrangements of flowers, grown and dried by Althea, which could sit in a fireplace until they grew too dusty. She had made her father lemon curd and potted kumquats which she'd put in pretty jam jars with doilies and ribbon and stylish, handwritten labels as well as the mince pies. Sylvia, as promised, got fudge, as did anyone else who didn't want dried flowers or bowls of hyacinths.

By Christmas Eve, at Juno's drinks party, wearing her scarlet birthday dress, she was feeling very tired and had lost any fondness she might have had for oscillating fairy lights and lametta. She was also missing Patrick and wished fervently she hadn't been so adamant about telling Juno she didn't want him invited.

But it would have been no good. He would have either wanted to talk or not wanted to talk, and either would have been a disaster. She contented herself with drinking rather too much mulled wine and eating too many healthy mince pies – neglected in favour of cheese straws by most of the guests. She spent most of the evening talking to her mother about Juno's chosen method of childbirth and reassuring her that Juno had no intention of eating the placenta, fried with onions. Her mother had heard about this on the radio and had immediately feared the worst. When William drove Althea home she was a little drunk but not at all happy.

And, as usual, she had forgotten to pre-pack the stockings and had to wait until her children were all asleep before she could do it. Since they had more stamina and less alcohol in their bloodstreams than she did, she found this difficult. At least they weren't expected at Juno's until after lunch. She and the children could have their traditional walk with Bozo and open their presents to each other before dressing in their best and presenting themselves for kitchen duty.

Why was it she wasn't looking forward to it? Last year she'd had Christmas at her house and was exhausted by nine o'clock in the morning. She had yearned for a chance for the four of them to spend Christmas morning alone, nothing expected of anyone except happiness. She'd had no man in her life then and had been perfectly content with that. So why wasn't she this Christmas?

Instead she felt a deep emptiness. She envied Juno both her coming baby and her kind and loving husband. Even her parents, who spent a great deal of time bickering, at least had each other to bicker with. No wonder the suicide rate went up at this time of year. Everything conspired to make the lonely feel lonelier and even the perfectly content feel unhappy. Next year she would arrange to be in a coma for the entire fortnight, send the children to Hong Kong and Bozo to stay with Sylvia. Bloody Patrick! Why did he have to go and seduce her like that? It thoroughly upset her carefully balanced life.

'Hello, darlings!' Althea's mother kissed her firmly, without waiting for her daughter to put down her armful of presents and cling-film covered trifle. 'Oh. You've brought the dog.'

'Hello, Mummy darling. How are you?' Althea returned the kiss with difficulty, ignoring the reference to Bozo, who was mincing along behind her.

Juno and her mother, who agreed on little, were in accord when it came to dogs on the furniture. Together they berated Althea for her slackness in this department. But they accepted that it was a long time to leave the little dog on her own and acknowledged that she looked extremely decorative curled up on a silk cushion. Bozo, knowing her presence was only just tolerated, always behaved very politely, sitting down whenever she was addressed and only speaking when spoken to.

The children billowed in behind their mother on a cloud of Happy Christmases, their arms equally full. It was four o'clock in the afternoon, and they had already exchanged their presents. The rest were to be opened according to the ritual Juno dictated, after tea. They came somewhat reluctantly. All their best presents had been left behind and they had nothing much to hope for now apart from extra-thick socks and educational tomes.

William, who was carrying a Linda McCartney vegetarian turkey dinner, a jar of brandy butter and several carrier bags, allowed himself to be kissed with good-natured calm. Rupert, who had a huge cardboard box full of presents he was controlling with his chin, was more reluctant. Merry was carrying the dog basket, in the vain hope that Bozo might sit in it. She put it down and flung her arms round her granny with genuine enthusiasm. Granny Vanessa got on better with girls than boys.

Juno was in the kitchen, looking flushed and tired. Althea remembered the Christmases when she had been pregnant, unable to stomach the sight of all that turkey fat, having to throw up between bastings. Althea dumped her load on the kitchen table.

'Darling.' She kissed her sister. 'You look all in. Go and sit down.'

'Actually, I do feel a bit poorly. Kenneth has done the turkey, but the potatoes aren't in yet and we need to open our presents.'

Althea remembered when this felt like a chore to her, too. 'What about the tea?'

'That's all set up in the drawing room. All you need to do is boil the kettle and make it. If you could just peel the potatoes first. The mince pies are heating in the warming oven.'

'You go and sit down,' urged Althea. 'I'll just go and say hello to Daddy and Kenneth, then I'll come in and set to.'

For once, Juno did as she was told. But being tired, sick and seated did not have a mellowing effect on her. She still insisted that everything should be done exactly as she would have done it, had she been able. Once Althea had made the tea in the silver pot, remembered the tea-strainer and the sugar tongs, presents were opened in strict order. Starting with the youngest, one present was opened, the paper folded and a note made of what it was and who it was from. Then the next youngest opened one, and so on.

It took hours. Their mother had brought with her all the presents she and her husband had been given, and as Mrs Kent exchanged gifts with an enormous number of people, she had more to open than everyone else. Thus, Althea's children were forced to watch their grandmother open endless boxes of bath cubes, pot-pourri and padded hangers from people they'd never heard of. Rupert and Merry started to bicker and Althea was forced to keep jumping up and down to replenish the tea-pot or see whether the potatoes had finally come to the boil and could go into the oven. Her father went to sleep. When the last carrier-bag-tidy had been duly admired and the fun part of the day was over, at Juno's request, Althea hoovered the drawing room, wondering as she did so if Juno wasn't pleading her belly a shade too much.

Then, rather than sit around and make polite conversation, she offered to set the table, but was forestalled by her mother.

'I'll do it, darling. It is a special occasion.'

'Can we go and watch television in the den?' asked Rupert.

'Ask Kenneth,' said Althea. 'Mother, I do know how to do it.'

'I'm sure you do, darling, but I never forget the time you put all the knives with their blades facing outwards. Mrs Higgins was coming to lunch and I was so embarrassed.'

'Mummy! I was ten years old!'

'Oh well, if you insist. I was only trying to help.'

Juno, who had been dozing, suddenly woke up and heaved herself upright. 'I'd better do it. Althea mustn't and Mummy always puts the spoons in the wrong place.'

'Nonsense! It's terribly vulgar to put them where you do . . .'

Althea retreated to the kitchen and started on the sprouts, mildly curious about what she did to knives and forks that was so offensive and which of those strong-minded women would get their own way with the spoons. She was just deciding that she'd peeled and crossed quite enough sprouts when Kenneth came into the room.

'Althea? I think Juno needs you.'

Kenneth had been stoically keeping Althea supplied with drinks, basting the turkey and generally making sure that his wife and her mother didn't fight, and that his father-in-law and his nephews really were happy watching television. Now, he sounded worried.

'Oh God. Where is she?'

'Gone upstairs to lie down. She's got backache, but when I suggested phoning the doctor, she bit my head off.'

'Oh dear, poor Kenneth. She's probably OK, just worn out. I did try to tell her not to have Christmas here.'

Kenneth nodded. 'So did I. Will you come up and see her?'

Juno was lying in the middle of her pure white silk bed with her hand over her eyes. 'It hurts, Ally.'

'I know. You're not due yet, you've probably overdone it. You're not bleeding? Your waters haven't broken or anything?'

'No.'

'No reason to call an ambulance just yet, then.'

'Oh Althea! Don't tell me you want to rush me off to hospital like Kenneth does! I keep telling Kenneth that I'm not ill, I'm having a baby. It's a perfectly natural process.'

'He's worried about you. We all are. And the baby's not due for another month.'

'I know when my baby's due, thank you very much.'

'Are you sure it's only backache?'

Juno turned on to her side and groaned. 'Yes.'

'Would you like me to massage it for you?'

Juno nodded, murmuring, when she had finished, 'Thank you, Ally. I feel much better, but I think I'll just lie here for a bit. I might get up later, when the dinner's ready.'

Althea left the room, content that her sister wasn't in danger, and wishing that she too could lie down and not get up until it was all on the table.

Her mother was in the kitchen, reassured about her daughter, but taking her anxiety out on the meal. 'I can't find the pressure cooker for the pudding. I know she's got one because I gave it to her!'

And Althea knew that Juno had got rid of it because it was made of aluminium. 'It's much quicker in the microwave, really, Mummy, don't worry.'

'And where does Juno keep her good china? These plain white plates are all very well, but they're a bit boring for Christmas.'

'Why don't you leave all this to me? I know my way round Juno's kitchen better than you do.' Her mother still hesitated. 'And Merry really wants you to teach her to knit. I put some needles and some wool in her stocking, but as I can't do it myself . . .'

'Really? Well then . . .'

Her mother thus removed, Althea considered the meal. Should she do it as Juno would have done it, seeing as it was her house? Or should she go with her mother, who had different ideas about the correct way to do things and was easily as dogmatic? Or, and this thought flitted across her mind like an evil fairy, should she do it as she would like it?

Althea sipped her drink, which had been upgraded to whisky, wondering what would happen if she served the meal in the kitchen, on boring white plates, with napkins folded in half, not like bishops' mitres, household candles stuck in bottles instead of silver candelabra, and only one knife, fork and spoon per person instead of rows of them. She was sorely tempted. Unfortunately her role was to be the conduit of stronger-minded women, who liked things just so, and Althea felt obliged to interpret their wishes as best she could, knowing that in the eyes of one, if not both, she would be doing it wrong.

Juno had just sent down a message to check that the chestnuts were ready to go in with the sprouts, and did Althea know which dish to use for the bread sauce; her mother had decided that the forks weren't clean enough and had set about cleaning them, a process which involved newspapers and most of the kitchen table; the children had all announced they were starving and that Grandpa had changed the channel before the end of the film, when the door bell rang. Althea decided the house was full of people who could open it and carried on worrying about the giblets, which her mother had insisted on boiling, filling the kitchen with steam and nauseating smells, and didn't stir. It rang again.

'Isn't anybody but me capable of doing anything?' she said to no one in particular and stalked to the front door.

There, his arms full of presents and a huge poinsettia, stood Patrick.

CHAPTER TWENTY

'What the bloody hell are you doing here?' Althea demanded.

'I was invited!' Patrick came in through the front door and dumped his presents on the floor. Then he opened his arms.

He caught her completely off her guard, and like a magnet she found herself pressed against him, unaware if she had gone into his arms of her own accord or if he had pulled her. They were like a haven, a steel corset which supported her even as it crushed her. There was a faint spattering of rain on the shoulders of his overcoat which wet her hair, and she had to stand on tiptoe to keep her balance.

His mouth, cold, hard, insistent, moved over her own with a tender thoroughness as he crushed her to him, and his collar caught at her earring.

All the separate, various emotions that Althea had been feeling homogenized into passion. She could have gone on kissing him for ever, feeling his tongue explore her mouth, causing a series of minor explosions over its sensitive surfaces. His teeth, hard against the softness of her inner lip, his lips pressing against her own made her knees weaken and her jaw tremble. Although she hadn't wanted him to come, couldn't breathe and was now nearly falling over with excess emotion, she didn't want him to let her go, ever.

'What's going on?' said her mother. 'Who is this?'

Patrick dropped her as if from a great height. Althea, short of breath and unsteady on her feet, desperately tried to get her mind and her limbs back into working order.

'Ah – this is Patrick Donahugh. Patrick, this is my mother, Vanessa Kent.'

Patrick stretched out a hand. 'How do you do, Mrs Kent? I was just wishing Althea happy Christmas.'

Mrs Kent took a deep breath, about to comment, when the

hall suddenly filled with people. Kenneth, her children and, finally, her father, appeared, brimming with curiosity.

Althea ran a hand hastily over her hair, grateful that she'd looked a total mess beforehand and that Patrick could have done nothing to make her look more rumpled, while Kenneth performed introductions.

Her father shook Patrick's hand, her children said 'Hi!' and her mother nodded, sizing him up with a critical eye. Like Juno, she had always adored Frederick.

Her children stood about for a minute before going back to the television. Althea knew they were hoping that Patrick's arrival would mean adult conversation in the drawing room, leaving the den and the television to them. Bozo, the last to greet Patrick, was by far the most effusive.

Althea slunk away to the kitchen. She couldn't have felt worse if they'd been caught *in flagrante delicto*. It was not being seen kissing Patrick which was upsetting, it was the fact that she'd let herself do it, after all her decisions and resolutions about telling him they couldn't see each other. How convincing would her arguments sound now, when she'd been so abandoned?

'Damn and blast, damn and blast, damn and blast,' she repeated to herself. She ran her fingers through her hair and found it damp with sweat. She wanted to burst into tears. Life was so complicated, Christmas was so complicated. And now Patrick!

She happened to have a knife in her hand when he came in carrying a bottle. She had the oven door open and was turning over roast potatoes. Seeing him, she turned round, brandishing the knife in what she hoped was a threatening way.

'Patrick, why are you here?'

'I told you! I was invited!' He was indignant. 'I was asked to come yesterday too, only I couldn't. Then Juno asked me for Christmas dinner. I thought you might be pleased to see me. You seemed pleased a minute ago.'

She stabbed a potato. 'That was a mistake! I know we haven't had a chance to talk about – about the night of the storm – but I really can't see you again.'

'Why the hell not?' He put down the bottle and placed his hands on the table.

'It's complicated. I can't explain now. Juno's upstairs having a false alarm and I'm cooking dinner. I told Juno not to invite you.'

Patrick sent a hand up into the thatch of his hair and regarded her, somewhat bemused. 'But she did. And I'm here. And I'm not going home, so you might as well make the best of a bad situation.'

'Oh hell!' she muttered, stabbing at the potatoes. 'You don't have to get all offended! Quite honestly, I'll be glad of your company . . .' Hell again, she shouldn't have said that, although it was true. 'I mean, I do like you, I am happy to see you, but I don't want you getting the wrong idea.' She looked up at him, willing him to take pity on her, to understand, not to make life any more complicated than it already was.

He sighed deeply and pursed his lips. 'We'd better take a rain check on this conversation. You're not making sense and we're bound to be interrupted. Kenneth sent me in to see if you need any help or another drink.'

He was right. It was no earthly good trying to talk in a house full of pregnant women, Christmas and inquisitive family members. 'Yes to both.'

'In which order?'

'A whole bottle of whisky first, and then I want someone to tell me which of these trays of roast potatoes are vegetarian.'

'I didn't realize potatoes ever ate meat.' He picked up the whisky he had brought in with him and poured a couple of fingers of it into her glass.

'This is no time for jokes. One of these trays has been cooked in oil only, and the other one has had turkey fat poured over it. Which is which?'

'Um – perhaps William won't know the difference?'

She eyed him balefully and put the potatoes back in the oven. Having poured her drink, he had retreated to the safety of the doorway, leaning against the door jamb, amused, confused and oozing sex appeal. Althea, who felt she must be oozing turkey fat and giblet gravy, wanted to run away and leave him to cook the dinner. She did the next best thing.

'If you'll excuse me,' she said with dignity, 'I must just go and see if Juno wants anything. I'll expect I'll remember about the potatoes soon.'

217

She met Juno at the bottom of the stairs. Her sister looked magnificent. Her hair was piled on top of her head and she was wearing a black, gold-trimmed caftan which made pregnancy seem like the only look to be wearing that Christmas. Her make-up was perfect and she smelt strongly of 1000, which was, she never failed to mention, the costliest perfume in the world.

'Hello, darling, bless you for holding the fort. I heard Patrick arrive and I felt so much better I thought I'd come down.'

'Juno!' For the second time in ten minutes, Althea felt like murdering someone she loved. She closed her eyes, opened them again, and felt just as angry. 'Shouldn't you be in bed?'

'Oh no. I feel fine. The pain's quite gone.'

'Oh, has it. Well, I'm sure there's something I could do about that.'

'What do you mean?'

'I asked you *not* to invite Patrick.'

'I can invite who I like to my own house.' The haughtiness in Juno's manner faded rapidly as she realized that Althea was genuinely angry and upset. 'I'll go and say hello to him,' she added quickly, moving with stately speed.

Althea retired to the downstairs loo. She ran water into the basin and splashed her scarlet face. All her make-up had long since been sweated off. Her hair was lank and she had flour on her cheek. Her apron was filthy. At that moment she hated her sister more violently than she had ever hated anyone. For Juno had spent most of the day lying down, albeit in a certain amount of pain, but had then had time to make herself beautiful before swanning in to greet Patrick.

Althea, on the other hand, had spent all afternoon cooking Juno's Christmas dinner, in Juno's kitchen, making allowances for all Juno's foibles about how things should be done. And having gone against her most sincerely expressed wishes about inviting Patrick without having the decency to warn her, she had caused Althea to meet him when she was looking like nothing on earth. It was so unfair. Althea wanted to scream and shout and go into the dining room and upset the carefully laid table and send all Juno's matching china crashing to the floor.

But she couldn't do that. She was a grown-up. Her children were here, her parents were here, she had to be the Perfect

Mother and the Perfect Daughter, not to mention the Perfect Sister.

Denied all the more satisfying ways of getting rid of her tension and frustration, she rummaged through Juno's bathroom cupboard until she found the Rescue Remedy, that homoeopathic cure-all which was particularly good for shock and stress. She briefly considered swigging the whole bottle; after all, it was a Bach Flower remedy, containing extracts of plants too small to measure, it couldn't harm her. But she decided she might need some later, and confined herself to just a few drops under her tongue. William said the effect of Rescue Remedy was psychological, and that it was just the alcohol content that made it work. Althea knew better.

She was brushing her hair, with the long, slow strokes which were supposed to be so soothing when the door rattled. It was Juno.

'Althea? Are you in there? You've been ages and everything is boiling over. You can't just go away when you're cooking dinner, you know!'

Althea unlocked the door and confronted her sister. 'You bitch!' she said, and swept past her into the kitchen she had so wickedly abandoned.

She felt calmer now. Either the Rescue Remedy or letting off some of her feelings to her sister had helped. She remembered which of the potatoes were vegetarian, and started on making the gravy. Then her mother came in.

'Althea, what has got into you! You've upset Juno! How could you, in her condition?'

Althea had a relapse. 'Mother! If I was in her condition, as you imply, I wouldn't need to upset anyone. Because I would be lying about on a sofa while someone else did all the work. Juno is a spoilt brat we've all been over-indulging for far too long.'

'Althea, how can you? She's invited us all –'

'I begged her not to. I knew it would be too much, but oh no, she had to have her own way. And it *was* too much for her, so who's having to save the day? Me. Sweet, kind, twittish old Althea.'

'But you'd have had to cook dinner anyway, if everyone had come to our house.' William had entered the room, and therefore the discussion.

'I know,' said Althea. 'But it would have been my kitchen, and I could have done things my way!'

'I don't think there's any call to be unpleasant.' But Althea's mother, seeing she was alone in this opinion, took the better part of valour. 'I'll go and see if I can calm Juno down.'

'It'll be a first if you manage that!' Althea said to her mother's retreating back.

'Are you all right, Mum?' William came and put his arms round her. He was a fine boy, and she loved him dearly, but right now, she didn't want a boy to hug, she wanted a man. But as she hugged him back, she found a little comfort in his bony form and a lot more in his caring nature.

'I will be. I just feel put upon. It's very childish of me.'

'But understandable. Can I do anything to help?'

'You can make your vegetarian gravy if you like. The packet's over there.'

He picked it up, casting a careless eye over the instructions. 'It was nice of Juno to get it in for me. She means well, you know. Her motivation is pure.'

'I'm in no mood for your Buddhist bullshit!' But she laughed.

Patrick appeared. 'Juno sent me in to tell you that you're half an hour behind schedule.'

'Oh did she?' Althea's hands went to her hips.

'Well, I wasn't her first choice, but no one else had the courage to do it.'

'And you didn't wonder why that was?'

'Uh oh,' murmured William.

'I didn't need to wonder,' said Patrick. 'I knew. But I thought I could cope.'

'Oh did you?'

'William, would you mind pushing off? There are some things I want to say to your mother I can't say in public.'

William obligingly pushed, absolving himself of responsibility for the gravy.

Patrick crossed the room and put his arms round Althea. She stood within their circle stiffly, wanting their comfort, knowing she shouldn't take it.

'Listen,' he said. 'Juno is being totally unreasonable. She's thoroughly out of order. You're being an absolute saint, slaving away here. She knows that in her heart, but at the moment she's too taken up with herself and her pregnancy to see things as they really are.'

'Huh!' Althea released herself. Patrick's arms were too seductive. If she stayed in them much longer, she'd relax completely, and they would never eat.

'Really – you're a star and you know it.'

'Do I?'

'And here's something you may not know.'

'What?'

'You look fantastically sexy in that apron.'

'Patrick! That is nearly as maddening as being told you're beautiful when you're angry!'

'And just as true.' His blue eyes danced with provocation and desire and for a moment she felt sexy and beautiful and a star – red face and shining nose notwithstanding.

Unable to manage anything more eloquent, Althea cleared her throat.

Patrick held her gaze for another moment before breaking the spell. 'Would you like me to see if the turkey is cooked? I mean, there are lot more interesting things we could be doing, like making love in among all that junk on the kitchen table. But with your parents and your children in the next room, you may not be able to concentrate.'

'And you would?'

'Oh yes. I've always been able to devote all my attention to the matter in hand.'

Remembering his attentions last time, she blushed and coughed, feeling weak and useless.

'Er – yes – if you could look at the turkey. I'd better make William's gravy.' She was trying to hang on to the thought that she'd resolved never to make love to him again.

She watched as he heaved the twenty-pound bird, free-range, corn-fed, organic, guaranteed to have roamed the stately acres of a local aristocrat, out of the oven. He stabbed it with a skewer, tipping the roasting tin to check on the juices.

'It's done. It can rest while we get the rest of the dinner organized. Is there a starter?'

Althea dragged herself back to the matter in hand with an

effort. 'Fruit cocktails. Juno's done them. They're in the fridge. I'll ask Merry to put them out. I think the table's OK, but I'd better check.' Better get out from his powerfully unsettling aura, too.

She was fiddling with the table decoration when Juno came in. 'I'm so sorry, darling, I never meant you to have to do everything. I've been a complete cow. Forgive me?' She put her arm round Althea in a sisterly way.

Althea hugged her back. 'Of course I forgive you,' she said, her words a few steps ahead of her heart. 'But it would be wonderful if you could just check on the details while I go to the loo and fix my make-up.' Juno looked hesitant for a moment. 'And I don't seem to have had time for a wee all day,' she added.

This time, Althea took her handbag with her upstairs to Juno's bathroom, determined to tidy herself properly, in the luxury Juno had had for her maquillage. She also decided to use Juno's mascara and lipstick, as well as her eyeliner brush to smudge in some shadow along her lashes. It was all very well for Patrick to tell her she looked sexy in an apron and beautiful when she was angry, but she wanted to look beautiful when she wasn't wearing the trappings of female servitude and flour on her cheek. She damped her hair, added some mousse, and used Juno's hairdryer to give it bounce and style. She spent a good fifteen minutes in the bathroom, and emerged feeling refreshed and expensively fragrant.

Juno was organizing where people were to sit. 'You look super, darling, but do take off your pinny. Kenneth is just opening some champagne. Go and have some, and then we can eat. Patrick's being marvellous, isn't he? Who'd have thought he'd be so good in the kitchen?'

Althea was pleased. 'Do you want some champagne?'

Juno shuddered. 'Good God, no! Actually, I've still got a bit of backache. Nothing violent. It's probably just a muscle or something.'

'You will tell me if you think you're really in labour, won't you?'

'Of course! Now go and tell the others to bring their drinks and come to the table.'

★

222

Juno's labour pains drew attention to themselves again while Althea was toying with her Christmas pudding. Juno had made a rich Benedictine sauce to go with it, and while it was delicious, it was also impossibly filling.

'Ally,' she said, sounding strained. 'Come upstairs with me, will you?'

Instantly, Mrs Kent sprung to her feet. 'Are you all right, darling?'

'Oh don't fuss, Vanessa,' said her father. 'Let Althea deal with it.'

'Don't be ridiculous. A girl needs her mother at a time like this.'

'Cool! Juno's having her baby!' said Merry.

'Don't you call her Aunt Juno?' demanded her grandmother, determined to take her worry out on somebody.

'No,' said Merry, unabashed. 'She doesn't need a label, she has a personality.' It was a direct quote.

Mrs Kent, suddenly feeling that she had lost status by allowing herself to be called Granny, appeared about to erupt.

'Why don't you have a brandy, Vanessa?' said Kenneth, quickly.

Althea got up and drew her sister out of the room.

'I'm coming up in a minute, darling,' called their mother.

'That's what I'm afraid of,' murmured Juno.

They were upstairs, sitting on Juno's bed when Kenneth came into the room. Althea was ringing the hospital, overcome with relief that Juno had, at the last minute, been talked out of a home delivery in a birthing pool in the presence of half a dozen alternative therapists.

'Are you all right?' Kenneth put his hand over his wife's, more for his comfort than for hers.

'I'm fine. It's probably just Braxton Hicks,' said Juno. 'But Ally's insisted on ringing to make sure.'

'Surely they won't be able to say what sort of contractions they are over the phone?'

'No, but they'll tell me what to do.' Juno patted the hand. 'It's exciting, really. I'm so fed up with being pregnant, I would be pleased if it came early.'

Althea put her hand over the phone. 'They think you should go in.' She spoke into the receiver again. 'We'll ring back when Mrs Reeves-Gill has decided what she wants to do.'

Although part of her would like Juno out of the way, where she could be looked after by professionals, she owed it to her sister to tell what she knew about hospitals and first labours.

'Now listen, Juny, even if you are in labour, you could be there for hours – days even. First babies always take forever. You'll get terribly fed up and might be better off at home.'

Juno, in spite of her tireless research into the business of childbirth, had lost some of her confidence. 'I think I'll go in. I mean, I know hospitals are ghastly, but you know what it'll be like if I hang on here. Mummy'll fuss so. And at least the hospital have got my birth plan and know I don't want unnecessary intervention.'

'Very sensible. Shall I pack your bag?'

Juno gave her sister a pitying look. 'I've had my bag packed for weeks now. It's in the wardrobe.'

Althea had gone on two-week camping holidays with small children with a smaller suitcase.

'What have you got in here? Has the Health Service got so bad you have to bring your own bed?'

Juno smiled weakly. 'I don't like to leave anything to chance.'

'No, you certainly don't.'

Kenneth came in. 'Are you ready, Poppet?'

'I think I'll just go and have a shower.'

'In case the hospital has run out of hot water?' said Althea.

'Exactly.'

CHAPTER TWENTY-ONE

Downstairs there was an argument going on about who should go in with Juno which Althea hadn't heard, but was expected to pronounce on the moment she appeared.

'Well, Kenneth should take her, of course,' she said, wondering how this was going to be the wrong answer.

'Yes, yes,' said her mother. 'Kenneth can *drive*, but I ought to be there, to see she's all right. See to her – feminine requirements.'

'Um – I don't think that's a very good idea, Mum. There'll be so much hanging about, and Kenneth'll be there to see she gets everything she wants.'

'I know, dear, but he's a man. Call me old-fashioned –' Althea could see Merry mouthing the words 'old-fashioned' behind her mother – 'but I don't think men have any place in the business of childbirth. And Daddy agrees with me, don't you?'

'You may have to lay the keel, but you don't have to be in at the launching,' he growled.

'What?' said Merry, familiar with the facts of life, but not seafaring terminology.

'Kenneth wants to be there, Mother.'

'Nonsense. He only says he does to pacify Juno. It's one of her little fads. I bet Frederick didn't stay in the room while you were having your babies.'

'No. We got divorced.'

'No, really. It's silly and undignified for women to be seen in that condition. He'll probably faint.'

'You'd faint, if you were there,' said her husband.

'Don't be ridiculous! I'd just be with her during the long first stage. First babies are always a long time coming.'

'That's what Mum says,' said Merry.

'I'll just go and get my things together. And find a nice book. I wonder if there's any Anne Rice?'

With her mother out of the room, Althea turned desperately to her father. 'You mustn't let her. She'll drive Juno mad, just when Juno really ought to be kept as calm as possible.'

Her father shrugged. 'You tell her. She never listens to a word I say.'

Patrick and William, who had been stacking the dishwasher, without rinsing the plates first, came in.

'Why don't Granny and Grandpa go in their car?' suggested William. 'Then, if they need to come home again,' he went on tactfully, 'they can.'

Merry, who was tired, sighed long and deep. 'Actually,' she said clearly, 'William should drive. He's the only one who hasn't been drinking.'

'Oh God! I never thought of that,' Kenneth groaned.

Juno cast despairing eyes to heaven and Mrs Kent, who'd reappeared, still looking for a suitable book, huffed indignantly.

'Well, everyone knows I don't drink. I'll drive her.'

'Sherry is alcohol,' said Althea. 'And you did have two glasses.'

In fact, Mrs Kent was one of those rare people whose driving might actually be improved by alcohol, given that nothing could actually make it worse. But everyone involved was very relieved to be given this cast-iron excuse for not letting her.

'Why can't William do it?' said Merry.

'It's far too far,' said Althea. 'And what would he do while he was there? He couldn't abandon Kenneth, and it would be difficult to get a taxi.'

'Well what are we going to do?' demanded Juno at last, when every other possibility had been aired and rejected. 'I won't go in an ambulance even if they did send one. You didn't have very much, did you, Kenneth?'

Patrick, who had kept quiet during the discussion, cleared his throat. 'Why don't you get William to drive Kenneth and Mr Kent to the police station. You can explain the situation and they can decide who can drive and who can't. If all else fails, William will have to do it.'

'That's an excellent idea,' said Althea. 'Off you go, with William.' And please God, she added silently, don't let William have

226

to drive Juno, Kenneth and my parents to hospital. It's just too great a burden for a seventeen-year-old.

Juno drummed her fingers on the arms of the stripped-pine windsor chair which she had picked up in a dear little junk shop which wasn't called dear for nothing. She, Patrick and Althea were in the kitchen, waiting.

'I wish they'd hurry up. If I'd known this would happen I would never have let Kenneth drink. Men are so selfish.'

Briefly, Althea wondered if Juno could possibly be in transition, to be so especially unreasonable. But more likely she was just strung up and anxious.

'Juny! It is Christmas, and you didn't know this was going to happen. He says he didn't have much. He might be fine.'

'Huh!'

'It was a good idea of Patrick's, wasn't it? Getting them to take a breathalyser test?'

Juno sighed. 'Yes.' She gave him a weak smile. 'Thank you, Patrick.'

'You're welcome.'

An anxious half-hour creaked by, punctuated by bright remarks from Althea and monosyllables from Juno. At last they heard William's ancient car in the drive, and a moment later, a jubilant Kenneth came in.

'I failed the test!'

'You what?' Juno was white with fury.

'I mean – I passed the test. I didn't have enough alcohol to make it turn red.'

'Oh good,' said Juno. 'Then let's for God's sake go, before Mummy has a chance to get in the car.'

'Hubert was OK too.'

Juno stood transfixed for a moment. 'I don't believe it! It's Christmas! Surely he must have had enough to make him over the limit!'

'Apparently he's been feeling liverish and has been on neat ginger ale.'

'Which I suppose means we'll run out of it tomorrow!'

'It could have been worse, sweetheart. If he'd been over the limit, your mother would be in the car with us.'

At this moment, Mrs Kent came in. She was furious. 'Honestly, everyone *knows* I don't drink! I don't know what those machines are doing! It's all totally unscientific.'

Althea caught Patrick's eye. He had obviously come to the same conclusion as she had and was struggling not to laugh. She was having difficulty biting back her smile herself.

'Mother,' said Althea, 'are you telling us you failed the test?'

'That's what their machines say, but I've never heard anything so ridiculous in my life.'

'It is to do with body weight,' said Patrick, well under control now. 'The tiniest thimbleful of sherry' – tactfully, he left out the brandy – 'would affect someone as slender as yourself, whereas a larger person might absorb it easily.'

Mrs Kent cheered up visibly. 'Well, that explains it. Now, come on everyone, not a moment to lose.'

'You really don't need to come, Mummy.'

'No, you'll get frightfully bored,' said Althea. 'We could play three-handed bridge, or something. I'm sure Patrick plays?'

'I'm afraid I don't.'

'Honestly, Althea dear, as if I could play cards while my darling daughter is having her first child!'

Althea had no idea of what her mother had been doing while she was having William, but she certainly wasn't at her bedside timing contractions.

Juno heaved herself to her feet. 'Thanks for trying,' she murmured as she proceeded to the front door, Kenneth carrying the enormous suitcase, her father arguing that their presence was quite unnecessary and her mother insisting that it was essential. Kenneth shouted over his shoulder that he'd ring when he knew anything, and at last the entourage was on its way.

Patrick regarded Althea with speculation. 'Now what?'

'We wait. You don't have to, of course. You could go home.'

If there was a hint in her voice that this was what he ought to do, he ignored it. 'Well then, what about a game of charades?'

The boys turned horrified eyes towards their mother. 'Mum! I know I shouldn't say this, and I was happy to drive everyone to the police station, but really, do I have to play charades as well?'

Patrick looked suitably contrite. 'Of course not. What do you want to do?'

'Go home,' said Merry. 'All our good presents are there. And we didn't want to come, anyway.'

'But I've promised I'll stay . . .' Althea was stabbed with guilty conscience.

'I'll drive us home,' said William, cheering up. 'We'll be fine.'

'There's a film by Quentin Tarantino I really want to record,' said Rupert. 'I could watch it here but you wouldn't want Merry to see it.'

'I wouldn't want *you* to see it –' Althea began.

Patrick interrupted. 'Why not let them go home? I'll keep you company, and they must be bored stiff.'

The children nodded in agreement.

'Oh, OK,' said Althea, feeling too tired to argue. 'But you will be careful driving, William? There's bound to be drunken drivers about.'

William, who had already driven through town, assured his mother that yes, he would be careful and yes, he always was, and led another party away from the house.

Just before the front door closed behind them Merry's voice could be heard asking, 'Do you think they'll make out? On the sofa?'

There was no chance that Patrick hadn't heard. He put his head slightly on one side. 'Well, what do you think?'

Althea felt persecuted, as if she'd somehow invited a boy she didn't trust up to her bedroom when her parents were out.

It was partly because that was how it was, except she hadn't invited him, Juno had. And of course, she trusted him. He wouldn't do anything to her she didn't want. It was herself she didn't trust. And without her children as chaperones, she felt terribly vulnerable.

'I think I'm a little old for that sort of thing.' Then, realizing how prudish she sounded, went on, 'I mean, we ought to clear up, unless you want some trifle?'

Patrick sighed. 'If trifle is all that's on offer, I'll settle for it.'

'I'm afraid it is.'

'You don't think we should talk? I mean, properly, not just chit-chat.'

Althea sighed. 'I suppose so, but I'm not sure now is the right time.'

'It's all the time we have! It's harder to get time with you alone than it is to arrange an audience with the Pope.'

'Not really . . .'

'Yes, really. And I want to know why it is that, when the last time we saw each other we were making mad, passionate love on the floor, now you won't give me the time of day.'

'It's not like that, Patrick! You don't understand!'

'And I never will unless you explain.'

'I did, ages ago.'

'You mean, all that stuff about the children and not wanting to disrupt their lives? It won't wash, Ally. The children would be fine about it, I'm sure.'

'I really don't want to go into it all now. I'm so tired. Let me get you some trifle.'

She was just serving it up when the telephone rang. She flew to it, every conceivable emergency rushing into her head like a swarm of flies. It was only after she'd picked it up that she realized it was far too early for news from the hospital. They would hardly have got there.

It was Merry, ringing to say that they had got home safely.

'Thank you darling,' said Althea. 'It was very considerate of you to call.'

She put the phone down. Patrick was sitting on the sofa, his long legs stretched out in front of him. He had finished filling a bowl and was eating his trifle. 'This is good,' he said. 'Have some?'

'No thank you.' She was too strung up to eat. Juno, Patrick, and the effort of Christmas had left her tense. If she'd had the energy to get it, she'd have prescribed herself another dose of Rescue Remedy.

'I bought you a Christmas present.'

'Did you?' She was horrified. 'I didn't get you one!'

'You didn't know I was coming. Would you like it now?'

'Might as well, I suppose. I mean – that would be lovely.' God! She was so agitated, even the most basic good manners had deserted her.

He got up and foraged for a parcel from a pile under the tree. It seemed he had brought presents for the entire household.

Althea's was flat and floppy. If it's underwear or anything like that, I shall die, she thought, fingering it gingerly, admiring the run-of-the-mill wrapping paper, putting off the moment of truth. It was a silk scarf. Gorgeous, but quite unthreatening.

'It's beautiful.' She draped it round her shoulders. 'I feel awful that I haven't got you anything. Almost all my presents this year were homemade.'

'A homemade present would be quite acceptable.'

'But I haven't made you anything.'

'You could give me a kiss, then you'd make me happy.'

'I can't make you happy. Oh, I could give you a kiss, but I can't do more.'

'Oh, yes you can.'

'I mean, I've explained. I don't – can't have casual affairs.'

'Define casual.'

'You know! We have different needs. I can't satisfy yours . . .'

'I'm sure you could with a little practice.'

'. . . And you can't satisfy mine.'

There was a silence broken only by the hiss of Juno's log-effect gas fire. 'Not unless you tell me what they are.'

She looked at him, all legs and casual elegance, spread all over Juno's cream leather sofa. How could she tell him what she wanted? How could she say she wanted love, commitment, happy-ever-after just like Topaz had? He would be embarrassed. There would be a tiny, significant pause before he answered. And then, what would he say? I'm sorry, Ally, I'm not that kind of man. I've tried it twice, and it hasn't worked out? If she was lucky he would, because although painful, it would at least be the truth. But he might just decide to string her along for as long as his interest in her endured, and then tell her kindly but painfully that he was moving on.

'And,' he went on, 'joking apart, how do you know that you can't fulfil my needs? You've never asked me what they are.'

'I don't need to, Patrick. Some things you just know by instinct.'

'Oh really?'

'Yes! And as for me telling you what I want from a relationship, there's nothing to say! I can't have – don't want any sort of relationship while the children are at home. It's too unsettling for them.'

'Have you asked them?'

Althea moistened her lips. 'Of course not! You can't ask children things like that in an abstract way, they would smell a rat, suspect the worst.'

'Why would you having a relationship be "the worst"? Why couldn't it be a positive thing?'

She was frantically trying to work out how to explain her feelings about selfish genes and step-parents without sounding offensive, when the telephone rang again.

She expected to hear Kenneth's voice and it took her a moment to realize that it was Frederick.

'Hello? Althea, is that you?'

'Yes.' She hid her sigh. 'Hello, Frederick. Happy Christmas. Did you want to speak to the children? They've gone home.'

She saw Patrick get up and leave the room.

'I know,' Frederick was saying. 'I've just spoken to them. It was you I was ringing.'

'Oh? Why?' She'd sent him a Christmas card and a very nice tie from the Oxfam shop, what more did he want? A lavish thank you for his gift voucher?

'Listen, I've got a proposition for you. We want to buy the house.'

'What house?'

'Your house. Our house.'

'What do you mean? I already own it.'

'Althea! Are you drunk? You remember I was setting up a new partnership when I was over in the summer?'

She didn't, but she took his word for it. 'Mmm.'

'Well, it's all worked out. They want me to come home almost straight away. Topaz and I want to buy you out, buy the house from you. Do you understand?'

Althea didn't think she was drunk but it took her a while to take in the enormity of his request. 'Yes, but I couldn't possibly sell it. It's the children's home!'

'William tells me you're having quite a struggle managing now you're out of a job. If I bought the house from you, it would still be their home, at least sometimes.'

232

'Frederick . . .'

'I know. It's a bit of a bombshell, but think about it. I'm prepared to offer you the market value, which, considering I already own part of it, is generous.'

'But . . .'

'I put it to the children, and they seem quite keen.'

'How dare you? It's nothing to do with them.'

'A moment ago, you said it was their home. You're overreacting, old girl. Give the matter some thought and let me know. But it's by far the best thing to do, believe me.'

'Look, you're not getting your hands on that house, or any money from that house, until Merry leaves full-time education. I've been paying the mortgage all these years, it's three-quarters mine!'

'I'm offering you the full market value – more, in fact – and you won't have to pay me anything. All the money will be yours. If you wait and sell it to anyone else, you'll have to give me my quarter-share.'

This took a bit of digesting. 'This is very out of character, Frederick. Are you sure *you* haven't had too much to drink?'

'Not at all. I just know what I want and am prepared to pay for it. Topaz has her heart set on that house.'

'But why? There are thousands of pretty houses, much more suited to a couple than my house. It's a family home!'

'Topaz thinks the conservatory is wonderful and you must admit the views are spectacular. She likes the garden, too.'

So the woman did have some taste. 'Won't she find the sitting room a bit small?'

'Fine for two of us. We don't entertain much. I'd knock your bedroom and the spare room into one, and make the bathroom en suite.'

'You've thought a lot about it.'

'Oh yes. And I want you to think about it too. As I said, the children are fine about it. They'll be able to keep their rooms for when they come and stay. Topaz is looking forward to getting to know them.'

'Won't she find it awkward, living so near Patrick?'

'Why should she? They're both civilized adults. As you and I are.'

'Oh.' It was a totally inadequate reply, but as her throat was tight with unshed tears, it was the best she could do.

'There's just one thing. We would like to proceed immediately. We're cash buyers, which would make you one too.'

'When would you want me out by?'

'End of March.'

'Frederick! That's impossible! I can't move house just before the Chelsea Flower Show!'

'That's in May, isn't it?'

Althea sighed. 'Yes, but I've to prepare for it. I can't move house just like that!'

'Don't be silly. A little organization . . .'

'Frederick, you're the limit!'

'So you'll think about it? It's a very good offer, you won't get a better when you do have to sell. And your money will buy you less.'

''Spose so.'

'Then I'll just send lots of good wishes for the season from Topaz and myself, and I hope to hear from you soon.'

Althea put the phone down without answering.

Patrick, who had tactfully removed himself, came back into the room as he heard her put down the phone. 'Bad news?'

She nodded. 'Yes. No. I don't know.'

'What?'

'Frederick wants to buy my house.'

'Oh.'

'He wants to live there with Topaz.' She gave him a tortured look as she thought about Topaz living in her house, sitting in her conservatory, mucking up her garden with bedding plants and dahlias.

'Ah. Well, you don't have to sell it, do you?'

'I have to think about it. This period without regular money has just about done for my savings and my redundancy money. And although it's only a small mortgage, the damn thing insists on being paid every month.'

'Is he offering you a reasonable price?'

'More than reasonable, provided I move by the end of March.'

'Hmm. Not much time.'

'No. I've got to find somewhere else to live, buy it, with all the hassle that involves, move out, move in – *and* organize my garden.'

'For Chelsea?'

She nodded. 'Still, I'll be a cash buyer, that should make things a lot easier. The only trouble is, I love that house and I don't suppose I'll find another I like as much.'

'Then don't go.'

'Frederick says he's spoken to the children about it – the bastard – and they're fine about it. But it's different for them, they'll go on living there, when they stay with Frederick.'

'And Topaz,' he added. If Patrick was holding a torch for Topaz, it was dim and well hidden.

'Apparently she's looking forward to get to know my children.'

Patrick laughed. 'Poor Topaz!'

'What do you mean?'

'I mean, they're challenging. She won't be able to treat them as cyphers. They won't put up with her controlling ways.'

'They put up with mine,' Althea reflected.

'I don't see you as a control freak, exactly.'

'No, well, perhaps not. And I can't ask them to live in poverty because of my sentimental attachment to my home.'

'You don't always have to put them first. You have rights too. And it's not them giving up their home, it's you.'

'I know. But they're at a dreadfully expensive age. Not having a mortgage and perhaps a bit of money over would make all the difference.'

'Are you very hard up?'

'No, not really! Not like some people are. But things like new clothes have always have been difficult to afford, and since I've lost my job, it's been worse. We bob along OK if nothing major breaks down, but things always do, just when you can least afford it.'

'Don't be pushed into anything you don't want to do.'

She shook her head. 'I may not be as forceful as my mother and my sister, but I won't let myself be bullied, I assure you. And if I can find a nice house – with a garden, views, plenty of space . . .'

'Everything you've got now.'

'Exactly. I might like it. I have always wanted a bedroom big enough to have a chaise longue in it. Like yours.'

'If you don't mind,' said Patrick, coming to sit by her on the sofa, 'we'll leave my bedroom out of the conversation at the moment. You've got enough to think about.'

'I only meant that it's big,' Althea insisted.

'Maybe, I have a better memory and a less pure mind.'

'Sorry.' Now she too was remembering what had gone on there and that, combined with his nearness, the subtle odour of his skin, his hair, and his aftershave, was all extremely unsettling. So she got up.

He took her hand and gently but firmly pulled her back. 'I'm not going to suggest anything drastic,' he said softly. 'It's just that it's Christmas, we're all alone in the house, and I don't think a little kiss would do either of us any harm.'

Althea swallowed, and allowed herself to settle deeper into the sofa. But after Patrick's mouth had been on hers for a few seconds, she doubted if he knew what a 'little' kiss was. She struggled upright, too aware of what might so easily develop from his wilful, skilful mouth and his sensitive, insistent hands which found their way so adroitly about her clothing.

'We mustn't! Supposing my parents came back suddenly? It would be too silly, being caught necking on the sofa. I'm thirty-nine years old!'

'Stop supposing, seize the moment.' He undid the third button of her blouse. 'You're always looking into the future and seeing trouble. Just relax and enjoy the now. Nothing terrible is going to happen, I won't let it. You can trust me, I promise.'

It had never been him she didn't trust, but always herself. But the self which kept her out of harm's way had knocked off for the holiday, leaving the wanton, womanly self who wanted a man, and whose body was responding so enthusiastically to his. But he was talking good sense: life galloped by, and if you didn't grasp the good times, the bright interludes between disasters, your soul shrivelled. Life became grey and monotonous.

They were lying full length on the sofa, still fully clothed, but as close as two people could be, when Patrick raised his head.

'What's the matter?'

'I heard a car. It's probably your parents.'

They got up and Althea hastily replaced her earrings and did up her buttons. And then to make quite sure that no one reached the right conclusions, she went to open the front door.

It wasn't her parents, it was Kenneth and Juno. 'They've sent me home!' she wailed. 'I'm not going to have the baby now after all!'

CHAPTER TWENTY-TWO

It took Althea a long time to get away. Kenneth eventually drove her home, having established his distraught wife in bed. Patrick had left hours before, and by the time she and Bozo finally cuddled up in bed together, she was deeply distressed and too tired to sleep.

It was because she was worn out. And she was disappointed about Juno's baby, too, although not as disappointed as Juno, who felt that having been sent home, because her contractions had stopped completely, meant that she would now never have the baby at all.

It was also the thought of losing her beloved home. Patrick was right when he said she didn't have to sell to Frederick if she didn't want to. But she didn't have a choice, not really. She couldn't expect the children to go on being poor when there was an alternative. And when she was rested, she would enjoy house-hunting. She loved poking her nose into other people's houses, and as a cash buyer, she was in a position to snap up a bargain. She decided to tell Frederick she would accept his offer.

The moving would be a real drag, of course. She would be flat out growing plants for Chelsea, the last thing she would want to be doing was going through eighteen years' worth of accumulated rubbish. And there were lots and lots of plants she would want to take with her. And where would she put them? Supposing she didn't find anywhere before she had to move? The thought of putting her furniture in storage was dire, but her plants? Was there a service which would give soil-room to beloved plants until their owner found a suitable garden for them? Unfortunately her clients' gardens were full to bursting, thanks to her policy of leaving no spare soil for weeds. Perhaps she should rent an allotment. No. Taking on an allotment would be lunacy. It would take her weeks to get one clear. She would have to think of something else.

And she was constantly worrying about her competition garden. Would she be able to produce enough plants of a high-enough quality? Would it work in real life? It had taken her a lot longer than three weeks to create the garden in the comfort of her own home. How would she manage at Chelsea, surrounded by all those professionals?

She turned over her pillow for the seventh time. She must go to sleep. Bozo was obviously very fed up with her tossing about, being disturbed every ten minutes or so. A dog needed a good twenty-three hours' sleep out of twenty-four. Everyone knew that.

A cool pillow and a determination to sleep did not keep the problem uppermost in her mind at bay. Patrick. She loved him, she wanted him, but she could not have him. Because her children had to come first and they wouldn't like a step-father, not just when their father was about to produce a step-mother, in the form of Topaz whom they would hate – even more than they had Claudia.

They did like Patrick and as a friend they would probably cope, but would he be prepared to be just a friend? No, was the simple answer. And having him as 'just a friend' would drive her mad, too. Nor could she visit him for illicit afternoons in bed while the children were at school. Even without the thousand logistical reasons why this was impossible, there were two thousand moral ones. She could not keep Patrick as a bit on the side, even if he were willing to be so treated. No, a clean break would be fairer to both of them.

Making this difficult decision still didn't settle Althea enough to allow her to become drowsy. Could she possibly ask Patrick to take a three-year rain check on their affair? No, she couldn't. She would get in touch with him tomorrow and tell him.

Althea woke on Boxing Day unaware that she'd actually been asleep. She was heavy of head and heart, totally unfit for the ongoing task of Christmas. She was even more unfit for the task of ringing Patrick and saying goodbye for ever, but she picked up the phone and dialled. His voice answered after three rings, and it took her a moment to realize she'd got his machine.

Dimly, some overheard snippet of conversation came back to her, reminding her that Patrick was spending the rest of the holiday with his sister before going to visit his daughters for New Year. She put the phone down before the long tone sounded. She couldn't say what she wanted to say to a machine. She would write him a letter. It might be a coward's way out, but it would be ages before she would have a chance to speak to him face to face.

'What are you doing, Mummy?' asked Merry. She was wearing her new outsized T-shirt, a pair of over-the-knee socks, and a denim jacket, all Christmas presents.

'Writing a letter. Why don't you put some clothes on? You'll freeze.'

'Have you forgotten we're going to Ronnie's house for drinks?'

'Oh no,' she lied glibly. 'I'll get ready when I've done this.'

'Who's it to?'

'Patrick,' she answered without thinking. This was the third draft, and if Merry didn't go away, there might have to be a fourth.

'What about?'

Althea put down her pen. 'He gave me a beautiful scarf as a Christmas present. I'm writing to thank him. Have you done your thank-you letters yet?'

'Der!' said her daughter. 'It's only Boxing Day!'

It did the trick. Althea didn't usually start nagging her children about their thank-you letters so early, but she did insist on them being done before they went back to school.

She turned back to her letter.

> *Dear Patrick,*
> *Sadly, I am writing to tell you that I don't think we can go on being friends.* [A nice, ambiguous term.] *I have enjoyed your company very much in the past, but owing to difficulties I have explained, cannot go on doing so. Best wishes.*

Then, as a gesture to Merry and to truthfulness, she added, *Thank you for the beautiful scarf.*

Because it was Boxing Day, and there would be no post for the foreseeable future, she delivered it by hand.

On December 28, she received a reply.

Thank you for your letter. I accept your decision and won't trouble you again.

Patrick

On New Year's Day, two weeks early, Juno had her baby. An exquisite little girl, weighing exactly seven pounds, was born with remarkably little fuss.

'I think having such a dreadful dress rehearsal, over Christmas, made it a much better first night.' Juno, flushed and radiant, held the tiny, sleeping creature in the crook of her arm as she lay propped up in bed.

'Can I?' Althea reached over and picked up her niece. She had had a lot of reasons to cry lately, but this was the only one she would admit to. 'She's perfect,' she choked. 'Just like you.'

'She's lovely, isn't she? But she's the image of Kenneth.'

'When's Mum coming down?'

Juno smiled. 'They're snowed in. The A9 is completely impassable. They won't be able to come before the weekend.'

'And when are you coming home?'

'Well. I booked in for a week's stay. I thought it best, you know.'

Althea hid her sigh of relief. The problems with Juno and her baby would only come after she'd gone home. Any little postponement of having to be the perfectly supportive sister would be gratefully received. She had problems of her own.

She didn't actually think Frederick had on purpose forced her to house-hunt when there were virtually no houses on the market, but it was doubly inconvenient. She had always thought house-hunting was fun, imagining herself living in each one, and what she'd do to the garden. But it wasn't fun. Imagining herself living in the houses they visited was deeply depressing, and the gardens, where there were any, were on solid clay, and after the fine, free-draining soil she was used to, this was an area where she just couldn't compromise.

She and the children trailed round what properties there were with ever-increasing gloom. The boys refused to visit the latest one, leaving Althea only her daughter as moral support.

'We can't live here,' said Merry firmly. 'It smells.'

Althea looked around hastily in case the owner of the house had heard. 'It wouldn't smell if we lived here. At least, not of boiling chickens.'

'I couldn't get to Ronnie's without a lift.'

Althea sighed. That was a point against the house. 'But otherwise it's OK isn't it? It's got four bedrooms . . .'

'No spare.'

'A luxury we can do without. A nice fitted kitchen, a beautiful sitting room with patio doors.'

'And a nice factory to look out at,' said Merry, glumly.

'Darling, I swear we've looked at every property even remotely suitable, and this is the best so far. We haven't long, if Daddy wants to move in by the end of March.'

'We've got two months, nearly. That's ages.'

'It's nothing! Moving house takes for ever, what with searches, surveys and whatnot. We're lucky we don't have to get a mortgage.'

'But you will have any house you buy surveyed, won't you?' Merry sounded anxious.

'Well, I might, but without a mortgage, it's not really necessary.'

'Yes it is! I met Patrick in town and he made me promise not to let you buy anywhere without having a survey done. He'd said he'd do it, if you liked.'

'I've told you, darling, Patrick and I have broken up our friendship.'

'But you can't –'

'Yes we can! You and your friends are always doing it!'

'But we're children! You and Patrick are grown up! I think it's tight the way you're being with him. And so does he!'

'Merry, darling, I really don't like you seeing Patrick, it's not right.'

'I didn't "see" him, I just bumped into him. Honestly, you're so unfair. If I'd ignored any of your other friends you'd be furious. But you want me to ignore Patrick, who's cool.'

'All right, you don't have to ignore him, but I would prefer it if you didn't tell him any of my private business.'

'Like what?' Merry was indignant.

'Like the fact we're house-hunting.'

'Oh God! I didn't tell him that! He knew! He asked me how it was going! And he said that about the survey.'

Althea sighed. 'Let's go home.'

'So we're not buying this house?' Merry's pretty face was pleading.

'I don't think so. Not unless we have to. Come on, let's go and see Juno and the baby.'

'If you don't mind, can you drop me home first? I love Candida, but Juno fusses over me so when I hold her.'

So Althea went to visit her niece alone, wondering, as always, how her sister could have named her daughter after a nasty micro-organism which had it in for women. Merry was right, Juno was maddeningly, if unsurprisingly fussy. But she was less so with Althea because the baby always stopped crying when Althea picked it up.

'They just like to feel cuddled,' she said, adjusting the volume on her niece's distress down to a quiet whimper with the aid of a hand thumping soothingly on her back.

'It says in the book,' said Juno, who, a mother of barely six weeks, still put a lot of faith in books, 'that if she's fed, winded and has a clean nappy, she should just be put down to sleep.'

'Wrong book,' said Althea, knowing that Juno wouldn't abandon books and rely on her instincts. 'Here . . .' One-handed, Althea rummaged through the pile of *How To Be the Mother of the Perfect Baby* books on Juno's bookcase. 'It says here that your baby should be carried around until it falls asleep naturally. According to this, it's only Western society which would dream of treating their babies like we do.'

'Oh,' said Juno meekly. 'Well, she's asleep now. Or do you have to carry them around all the time?'

'No,' said Althea hastily. 'Once they're asleep you can put them in their cribs. As long as you pick them up as soon as they cry.'

She led Juno gently away from her sleeping babe, having assured her that the baby alarm was switched on and working, and made her a cup of tea. Althea could have told Juno all that without reference to the printed page, but Juno would not have accepted it. Words of wisdom had to be in print, between glossy covers, with lots of shiny photographs, to be of any value.

'How's the house-hunting going?' Juno sipped her tea and put her feet up on the opposite chair, a thing she would never have done pre-baby.

'Lousy. If the house is OK, the soil is terrible, and if the soil is OK, it's too far from school and town and so on.'

'I'd have thought being a cash buyer would put you in a very good position.'

'It would do if there was anything to cash buy. But there's nothing on the market at this time of year. Bloody Frederick, wanting to move in March. Couldn't he have waited until after the Chelsea Flower Show?'

Juno, who was low on sleep, took a moment to grasp the significance of this. 'I don't suppose he could choose when to start his new job.'

Althea sighed. 'No.'

'And perhaps you could rent?'

'Perhaps, but what about my plants? You can't put those in storage.'

'Wouldn't Frederick let you keep them in his garden, until you find somewhere?'

Althea made a face. 'The plants in the garden, yes, but not the forest in the conservatory. It's Topaz's favourite part of the house; she'll want to put furniture in there.'

'I always thought there was far too much greenery.'

Althea stood up. 'I must go, the boys will need feeding. And don't worry about Candida. Just pick her up if she cries and latch her on. It doesn't matter if she doesn't go four-hourly at this stage.'

'I don't want her getting fat.' Juno was a reluctant breast-feeder. 'She might have your genes. Remember what a pudding Merry was?'

'She's a stick-insect now! Breast-fed babies regulate their own weight. Don't worry about it.' She kissed her sister. 'And let Kenneth play with her too.'

If Mrs Jenkinstown hadn't rung her up to remind her, Althea would have forgotten all about the governors' meeting. She rushed there, late and flustered, thanking her lucky stars that at least circulating the minutes was no longer her responsibility. She only had to type them.

As she locked her car, she spotted Patrick's across the car park. Damn! He might have had the decency to send his apologies and not show up. And on time, too. It was just too unreasonable. She'd been so busy, there was very little time to think about anything except what a Tyrolean finish was, and how much space would be over when you put a single bed into a room ten feet by ten feet. But he'd been hovering there in the background, and with him a deep depression which was harder and harder to fight off. Seeing him now would bring it all into the foreground and make it far worse.

She was seeing that every place had a copy of all the multitudinous bits of paper to be distributed when Geoffrey Conway and Patrick came in.

'Mr Donahugh has had a tour of the site. We should be ready to start building soon. Any chance of making us a cup of coffee before we start, Mrs Farraday?'

She smiled with all the charm she could muster. 'I'm afraid I just don't have time. Why don't you ask Janet? I'm sure she wouldn't mind making you both a cup.'

She didn't mind making tea at half-time, that was part of her job, but she was not going to do it now.

'The cups and the kettle are all laid out ready, Mrs Farraday.' Geoffrey Conway was reminded why he hadn't chosen her to be his secretary – she couldn't be relied upon to jump to his every whim.

'Then do carry on. I'll just finish what I'm doing here, but don't bother to make me a cup.'

She glanced at Patrick to share a smile at Geoffrey Conway's expense, but he looked at her, as stony as his buildings would be when they finally went up.

Patrick continued to glare at her whenever she caught his eye, which, after the first couple of times, she avoided doing. She saw his pile of papers were rapidly being covered in angry doodles. Why was he still angry with her? She knew he'd taken Sylvia out to dinner, because Sylvia had told her. She'd also revealed that he and Jenny had been seen together. So why the dagger looks?

She saw Mrs Jenkinstown intercepting one while the school plan for sex education was being debated by the vicar and the teacher-governor who would have to carry it out. Althea blushed under her disappointed gaze. If she and Patrick had been holding hands and playing footy-footy it would have been all right with the chairman of the governors. Such blatant evidence of a breakdown in communications was not.

After the meeting, Althea stayed behind to type up her notes on the school PC, partly so she wouldn't have to come back and do them another time, and partly to give Patrick and Mrs Jenkinstown a chance to leave. She stayed talking shop to Janet for minutes she couldn't really spare to make quite sure the coast was clear before finally pulling on her coat. She had a house to go and see – the last house, she swore – before she finally gave up.

If Janet hadn't been nearly ready to leave, Althea would have gone back inside the door again in spite of the house. Patrick's car was still there. And Patrick was leaning against the driver's door of her own car. Bugger!

'Can I help you?' she asked him as she approached. 'I am in a bit of a hurry. I have a house to see.'

'I know. That's why I waited.'

'Oh?' She got out her keys, wondering if she would have to stab him with them to make him move.

'If it's the house I think it is, you shouldn't touch it with a barge-pole.'

Althea had had her doubts about it herself. Hearing Patrick being so sniffy made her determined to live there. She produced the details. He snatched them from her and glanced over them with cursory disdain.

'Ripe for renovation. Have you any idea what that means?'

'I have an excellent builder who can advise me. He's very reasonable.'

'I'm coming with you. Your car or mine?'

'Patrick, what is this? What gives you the right to be so high-handed?'

'Friendship! And not, before you refer to that damned insulting letter you wrote me, between us. I'm talking about my friendship with your children. They're nice kids. They deserve somewhere better to live than that health hazard. So, whose car?'

Sensing herself about to give in, she made one last stand. 'Don't try and be masterful with me! I'm perfectly capable of deciding whether or not a house is about to fall down. And I'm extremely good at DIY.'

He took hold of her keys, unlocked the door, unlocked the passenger door, and shovelled her into the driving seat. She tried to drive off and leave him standing there, but he was in the car before the engine fired.

Her car groaned as they went up the hill. The worst part of this whole situation was, she decided, that she was secretly pleased to have someone else to look at the house with.

'It won't do, you know.'

Althea did know. Being told didn't help. 'It's got a lovely garden. The soil's OK.'

'Is that all you care about?'

'No, but it is important. And the master bedroom is big too.' She fought back the memory which rapidly followed this statement, and hoped he would too.

'The other bedrooms are tiny and it's miles away from anywhere.'

'Merry could have a music room. It would be nice for her to be able to practise the piano without the boys moaning.'

'Merry would rather a bedroom big enough for a bed *and* a chest of drawers in a house which didn't feel spooky even to those without an imagination.'

He was leaning against the kitchen worktop across the room from her. The kitchen was a good size and would be nice if someone removed the decaying plywood units and put in something more substantial. Althea contemplated Patrick, acknowledging the fact that if he crossed the room and took her in his arms she wouldn't protest, she'd settle into them like a bird into its nest. But he didn't cross the room. He stayed where he was.

Althea sighed. 'I think I must have looked at every house on the market,' she said quietly. 'This is the last one even half-way possible. I have to be out of my house in six weeks. I'm in no position to be fussy. I could buy this and then move again when there's more on the market.'

'You'd lose almost ten grand doing that.'

'Maybe! But I don't have an alternative! I could really do with a little support just now. This house is really perfectly adequate.'

'It's structurally unsound. Only you would dream of buying a house without a survey. With one, this would be virtually unsellable.'

Althea turned away. Rightness is not an attractive quality, and she didn't want to see it in every line and crease of Patrick's body.

'There is an alternative you know.' His voice was gentler than it had been for a very long time. 'You could rent.'

'Where?' She'd thought of this after the first six hopeless properties.

'At my house.' Her jaw dropped, and while she was thus silenced, he went on: 'There are six good rooms which are leak-proof. You could get your builder to do them up a little to make them habitable. You could stay there until after Chelsea, when you've more time and there would be more properties about.'

He stopped talking but still she couldn't get her mouth and brain to function in unison.

'I suggested it to William. He saw it as a perfect compromise.'

She sighed. 'He's a Buddhist. He would.'

CHAPTER TWENTY-THREE

❁

She'd done most of the easy part. Wrapping each glass, cup and plate in newspaper and finding space for it in the mismatched collection of cardboard boxes, bread-crates and tea-chests had taken a long time, but it didn't take any hard decisions. The books, too, she had weeded thoroughly and then packed. The furniture was all labelled and colour-coded and the things which were going into storage had already gone.

But the attic was a minefield of sentimentality which Althea had not wanted to tackle. Only a furious telephone call from Frederick, swearing that if her junk still cluttered up the attic when he got to England he would cancel his damn cheque, got her to drag the problem to the forefront of her mind. Apparently Topaz wanted to turn the attic into a home-fitness centre.

Sacks of worn baby clothes; boxes of favourite broken toys; suitcases full of school work from the ages of five upwards: it was not a job to be tackled alone, Sylvia had declared, and had arranged to come and give assistance. Sylvia knew that without her unsentimental influence, Althea would carefully pack a pantechnicon with junk which would either have to be stored, or found space in Patrick's stables. And although these were capacious, he had a fair amount of his own things in there, and wouldn't want to stumble over splitting plastic sacks to get to them. Particularly if he discovered what he was stumbling over.

'You can't throw away that babygro!' Althea implored as Sylvia held up a withered scrap of blue-grey cotton towelling. 'They all three of them had that and looked so sweet!'·

'Haven't you any photos of them in it?' demanded Sylvia.

'Of course. Loads.'

'Then throw it away. The toes are completely worn out and half the poppers don't pop. Honestly,' she went on, seeing Althea meant to argue, 'your grandchildren won't want to wear it. Your children won't remember wearing it and so it won't mean a thing to them. And you're surely not going to offer it to Juno. Chuck it!'

'OK,' sighed Althea. 'I suppose you're right.'

'Of course I am. Now you see this handful of binbags?' Althea nodded. 'We are going to fill them with things to throw away.' She put in the offending babygro. 'And when we have, we'll go downstairs, open the wine I brought, and order pizza. I'm paying.'

'Yes, Sylvia.' Althea put her head on one side and regarded her friend. 'Has it ever occurred to you that being a nursery nurse is insufficiently demanding? I see you as a potential head teacher, myself.'

Sylvia chuckled. 'So I'm bossy. But I'm good.'

She was. She forced Althea to guess which of her children had completed which work sheet, or drawn which picture, and if she couldn't tell, it got thrown. After this had gone on for an hour, during which time Rupert came up with tea for them both, and mentioned that he didn't care if he never saw any of the stuff he did at primary school again, she chucked a lot more.

Eventually they staggered down from the attic, carrying the last load of bags, and upon Sylvia's insistence, put them straight in the back of Althea's car, so she couldn't change her mind. Tomorrow, they were going to the tip. Sylvia found a corkscrew and a couple of chipped mugs and poured the wine.

'Now, when are the removal people coming?'

'Tomorrow. At eight.'

Althea had wanted to move herself, with the help of a van and a few friends. But her mother, who was very helpful and supportive when at a safe distance, insisted on paying for a firm.

'It's bad enough moving when you've got professionals!' she declared, her voice carrying stridently down the telephone. 'Doing it yourself never works. You'll only damage your back, and then where will you be? In bed, staring at the ceiling for weeks!'

And as Althea couldn't spare the time for bed rest, she got quotes, told her mother the least iniquitous amount, and allowed her to pay it.

The other advantage of having professional removers was that it meant less contact time with Patrick. In spite of his generous offer and his obvious concern for them as a family, he was still avoiding her. She ought to be pleased, of course. She had wanted not to have to see him at all, and had told him so, in writing. But every stony glance cut her. He was so warm and friendly to the children, and so cold to her. He was, it appeared, willing for her to share his house but not his air-space. Still, she hadn't time to worry about things like that, not when Chelsea was only just over six weeks away.

'What sort of pizza do you want?' Sylvia was asking, as Althea clung to her mug of wine, contemplating her broken heart and the Chelsea Flower Show with equal misery.

There was a lot of discussion and changing of minds before Althea was forced to make a decision. 'Oh, whatever you're having,' she said.

'But you hate pineapple on pizza,' said Merry. 'Get a grip!'

'Well, without the pineapple then.'

'You must be really sad leaving here,' said Sylvia, when they retreated to the conservatory. It was a little chilly at this time of year, but the children were watching some film which involved a lot of cops, cars and unsuitable language in the sitting room.

'I am, of course. But I'm more worried about the future than I am about leaving the past. We were happy here, when it was just the kids and me. And it's been my home for a long time. But I've also been more unhappy here than I ever hope to be again.'

'I suppose you have. You always seem to be so relaxed and laid back, one tends to forget the pain you must have been through.'

'It's all water under the bridge now, of course,' Althea said brightly, not caring to see pity in her friend's eyes.

'And you're happy to be living with Patrick? I gather you've had – er – a little breakdown in communications.'

'For a start, we're not living *with* Patrick, we're just using part of his house. And for a second, we're fine with each other. We're just not an item.'

'Has he broken your heart?'

'Of course not! What rubbish you talk sometimes, Syl. We just don't get on as a couple, that's all.' She regarded her friend speculatively. 'I must say, I thought you fancied him yourself. Why aren't *you* going out with him?'

Sylvia looked embarrassed and uncomprehending. 'I must confess, I did ring him up on a pretext and tacked on another invitation to dinner, but he turned me down.'

Some emotion very like relief flickered for a moment in Althea's diaphragm. She quenched it firmly. 'Oh? Actually, I think he's interested in Jenny. He likes younger women.'

'I'm younger than you!'

'But not as young as Jenny.'

'No, well. Still, I might give him another chance when I help you to move in. He might have forgotten what I looked like.'

Althea laughed merrily, hiding the pain her friend's casual remarks were causing. 'Why not? And are you sure you can help? I don't want to wear you out.'

'No, you won't. I'll get Jenny to come along too. You'll need all the help you can.'

'So I will,' said Althea glumly, not looking forward to witnessing Patrick being fawned on and flattered by two such up-front young women as Sylvia and Jenny. Still, moving was supposed to be the most stressful thing next to a bereavement or a divorce, a little added stress probably wouldn't make any difference.

It was somewhat of an embarrassment to Althea to discover that Patrick had allocated the rooms he had been living in to her family, instead of the rooms he had shown her. There was some explanation which William related but Althea, her mind on other things, didn't quite grasp what it was. She was too busy telling removal men what she wanted where, a difficult task at the best of times, made harder by the rooms not being the ones she had expected. They were much larger, and would allow for a bed-room each and a sitting room. But Althea had planned things differently.

What had been Patrick's bedroom would be the sitting room. It was extremely spacious and had wonderful views. But the real reason behind the decision was her hope that once the room was filled with family clutter, she would forget that stormy night when passion had got in the way of reason.

Sylvia, who, Althea decided, had come as much for the

talent-spotting as to help, regarded the two husky young removal men. 'Don't fancy yours much,' she murmured to Jenny.

Althea compressed her mouth into an expression of disapproval. She didn't fancy either of them.

Instead of the traditional brown coats, they wore ripped T-shirts and Levi's. Muscles rippled proudly in their arms, but, in spite of their bulk, they didn't seem very strong, and what went on in their heads was anybody's guess.

In sharp contrast was the foreman. He was an aged, wizened person who would probably have managed better on his own. He coaxed furniture up the stairs, round narrow bends, and over banister rails as if it were flexible. He went in for none of the heavy breathing, gasping and subdued swearing which the younger members of the team found necessary. Althea kept expecting him to wave a wand over a box of books and get them all to leap out and into the book cases, like Mary Poppins.

'I like them older,' she muttered, watching the brown-coated foreman instructing the young men on how to pick up a tea-chest without incurring a permanent injury.

'So do I,' said Jenny. 'But not wrinkly-older. Someone nicely mature. Knows his way round the world, how to treat a woman.'

'Like Patrick?' asked Sylvia.

Jenny may have blushed. It was hard to tell under the accumulated grime and her usual healthy glow. 'Uh huh.'

'Come on, girls. We've got a lot to do,' said Althea.

'So which of these rooms is your bedroom?' asked Sylvia. 'Or will you use Patrick's?'

'What do you mean?' It was Althea's turn to blush now, but in her case, it would be put down to exertion.

'I mean, this big room' – Sylvia led the way into it – 'was Patrick's bedroom.'

'Was it? How do you know that?' Somehow Althea managed to sound arch instead of desperate.

Sylvia shrugged. 'He showed me round once.'

'And me,' said Jenny, not to be outdone.

Whether he'd done more, Althea couldn't tell. 'Oh. Well, as it's the biggest,' she said, 'I thought I'd have it as the sitting room.'

'So, which bedroom?'

Althea led the way to the smallest. 'Here. That way the boys don't have to share.'

'There is such a thing as being too unselfish, you know,' said Jenny. 'You should be more assertive. Perhaps you should go on a course.'

'I like this room.' Althea tried assertiveness and found she liked that too. 'It has a lovely view.' It was the same view as from what was now the sitting room. But if Sylvia or Jenny even noticed, they didn't comment. They wouldn't know why Althea was so fond of it – unless, of course, they had the same reason for liking it.

'I'll go and tell the men that,' offered Jenny, and disappeared.

Sylvia and Althea went back to the sitting room. 'Your furniture will be lost in this vast space,' said Sylvia. 'What it needs, of course, is a four-poster bed.'

'What it's getting is a sofa and a couple of armchairs which need re-covering. Now pass me that broom, and I'll give the floor a sweep.'

Most of their furniture had gone into a portakabin, a costly habitation necessary, she hoped, for only a short time. The very minimum had been moved to Patrick's. School books, gardening books, a few pots and pans, some treasured possessions. Most of these, Althea realized with resignation, were designed to make a noise – CD players, tape decks and televisions. Perhaps that was why Patrick had moved into an area of the house quite removed from this one.

Sylvia, backed up by Jenny, insisted on inviting Patrick in to share the wine they had brought with them. Althea protested, saying the place was a mess, he'd be tired, etc., etc., but they took no notice. Althea gave up assertiveness as a bad job.

He came, but managed to avoid Althea almost completely. Only Althea was aware of it, but to her it was plain. She resolved to get her family, herself and her plants out of his way just as soon as the Flower Show was over. Now, she couldn't afford grand gestures.

She watched him flirt with the girls and chat with her children, all of whom were lounging around the furniture, which was indeed lost in the vastness of the room.

'This is a two-sofa sitting room, really,' said Merry. 'Or even three.'

'Cool! Can we get two more sofas?' asked Rupert. 'Then we can all lie full length and watch telly.'

'And where will your mother sit?' asked Patrick.

Rupert shrugged. 'She never has time to sit down these days.'

Patrick turned his gaze upon her, managing to hide any concern he might feel under bored disapproval. 'Oh, really?'

'Yes,' said Althea. 'Now I must go and fetch the animals from Juno's house before she releases them into the wild.'

Things were not going well in the greenhouse. A whole tray of ivy-leaved toadflax had resented its removal from the garden wall and had died. The nigella seedlings had all grown to a great height and fallen over, and the seedling ash tree had lost its leaves. With the build-up to the show only two weeks away, she would be hard pushed to produce more, and decided the toadflax would have to be picked a couple of days before the judging, as would another ash tree. Frederick and Topaz would have to endure another raid on the garden by Althea.

But they were being very supportive, as indeed was everyone. Only Patrick ignored Althea. He didn't ask how things were going or offer help in some way.

Sylvia had told her mother and step-father that Althea would need to stay with them on and off for at least three weeks. Her step-brother had been ordered to be her hired help. Althea, who followed up Sylvia's assertiveness with a lot of politeness, gratitude and offers of payment, which in Sylvia's brother's case, was accepted with alacrity, was smiled on and made welcome.

Jenny, whose cousin 'from Oz' was in the UK on the grand tour, was to be employed as a labourer on one of the posh magazine gardens. She promised to introduce him to Althea before the public were forbidden the showground, just so Althea would know someone. Althea was truly grateful for the offer, but she wondered how willing Jenny's cousin would be to be nice to a woman past her first flush of youth. The showground would be full of attractive young horticulture students building gardens for the colleges. But still, it was a nice thought.

Althea turned her mind to more immediate nice thoughts.

Merry's birthday party. Coming as it did towards the end of April, Merry's birthday should have heralded the beginning of summer but the boys never failed to remind Althea that one year it had snowed. Not that year, thank heaven, and the party, consisting of five exotically dressed and highly made-up young girls, went as planned. They played pass the parcel, musical statues and charades, stayed up all night talking and went home in the morning, dark-eyed and yawning, assuring Althea that they'd had a great time.

Rupert, who'd been very helpful and un-big-brotherish, operating the tape player for the music, commented: 'Those girls, they look about twenty and they act like they were nine.'

Ignoring the disdain in his voice, Althea smiled. 'I know. Great, isn't it? They look so grown up and sophisticated, but underneath they're still little girls.'

CHAPTER TWENTY-FOUR

It was raining heavily. Having come up from Gloucestershire on the early train and left her bags in Fulham with Sylvia's parents, Althea stood in the foyer of Sloane Street underground station feeling a completely country bumpkin, reluctant to dart out into the alien world of hurrying feet and eye-threatening umbrellas. Everyone around her seemed to know where they were going and what they were doing, and Althea felt that if she hesitated she would be mown down.

And although they were entirely suitable, given the weather, it felt wrong being in London in her gardening clothes. All about her people were wearing slick city suits and neat navy-blue macs or clear plastic ones over bright, short skirts. She spotted the occasional Burberry over a Liberty print dress which went with sensible loafers and an executive briefcase. No one else was wearing lace-up walking boots, loose trousers and a cracked wax jacket which hadn't ever been a Barbour, even when it was new.

She already felt a failure for taking the tube, instead of the bus as recommended by Sylvia's mother. Althea didn't trust buses, you couldn't tell where you were supposed to get off. With the tube, at least you knew when you'd arrived. She took a deep breath, pulled up her hood, and ducked out into the street, setting off in what she hoped was the direction of the Royal Hospital grounds. Although Althea had been to the Chelsea Flower Show before, she'd been taken by a friend and so couldn't quite remember the way. She had a map tucked into her pocket, but in such heavy rain she didn't want to have to refer to it.

She had instructions about when she was to meet the organizer of the competition, her fellow exhibitors and the small amount of hired help they were allowed, but had been given no details about where they might be.

They can't be that hard to find, Althea muttered to herself, risking the map's disintegration by a quick look under the awning of a shop which sold hand-tailored waistcoats for more than Althea would spend on clothes in a year. That's definitely the barracks, she assured herself. I must be nearly there.

At last, she stood in a corner of the huge, municipal gardens which would, by a lot of hard work and not a little magic, soon be transformed into the Chelsea Flower Show. There were early signs of this metamorphosis. Groups of people in boiler suits stood about in the rain holding ropes, shouting instructions, and beckoning to reversing vehicles. Lorries drove up and down the paths loaded with polythene-swathed crates. Sheets of plywood and piles of timber and bricks were placed at regular intervals around the vast empty space which would soon be the giant marquee. Vans with the names of garden-design firms, municipal parks departments from far away, turf and timber suppliers, seemed frighteningly professional. One tent was already erected, and had a stream of people queuing up outside it. It was the coffee stall.

Now where do I go? She peered cautiously from under her hood. They must be somewhere here. She started to walk round the vast space. With luck, I'll see two other lost-looking souls.

Althea smiled hopefully at everyone she saw. There were not many, and although they all returned her smile they none of them bustled up and said, 'You must be Althea.' She passed hundreds of ceramic lavatories which looked like the winner of a sculpture competition. She saw a huge farm cart travelling on the bed of a low loader, followed by what appeared to be the trunk of a mature and ancient oak tree. Her spirits began to lift. While her garden was going to seem boring and pathetic amongst so much innovation, watching the other gardens develop would be fascinating.

At last she spotted a woman standing by a small placard with 'Gardens Grow' written on it by a careless marker pen. 'Hi!' she said with relief. 'You must be Felicity Clarke?'

'No,' said the woman. 'I'm Veronica Edgeworth-Harvey, one of the prize winners.'

The woman was carrying a huge green umbrella and wearing the authentic version of Althea's waxed jacket, without the hood, at the collar of which were revealed a white silk blouse, an Hermès scarf and a string of pearls. Beneath the jacket was a tweed skirt which ended just above a pair of very shiny Hunter wellington boots, navy blue and spotless. She had pearl studs in her ears and a perfect complexion. She didn't smile.

'Oh, hello! How nice to meet you! I'm Althea, Althea Farraday. I'm one of the contestants, too.' She held out her hand, forcing the woman to take one of hers out of the pocket of her Barbour. It felt cold to the touch. She's not stand-offish, Althea told herself, hoping passionately that she was right, she's nervous and shy.

'I wonder where Felicity Clarke is?' Althea went on. 'She said nine-thirty.'

'I know,' said the woman. 'She's late.' She sounded annoyed.

'I wonder who the other contestant is?'

'It's a man. A friend of mine's nephew. It's terribly unfair because he's practically professional. I've only done a six-week course in garden design.'

'Oh.' Althea wondered if she ought to confess she'd done a no-week course in garden design but decided her confidence was eroded enough already without having well-bred scorn poured on her by this English rose.

'But my man is coming to help me with the planting up.'

'What do you mean? What sort of man?'

'My *gardener*.' The woman regarded Althea as if she must be stupid. Althea felt stupid under her critical gaze. She couldn't remember the details, but she was fairly sure there had been things in the rules about having to create the garden yourself. But a moment's depressing tussle with her memory didn't come up with a clause prohibiting people with gardeners, stately homes or unforthcoming manners. Damn.

'Oh.'

A young man with an anxious expression loped up to them. 'Are you Althea and Veronica?' He put a warm hand into each of theirs in turn. 'I'm Michael. Felicity asked me to welcome you. She's got held up. Alistair Crowthorne, the other contestant, is over in that little hut. Come and join us.'

Althea and Veronica followed him in thoughtful silence. Althea thought he was a pleasant young man who at least gave

259

the impression of being friendly, even if it was part of his job as a public-relations man. Veronica's expression gave no clue to what she was thinking, but Althea would have laid money she was raging against people who used your Christian name even before you'd been introduced, let alone invited them to use it.

Alistair Crowthorne was tall, dark and undeniably handsome, and slightly less forthcoming than Veronica Edgeworth-Harvey – if that were possible. His wellies were green, but just as pristine, and went with a Burberry and a hat which would have looked unbearable on his grandfather. He appeared to be about twenty-five and sounded, when forced by Michael to speak, about fifty.

'Well now, Flick'll be here soon to show you the plot' – Michael was working hard – 'but I may as well run through the rules while we're waiting.'

He produced a roll of plans. 'We're here.' He pointed to a square. 'And the plot's divided into three. One for each of you.' He smiled briefly. Only Althea smiled back. 'You're allowed three days' use of our digger and our three lads, to get the ground broken, but after that, any labour you'll have to pay for. OK?'

Everyone nodded.

'I'm sure you'll have a great time. It's a wonderful chance to exhibit at Chelsea. I think "Gardens Grow" have done a super thing giving you all the opportunity.'

'Yes,' said Althea, when she realized that no one else was going to say anything.

'Well . . .' Michael glanced at his watch, hunting his mental timetable for an escape route. 'As Flick isn't here yet, I'll take you along to the plot. The chaps'll be here soon with a digger, so there's not much time to lose. We'll soon have you covered in mud.' He laughed. He would soon be somewhere else.

The four of them walked to the site in silence. With so little encouragement, Michael's supply of enthusiastic conversation dried up; Veronica looked pained and put upon; and Alistair so far above the rest of the world it seemed strange that his boots actually were picking up a little soil.

Althea was forcing herself to grasp the fact that not all people who gardened were nice. This was an assumption she had clung to for years and it was hard to be disillusioned at this particular moment. But unless her fellow contestants unbent several miles, there was little chance of the camaraderie she'd anticipated. They might all be in the same boat – sharing a comparatively small plot of land – but that didn't mean it was necessary to socialize.

This was disappointing, but even more so was the discovery that, as she trembled on the brink of the most important and exciting opportunity of her life, she didn't feel excited, or even scared, particularly. She just wanted to go home.

And not to the big, dusty rooms with beautiful views and fine period details, dotted about with her tatty furniture where her children were now ensconced. No, to the home she'd loved and tended for so many years, which was now inhabited by Frederick and Topaz, and which she hadn't had time to say goodbye to.

CHAPTER TWENTY-FIVE

Althea wished she'd brought a flask, like the generous, leather-covered ones Alistair and Veronica had, then she wouldn't have had to walk the mile or so across to the stall by the entrance to get a cup of coffee. She'd have shared her flask, if she'd had one, without a second thought. But Alistair and Veronica weren't into sharing. In fact even sharing the labour and digger was hard for them. They watched, feet tapping, hands on hips, while another person's plot was being churned into workable mud, muttering 'At last', when it was their turn.

Althea knew that while she was away, they would try and persuade the jolly digger-driver to leave her plot and do something to one of theirs, and hoped he would refuse. He was friendly, oblivious to the pouring rain and worsening conditions. She bought him a cup of coffee and a KitKat – she needed him more than they did as Sylvia's brother had done something to his back and couldn't come. Sylvia had said it was typical. Jenny's 'cousin from Oz' hadn't materialized either.

'So, if your site's supposed to be sloping,' the digger-driver asked her, sipping the brew which was now luke-warm, cooled by the rain and the long walk from the coffee stall, 'when's your soil getting here?'

'Oh God!' Althea murmured behind clenched teeth so the others wouldn't guess the vastness of her mistake. 'I never thought of that.'

'Well,' went on Jerry, the driver, 'loads of sites are getting rid of soil. You want to stop the dumper trucks as they go to the tip and get them to off-load here. Then you want a few railway sleepers to build up the back.'

She'd have offered him her body if she'd thought he'd want it. 'Thank you so much. It never occurred to me to think about soil. I was too bound up in the plants.'

'Go on, ask that truck there.'

Although a friendly soul, Althea was actually quite shy about stopping young men in the road and asking them to reverse and dump a load of soil into a very confined space. But she forced herself to do it, and was surprised how obliging the young man was.

'We're getting rid of a whole load of it, do you want it all?' he asked.

'Well, I probably need quite a lot.'

'Tell you what, I'll bring it all until you tell me to stop. OK?'

'Very OK. You're so kind, thank you very much.'

He grinned and made a dismissive gesture. 'Glad to help.'

As the day went on, Althea discovered that it was only her fellow winners of the 'Gardens Grow' competition who were so unbending. Everyone else she came across was extremely friendly and willing to help. The railway sleepers she acquired from someone who'd over-ordered and didn't want to use the less good ones. Althea was tipped off about these by the man who brought the soil. Once Althea had asked permission, he brought them round to her. They were exceptionally heavy, but with Ned and Tom, the hired help provided by 'Gardens Grow', to heave them into position, she eventually had a back to her sloping site.

Unfortunately, Veronica complained that her sleepers in-fringed on her plot by an inch. And although Veronica had an antique summerhouse for that corner and it made no difference to her design, she insisted on Althea sawing off the surplus. The railway sleepers could have been of solid iron. Althea's borrowed saw was not up to the job and after half an hour of sawing she had made no impression. Either Ned or Tom (Althea never did get them sorted out) watched for as long as they could bear it and then took over. Whichever one it was gave up after fifteen minutes with no visible result. The three of them slapped a coat of wood preserver over the ends while Veronica was at lunch, assuring her when she came back that yes, they were now the right length. Althea refused to feel guilty, especially when, having measured the plot again, she found it was three inches narrower than Veronica's. She took the tube back to Fulham Broadway, tireder and wiser. Veronica, who swept by in a Mercedes, didn't stop to give her a lift to the station.

Sylvia's mother was motherly in the best sort of way. She made Althea a cup of tea and ran her a bath while she drank it. Then she insisted on giving Althea her supper – shepherd's pie, peas and carrots – on a tray in her room so she could eat it in her dressing gown and not talk if she didn't want to. Althea didn't want to, but she managed to tell Mrs Jones how grateful she was for her kindness before collapsing into bed at nine o'clock.

The next day she left the house at seven a.m. braving the bus. Thus she had a couple of hours on the plot alone, before the others came. And as it wasn't raining quite so hard, she felt more cheerful.

'Cup of coffee, Al?' Ned – she was sure it was Ned – held out a polystyrene cup half full of liquid. 'I owe you it.'

Althea sipped it. 'Wet and warm, as they say.'

'Unlike Lord and Lady Snooks.' He nodded towards Veronica and Alistair. 'They may be wet, but the entire ozone layer would have to disappear before they'd warm up.'

'I expect they had difficult childhoods,' said Althea.

'They were born old.'

Althea rummaged round in her bag. 'KitKat?'

Ned took one. 'Ta.'

While the other two were arguing over what they wanted Ned to do first, Althea took herself off to visit the other gardens in the making.

They were all far more ambitious and exotic than hers was. There was a conservatory in a tree, built round one of the mature trees in the grounds. It was splendid, like the bridge of a ship, and promised to be one of the stars of the show. Someone else was building a miniature replica of the Grand Canyon, re-producing all the strata of rock in their proper order. Another was recreating an Irish hermit's garden, with nine bean rows, a crumbling stone dwelling, a bog and fantastic wild flowers.

Her time away from the preciousness of Veronica and Alistair was cheering and inspiring. While she felt her garden would never be able to hold up its head in such illustrious company, the energy and atmosphere inspired her to greater heights. And it began to amuse her that Veronica and Alistair, who were as amateur as she was, were the only ones, among all the most illustrious names in the gardening world, who seemed stuck up.

*

Althea went home for the weekend. The three children and Bozo had all come to collect her from the station. Seeing them waiting on the platform melted her well-developed stiff upper lip into a quivering heap of emotion.

'I've missed you all so much!' she said, hugging them in turn and eventually picking up Bozo who was scrabbling at her leg.

'Aren't you having a nice time?' asked Merry. 'I thought you wanted to go to the Chelsea Flower Show?'

'I do, and I am having a nice time, I suppose. I just missed you lot. Have you missed me?'

'Of course,' they said.

But Althea could tell they hadn't. And although she was very pleased they weren't all clutching her trouser legs like orphans, she couldn't help wondering why they hadn't.

'So is William looking after you all?' she asked, holding Merry's hand.

Merry, having quickly checked that none of her friends were around and would see her thus attached, nodded. 'Sort of. And Patrick has.'

'What do you mean, Patrick has?'

'Well, he's been seeing we're OK and stuff.'

Althea was about to protest but realized that she couldn't. If it had been anyone else keeping an eye on her children, she'd have been delighted and grateful. 'What about Juno? Has she been looking after you, too?'

Rupert shook his head. 'We look after her. She's so neurotic about Candy – we're not supposed to call her that, by the way – she hasn't any energy for us.'

'No, well, new-born babies are exhausting.'

'So we go over and carry her about, so Juno can get some rest. She's longing to see you.'

Althea gulped. 'Well, she can't, not till I've had a bath, a big drink and a long nap. I'm knackered.'

'Mum! I thought we weren't supposed to say that?' said Merry.

'Nor am I, but no one's perfect.'

Patrick was nowhere to be seen when William drove his family into the courtyard of their temporary home. Althea was heartily relieved and bitterly disappointed. She put her ambiguity down to extreme fatigue and over-excitement. But she resolved that tomorrow, she would seek him out and thank him for keeping an eye on her children.

Althea visited her sister on Saturday afternoon. Patrick's car was still missing, and it was only when they were nearly at Juno's that Merry mentioned he'd gone away for the weekend.

Juno was pleased to see her, fairly interested in what she'd been doing, but mostly she badgered Althea for advice and then told her it was all wrong.

Althea was never offended if people rejected her advice. Why should they take it, after all? But Juno seemed to want it just so she could tell Althea how foolish, old-fashioned, new-fangled or dangerous she was. Only Candida herself, an adorable bundle smelling of fabric conditioner and babies, who slept obligingly the moment Althea took her into her arms, made the visit worthwhile.

On Monday Althea was being driven up to London with her first consignment of flowers, trees, and turf, which she now referred to as 'plant material'. She was going in a dilapidated van belonging to Daniel, a Buddhist friend of William's. He was doing it to gain merit and earn twenty pounds. While she was distinctly uneasy about travelling in such a vehicle, it seemed the only solution to the problem. The alternative was to hire a van, drive it up, drive it back and then travel back up by train – a hugely costly and time-consuming exercise. For although Althea now had a handsome sum of money in the bank, the habits of economy were too ingrained to break. Besides, they would need every penny for their new house, if they ever found one.

Thus, at five o'clock on a beautiful May morning, she and Daniel set off for London, the van full of dewy plants. It was the most perfect morning Althea could remember seeing. Although she had only had four hours' sleep and felt slightly muzzy in the head, she marvelled at the mist threading over the valleys, hiding the factories and motorways, leaving only the hills and trees. Daniel was obligingly silent, and she gazed at the beauty around her awestruck and pensive.

She realized, after about twenty miles, that in different circumstances she would have thoroughly enjoyed Chelsea. She liked the people building the other gardens. The atmosphere was powerful and energizing. With a team to work with, instead of people to compete against, she would have been really happy. But she'd had too much upset recently.

It wasn't only moving away from the house she'd lived in so long. It wasn't only Patrick, his hold on her no less than it ever had been, in spite of her not seeing him. Nor was it just the uncertainty of her future: where she would live; how she would earn her living. Or the worry she inevitably felt about the boys' coming exams. The GCSE's weren't so important, as long as Rupert got good enough results to get into the sixth form. But William's A levels were vital. And he hadn't thought so until recently, possibly when it was too late to catch up.

No, what was stopping her being content was the painfully acquired knowledge that one of her most fondly held beliefs was wrong: sacrificing your own need for happiness every time, in case the children didn't like it, was an unreasonable demand. She had gradually come to realize that she should have continued her relationship with Patrick and dealt with any distress the children might have felt. And this was a particularly bitter pill to swallow, as she was now fairly confident that they would have coped perfectly well. But it was too late. Patrick wouldn't have her now if she came chocolate-covered and gift-wrapped. And why should he? She was a neurotic female who didn't know her own mind and had happily messed up a promising relationship just in case her children objected, without even asking the children the question whether they did or not.

'All right?' asked Daniel. 'You seem a bit quiet.'

'I'm just tired, that's all.'

It was odd, she thought, that she had reached this conclusion when her head was almost totally absorbed with the Flower Show. It was as if one's brain was so used to going along its old established track, that to change a long-held belief you had to be so preoccupied that your mind was caught unawares, and thus able to alter.

'Would you like a peppermint, Daniel?'

'No thanks,' he replied.

And that was all they managed by way of conversation until they got to London, and Daniel needed direction.

Althea was heartily glad that her companion was a Buddhist, and therefore not given to road rage, irritation and impatience. Otherwise their journey, including the inch-by-inch procession from the entrance to the showground to her plot, which took over an hour, could have been extremely stressful. Not for the first time, Althea wondered if there wasn't something in this Buddhism after all.

Daniel helped her unload, took his money, and set off to Hampstead, where he was going on a retreat. Althea jokingly suggested she met him at the exit with a cup of coffee.

'I could have planted up my garden, gone across to the refreshment tent and carried the cup to you in the time it'll take you to get out of here.'

He grinned and shrugged. *'Samsara!'*

'That boy,' she said to Veronica, who happened to be standing next to her, 'used to be a law student.'

'Oh? And what is he now?'

'A Buddhist.'

'Oh. I didn't know that was a profession.'

Althea sighed. 'It isn't. But how I wish it was.'

Time ran away like water going down a drain. First came the closing of the ground to the public, with no entry without a Build-Up pass. Then the real changes began. Building sites grew grass, mature trees were planted by crane, their massive root balls wrapped in polythene. Althea took time to watch as a grove of hundred-year-old olive trees took up residence on a false hillside, the crane-driver working with as much skill and precision as a surgeon. Conservatories, sheds, even boats, flew up overnight. The biggest marquee ever was erected; the atmosphere buzzed.

And disaster became a daily occurrence. Veronica's standard wisteria in white took a fit and went brown. She spent a harassed morning on her mobile phone trying to track down another. Alistair's fig tree refused to come into leaf, even when he draped it in plastic and turned on the heaters. A crane broke several panes of glass in the conservatory/tree-house. Plants wilted for no apparent reason.

Every day Althea went to the site in fear and trembling

about what would have happened to her little plot, now nearly complete except for last-minute touches. And every day she found it all in order – until the Friday before the judging, which would take place on Monday. Then, what she saw was so awful, it put everyone else's problems into the pinprick category.

On Thursday night a stop-cock had burst, allowing the Thames to gush in a powerful stream across the corner of the 'Gardens Grow' plot. No one had noticed until some night-owl bonsai-grower spotted it a couple of hours later. By which time the area was knee deep in water and Althea's garden was partially washed away.

She discovered it at seven a.m. on Friday morning. All her belatedly garnered soil had been washed into a stream of mud. Her pond was sliding down the hillside she'd so carefully built. Her trees leaned as if about to topple over completely. The whole plot looked like a plastic model put too near the fire.

She took a deep breath and said nothing. Veronica, early for once, came up to her.

'Are you all right? I've rung Felicity. She says she's on her way. You seem very calm.'

'It's shock,' said Althea. 'And expediency. I really haven't got the time to have a nervous breakdown now. I'll have to wait until next weekend.'

'Is there anything I can do?' Veronica was obviously as shocked as Althea. It was only sheer chance that it hadn't been her garden.

'Can I borrow your phone? I need to ring my son.'

'Won't he have to go to school?'

She shook her head. 'No. He doesn't go in on Friday mornings.'

William was monosyllabic but reassuring. Everything that Althea asked him to do, he agreed to. 'Yeah, yeah, sure, Mum. Fine. No problem. I'll be there. I'll see if I can get Daniel: if not, it'll take longer. But I'm sure it'll be OK. Try not to worry.'

It was only then that Althea allowed herself to retreat to the Ladies. She was splashing her face with water when someone came up behind her.

'Hey! You're the one whose garden's been washed away!' It

was a woman in her early twenties with long brown hair tied in a plait and a sympathetic expression. 'How awful!'

'Yes.'

'But "Gardens Grow" are the sponsors, aren't they? They'll probably arrange for you to have another plot next year.'

Althea shook her head. 'Nope. It's this year or never for me. So it had better be this year.'

'You're very cool about it.'

Althea almost smiled. 'As I said to someone earlier, I've no time for a nervous breakdown until next weekend. My son is being driven up by a friend to help me sort it out. He's a Buddhist. Very calming.'

'What was your garden like? I've only just got here and I didn't see it before the disaster.'

Althea leaned on the sink. There was nothing practical she could do about it just yet, anyway. She might just as well tell this interested soul about her cheap, instant garden, designed for amateurs to achieve quickly.

'All the books tell you to buy plants in threes and fives. But what young couple on a mortgage can afford that? It's hard enough to afford single plants. Most of my garden – at home I mean, although I've moved from there now – was created from people giving me bits and buying plants at boot sales and fêtes. That's a good way to do it, of course, but it can take ages. And the couple I have in mind – I feel I almost know them – are starting completely from scratch. They're in a starter home and all they've got is a patch of not very good lawn and some topsoil. And it's all on a slope.'

'Why? Are starter homes always on slopes?'

'No. But in my garden, the only bit I could spare was. And I come from a very hilly part of the Cotswolds. Flat gardens are at a premium.'

The woman seemed so fascinated that Althea let herself ramble on. It was soothing to share her dream and ideas with someone who seemed interested. Veronica and Alistair were so cagey about their plans, she hadn't felt she could talk to them about it. And at home, no one would have understood. They were still talking when Veronica came in.

'Oh there you are. Felicity's here. Everyone's looking for you. She wants you to pull out and do it again next year.'

'I'd better go. Thanks,' she said to the woman. 'It was nice talking to you. Cathartic. I feel better now.'

The woman grinned. 'Nice talking to you too. I think you've got some really good ideas.'

Althea refused to be talked out of repairing her garden. She didn't want to wait a whole year for another chance.

'OK, then,' said Felicity, sounding tired. 'You can have some help with the landscaping, but I don't know about the planting. It might not be fair.'

'It wouldn't be,' put in Veronica, who had been supportive only for a short time.

'My son is coming. If you could arrange a Build-Up pass for him, he'll help me.'

'Right,' said Felicity. 'What's his name? I'll leave one at the gate.'

Althea thought she'd used up her supply of astonishment and shock, but when she saw Patrick and not William striding through the traffic which still thronged the road round the marquee, bearing purposefully down on her, she felt remarkably shaky. She'd been so brave up to then. Seeing Patrick made her want to burst into tears – an event everyone had expected to happen earlier.

She couldn't speak for a few minutes. 'Hello. What are you doing here?' she managed, croakily.

Patrick didn't hold open his arms to her, or even smile. He just grunted at her. 'William told me the problem.'

'But you didn't need to come! William would have been fine!'

'William's got his A levels to take, in case you've forgotten. He needs to work every hour he can.'

'I know! I wouldn't have asked him if it hadn't been a real emergency!'

'Which is why I'm here. And before you say anything, you don't need an expert gardener, you need a builder. What do you want me to do?'

Althea smiled. It seemed like the first time for ages.

Patrick's athletic form, stripped to the waist and shovelling soil about like a navvy, made an impressive sight. Piles of soil moved from one side to another with lightning speed while Althea stood at the top, tamping it down, replacing her sheets of plastic, replanting her plants. They worked almost non-stop, all day.

It was tea-time when the woman Althea had met in the Ladies reappeared. 'Cor,' she said.

Althea didn't know if she was 'corring' at Patrick who was nicely tanned, slicked with sweat and moving with an elegance and speed which could elevate digging to an Olympic sport, or if it was the improvement that had been wrought since she'd last seen Althea's garden.

'Mmm,' Althea replied ambiguously. 'I'm not sure if I can get it right in time, but at least I'll have tried.'

'You know they'll mark you down if one single pot rim is showing, or if one blade of grass or twig is out of place.'

'Yup. But I don't think I care about winning an award any more. I just want to make a respectable attempt.' She regarded the neighbouring plots, both by now almost perfect. 'And not feel too embarrassed next to this lot.'

Patrick put down his spade and leant on it. 'They're both extremely professional.'

'I know.' Althea sighed. 'I should have gone on a course, really. But I've always been a learning-by-doing sort of person.'

'Really?' said the woman. 'You haven't got a card, have you?'

Althea's brows drew together in confusion.

'She means a business card,' said Patrick. 'And no,' he said to the woman, 'she hasn't.'

'Well, just jot down your name and address on something, then. And your telephone and fax numbers.'

Althea was about to say she didn't have an address or telephone number either when Patrick pulled out his wallet. 'Here.' He scribbled on one of his cards. 'You can reach Althea here. If she's not in, she'll get a message.'

The woman was impressed and gave Althea an envious, respectful glance. 'Thanks. Here's my card.' She handed it to Althea. 'I may well be in touch.'

'I wonder why?' said Althea, when she'd gone. 'Is her six-foot square of grass and golden privet giving trouble?'

Patrick picked up his shirt from where it was draped on one of Althea's sections of trellis and put it on. 'I don't know. It's hard to tell.'

Althea forgot about the woman when she saw Patrick getting dressed. 'Are you going?' She heard the desperation in her voice and smiled to try and erase it. Veronica had come back and she didn't want her seeing her looking anything but cheerful.

'I must. I've got a lot of work to do.'

Althea's cheery grin broadened agonizingly.

'I really appreciate your coming. I couldn't have managed without you.'

'Yes, you could. Someone else would have helped out. I came for my own reasons.' Then he bent and kissed her, very hard, on the mouth and strode off into the crowd.

'Is he your manfriend?' asked Veronica.

'I don't think so,' said Althea, confused.

'Then why did he kiss you like that?'

'God knows!'

CHAPTER TWENTY-SIX

Althea awoke for the last time at four on the Monday morning. It was then that she gave up trying to get back to sleep again. She had slept, she was sure of it, but very little. Most of the night had been spent contemplating the kaleidoscope of change which seemed to be her life. Rather than go on trying to make sense of the confusion in her head, she got up and went to the window.

The spare room in Sylvia's mother's house was in the attic, and her view was of the myriad roofs and chimneys of Fulham and Chelsea. And this morning even Battersea Power Station seemed beautiful, veiled in pink-tinged mist and garlanded with jewels of sunlight.

How much more beautiful would the view from her bedroom in Patrick's house have been? This ungrateful, foolish thought came into Althea's mind the same minute she realized her stomach was making urgent demands and that she must go to the loo. She felt like an elastic band wound round something nearly to breaking point, waiting for the snap which would release her pent-up energy and send her lurching into action.

And there seemed no way to release it in this small place. Sylvia's mother and step-father slept directly underneath and would be disturbed by pacing. She'd finished her book, and even if she hadn't she felt it unlikely she could concentrate sufficiently to read. And she was far beyond the aid of Rescue Remedy. She doubted if large quantities of neat spirit would have any effect other than to make her violently sick.

After the fourth visit to the loo, she decided she'd be better off on the site. Sharing her nerves with other exhibitors would be preferable to the solitary, silent knots of anxiety which turned her body into a single mass of worry. Exercise or work was her only hope.

She tried both. She walked briskly all the way from Fulham's back streets to Chelsea's town houses, rapidly building up a sweat. It took her just over an hour. And as the houses grew grander, so their gardens grew more exotic and, gradually, her admiration of what people had done with their small, unpromising spaces penetrated her nerves. London was not such a bad place, she concluded. In fact, even the poorer areas took on a beauty in the pale golden light of dawn. But although it was only five a.m., the city was on the move. And when she arrived at the showground, she realized that the Flower Show had never gone to bed at all.

'The flower-arrangers have been up all night,' said the guard on the gate when Althea commented on the activity. 'And they're none of them young, mind.'

'Goodness me,' said Althea. 'I'm exhausted and I went to bed at nine o'clock.' She'd gone to bed, true, but she hadn't gone to sleep, not for a long time.

'They've got stamina, I'll say that for them.'

Althea stayed chatting for a moment or two longer before taking a deep breath and facing her fate.

It was amazing what had been achieved overnight. Some of the sites which had seemed raw and new had suddenly matured into beauty. She spoke to one designer, obviously as unable to sleep as herself, whom she had seen a few days before.

'Your furniture arrived then?'

He gave her a smile of relief. 'Yup. I never thought it would be made, let alone get here on time. I rang the man on Thursday – *Thursday* for God's sake – and he said, "I've got the wood."'

'How awful! Did you scream at him?'

The designer shook his head. 'No point. These craftsmen don't respond well to screaming. He knew when I had to have them, and I had to trust him to get them to me.'

'They look fabulous, as if they're growing into the soil.' Two chairs with arms and a bench encircled a fountain consisting of a pile of moss-covered rocks, creating a miniature waterfall. Her eye drifted enviously from this sylvan scene to the antique summerhouse in the corner, the ripe fruit bursting out of fruit-nets, a tunnel of white roses, dew-kissed and fragrant. 'In fact, the whole garden looks fabulous. You're bound to get a gold.'

'Who knows? It's my first Chelsea. It's been done, I suppose, but it's highly unlikely.'

'I'm just hoping not to embarrass myself. Veronica said she thought my sort of garden would go down better at the Hampton Court Show and she wasn't paying me a compliment. According to her it's very downmarket – they let children in.'

'I think your garden's fine, considering you haven't had any formal training. Not to mention it being nearly washed away.'

Althea smiled in a way she hoped showed due gratitude and humility and moved on. Why oh why had she let herself be seduced into believing she was going to do anything other than make a complete fool of herself? She might as well have offered her humble cooking skills to the head chef at the Dorchester. 'Gardens Grow' had a lot to answer for.

Althea didn't rush to reach her plot. She knew it would look a miserable effort after the wonders she had passed: lichen-covered statues overlooking lily-covered ponds; scented arbours; minimalist Japanese stone gardens, every piece of gravel leaning the right way; and lush swathes of Spanish moss drifting round a house straight off a film set, Tara before the fire. No, her homely Cotswold sloping garden would seem pathetic.

However, getting there at this ungodly hour would mean she would get a few precious hours to herself, without Veronica's nasal tones, which managed to sound complaining even when she was pleased. And without Alistair's superiority which made her feel older, fatter and more provincial every minute. He probably regretted the days when his estate was kept fertile by serfs. His love of gardening should have made him human, but instead seemed more like a desire to impose his will on everything, even nature. The only natural things permitted in his garden were the massive granite blocks, brought down from the family acres. But it was beautiful – even though everything in it deviated from nature's original plan, and was either variegated, golden, un-naturally large or miniature, the effect was stunning. The judges were bound to be impressed with such perfect blooms.

Althea deplored vandalism, but some municipal planting schemes made her yearn to scatter marigold seeds, nigella, or even Virginia stocks, in among the ordered ranks of begonias, salvias and lobelia. Alistair's garden was infinitely tasteful, with not a bedding plant in sight, and it created in her the same urge to strike a blow for disorder, even though it would not be there long enough for the seeds to take effect.

Her own garden, bang next door to his, looked extremely homespun and unsophisticated. Although, without his for comparison, she would have been pleased with it. It looked better than it had at home because here she was able to dictate the level of the slope, rather than put up with the ground's ideas on the matter. And she'd splashed out on some beautiful woven-willow fencing to divide the sections and create a pathway. At home she'd used recycled trellis. Here, her pond lining was covered with the finest compost, instead of the stony spoil she had used before. And somehow the common plants she so loved looked much more exotic against a background of darkest brown.

The pond area was her favourite section. A mere two feet by four feet, every nook and cranny was planted. Hart's-tongue ferns, fragrant Corsican mint, with its minuscule pink flowers, and kingcups crowded round the tiny pond where frog-bit, its leaves like miniature lilypads, wild forget-me-not, water-mint and water-hawthorn filled the space. It gave the impression of being very deep and very mysterious, its origins as well hidden as the pots the plants were growing in. And this morning a pair of dragonflies hovered like slivers of turquoise above the tiny shimmering pool.

Greatly cheered by this vote of confidence from Mother Nature, she went on to the bog garden which moved out from the pond. So far, she'd stuck to her plan and left out the beautiful showy hostas which would add a necessary touch of sophistication to the section. Her reasons for this were perfectly valid: hostas were expensive and likely to be decimated by slugs and snails, at least in her part of the world. But the kindly designer on the 'Aid to the Aged' garden had told her he'd several fine plants he didn't need and would be glad to contribute. Looking at it now, still slightly askew from its encounter with the Thames, this section was definitely less than perfect. As a gesture to Chelsea she decided to accept his offer. Her explanatory notes, laboriously worked on and reproduced, mentioned hostas, and did say that you could do without them if you had a slug problem; however, as for this one week of her life Althea hadn't, she decided to indulge herself.

Walking through to the annual or children's garden, Althea passed her tiny rockery. A pebblery, William called it, it was so small. But the plants in it were equally little and set it off charmingly. Creeping thymes covered the only reasonably large stone. Althea had dug it up from her own garden, stone, thyme and all. It looked instantly at home and added much needed maturity.

Alistair had described her annual garden as 'a riot of colour', and hadn't meant it as a compliment. True, there was a huge variety of colours which weren't usually put together, but Althea felt that every garden should have a corner for pure vulgarity, and a children's garden was often the very spot.

Through an arch was Althea's Temple of Taste, described in her leaflet as her white garden. Here, carefully selected self-seeding foxgloves, as pale as cream and speckled with cinnamon spots, white nigella, honey-scented alyssum, hardy geraniums, including a white phaem and a Kashmir white, and some white lavatera, were backed by white sweetpeas, a clematis and a climbing rose she had been nursing since last May. This area, mercifully, had been more or less unaffected by the burst pipe, which was just as well, Althea reflected, as it would have been virtually impossible to reproduce.

At the end of the garden was a well-weathered garden seat, a throw-out of Juno's, lovingly restored and repaired and now the focal point of her garden. Althea always felt tired by the time she had reached it, as if it really was a long way from the start of the garden to the finish, instead of a matter of a few yards.

The seat was encircled by more roses, most of which had come from cuttings, and one, the *Rosa glauca* she was so proud of, had grown from a self-sown seedling. Honeysuckle was twined among them, so the whole seat was a scented haven from the world. William would have pointed out that unless the roses were kept very well pruned, it might be rather a prickly haven, but it looked stunning, and at Chelsea, that was what counted.

Althea sat on her bench, avoiding damaging the delicate blooms which gently brushed her cheek. She sniffed the air, the appley smell reminding her of when she had rescued it from the storm in Patrick's greenhouse. Inevitably, she remembered what happened afterwards. Inevitably, she felt a stab of longing. She shook her head to clear it, and got up. She had work to do, lots of it, even though it was only a quarter to six. She wanted her garden perfect before Alistair and Veronica arrived. She noted, not without a thread of satisfaction, that Alistair's fig tree was still bereft of even a single leaf.

'So tell me about *your* garden.'

It was Althea's friend with the kind face and the plait, whose name she couldn't remember. This time she was carrying a microphone and a tape recorder and she had asked Veronica, Alistair, indeed almost everyone about their gardens. But as Althea already felt this woman was a friend, she ignored the microphone and began with enthusiasm.

'Well, the whole point of my garden is that it's cheap . . .'

She went on to tell the woman about the wash-basin pond, and the hart's-tongue ferns and ivy-leaved toadflax taken from walls. She even admitted to buying nice fencing, and to planting hostas, just because it was Chelsea.

'But it would work just as well with cast-off larch-lap and borage – you know, the wild one with huge leaves and tiny, very blue flowers?'

'You sound very enthusiastic.'

'Well, I am. Gardening has always been a passion and a part-time job, and now I hope it will be my work.' Althea found herself explaining how she'd been made redundant. 'But my main hobby-horse is that gardening should be seen to be accessible to everyone, not just people with south-facing walls and the run of the garden centre. This garden could look good in one season and even better next.'

'So what will you do when the show is over?'

'I shall advertise my services in all the usual places, but there are so many garden designers about and unless you've got a name, there isn't much work. Most garden designers have rich husbands to support them.'

'So how will you make ends meet? Carry on gardening?'

'Oh yes. I couldn't give it up. But I'll probably have to find a day job.'

'Well, thank you, that's very interesting. Inspirational. Now, what do you think of your chances for winning?'

'You mean getting some sort of award here? Nil, frankly. I've already won getting this far. "Gardens Grow" offered this opportunity as a prize, and I've more than won it. I've learnt so much I don't need any more prizes. And' – Althea smiled confidingly – 'do you truly think my garden, proud of it as I am, is really going to compete with all these professional designers? It's like putting a Shetland pony in for the Grand National. Getting over the first fence is miracle enough.'

'Well, thank you very much. I've thoroughly enjoyed hearing about your garden and I'm sure our viewers will too.' She switched off her tape recorder. 'You have still got my card, haven't you?'

Althea felt her mind go blank.

'No, of course you haven't. Here.' The woman handed her another one. 'I'll be in touch anyway, I'm sure I will.'

Althea had glanced at the card before stuffing it in the pocket of her dungarees. *Phillida Stancombe. Flourishing Ideas Productions.* She had time to wonder who the hell they were when they were at home before Veronica came up. 'The judges will be along in a minute. Hadn't you better get changed?'

Veronica was immaculate in a Liberty-print tana-lawn number which showed off her English rose complexion, pearls, and bone-fine ankles to perfection. If only she wasn't so haughty – not to say horsey – she would have been beautiful.

'The judges? Hell and damnation! I'm off!'

'You're not waiting?'

'No way! I'll find out soon enough.'

Althea found a small, forgotten area of the showground behind the Disabled Ladies Toilet. It was a permanent grassy bank well concealed by canvas and guy ropes. She lay on her back, her face offered to the sun, and tried very hard to relax.

'Nervous?' It was the woman with the tape recorder, Phillida someone or other.

'Yes, believe it or not. Although I must look as if I'm just soaking up the rays.'

The woman chuckled. 'I bet you didn't sleep and I bet you've been to the loo at least twenty times.'

'Twenty-two, actually.'

'Here, have a sip of wine. I've got a can in my bag.'

'At this time in the morning?'

'If you've been up since before dawn, it's probably opening time to you. Here, have some.'

She handed over the can and Althea took a sip. 'That's surprisingly nice.'

'I got red rather than white because I knew it would be warm before I got round to drinking it. Have some more.'

'Don't you want any?'

Phillida shook her head. 'I got up at seven. It's still morning for me. Go on, drink it. Then you may be able to have half an hour's quick kip before Royalty arrive.'

Althea groaned. 'Can you die of nerves, do you think?'

'Why are you so nervous? Is it the Royal party?'

'Oh no. I mean, I suppose it ought to be. But they're just people, and there's always some way to get through to people, if you try hard enough. No . . .'

'What then?'

'It's the disappointment everyone's going to feel when my garden bombs. I mean, I said to you earlier, I've had my reward. But there are' – Patrick's laughing eyes appeared in her mind – 'people, family, who've been very, very supportive. If I fail, they'll be miserably disappointed.'

'Success is a funny thing. You never quite know the exact moment that you achieve it.'

'Sorry?'

'Never mind. You finish the wine, eat my sandwiches and have a doze. I'll catch up with you later.'

Very much to her surprise, Althea did doze. She woke up with a start in a panic, wondering where she was. A glance at her watch showed her that she'd only been away from her plot for an hour.

She was not in a hurry to find out her fate. She went to the Ladies, washed her face, changed into her dress, an old favourite which always gave her confidence and slowly went back to the 'Gardens Grow' plot.

For a moment she thought it was a mistake, stuck there on a card in the middle of her garden. And then she thought that perhaps the plot as a whole, incorporating all three gardens, must have achieved the award. Then she saw a card in Alistair's garden. She looked back at the card and let herself take in its legend. It appeared that her garden, her cheap, makeshift, nearly-washed-away garden, had won a Silver-Gilt Medal.

Felicity appeared from behind a Japanese Pagoda. 'Darlings! I'm so thrilled! A Bronze for Alistair and a Silver-Gilt for Althea. You mustn't take it personally, Veronica. These things are purely subjective.'

Althea, on whose face a smile had begun to work its way from one corner to the other, was impressed. It couldn't be easy for Felicity to tell two contestants how well they'd done and another that it wasn't important in the same breath.

'Of course, if it hadn't been for my fig tree not being in leaf, I'd've got a Gold,' said Alistair.

'I'm sure,' said Althea, who could hardly prevent the joy and excitement not to mention smugness at having done better than him, spilling out of her.

'Well, I'm going home,' said Veronica. 'If they think I'm going to hang around here for a week, being nice to the *hoi polloi*, they'd better think again.'

'Well, be nice to the Queen first,' said Felicity. 'Then you can do what you like. Here, Althea, do you want to borrow my mobile so you can tell your family?'

After a few false starts, Althea got through to Patrick's answer phone. She left her message, sad that no one was there in person, but delighted to be able to give such good news. The children would hear when they got home from school. Patrick might take them out for a meal. Ah, Patrick. She sighed deeply, her happiness shaded briefly, like a cloud passing in front of the sun. But at least, thanks to her Silver-Gilt, he and the family could feel their efforts weren't wasted.

It was some time after the official party had visited, Royal hands were shaken and many questions asked, that a gleeful Phillida came up, barely able to suppress a skip. 'Yes, yes, yes!' she said to Althea, punching her fist in the air. 'I knew you could do it!'

'Well, thank you for being so thrilled for me.' Althea was a little surprised that someone she had barely met should be so excited by her success.

'Now you've got a Silver-Gilt, it means I can go ahead with my plan!'

'You have a plan?'

'Yup! I don't know how you'll react to it, of course, but basically, how would you like to present a gardening programme?'

'What?' Althea felt she must have misheard.

'On television? I'm with *Gardening Go-Round* and our regular female presenter has gone on maternity leave. I've been saying for ages that what we need is a non-professional gardener – no, don't take offence – I just mean one that hasn't spent years and years at Kew with a degree in botany. You haven't got one, have you?'

'A degree in botany? No!'

'But you love gardening, and can talk about it?'

'I don't know.' She thought for a moment. 'I suppose I do talk about it, given half a chance. Not many of my friends are that interested.'

'It would only be a three-month contract at first, but if you took off, it would be renewable. I know Marj Fenton has no intention of coming back after she's had the baby.'

'You're saying you want me to go on television?'

'Yup! I think you'd be perfect. You'd be accessible, just like you think gardening ought to be. And it'll be well paid. You'd be able to save to keep you going through the hard times. And even if your contract wasn't renewed, you'd be a name!'

Veronica who hadn't gone home, in spite of her earlier protestations, broke in. 'Do you realize that Althea has had no training? At all?'

Phillida regarded her. 'What, no diploma or anything? Not even a recreational garden design course?'

Well, she'd thought it was too good to be true. 'No, I'm afraid not. I'm entirely self-taught – though I did have a bit of help with my drawing. A friend taught me how to do it.'

'But that's wonderful! Just what we need! I can't wait to tell Nathan. I'll bring him to meet you sometime during the week.'

Phillida eventually left, carried away on a bubble of enthusiasm.

'Some people have all the luck,' said Veronica.

Althea considered this. Could being abandoned with three children, subsequently made redundant, having her plants threatened by a storm and then her garden nearly washed away by a burst pipe really be called lucky? Well, compared to Veronica, who was thin, rich and probably beloved by her husband, but who didn't know she was born, she felt bloody lucky.

CHAPTER TWENTY-SEVEN

❀

'Hi, Mum!'

Althea turned, amazed to see William, Rupert and Merry all standing in a line, a bit uncertain how to greet their mother in this exotic setting.

She stepped over the barrier round her garden and flung herself at them. 'Darlings! How did you get here? You're not members!'

'Patrick arranged it. He was at university with one of the major designers.'

'Oh? Who?'

'Barbara Wynne-Jones. Have you heard of her?'

'Of course I've heard of her! She's one of the most successful designers there are!' She was also talented, very glamorous and married to someone Big in the City.

'Well, apparently she and Patrick are great mates.'

'But how did you get here? By train?'

'Yup. Juno rang school to get permission for us to be absent.'

'That was jolly kind of her.' Not to say completely out of character.

'Well, Patrick . . .' Merry subsided into silence under the baleful looks of her brothers.

'Patrick what?'

'Told her to,' Merry mumbled.

'And when has Juno ever done what she was told?'

'*I* don't know.'

'Sorry,' said Althea, 'but how did you get from the station? The *underground*?'

'Course! Honestly, Mum,' William went on. 'Anyone would think we were kids.'

'Well, you are,' Althea muttered to herself.

The boys, hearing, exchanged pained glances.

'Oh well, you obviously managed to get here safely. So, what do you think of it?'

'It's amazing,' said Rupert. 'Better than the one you made at home.'

'Is it?'

'Yeah, it looks nearly as good as this one.' He indicated Veronica's garden.

'Can I pick the flowers?' asked Merry.

'No!' Althea squeaked.

''S all right. Only joking.'

It was lovely seeing the children again and hearing all their news. Telephones didn't compare with talking face to face. Their conversation was somewhat disjointed, as crowds of people kept coming up to Althea and asking her questions. She couldn't get over being referred to as an expert, when all her life her opinion had counted for so little.

'Juno's coming up,' Merry informed her during a lull. 'You can bring babies in, but not pushchairs.'

'Oh good. I hope she'll like it.'

'Well,' said Merry, 'I expect she'll prefer the others, but she was over the moon. Look,' she went on quickly, 'would you mind if we went off shopping and met you here later, say at five o'clock?'

Her children, innocent country-lambkins, loose in London? William, reading her mind, broke in. 'Honestly, Mum, I'll look after them. And this is Chelsea, not Brixton. The worst that can happen is some Sloane'll kidnap us and force us to speak with posh accents.'

'Don't joke about things like that, please! And OK. But stick to William like glue, you two. Have you got any money?'

'No.'

'Well, you'd better take my card.'

Althea shot a furtive glance over her shoulder as she handed it to William. Juno had been appalled when she discovered that all Althea's children knew her PIN number. Just as well she didn't know they used to lean over her at the cashpoint machine, chanting the digits to her in case she forgot. Now she was frightened they would be mugged and forced to confess it.

'What shall I get? A nifty fifty?'

'Yes, but I want change. You can buy lunch and something small.'

'It will be small,' grumbled Merry. 'Fifty pounds isn't a lot these days.'

'But I don't live in these days. I still think fifty pounds is enough to take a family of five on holiday in Majorca for a fortnight. We'll go out for a really nice meal tonight,' she added.

They went to one of the many Italian restaurants in the area.

'You can have anything on the menu except pizza,' said Althea. 'You can have that at home.'

This stipulation made, the choosing became animated and noisy. But at last everyone had made up their minds. A friendly waiter took their order and came back with a tray of drinks.

'So, how have you all been getting on in Patrick's house?' Althea asked, having taken a long sip of her wine. 'I expect you're looking forward to us having a place of our own.' She was herself, but the thought of house-hunting was too terrible to be given headspace just at the moment.

'It's really great, actually,' said Rupert. 'I wish we could find a house like it.'

'So do I,' said Merry.

'It's a bit grand for the likes of us, I'm afraid, poppet.'

'Well, we could buy half of Patrick's house, then,' said Merry. 'I mean, we're living in some of it already, and there's still loads left.'

'It's too big for one person, that's for sure,' said Rupert, who had scruples about personal wealth.

'I don't expect he'd want to share it on a permanent basis,' said Althea, not sure if she cared much for the idea herself. 'He probably values his privacy.'

'There's privacy, and there's isolation. That house is big enough for an army,' said William.

'Well, you could ask him if we can go on living in it,' said Merry. 'It would save all that grisly house-hunting. Remember the one that smelt?'

'And all those with no proper-sized bedrooms?' Rupert obviously did.

'I must say I think sharing Patrick's house is a good idea,' said William. 'Patrick's great.'

'Yeah. He's cool. Why are you always so tight to him, Mum?' asked Merry.

Althea was saved from having to answer by the arrival of the food. 'Are you going to manage all that, Merry?' she asked, as her daughter disappeared behind a mountain of pasta.

Her daughter gave her an impatient glance. 'I'm not a baby, Mum.'

William was examining his antipasto suspiciously, in case he discovered a whole baby squid or bit of chicken. 'Is that nice, William?'

He sighed. 'I'm not a baby, either.'

'This is lush, Mum,' said Rupert. 'What about yours?'

Althea tasted a forkful of cannelloni filled with ricotta cheese and spinach. 'Heavenly.'

'So, why don't you and Patrick get on, Mum?' asked William, dealing deftly with a spear of asparagus.

'We do get on, where did you get the idea that we didn't?' Althea sounded indignant.

'You told me after Christmas that you'd broken up being friends,' said Merry.

'Well – we made it up. Sort of.'

'He doesn't seem to think you have,' said Merry.

'Perhaps he doesn't like me very much.'

'Yeah, right,' said Merry. 'Like he really would come rushing up to rescue your garden if he didn't like you.'

'I think he fancies her.' Rupert blushed at the thought of his mother being sexually attractive, and speared a square of ravioli.

Merry regarded her mother strangely, as if seeing her through new eyes. 'Really? Cool,' she said, pleased but mystified.

'I'm sure he doesn't,' mumbled Althea, rearranging her napkin.

'Anyway, what's that got to do with his house?' asked William. 'Shall I ask him if he'd like you to buy half of it?'

'William, if you so much as mention my name and houses, in the same breath, to Patrick, I'll stop your allowance until you're forty-nine.'

'Mum! He won't need an allowance when he's forty-nine!' said Merry.

'Yes he will,' said Rupert, 'if he's still a Buddhist.'

'But he might be really glad to sell you half. Juno reckons he's running out of money.'

'Oh? And is Juno best friends with his bank manager's wife?'

'I don't think so, but she came over the other day and commented that nothing much had happened to the house since she'd last been.'

'That doesn't mean he's run out of money, necessarily.'

'I'm only passing on what Juno said,' said William, who was bored. 'Now can we drop the subject?'

In spite of the hordes of people whom Althea spoke to during the next three days, she couldn't help worrying away at what her children said about buying half of Patrick's house. In spite of her denial in the restaurant, the cessation of work did indicate a lack of money and it was a huge property, which needed lots more doing to it. Barnet House was also one of the nicest houses in Gloucestershire. And none of the many houses she'd seen were even liveable in, let alone lovely.

Of course, she'd been house-hunting in the dead period after Christmas; there would be a lot more houses on the market now. And if the television job really did materialize, she'd be able to afford a proper mortgage, as well as having a substantial amount already.

But in her heart, she knew she wanted Patrick's house . . . nearly as much as she wanted Patrick.

Juno duly came, in a ravishing hat, with Candida, as pretty and elegant as her mother in organdie and broderie anglaise, strapped to her mother in a contraption which could never stoop to the name of 'sling'.

'Oh, Ally, I'm so proud of you!' she said, when Althea had managed to kiss her without dislodging the hat or crushing the baby. 'I knew you could do it! A Silver-Gilt! Why do you think you didn't manage a Gold?'

If she could guarantee Juno could stay quiet for a couple of hours, Althea felt she might be able to explain. But as this was far harder to achieve than a Gold Medal she didn't bother to try. 'I don't know, really.'

'That one over there is nice,' said Juno, looking over Veronica's reconstructed dry-stone wall.

'Finish looking at mine and I'll introduce you to Veronica,' Althea promised.

'Really, I'm very impressed.' Very surprised, too, by the sound of her. 'It isn't one of your usual wild designs. Dear little pond. Oh, but isn't that a weed, darling? That little thing with the tiny mauve flowers? Did you miss it when you weeded? Is that why you didn't get a Gold?'

'That's ivy-leaved toadflax and I think of it as a wild flower.'

'Oh.'

After Juno and Veronica had exchanged greetings and discovered distant but mutual acquaintances, Juno swept Althea off to buy her a glass of Pimm's.

'Patrick came to dinner last night. He was frightfully good with Candida, wasn't he, sweetie?' Since she'd had a baby, Juno's voice, which was usually precise and business-like, would suddenly become sort of soft and gooey while she spoke to the baby, and then revert to sharpness with unnerving rapidity. 'He didn't say a word when she brought up some milk on his jacket, did he, angel one? Poor man,' she added, crisply.

'Well, I shouldn't think he minded.' Althea ate a piece of cucumber, wondering if Juno ever got it wrong and snapped at her daughter and cooed at Kenneth. 'Some men love babies.'

'Oh, I didn't mean that! No! I meant it was sad about his house.'

'What about his house?'

'Well, he didn't say anything directly, but I was there the other day and he hasn't done any new work on it. And I gather from Diana he's actually sent the builders away. He must have run out of money.'

'Did he tell Diana that?'

'Oh, no. I don't think they know each other. It's just that her neighbour is having a patio and the builders had been working at Patrick's house. They told her.'

'That doesn't mean anything. If they finished the job –'

'The thing is, they hadn't! He paid them off before they'd done what he'd asked for originally. I think he'll have to sell.'

'That's awful!'

'Do you think so? It is a terrible great barn of a place. Beautiful, of course, but far too big for one. I think it would be only sensible to get rid of it if he can find a buyer.'

Althea, who'd sold her own house because it was 'only sensible', didn't want Patrick to have to do the same. 'Would you like another drink?'

'No, thank you, sweetie. When you're breast-feeding you have to be so careful.' She gave Althea a look which said there were many reasons for being careful, and given half a chance she would tell Althea every one.

It was towards the end of Thursday evening, Althea, thinking she would drop where she stood if she didn't sit down, had taken refuge at the top of her plot and collapsed on to Juno's garden bench. She was sitting with her eyes shut, blotting out the sounds of the crowds, when someone spoke directly to her. Her eyes flew open and she saw a young man with a pony-tail carrying a video-camera. He was pointing it at her. She was about to protest when Phillida Stancombe appeared from behind him.

'Sorry, love, I bet we're the last people you want to see, but this was the only time Tristan could do.'

'Er – What?'

'I wanted to have you on tape, so the powers-that-be can see what a wow you're going to be. I'm so excited!'

Phillida remained excited and Tristan went on filming for some time. They shot Althea explaining her garden to the visitors, describing it to camera, looking over the wall to Veronica's and pontificating on that. They would have taken her into the main marquee and filmed her reactions to the exhibits there if she hadn't managed to convince them that all they would get near would be the bonsai.

'You're a natural, a complete star,' Phillida enthused. 'I'm bringing Nathan, he's the man you need to impress, with me tomorrow. But we'll come early, so you won't be so tired.'

'Good,' said Althea, who, having had a discreet paddle in her pond – unaware that Tristan was still filming – was feeling a little better. 'I'll look forward to it.'

William and Daniel were due to appear at five on the dot on Friday, to help Althea dismantle her plot and carry home all the plants she didn't manage to sell or couldn't bear to part with.

In fact, she had agreed in principle to sell quite a lot of her plants, but strangely, no one wanted a pond made out of a wash basin and quite a lot of her wild flowers had become distinctly weed-like since Monday.

At twenty past five, when she was starting to get impatient, and to worry about the vast number of plants she had arranged to buy, a very smart van drew up by her garden. Trust Veronica to have such a posh vehicle, she muttered to Gerry, her friend who made orangeries. It was Patrick.

She wasn't as surprised as she should have been. He had turned up in her life unexpectedly so many times, she had come to expect it. But she was nervous and felt very shy.

'Well, are you ready to dismantle?' he asked her.

It was a very hot day and his cotton trousers were very crumpled and his shirt was open at the neck. Veronica, who was giving orders to her chauffeur as to how her passion flower was to be packed, paused to admire him for a moment.

'Where are William and Daniel?'

'You're in danger of treating your son like a husband. He's at school, where he ought to be.'

'I haven't got a husband.'

'I know. That's why I came.'

And having tossed this somewhat ambiguous remark into the state of chaos which was Chelsea at closing time, he started to load up the van.

'Um, I've arranged to buy a few plants. I'll just pop along and collect them.'

'Pop' wasn't a particularly apposite choice of word, she decided, forcing her way against the tide of hundreds of people, many of them blinded by armfuls of plants and flowers. But she battled through and came back with mounds of wonderful bargains which would have been tossed into skips if she hadn't bought them, and had a van to take them home in.

At last, Althea was sitting up in the front of it next to Patrick. In silence he inched his way out of the showground. In silence Althea watched the pandemonium, the destruction of all the combined forces of nature and art, toil and inspiration which had existed just a short time before. It was sad, very sad. But it was Chelsea. At least 'Gardens Grow' had undertaken to flatten their site, otherwise she'd have had to be there all weekend, to leave it all as it had been less than a month earlier.

'You must be very proud,' said Patrick when at last they were crawling along the Embankment towards Fulham, so she could collect her things from Sylvia's mother's house.

'Yes, but I couldn't have done it without you.'

'Of course you could. All I did was show you how to hold a pencil.'

'It wasn't only that . . .'

'It was you who won the prize, all on your own. Just take the credit.'

The traffic was still appalling. After half an hour, they had hardly progressed at all.

'It was terribly kind of you to come. The traffic is hell and it's such a long way.'

'The traffic would have been just as bad for William and his friend.'

'Yes, but I would have paid them.'

He looked at her.

'I don't suppose you'd like me to pay you.' She kept her gaze firmly out of the window.

'No,' he said shortly.

Althea was about to insist on at least paying for the petrol – after all, if he was short of money it was only right. But she stopped herself in time. He would probably make her walk home, with all the plants.

'Where did you get the van from?'

'It's the firm's.'

'The children told me you know Barbara Wynne-Jones?'

'Yup. We were at university together.'

'They told me that, too. You must have kept in touch if she could arrange tickets for my lot.'

He regarded her again. 'Yes, we've kept in close touch.' His mouth gave a little twitch. 'Especially since her marriage has been so rocky.'

'Oh.'

'The children told me,' he said after a few minutes, 'that you've been offered a job on television.'

'Yes. It's quite funny. Do you remember that woman with the plait? You saw her and gave her your card?'

He nodded.

'Well, it seems she's a producer for a company which puts on an afternoon gardening show, and they want a female presenter.'

'You?'

'Me. Not just me, of course. But I'm to have a sort of low-budget, low-experience spot.'

'Well done!'

'The thing about it is, even if I'm taken off after one series, I'll be a Name. People might have heard of me when I advertise my services.'

'That's true.'

'I met the boss of it all – can't remember what he called himself. Nathan somebody. He was sweet. Very keen on me. Said he'd write and confirm today.'

'That's terrific.'

Althea had run out of polite conversation. 'But not terrific enough to put a smile on your face?'

He did smile, briefly. 'I'm absolutely thrilled for you, of course. You'll be extremely good and I'm convinced you've a stunning career ahead of you. Barbara was very impressed.'

'Barbara Wynne-Jones?'

'None other.'

'Really? She didn't just say that because she knew I was a friend of yours?'

'Barbara doesn't say things to be nice.'

A warm feeling started in Althea's stomach, like the first mouthful of hot soup after a cold, wet walk.

'But things aren't going so well for you?'

'Sorry?'

'It's Juno. You know what a networker she is. She told me . . .' She paused. 'She told me she thought you may have to sell the house.'

'Yup.' His eyes were on the road and she could see no

emotion on his face, but he must be devastated. Gutted, her boys would have said.

'You must be awfully upset.'

'There's no point in being upset. It's just how things have worked out. I over-reached myself.'

Althea knew she had to go on. 'The children have got a plan.'

'Oh?'

'Yes. They think I should buy half your house. Then you'd have enough to finish the restoration.'

'Oh?'

This wasn't very promising. 'Of course, they want to buy the half we're living in.'

'Of course.'

'So, what do you think of the idea?'

He didn't answer and Althea was too stressed to endure silence for long. 'I told them I didn't think it was a good idea because I didn't think you liked me very much.'

'I see.'

'Well? Do you like me?'

'You're all right sometimes.' He changed gear and managed to squeeze past a bus.

If that was the best he could do he could sell his house and be damned. 'So I'll start house-hunting immediately and move out as soon as I can.'

'There's no particular hurry. I don't think there'll be too many people willing to pay a fortune for a crumbling mansion.'

'Perhaps I'll buy it all.'

'You couldn't afford it.'

'How do you know? I've got all the money from my house and I could get a massive mortgage on the salary I'll be earning.'

'Not on that house you couldn't. Even if you could, you couldn't make the payments.'

'Oh! You're such a miserable so and so sometimes!'

He shook his head quickly, like a dog freeing his ears of water. 'I know, I'm sorry. I'm raining on your parade and being a total jerk.'

Instantly mollified, Althea put out a hand and only just managed not to put it on his leg. She put it back in her lap. 'You could borrow money and divide it up into flats. You'd make a fortune.'

'No. My dream has always been to see it restored to its former glory. Flats are rarely glorious.'

'It's such a shame!'

'What is?'

She tried hard to sound brisk and business-like, as if there were nothing whatever personal about the offer. 'That you don't want me to buy half the house. It would solve both our problems. I'd have somewhere nice to live and you'd have enough capital to carry on with the restorations. We needn't get in each other's way. In fact, if we were careful, I should imagine we could avoid each other completely.'

'That is the most ridiculous thing I've ever heard of.'

Althea felt as if he'd punched her in the stomach. She subsided into the seat, wishing she had the energy to jump down from the van and find her own way home.

'Unless of course,' he went on, overtaking a pizza-delivery bicycle too close for Althea's comfort, 'we were married. And I don't suppose you'd be interested in anything like that, would you?'

Althea went hot and cold, uncertain if she'd heard him right. Then, deciding that she had, made a tough decision. It would be so easy to mumble, to carry on looking out at the traffic, to appear to agree with him. But he had once told her to seize the day. It would be his fault if he didn't like it when she did.

'I would, actually.'

He braked suddenly, then accelerated hard. 'Would what?'

'I would be interested in marriage, things like that.'

He cleared his throat. 'In general? Or with anyone in particular?'

He wasn't making it easy for her. 'With someone in particular.'

He drove on in silence but he didn't seem to have his mind on the road. 'With me?'

'If you were asking, yes, with you.'

He indicated and suddenly swung the van into a side street and pulled up. They were on a double yellow line. 'Could you say that again?'

'I said, if you were asking – about marriage – to me, I would be interested.'

'You mean you'd say yes?'

'Yes. But you would have to ask me. This conversation is so confusing, I wouldn't know what I was agreeing to, otherwise.'

He took a deep breath, raised his shoulders and lowered them again. 'Will you marry me?' he said eventually, looking out into the street beyond.

'Yes,' said Althea. She watched a black cat cross in front of them and panicked because she couldn't remember if it was lucky or unlucky. A traffic warden was walking towards them. This was easier: she knew they were definitely unlucky. 'There's a traffic warden.'

'I don't care.' He turned to her, put his hand firmly behind her neck. 'Do you really mean that? That you'll marry me?'

'Yes – but the traffic warden!'

'Bugger the traffic warden,' he said, and kissed her.

CHAPTER TWENTY-EIGHT

❀

Having left Sylvia's parents with a houseful of cut flowers which, according to Sylvia's step-father, made the place look like a funeral parlour, they found their way through the back streets to the main road.

Althea sighed and closed her eyes. 'Are you all right?' asked Patrick.

'I'm just peopled up to the eyebrows. And I would kill for a shower.'

'Well . . . supposing we didn't go straight home? You know when we get back everyone will be there.'

'What do you mean, everyone? Only the children, surely.'

'That's what I meant. But I'd quite like to have you to myself.'

'The children are part of my life –'

'I know,' he went on quickly, hearing the sudden tension in her voice. 'I'm quite willing to share you with them. And I really like them for their own sakes, nothing to do with you. It's just, if you're tired, I know a lovely hotel by the river at Henley. We could spend the night there, set off early and be home by breakfast tomorrow.'

Althea sighed. 'It sounds blissful.'

'I'll find somewhere to phone from and see if they've a room. Yes?'

'And I'd better tell the children I'm not coming home.' She frowned. 'What shall I say? That we broke down?'

'Tell them the truth. That you're tired and need to go to bed.'

She bit back a smile that was in danger of becoming a smirk. 'So we're going to this hotel so we can have an early night?'

He didn't conceal his feelings. He looked as lecherous and lustful and meltingly attractive as was possible. 'Exactly.'

'Patrick, I know they're awfully fond of you and everything,

298

but this is something I'm going to have to break to them very gently.'

'Althea, my darling, my dearest love, my angel, would you be very horrified if I told you the children more or less insisted I propose to you? That Merry in particular will be very disappointed if she isn't tripping her way down the aisle behind you in purple taffeta by the autumn at the latest.'

Althea sighed. 'It's not Merry I'm worried about. It's the boys.'

'The boys are fine about it. They're just confused as to why you've been being "so tight" to me.'

'You mean you've discussed this with my children? Without saying anything to me? You're as bad as Frederick!'

'I'm worse than Frederick. They are at least his kids. But I knew I had no chance with you unless the children approved.'

Althea banged her fist on the dashboard of the van. 'It's role reversal all over again. The bridegroom asking the children's permission to marry their mother!'

Patrick chuckled. 'Well, they said yes, so why should you object? In fact it was William who suggested –' He stopped abruptly.

'What?'

'Nothing, never mind. And I'm sorry. I wouldn't have said anything to them, but they approached me.'

'What! Patrick! This is terrible! Even worse than I thought!'

'It wasn't quite how I've made it sound. We were chatting one evening, and Merry said –'

'Merry! How could she!'

'Merry said, why didn't we shack up together.'

Althea covered her face with her hands. 'My mother would turn in her grave if she was dead.'

'And I said, it was complicated, and that I didn't think you'd want to.'

'Oh God!'

'But she said she was sure you really liked me because you were so upset when I went out with Jenny. Where did you get that idea from, by the way?'

'It doesn't matter,' she groaned.

'Well, anyway, we discussed it. And the boys agreed you did care for me, and William said you were probably holding me at arms' length because you thought they wouldn't approve.'

'True.'

'But as they did approve, they thought I should make a move.'

'This is so embarrassing.'

'Not really. Go-betweens are a fine old Irish custom. I'm all in favour of them. Now let's see if we can find a couple of phone-boxes that work?'

'Hello, Merry? It's me.'

'Oh, hi, Mum!'

'Darling, would you and the boys be terribly disappointed if we didn't come home tonight? We . . .' She felt herself blushing. Admitting to your thirteen-year-old daughter that you had a sex life was embarrassing. '. . . Patrick wants us to spend the night in a hotel. It's such a long journey and I'm so tired.'

'Oh . . . it's Mum.' Althea heard them muttering in the background before Merry's hand went over the receiver, 'That's OK. William's going to drive me over to Juno's. She said she might let me give Candida her bath.'

'How lovely.'

'You will bring me the freebies, won't you?'

'Of course. If there are any. Do the boys want a word?'

Althea heard Merry ask. 'Not particularly. They send their love. And to Patrick. I'd better go now. Byee.'

Althea put the phone down not knowing whether to be pleased or sorry. It was wonderful that her children were so in-dependent and could manage without her. But it was a bit strange.

The hotel had gardens which went down to the river. It was approached from the back, the drive sweeping round and passing velvet-smooth lawns dotted with mature trees and well-managed flower beds.

'It's beautiful!' said Althea. 'You can just imagine elegant Edwardian ladies strolling about and taking tea in their huge picture hats and tiny parasols.'

'They must have been dreadfully hot. No wonder they kept fainting,' agreed Patrick.

What was harder to imagine was herself, hot, tired and crum-pled, facing the desk clerk with equanimity. She dawdled behind

Patrick as he carried their things up the steps and in through the doors.

He must know we're not married, she thought, as the young man took down their details. She was overcome with self-consciousness and concentrated hard on the arrangement of silk flowers in the fireplace while Patrick signed them in. Here I am a grown woman – knocking forty, for God's sake – feeling embarrassed about being seen checking into a hotel with a man. Patrick smiled at her reassuringly. 'Shall we go up?'

Althea nodded and followed him up the shallow, sweeping staircase to their room, grateful that he had declined the services of a porter.

The room was embarrassingly bridal. A white bedspread covered a huge bed, and floor-length gold curtains graced the windows, which looked over the gardens and the river beyond. The bathroom was full of thick towels and enough little sachets of bath oil, shampoo and conditioner to satisfy even Merry's heart.

'We're quite late for dinner,' said Patrick, dumping her squashy bag heedlessly on to the pristine bed. 'We should go down quite soon, if you want to eat.'

Althea never wanted to eat again. Her appetite had vanished. She felt as nervous as any virgin bride confronted with an enormous bed and a bridegroom who suddenly seemed a stranger.

'Have I time for a quick shower?'

'Of course.'

The water came out hot and strong, sandblasting her body of the dirt and grime it had accumulated during the long, sultry day. But her mind was still unsettled. Here she was, a successful garden designer, the fiancée of a gorgeous, kind and sexy man, and about to be financially independent – properly – for the first time. But when she should have been feeling euphoric, she just felt strange and unsettled.

The bedroom was empty when she came out of the bathroom. She put her clothes back on and dried her hair. Then she applied her make-up very carefully. She was just putting on lipstick when Patrick came in and she realized what was bothering her.

He flung himself full length on the bed, his heels carelessly against the bedspread.

'Patrick, I don't quite know how to put this . . .'

He sat up, no longer relaxed but pale under his tan, his expression strained. 'But you've changed your mind. You don't want to marry me after all.' His tone was light and he smiled, but she could hear the tension in him.

'No, nothing like that. But I just feel . . .'

'What? For God's sake, don't keep me in suspense.'

'I want to go home. To *our* home.'

He closed his eyes and let out his breath quickly. 'Is that all? God! For a minute I thought there was something serious.'

'You don't mind?'

'No, not really. It's just . . .'

'What?'

'Nothing. We've got the rest of our lives together, after all.' Seeing Althea's confusion he went on. 'To spend nights in hotels, I mean.'

She nodded. 'Will they mind very much?'

'Will who mind?'

'The hotel. If we don't stay.'

'Of course not. I'll go and explain. You finish doing whatever you were doing and I'll come up and get you when it's all settled.'

'Patrick?'

'Yes?'

'I love you.'

The warmth of his expression made her glow with anticipated pleasure – and with love. 'Hold that thought until I can do something with it.'

Althea felt suddenly lighthearted. It had been the hotel which had been wrong, not her life, or her choice of partner. She put the few things she had taken out back into her bag, tidied the bed and selected one sachet of each type on offer and tucked them in her sponge bag for Merry.

Fortunately for her conscience, the foyer was empty when they finally left.

'Did you have to pay?' she asked him as they drove off.

'Don't worry about it. Have a nap. You must be shattered.'

302

If she was a little surprised at this order, Althea was quite willing to comply and slept soundly for the entire journey home, waking only briefly when he stopped for fuel.

'Wake up, we're here.'

Althea opened her eyes. 'Gosh, I must have slept the whole way home.'

'Just as well. Althea . . .' He took her hand. 'There's something that perhaps I should tell you.'

Her heart lurched in panic and she took back her hand. 'If you're going to tell me you're really married to Topaz or have a wife and family who think you're a long-distance lorry driver tell me inside. I want to get out of this van now.'

'OK, have it your own way.'

She clambered stiffly down, waiting for him to join her with a key. He leapt down easily, walked up the path and put his key in the door.

Almost before he had time to turn it, the door opened.

'Surprise!'

The hall was full of people all in party clothes, shouting, 'Well done.' Balloons printed with 'Congratulations' almost blocked the doorway. Banners covered in stars and hearts echoed the message in multi-coloured felt-tip pens. Merry had obviously been hard at work, aided by her friend Ronnie, whom Althea spotted peeping out from behind the adults.

Merry flew into her arms. 'Hello, Mum! It's wonderful that you came! We were so disappointed when we thought you weren't going to!'

She was pushed aside by her brothers, and then everyone else in the world hugged and kissed and congratulated Althea.

'Juno, is this your fault?' Althea demanded, when her sister, baby still attached, gave her a hug. 'Why didn't you tell me? We nearly didn't come!'

'Aren't you pleased?' Juno demanded. 'Merry promised me you've always wanted a surprise party, but Patrick wasn't sure, so he wouldn't promise to bring you.'

'But supposing we'd stayed at that hotel?' Althea waved at the banners. 'All this would have been wasted!'

'Oh no,' said Merry. 'We were having the party anyway. We thought we might as well.'

'But you *are* pleased?' said Juno.

'I'm thrilled.'

Less thrilling, but typical of Juno, was the presence of Frederick and Topaz, lurking towards the back of the crowd.

'That's a bit unconventional for you, isn't it, Juno?' Althea said. 'Asking the exes to an engagement party? Not that I mind, of course . . .'

Juno blinked. 'You mean – you and Patrick? You're engaged!' She screamed, waking Candida who joined in. 'Everybody! They're engaged!'

Althea felt herself flailed again by hugs and kisses and slaps on the back. 'I thought she knew!' she mouthed to Patrick, equally belaboured. 'Why else the congratulations?'

'Your Silver-Gilt medal, of course, you dilly! Still, they had to know sometime.'

'Well done, Mum.' William gave her an awkward hug. 'I'm very happy for you.'

'But what about you? How do you feel about it?'

'It's fine, really. It'll be great having a rich step-father.'

'But darling, Patrick isn't rich.'

William shot Patrick a confused look. 'Isn't he? Sorry, must have got it wrong.'

'Find Rupert and Merry for me, there's a love. I want to know they're all right about this.'

Rupert and Merry were fine about it. Merry asked instantly if Ronnie could be a bridesmaid too. 'After all, I have to have someone else and Candida's far too young. Even if you wait ages.'

'Honestly, Mel, they may not be having that sort of wedding,' said Rupert. 'They may want to slip quietly away to a register office.'

'Well, tough. I'm not having my mother getting married to a millionaire and not having a proper wedding.'

'Darling, where did you get this idea that Patrick's a millionaire?'

'Oh, never mind about that. Just say you'll have a proper wedding and that Ronnie can be a bridesmaid.'

'All right, darling. If I can find a priest who'll marry us. We're both divorced, you know.'

'Lush! I'll go and tell Ron.'

There was a certain inevitability about retreating to the kitchen for a drink of water and finding Topaz there.

'So, you finally got him to agree to marry you?' Topaz leaned her long body against the rickety enamel table which was Patrick's work surface.

Althea shrugged. 'I offered him money, how could he refuse? Marrying me means he can keep his house. How lovely it is being rich enough to be married for your money!'

'What do you mean?' Topaz raised an over-plucked, sceptical eyebrow. 'He doesn't need your money! He's rolling in it! Don't you know about the family trust fund? They're due for another share-out next year. He's virtually a millionaire!'

Althea felt all the wine she had drunk go to her knees. She felt suddenly weak and had an overwhelming need to see Patrick. He was in his sitting room – a room which she planned to use as a study eventually – talking to Kenneth about babies.

'What is it, darling?' he said, seeing her anxious expression.

'I just need a word.' She led him down the passage and through the door to what would one day be a very comfortable kitchen. 'Topaz has just told me you're enormously rich! You weren't going to have to sell the house at all!'

He bit his lip, shrugged and shook his head. 'I'm sorry. It's William's fault. He told me not to mention it. He felt it would damage my chances. And as my chances seemed blown to bits anyway, I couldn't risk it.'

'"Men were deceivers ever",' she quoted. 'So if you're so rich, why did you stop work on the house? You haven't done a thing since I've been away.'

'Come and see what I have been doing.'

He took her arm and marched her through the house into the garden. It was a haven of peace away from the noise and confusion. She wanted to linger in it. It was a sultry evening, the stars were bright and she was a little drunk and a lot in love. But he permitted no loitering until they reached the greenhouse.

'There.'

It had been totally restored. Every window-frame and every pane of glass had been repaired or replaced. And someone,

Merry probably, had filled it with nightlights and little flames were now reflecting from every surface, magnified indefinitely so there seemed to be candles for miles.

The benches were now sturdy, bright and fragrant with new wood. The floor-tiles had been renewed. There was nothing she couldn't grow in a greenhouse like this.

'There's automatic shading and watering systems for when we go away,' he said. 'And there are flower beds on the floor so you can grow vines.'

'It's wonderful!'

'And it's not all.'

He led her to the end of the greenhouse which suddenly opened out into another glass-enclosed space, also candlelit. But this time the candles were in splendid wrought-iron candelabra. It was an orangery, just as beautiful as any she had coveted at Chelsea. The air was warm and the candles shimmered. Not only an orangery, but a swimming pool. At the gable end, a huge, half-moon-shaped window, bathed in golden light, looked on to the setting sun.

'That is glorious,' she whispered, awed by the vast expanse of glass, divided into panes, reflected in the pool.

'It's a Diocletian window. It is nice, isn't it?'

'It's fabulous.'

'And I know you're not keen on swimming, but it's heated and the humidity will make it possible for you to grow all sorts of exotic plants. And as I can't stand gardening, it'll give me something to do while you potter about.'

'I might get to like swimming.' The thought of swimming, naked, in this beautiful pool with Patrick was fairly bearable. 'How on earth did you get it done in the time?'

'You've seen what they can do at Chelsea in a couple of weeks. It's the same. You just need enough people who know what they're doing.'

'But are you sure you can afford it? I know Topaz said you were rich, but you did sack those other builders – the ones who are doing Diana Sanders's neighbour's patio.'

'I did. Patios are probably about their speed.'

'So you didn't run out of money?'

''Fraid not.'

306

'So you don't need my money so you can restore your house?'

'No. Do you mind, very much?'

She sighed deeply. 'I did like the idea of being married for my money. It made me feel so rich.'

'You're the first woman I've ever known who could possibly feel disappointed to discover her husband is well-off. The others – and Topaz was the worst, I suppose – seemed to want nothing more from life than a man to keep them in the style to which they'd like to become accustomed.'

'How awful of them.'

'But you wanted to give *me* money, all your money, when you've never had any before.'

'It's because I love you,' she explained. 'You want to share things with the one you love.'

'But feeling rich isn't important to you?'

'No. It's just novel.' She hesitated. 'Feeling loved is what's important to me.'

'I intend to make you feel that for the rest of your life.'

'Oh Patrick.'

'And besides, I want you for much more important things than money.'

'Oh?' She smiled, waiting to hear his sweet nothings.

'Mm. I want my garden designed free. A zero-maintenance garden, nothing but stone slabs. No beastly flowers.'

She chuckled. 'If you hate gardening so much, why did you take up with a garden designer?'

'It wasn't on purpose, believe me. I thought I was immune to commitment and all that goes with it. And here I am, committed, well and truly, not just to a woman, but to her three children, umpteen animals and about a million plants.' He sighed. '*Samsara!*'

'You've been spending time with William!'

'I have, and while I'm in a confessional mood, I'd better tell you I haven't bought you an engagement ring yet.'

She indicated her surroundings. 'This is better.'

He squeezed her tightly. 'It was a lure. I thought you'd never be able to resist me if I offered you all this. I knew you'd resist money easily, but not a proper greenhouse.'

'It's a funny thing, Patrick, and you might find this difficult to believe, but I would have been just as willing to marry you if you lived in a bungalow on a north-facing precipice.'

'Unless the soil was pure clay, and the children had taken against me.'

'Well – love has its limits.'

He grew suddenly serious. 'But you do like it? It is all right, isn't it?'

'It's better than any ring. It's the most wonderful greenhouse in the whole world.' He came towards her and took her into his arms. 'It's perfect in every detail,' she murmured into his neck.

But the floor, they discovered a little later, was rather hard.